. . . but in his dark expression, she saw something else entirely, something that reflected back into her own eyes, primitive and all-consuming.

"It is well and good that we finally clear the air between us, Christine," he breathed against her mouth.

Her lips parted, but whether in protest or invitation, she knew not. He seized upon her hesitation and covered her mouth with his. A hot open mouthed kiss that pinned her to the bench. Like the clever black-hearted devil he was, he swooped between the cracks of her defenses. She made a token effort to deny him. But he dragged her across his lap, bringing her down to the bench beneath his weight.

His tongue swept deeply into her mouth and met hers, a tempestuous battle that shattered all boundaries between them and made her earlier resistance seem childish. As if an earthquake swept through her psyche, the past crumbled, and she was without pride, returning the force of his passion and reveling in sweet desire. He tasted like rich coffee and brandy and hot gratifying sex in an elemental way that made her feel alive.

MELODY THOMAS

Beauty
And The
Duke

AVON
An Imprint of HarperCollinsPublishers

This is a work of fiction. Names, characters, places, and incidents are drawn from the author's imagination or are used fictitiously and are not to be construed as real. Any resemblance to actual events, locales, organizations, or persons, living or dead, is entirely coincidental.

AVON BOOKS
An Imprint of HarperCollins*Publishers*
10 East 53rd Street
New York, New York 10022-5299

Copyright © 2009 by Laura Renken
ISBN 978-0-06-147267-1
www.avonromance.com

First Avon Books paperback printing: August 2009

Avon Trademark Reg. U.S. Pat. Off. and in Other Countries, Marca Registrada, Hecho en U.S.A.
HarperCollins® is a registered trademark of HarperCollins Publishers.

Printed in the U.S.A.

10 9 8 7 6 5 4 3 2 1

For my husband, Thomas. My own personal hero.
Thank you for all that you do. I love you.

Beauty
And The
Duke

Chapter 1

London
1840

"**L**ondon is becoming overrun with tourists and children," Christine Sommers stated to her friend and assistant, Amelia, from her seat atop the stone steps leading into London's popular museum of antiquities. Shifting her attention from the children running around wildly and screeching like banshees in the park next to the massive hydra fountain, she folded her hands over her reticule. "I have always lived by the dictum that all children are best kept locked away until they can behave like adults."

"Which is why I am a teacher and you are an administrator."

"I am a paleontologist."

Behind her, a footman opened the museum's double doors and laid out the red carpet in preparation for the evening's private gala. A thousand invitations had gone out last month. Fifteen hundred had come back. Tonight would be a crush.

She relaxed her death grip on her beaded reticule as she continued to observe the last stragglers trickling out of the museum and onto the walks. She told herself she was not suffering nerves. Why should she be? The early evening air was pleasantly warm for May, the sunset only slightly dulled by cloud cover. The evening could not be more perfect.

As usual, Christine had arrived too early. Why couldn't she be fashionably late to an event just once in her life? And perhaps, in hindsight, it would have been wiser had she taken into account her need to breathe before she let Amelia stuff her into the corset that squeezed her torso. She felt like a sausage ready to be hung on a rack and cured.

"You look beautiful," Amelia said as if reading Christine's thoughts.

Christine looked down at her skirts. The cornflower-blue satin trimmed in blond matched her eyes. "You don't think this gown makes me look like a courtesan, do you?"

Amelia's musical laughter turned the heads of a group of gentlemen loitering on the cobbles below them. Her shining gold hair beneath the hood of her pale yellow cloak seemed to draw the weak light to her face and she positively glowed. Amelia was one of those rare individuals in Christina's life who possessed the power to pull light from the very air around her. Moments like this, Christine found herself jealous of her friend.

"And if it does?" Amelia asked. "What do you care what others think? You certainly haven't cared at any other time. It is all right for you to step out of your lab and look pretty once in a while."

Adjusting her silver-framed spectacles, Christine was about to protest when Amelia suddenly popped to her feet and began pacing like a restless mare before a race.

"I do wish Mr. Darlington would hurry." She stopped her pacing and tented a gloved hand over her eyes. "He should be here by now. Tonight is important."

Tonight was the Fossil Society's annual spring gala and the most passionate bone collectors and hobbyists were beginning to arrive. Collectors from as far away as America had come to be the first to view the new exhibits that would open to the public next week, of which Christine's contribution was a part—a fossilized metacarpal she and Joseph Darlington discovered last month in Dorset.

Tonight, the famous C. A. Sommers, author of the scandalous book that pit the infant science of paleontology against old-world mythology was also a candidate for the Fossil Society's highest award. Christine had kept her promise to her father to publish the book, a book examining the theory that great beasts once roamed the earth, and touting the possible existence of dragons. A book that historians mocked, and a theory that eventually destroyed her father's once lucrative career.

The book would never be a contender for next year's distinguished Copley Medal award, but Christine had every confidence *No Beast of Myth* would win tonight's less-than-prestigious honor. It was given by an organization that consisted of stargazers and romantics, all of whom thrived on the preposterous fringes of the absurd.

But tonight was important to Christine for another reason altogether. Sometimes a woman simply had to take matters into her own hands when it came to determining her future.

Joseph Darlington had once been her father's most promising assistant. Two months ago, he had finally returned from a fellowship at Edinburgh, and Christine realized she had come to a bend in her life. She was eight and twenty, after all, and though she had long since risen above the romantic inclinations that seemed to assail youth, she did not want to awaken ten years from now and find herself irrelevant in a world that had passed her by.

Last week, she had applied to the museum board of trustees to head up an expedition to Perth, Australia. The team leader had recently expired of a heart attack. She knew the trustees were in desperate need of a paleontologist and stood to lose their funding if they could not secure a team before the end of the month. Even if Christine was a woman, no other scientist had her credentials and could save the expedition on such short notice. They could *not* deny her this time, and she was convinced she would be given the appointment tonight during the award ceremony.

To that end, she wanted to share her passions with a like-minded man. She was a woman of action and circumstance, after all.

Tonight was one such occasion where action was required to make something happen. Joseph Darlington might be as brilliant a paleontologist as she, but he was also a man. And beneath her velvet evening mantelet, Christine knew she looked as bold as she could manage for a woman who was about to ask a man to wed her.

Amelia's pacing stopped. "Mr. Darlington is here."

Christine turned her head and glimpsed Joseph Darlington stepping down from a carriage that had stopped behind a long line of carriages from which finely dressed patrons of the museum descended. Her heart did a flip-flop, and she rose from the stone bench where she had been sitting to better observe him over the growing crowd.

As always, he looked handsome and dapper. His wheat blond hair, brown eyes and perfect smile were all attributes that distinguished him in a scientific community filled with stodgy old windbags who would as soon steal a fossil from a fellow scientist as find one themselves.

"I wish I were not so nervous." Amelia raised her hand to wave.

Christine grabbed Amelia's wrist before her friend could yell *helloo* over the heads of the crowd. "What are you doing . . . ?"

But her words died on her tongue, for Joseph Darlington was not alone.

Behind him, another man filled the carriage doorway, his dark evening cloak delineating a pair of broad shoulders. Christine stilled. Even the bouncy Amelia grew silent. Christine knew at once who he was. As the man stepped out of the conveyance and unfolded to a great height, the setting sun's fiery glow threw his saturnine features into harsh relief. A swath of silver showed in his dark-as-night hair. As he settled a top hat on his head, Christine held back a gasp.

Amelia leaned nearer. "It is *he*! *The Duke of Sedgwick*. Mr. Darlington said Lord Sedgwick had written and expressed an interest in attending this event. Lord Bingham will be beside himself that someone is here tonight of higher rank than he."

Normally that thought would have made Christine smile. Bingham was a pretentious snob.

At the sight of the notorious duke, a frisson of awareness aroused a familiar unpleasant sensation in Christine's chest. It was not unlike the way she felt when she smoked her father's old cob filled with strange tobacco from Bolivia or breathed in the fermented distillates that preserved her collection of lizards and frogs. The duke held out his gloved hand to a pretty girl, swathed in pink flounces, who looked no older than the students in Amelia's class.

"That must be his sister," Amelia added behind her gloved hand.

Then Joseph spotted them at the top of the stairs. And just that quickly, the joy she felt being near her oldest friend suffused the restiveness that had momentarily sparked memories of a time in her youth she wished only to forget. Joseph had a way of putting her in control of her feelings and refocusing her purpose.

"When did Mr. Darlington tell you that Lord Sedgwick had written to him?" Christine asked Amelia.

Amelia flitted her hand airily. "I don't know. Last month," she answered without turning. "Somehow I thought Lord Sedgwick would be . . . less, um . . ."

"Less what?"

"Young?" The fan that had been dangling from Amelia's wrist suddenly popped open and her voice lowered to a whisper. "They say he bears the mark of the Sedgwick curse. His first wife died of scarlet fever. His second wife . . . well, no one knows for sure what happened to her. But her ghost haunts the crags around Fife. Do you suppose his grace is attending tonight with his sister because he is cursed and no other woman will go near him?"

Sometimes Christine could not believe Amelia was only three years younger. "He is a duke, Amelia. He can be with whomever he wants."

The ton's scandalous vagaries were normally a matter of limited interest to Christine. But when it came to the infamous Erik Boughton, Duke of Sedgwick, who lived in his castellated estate north of Edinburgh and rarely ventured to London, she knew more than most.

He had not been born into wealth and power, but one would never know that, looking at him now. He'd been a child of two when the death of a cousin left him the sole heir to a duchy that made up a sizable piece of Fife. At seventeen, he'd won a very public trial that forcibly removed his stepfather as tutelary to the Sedgwick estate and bestowed on the young duke sole custody of his half-sister. Twenty-one when he made his fortune in the iron-ore industry and twenty-four when he married for the first time.

Men like Sedgwick who ruled small empires did not seek their amusement at a gala hosted by the London Fossil Society. Of that, Christine was sure.

But as she watched his approach, a current went through her, a faint resonance of the awareness she had felt just moments ago when he had stepped out of the carriage, the same restiveness she had felt the first time she met him years ago during her first and only season. Unsettled, she looked away and found a row of beads on her sleeve to study.

Beside her, Amelia waved at Joseph, making a spectacle of herself on the steps as he approached. "Does not Mr. Darlington look dapper tonight? I will have to tell him so, I think."

And Amelia did, the instant he arrived in front of them—words that faded to the background of Christine's thoughts as Sedgwick followed behind him and Christine could not help staring at him. He still possessed a face more harsh and riveting than handsome. He was not smiling as his eyes came to rest on her face.

Christine was tall for a woman, and tonight she had worn flat slippers to make her height less awkward to Joseph. But standing next to Lord Sedgwick, she did not have that problem. In fact, he was one of the few men of her acquaintance with whom she had to tip her chin to look into his face. She had not stood this close to him in ten years.

The girl beside Lord Sedgwick clasped her hands, gazing across the courtyard. The newer east wing extension of Montague House housed the Library Gallery, a magnificent addition to the museum. "Have you ever seen anything so . . . so wondrous, Erik?" The girl faced Christine as Joseph introduced Lord Sedgwick and his sister, Lady Rebecca.

Lady Rebecca dipped and her frothy pink gown rustled. Glossy black hair drawn to the back of her head fell in an abundance of curls over one shoulder. "It is a pleasure to finally meet you, Miss Sommers. Truly. Professor C. A. Sommers's book sits in our library. Tell her, Erik."

Then Christine was looking into his sherry-colored eyes, surprised that a man with Erik's background and aptitude would read what many in the literary and scientific communities considered intellectual twaddle. "You are familiar with my father's work?"

"He read the book," Lady Rebecca said, forging onward like a snowball rolling downhill, gathering girth and speed. "And he did not throw it away, which is always a good sign. Erik is very strict about what he will allow me to read. We are here tonight because he promised that while we are in London we could see this exhibit." She smiled up at Joseph, and Christine sensed Amelia stiffen. "It was our good fortune that my brother met Mr. Darlington at Edinburgh University some months ago and knew whom to contact." She shifted her attention to the massive hydra fountain. "Is it not remarkable, Erik?"

Curious about the girl's reaction, Christine adjusted her spectacles and peered at the fountain.

Carved from stone, the life-like many-headed reptile painted red and gold and with claws extended dominated the square in a spectacular watery display. It looked as if it had swooped down from the sky to snatch up—and deservedly so-—those unruly pint-sized humans destroying the flowerbeds in a game of cricket and violating the ambiance inspired by the drama.

Amelia's gaze also landed on the fountain. "'Tis a hideous sea serpent, to be sure." She shuddered, her delicate features incapable of frowning, no matter the occasion.

"Hydra," Christina corrected, unwilling to allow even a friend to blaspheme such a work of art, even unintentionally. "The fountain is a dragon."

"Hydra, basilisk, sea serpent, *dragon*—" Amelia fluttered a dainty gloved hand. "Is your father not the one who told us they were all the same beast beneath the myths? Is he not the one who told the Fossil Society last year that whatever they had learned about monsters not existing was a lie? Mrs. Hubble's husband still refuses to allow his wife to return to the meetings for the nightmares he caused her to suffer."

"What about you?" Lord Sedgwick queried. Four pairs of eyes turned to him, but *his* eyes were focused on Christine. "Do you believe in dragons, Miss Sommers?"

Only fools and children allowed themselves to believe in myths and fairy tales. "I am a scientist," she said after a moment.

Amelia suddenly laughed. "Good heavens, Miss Sommers is much too serious to believe in anything fantastical. She is a woman of discipline. Not romance."

Christine looked at Amelia. The first time she had made that remark, Christine had laughed and agreed, but that observation now disturbed her.

Lady Rebecca peered shyly at Christine. "Miss Sommers. Mr. Darlington said you are a passionate paleontologist. I guarantee it is of no offense to find another kindred soul in a woman." She pressed a fisted hand to her breast. "I, too, am passionate. I so envy Mr. Darlington's expedition to Australia. You must as well. He was telling us all about it on the way over here."

Lord Sedgwick coughed into his gloved hand. "I believe he also said he had not broken the news to anyone, Elf."

Christine did not understand. The look in Joseph's eyes left her floundering and sifting through the past week's conversations for clues as to Lady Rebecca's reference. "Perth? Australia?" *Her* Perth?

"Yes. Perth," Joseph said and she saw a sheepish look in his eyes. "I approached them last week."

"He is the new team leader," Amelia said, pride obvious.

Joseph slid his hand over Amelia's, pulling her nearer to his side. "We could not tell anyone until Lord Bingham informed me of the final decision this afternoon." His gaze slid to Amelia. "Now is as good a time as any to share the rest of our news. Amelia has consented to be my wife and will be traveling with me as my assistant."

Christine stared at them, dumbfounded. The bile of bitterness rose in her throat and she desperately tried to swallow it, but could not.

After a moment of awkward silence, Lord Sedgwick cleared his throat and took his sister's arm. "I think this conversation no longer concerns us, Elf."

"But this is all so terribly romantic," Lady Rebecca said, her melodic voice fraught with youthful romanticism. Her brother dragged her away before she could say more.

Christine suffered momentary panic that she might actually tear up. This made no sense. Amelia took Christine's hands into her own. "I so wanted to tell you everything, but Joseph wanted us to be together when we shared the news. I thought for sure my excitement tonight must have given something away." She peered up at Joseph with utter adoration in her eyes. "But we couldn't be happier."

A cool gust of wind pushed against Christine's mantelet and stirred the refuse on the streets, bringing with it the unpleasant scent of the Thames. She tucked a wisp of her hair behind her ears and remained silent.

She had planned everything so perfectly. And even if she had not, the stipend Joseph would receive from the museum was hardly enough to support a wife. Swallowing the constriction in her throat at last, Christine focused again and realized Joseph and Amelia were waiting for her to respond. And she still did not know what to say.

"This project is important to me, Christine," Joseph finally said when she remained speechless. "I have a chance to make a name for myself. That won't happen at Sommershorn Abbey. You must know that. I'm sorry, but there it is."

Joseph then peered down at Amelia, the action so tender, Christine was left even more confused. "We will be traveling to Gretna Green later tonight," he said. "You will understand why we cannot remain for the entire ceremony this evening. I will have to leave after they make the announcement about my appointment."

Amelia touched Christine's arm. "It is not our want to hurt you."

And yet they had hurt her. She felt as if Joseph had plunged a knife into her heart. Behind him the sun was about to leave the sky. The same sunset that tinted the clouds amber also colored the tips of his blond hair. For the first time in all the years since she had known him, she realized she had never taken the opportunity to slide her fingers through that golden hair or to tell him how she felt about him. Seeing his affection for Amelia made her feel the loss even more for she was losing them both.

She swallowed again. "Why didn't you tell me?"

"Because you would have said something unhelpful and neither of us wanted to be made to feel guilty," Joseph said quietly. "You have Sommershorn Abbey. You don't need Amelia and me," he added, as if that adequately explained everything, as if Christine had not worked hard and sacrificed her own dreams to make the school a success.

"Unhelpful, as in . . ." she fumbled through her thoughts. "How can you support a wife on a professor's stipend? I know how this museum finances its expeditions. Most of the expense will come out of your pocket."

"Sometimes one has to have the courage to act, Chrissie," Joseph said. "Or the moment will pass, and it will never come again. I will not be that man who wakes up tomorrow regretting what I did not try today. Your father once told me that it is far better to have failed trying than never to have made the effort at all."

Someone bumped Joseph, interrupting his conversation. Torchlight whisking in the breeze caught the sheen of long satin gowns, polished silver cufflinks, and tiaras. The last of the crowd was moving through the doors. Christine could hear the orchestra warming up.

Christine wanted to speak, to say anything to mend the rift that had opened between them. Her emotions were illogical and incongruous, completely reckless and without regard to the fact that she was happy for Joseph and Amelia. But the words would not come. She could not accept that all her plans of five minutes ago had been dashed to the rocks and devoured by sharks.

She could not!

Then Joseph laid his hand on Amelia's arm, and the moment for talking was gone.

He pressed his other hand against Amelia's back, his gaze hesitating on Christine as if accepting that she would not follow. "You'll be sitting at the head table with Lord Bingham and the other dignitaries," he said. "We probably won't have an opportunity to speak to each other later. I just wanted to congratulate you for having the courage to publish your father's work. I know it would have meant a lot to him."

Before she could tell Joseph to go to blazes and that she loved her father, despite what people may have thought, he had already turned away, placing Amelia slightly ahead of him, a stance that safeguarded her from arms and elbows. Christine watched them disappear, her height allowing her to follow his progress easily amid the thinning crowd. They were an attractive couple, she admitted, as they shuffled through the doors. The same doors Lord Sedgwick and his sister had entered minutes before. The urge to weep suddenly vanished.

Erik.

Here in London. At this very gala.

And a newer more terrible thought than Joseph and Amelia traveling to the other side of the world took hold in Christine's mind. Lord Sedgwick was a duke. He and his sister would probably be sitting at the same table of honor as she.

She raised her gaze to the heavens. And the night had only just begun.

Erik watched as Christine accepted another glass of champagne off a tray presented her by one of an army of footmen. Her fourth, Erik considered, as he sipped his own glass. Beneath an enormous chandelier, footmen threaded their way among the tables carrying large silver platters crowded with demitasse-size cups of melting sherbet. At the far end of the hall, an orchestra played a jaunty reel and most of the younger guests had already made their way onto the floor.

He found his sister enjoying the lively music. Becca was the reason he'd consented to come here tonight. But she was not the reason he stayed. He looked past her toward the elaborate entrance to the exhibits. The museum had closed its doors to the public hours ago and only the guests of the gala roamed the inner sanctum of the museum. Towering planters of palms and strands of orchids festooned the rotunda recalling the garden of Babylon, a place in history noted for wealth, luxury, and wickedness. He thought it an amusing contrast for the Fossil Society, an organization that fostered images of carnivorous monsters that once roamed the earth.

An hour had passed, during which the members present ceremoniously honored the achievements of their dead Society members. Christine sat farther down the table from him, her father's plaque beside her, a simple tribute given to her for Professor Sommers's work. Erik watched her gently polish it twice when she thought no one was looking—only to look up this last time and discover someone was watching. She eased a serviette over the plaque.

They had not spoken since their introduction outside on the steps of the museum. Tonight was the first time Erik had seen her in ten years. Her body was a little fuller and rounder, and looked softer in all the places a man would find his pleasure. She had the same full mouth he remembered. She had not worn spectacles when he knew her before, but she still had the same large, intelligent blue eyes that surveyed the world with a mild skepticism. Eyes that had a way of looking inside you.

The way she had always looked at him.

The way she was looking at him now. Half-annoyed—flushed, as if he'd caught her performing fellatio rather than the simple human act of remembering her father.

He grinned into his glass as if to tell her she could glare him to hell and back and it made no difference. He'd do as he pleased. She was still self-governing, opinionated, and willful, and completely unaware of the way every man at the table watched her, he thought as he shifted his attention to the boor beside her. If Lord Bingham ogled her any closer he'd have his face in her bosoms. But Christine, as usual, was oblivious.

Before his thoughts could overrule his restraint, Erik forced himself to turn in his chair and look back to the dance floor. Bingham was just one of dozens Erik had met since arriving in London two days ago.

Someone suddenly jostled his elbow, nearly spilling his champagne. Erik saved his glass as Lord Bingham plopped his large form down on the chair next to him. "How are you enjoying our little soiree, your grace?" Bingham jovially offered a glass of champagne, then frowned slightly as he noted the glass Erik already held in his hand. "Capital stuf' for putting the life into you. Only the bes' for those who know the difference between quality and mere French swill." He winked. "Men of our means like their quality. Right-oh chap? Drink up, I say." He tipped his glass and drank.

Erik's gaze moved past Bingham to where Christine had been sitting a moment before. Her chair was empty. A quick search of the crowd found her moving among the tables toward the door. He'd noted Darlington and the little blond who was to be his wife had slipped out after the awards ceremony. Christine was no doubt headed home.

"You're wasting your time with tha' one," Bingham sniffed. "Set in her ways. A cold fish. Spends most o' her time at Sommershorn Abbey managing the education of a bunch of girls. Can't do much else since her father passed. Doesn't run with our crowd. Not the right experience."

Erik gave Bingham his full attention. For the most part people avoided Erik as if he were a case of poison ivy. They skirted around him—unless they wanted something from him. It always amused him when a person thought he knew Erik well enough to be his friend, a fact that would make some conclude he had a sense of humor.

Bingham cleared his throat. "Pleasant enough assistant when she is volunteering here though," he hastily added. "Indispensable. Wouldn't know what to do without her help cataloging the exhibits. Has one here herself, someplace."

"Yes, I saw it. I believe it is located in the basement."

Bingham swallowed more champagne. "We've not had anyone of your stature take an interest in our organization in quite some time. You are here in London for the Season, your grace?"

"Business only."

"That's right. You've not participated in our London Season in . . . how many years?" When Erik did not reply, his grin faded and he gave a little cough. "Darlington mentioned you had an interest in fossils. You have certainly come to the right place. Are you a collector? Or a seller?"

Adjusting his evening jacket, Erik rose. "My sister is the collector. Not I."

"I see." Bingham hastily followed Erik to his feet. "Frankly, I was surprised when Darlington came to me and asked for two invitations to this gala. He said you corresponded with Lord Charles Sommers. Professor Sommers to all of us who knew him well. God bless his saintly soul wherever it may be." He chuckled, and the champagne in his glass slopped over and splashed on the man's waistcoat. "Most thought the man belonged in Bedlam. Soft in the head, if you know what I mean. But his book is wildly popular with this society. Do you have an interest in the existence of dragons?"

Erik remained silent, waiting for Bingham to get to the point.

"I only ask because Professor Sommers rarely corresponded with fossil hobbyists," Bingham said in an undertone. "His interests tended toward the serious collector. A person would have to have something valuable in his possession to hold Sommers's interest. Perhaps more than personal business brings you to London?"

"Business is never personal, Bingham." *Ever.* He'd learned long ago there was little he could not buy. "Now"—Eric looked toward the doorway through which Christine had just disappeared—"if you will excuse me."

Bingham sputtered. "Yes, of course."

But Erik was already walking away.

* * *

"Good night, Miss Sommers," the watchman said as Christine passed him in the darkened hallway.

"Good night, Mr. Traverse. Please tell your mother I said hello."

Cloak in hand, Christine hurried through the Hall of Unicorns toward the back door. This wing of the museum was only slightly quieter than the corridor she had left, as it was closed off to the public. But music from the orchestra reverberated against the ceiling.

She'd made a brief detour to the cloakroom, but other than the few times a guest stopped her, congratulating her on Papa's award or asking about Joseph's new appointment or why Aunt Sophie had not attended the festivities tonight, she had made a successful exit. No one could accuse her of running away if no one knew she'd escaped.

As Christine rounded a corner, she nearly collided with . . . Erik! A gasp escaped her.

He was standing with his arms crossed, his shoulder leaning against the doorjamb, quite at his leisure with her effort to elude him. He had the most piercing eyes she had ever known, and they did not waver from hers. All night she'd been forced to smile and pretend Erik Boughton was not sitting five feet down the table from her. And now she no longer need pretend. Such was the irony of her life. She was almost relieved to finally face him.

"It warms the cockles of my heart to know you've na' changed, *leannanan*."

The gently spoken Gaelic endearment he'd once bestowed on her lifted her chin a notch. She vehemently disliked the familiar thrill that arced through her. "Do not presume to still know me, Lord Sedgwick."

The faintest smile lifted the graceful curve of his mouth. He had made no move to detain her. He didn't have to. His very presence held her immobile in invisible arms of warmth. She had the uncomfortable impression he knew exactly the turmoil his presence was causing her.

"How have you been, Christine?"

"Very well." She paused as her mind cast about for something more intelligent to say. "And you?"

He answered the same.

Ten years all summed up in two little words. It wasn't even as if they had parted on poor terms. Not completely anyway. She had simply departed and vanished to another continent, and he had wed her cousin Charlotte.

But the fact that he was here, not only in her part of England but at the museum, was an infringement. "Why are you here at the Fossil Society gala?" she asked. "I cannot imagine that these people would interest you."

"No, I imagine you cannot *imagine* any such thing. Becca has an interest in fossils. I am in London on business and so I thought to bring her. Darlington arranged for the introduction to your Lord Bingham. And so here I am."

The corner of her mouth crooked slightly at the memory of Bingham having to surrender his seat of prominence at their table to Sedgwick. "*My* Lord Bingham is not used to being outranked or -flanked. He likes to think himself king even if it is only the Fossil Society he rules. Few remember it was Papa who founded the organization."

After a pause, he said, "I was sorry to hear about your father's passing."

She studied Erik Boughton's handsome face in the sconce light. The last time she had stood this close to him she had been deeply, irrevocably in love. "He always liked you."

Erik gave a humorless laugh. "Despite the fact no one else in your family did?"

"If Papa found fault with you it wasn't because he believed you gave my cousin scarlet fever," she said.

For a moment, Erik started to say something more.

With each heartbeat, Christine felt herself pulling back into her comfort zone where everything was safe and in its place. A place she could control. For the space of a few breaths, neither of them spoke. Then he asked, "What happened to you after you left England?"

"I spent seven years with Papa and later Mr. Darlington, going from dig to dig, from the Rhineland to South America, only to return to England and unearth our largest discovery ever, near Lyme Regis. It was either that or learn to play the pianoforte. I was never any good at playing the lady." Normally she did not allow herself to blather and her impulsive words made her blush. She cleared her throat. "But that does not mean I do not have standards. I have the school's reputation to think of, after all."

"Obviously no student's doting papa has seen you in that gown."

She peered down at herself, pleased that he had not only noted what she wore, but also considered it provocative. She rarely had the opportunity to wear such a dress . . . and tonight was supposed to have been a special occasion. "What is wrong with this gown?"

"Nothing," he said. "You put the highest-paid demirep to shame." Leaning nearer, he said, "And I mean that as a compliment."

Disdain for his humor flattened her smile. "Clearly you have developed the manners of a poet. A very poor one."

"I never had manners of a poet. I thought that was why I interested you."

The triumphant end of a lively reel rattled the artifacts in the preview case. Silence followed, startling in its intensity, as if it signified more than the end to this evening's festivities. Yet, neither of them hurried to be the first to say good-bye.

Then he stood aside for her to pass. But as she slipped past him, his hand snagged her arm, turning her. His tension was so great he might have been made of pressed iron. Aware of a sudden burn behind her eyes and his breath against her temple, she lifted her chin.

"I am glad to see you doing well, Christine."

"You as well, your grace."

His expression changed subtly, unmistakably.

Then she was walking past him into the fog that had settled over London like pea soup tonight. As she hailed a hansom and then leaned back against the aged, cracked leather seat in the cab, she drew in her breath, recognizing tonight had not gone well for her self-confidence, which was normally unflappable under the most dire of circumstances. Everything had seemed to escalate to more than it should have. Erik's presence had only added to the burden of Joseph's rejection for it reminded her of a far more painful time in her life when she had watched the man she'd once loved wed another.

She had met the infamous duke of Sedgwick her first Season in London at a ball given for her cousin Charlotte at the Somerset manse. That year had been the only time in her life when she'd contemplated trading her scientific passions for something . . . something elusively magic. She'd been young enough to feel her heart awaken to the first stirrings of love—or what she had believed was love. At eighteen, her world could not have been brighter or filled with more promise.

Theirs had been a secret courtship, precipitated by her, ended by him, a fleeting interlude in her life that had managed to imprint itself on her memory with an impunity that had shaped her relationship with men in her life since.

Christine had always wondered in the deepest recesses of her mind if Erik had chosen her cousin Charlotte because he'd thought her more beautiful, less willful. Or because Charlotte's dowry would add massive wealth to his holdings. The Sommers family had certainly misjudged the profitability of the land that came with Charlotte, just as they misjudged the young duke of Sedgwick. To this day, Charlotte's father, Christine's uncle, still contested the agreement that gave Sedgwick the York land in exchange for a mere two-week marriage to his daughter. Her uncle still harbored the hope that at the very least, Sedgwick would go to the gallows for the murder of his *second* wife, of less than a year, after *she* vanished. That had been seven years ago. Christine knew he'd had a daughter by his second wife.

Christine did not know if all the gossip about Erik was true. Through the years, she'd learned to dismiss the scandal rags.

But strangely . . . that night as she lay awake in bed staring at the plaster ceiling, instead of thinking about Joseph and Amelia on their way to Gretna Green and feeling sorry for herself, she was thinking about the man who had long ago introduced her to more than her first tempestuous kiss.

It bothered her that Erik was still as handsome, just as perilous as he had always been.

He had a little more silver at his temple. But she doubted little else had changed. She would wager he was still prideful, stubborn, and determined to have the world served to him on his own terms. Now, after ten years, Erik Boughton, the devil Duke of Sedgwick, had returned to London, almost on her doorstep, and Christine found herself wondering why.

Chapter 2

Christine awoke as the sunlight burned away the darkness and the birds commenced their happy chatter. Dozens of happy birds lived in the trees outside her window. Where was her cat when she needed him? No pillow over her head could snuff out the din of cheerful chirping.

With a groan, she finally turned and peered over her shoulder at the clock across the room. She kicked off the eiderdown. Not because it was time to be out of bed but because she had forgotten to wind the clock again. She was usually ever so sensible about such things. Punctuality was a virtue. She washed and dressed before her maid arrived, and hurried downstairs.

Great Auntie Sophie was already at the table, bent over the morning broadsheet, poring over every word in the society columns. No frivolous periodical, newspaper, or book in all London went unread in the Sommers household.

Lady Sophia was Christine's paternal grandmother's sister, and had been living at Sommershorn Abbey for as long as Christine remembered. She was a brilliant archeologist, the first in the family. Christine loved no one more, but she and Aunt Sophie could not be more different in character.

While Christine maintained a dutiful, sensible approach to life, her aunt smoked and drank and scandalized proper society at every opportunity. It wasn't that Christine was an angel or had never lied, but Aunt Sophie never lost her fear of the fight and remained proud of her sedition. Even this morning, her rouged cheeks and scarlet gown shouted defiance.

"Good morning, Aunt Sophie."

"Morning, dear." Aunt Sophie spoke, looking up as Christine kissed the proffered withered cheek.

She walked to the breakfront and poured coffee from the silver service Mrs. Samuels set out every morning. "You look very bright this morning."

"And you look as if you are attending a funeral. Who died *this* time?"

Christine stirred cream into her coffee. Other than the return of an old love and all her dreams passing into an ignoble demise, nothing in her life had changed from yesterday. "I am teaching classes this afternoon."

"That explains the somber look. Try to be tolerant of them, dear. The girls at this school truly do look up to you. You are a wonderful mother figure to them."

Aunt Sophie made her feel like a white-haired crone. She set down her spoon.

"*Why* are you teaching today?"

"Amelia and Mr. Darlington have left Sommershorn Abbey," she said without turning. "They eloped."

A tiny gasp came from Sophie's throat. Little could shock Aunt Sophie. "Mr. Darlington and *Amelia*?"

"The museum appointed him to lead the expedition to Perth next month. He'll be gone for years." Christine slid her finger around the smooth cup rim. "Amelia will make him a good assistant."

"Oh, my. Oh, dear."

"This is an opportunity for Mr. Darlington."

"What about the projects the two of you were working on together?"

"We have had no projects since his return from Edinburgh. With Papa gone, there is nothing I can offer him here at Sommershorn. The historical and archaeological societies denied every application I submitted. The museum was my last chance to prove I could undertake an expedition. They chose him." She was thoughtful as she turned and sipped from her cup. "Do you ever regret not marrying and having children?"

"Regret is as useless as a three-wheeled cart on a bumpy road. *Never* go through your life regretting anything, dear."

Sunlight spilled through the windows behind Lady Sophia and warmed the air. The green walls topped with classical frieze matched the room's enormous fireplace and served as a background for the many antiquities the family had collected during years of traveling abroad. Christine always found as much comfort and inspiration in this room as she did in Sophie's sage advice.

"I see Lord Sedgwick attended the gala," Sophie said.

Christine stiffened. Aunt Sophie had to go and bring up the inevitable. "If you are wondering if we spoke, the answer is yes," she replied, dumping another hefty spoonful of sugar into her coffee. "He attended with his sister."

"His grace is courting the *ton* for another bride, who will give him an heir. They claim no proud papa is standing in line to wed his daughter to him."

"Truly, Sophie," Christine said quietly. "You are as bad as the rest. It is no wonder he chooses to remain in Scotland, the way people treat him here. Besides, he doesn't need an heir. He has a daughter. Scottish law allows a daughter to inherit."

"His duchy is an English patent, dear. Not Scots."

"Oh."

Aunt Sophie studied Christine, then returned her attention to the paper. She chuckled. "Your uncle must be apoplectic. My sister's side of the family never did have the sense of an acorn, which is why they are now poor."

Christine carried her cup to the window and stared outside at the azaleas. This was not a conversation she wanted to have. "C. A. Sommers won the Fossil Society's award last night," she said after a moment, changing the topic.

"I never doubted that outcome for a moment," Sophie said.

Christine turned. "I wish you could have been there."

Sophie looked up, her blue eyes blinking. "What would I do at a function where I would be required to be nice to those bloodsucking windbags you want to impress? You had Amelia and Mr. Darlington to accompany you. I'm just sorry Bingham, the old blatherskite, chose him over you to lead the Perth expedition. Joseph was always a better geologist than a paleontologist."

Christine pulled out the chair next to Sophie's and sat. "Oh, Sophie." Passion infused her voice. "What I wouldn't give to make an earth-shattering discovery. A discovery so magnificent . . ." Setting her coffee cup on the table, she focused on Aunt Sophie's kind face. "The entire world would be forced to admit that what I have to offer is important."

"Is that what is truly bothering you, dear?"

Of course it was. Didn't Sophie understand her better than anyone? "I want to be like you, Sophie. Free of the *ton*'s prying eyes and suffocating rules. I want to seize the moment. I want to be taken seriously."

Sophie patted Christine's hand. "One day, you will show every stodgy scholar in Britain a thing or two about the female intellect, dear. But you must carefully plan and be patient about these things. Something always comes up, and when it does, *then* you seize the moment."

"Patience." Christine sat back in her chair. "How can I be patient when the entire world is passing me by? *I* should be the one going to Perth."

"But you are not, dear. The museum trustees did not choose you. Mr. Darlington did not choose you."

Christine picked up a folded serviette from the table, snapped it open and dabbed the corner of each eye. "This house will not be the same without Amelia. I shall miss her laughter most, I think."

"If it is any consolation, I am still here," Sophie pointed out.

"Thank you, Aunt Sophie. You have always been dependable in that way." She smiled. "Perhaps we could spend more time together now that Amelia isn't here."

A knock on the front door signaled an end to their *tête-à-tête*. Sophie patted Christine's cheek. "That would be wonderful, dear. We can share a spot of tea later this week."

A footman entered the dining room and announced that Lady Bosworth's carriage and party had arrived.

"I am off to the races, dear."

"I thought you didn't like Lady Bosworth."

"Pish-posh." Aunt Sophie tugged on her gloves. "That was yesterday. She has apologized for whatever it was she did that caused the tiff. At my age, it is never wise to hold grudges for too long. You will understand soon enough, dear."

Aunt Sophie hurried out of the room, leaving Christine alone with her thoughts and listening as the horses and carriage pulled away from the drive. At sixty-eight, Aunt Sophie showed a remarkable lack of regret for any of the choices she had made in life. She was who she was and to the devil with anyone who found exception to her character.

Her cat meowed at her feet. Christine looked down. Beast, her fat tabby, rubbed against her legs. She lifted the large tomcat onto her lap. He began to purr against her hand, his front paws kneading her arm. She'd found him years ago, after the poor thing had been run over by a beer wagon, and she had nursed him back to health. He had one golden eye and parts of his body were missing fur, but to her, he was a beautiful cat.

Nuzzling his head, she picked a piece of cheese off Aunt Sophie's plate and rewarded him for his affection. "You know who loves you best, don't you?" she cooed.

But after a while Beast abandoned her for the outdoors, where an abundance of mice awaited the patient hunter and he could be king of his world.

Christine made her way through the empty and hallowed corridor of the school where the young women who attended learned about something more than manners, etiquette, and needlepoint. Many of the students here were younger daughters of genteel landowners, bereft of the needed dowry to marry well. They would never see a Season in London. But for most of the sixteen girls enrolled at Sommershorn Abbey and for the three teachers, former students who spent the year living among the girls, the experience this school provided gave them the means to better their lives.

Christine picked up her pace and felt a pin drop from her tightly wound chignon. It fell to the wooden floor with a soft click, but she couldn't stop to find where it had fallen. Already she was late.

She paused outside the classroom. It would not do
to allow the girls to see her harried, especially when
she preached the importance of self-respect and control. She opened the door. The girls were congregating
around the desk, clearly not expecting to see Christine.
They straightened guiltily, their excited chatter coming
to an abrupt end as if someone had doused them with
ice water. Each of them scattered to take her place
behind her wooden desk.

"Miss Amelia has left us," Christine explained when
she had their attention again. She walked across the
room to stand behind Amelia's disorganized desk. "I
will be taking over her classes until the end of the session this week."

The girls looked at each other and giggled. Dolly,
a lanky seventeen-year-old with a mop of red curls
spoke first. "Did she and Mr. Darlington really
elope?"

Startled, Christine looked at the girls, their expressions intent as they awaited her reply. "Did Miss Amelia
inform you of her plans?"

The girls grew more excited and animated. "Not in
so many words, Miss Christine," Dolly replied, clearly
the class spokesperson. She was the oldest.

"It's the magic ring what done it," the school's
newest acquisition blurted. Babs was the fifteen-year-
old granddaughter of Aunt Sophia's whist partner.

"Two months ago she made a wish that Mr. Darlington would marry her," another girl replied to a chorus
of animated gibberish.

" 'Tis true, Miss Christine," Dolly said with heartfelt
passion.

"What is true?"

Dolly stepped forward. "This morning we found the
ring on her desk. It must have finally come off her finger

yesterday. The ring is truly magic. She wanted to wed Mr. Darlington. And now she is wed."

Christine held out her hand. Dolly dutifully dropped a band of silver into her palm. Christine had in fact seen this ring on Amelia's hand.

"There is no such thing as magic."

"But there is, Miss Christine," Dolly insisted. "Miss Amelia proved it. She wanted Mr. Darlington to fall in love with her and he did."

Christine took a seat at the desk and peered sternly over the rim of her spectacles at each of the girls. "Have you considered that he fell in love with her because she was worthy of his affection?"

From the blank response on their young faces, they had not considered the possibility. Christine turned the ring into the light, noting an odd Celtic inscription carved within the band. *Chance not. Win not.* The ring itself was made of braided antique silver laced with something black.

"Where did she get this?"

"Lady Sophia gave it to Babs last year and said it was a special ring just for special girls," Dolly said. "If a person puts it on then what she wants most in the world will make itself known *all* within five minutes. Babs really wanted to come to this school. When she put the ring on, she asked her papa if she could attend Sommershorn Abbey this year and he said yes. Isn't that so, Babs?"

The girl in question nodded vigorously. Christine shook her head and tried not to make light of the girl's supposed miracle.

"Oh, but 'tis true. He'd been adamantly against the school, Miss Christine," Dolly insisted. "Only when Babs came here did the ring come off. Then six months ago, Sally put on the ring. Didn't you, Sal?"

The young blond girl in a black-and-white pinafore beside her nodded. "Papa was going to betroth me to that lecherous Viscount Alton. A letter arrived calling me home. But when I arrived, Lord Alton had run off with my older sister. Then Miss Amelia put on the ring. We were in your office upstairs, standing beside your desk when Mr. Darlington arrived just then, back from Edinburgh. He'd come to see you, but when he glimpsed Miss Amelia"—Dolly clutched her fist to her chest—"we all knew it was she he would pick."

For a moment, the words almost made Christine look away. Of course, Joseph had come to Christine's office first. But she had been in the "dead room" that day cleaning up a fossil. She looked at her young protégés. "This is exactly the kind of balderdash that gives women a bad name."

Dolly lifted her chin. "You are always about facts and truths, Miss Christine. What if something else does exist that cannot be explained by physical evidence? Isn't it our responsibility to explore these possibilities as well? What if we want to believe in something more?"

Christine looked at the girls and felt a strange kinship to each of them. All of them in some way stood outside society. "You cannot wish your problems away," she quietly said. "Your destiny is not inscribed in the stars. There is no such thing as magic or fairy tales . . . or curses . . . or mystical phenomenon. This is only a ring."

None of them looked convinced.

"Would it satisfy you if I put it on? Would you then be convinced that everything that has happened thus far has a clear and logical explanation and there is no such thing as magic to grant you something that you are not willing to earn for yourself?" She turned in the chair and found the regulator clock on the wall. "Five minutes, you say."

The girls nodded and pushed close to the desk. Christine peered at each face. "All right. In five minutes, you will all forget this ring and allow me to get to the business of teaching you something important. Are we in agreement?"

"Yes, Miss Christine," they all answered in unison.

"Very well." She looked down at the ring, felt a strange tingle in her palm just then, and hesitated. The sliver warmed her flesh, an odd sensation. She attributed the sudden flush of heat to everyone standing too close.

"Perhaps you should all find your seats first," Christine suggested.

After they did as she asked, then watched her expectantly, Christine slid the band onto her right ring finger and held up her hand.

"Five minutes," she said.

She folded her hands in front of her and waited for the clock to tick away five minutes.

Tick. Tick. Tick.

Her senses picked up each second. The birds outside the window suddenly sounded too loud. She could hear the rush of blood in her ears. Then her breathing calmed and she felt a strange sort of euphoria fall over her. When she looked at the clock again, three minutes had passed.

"What did you wish for?" Dolly asked.

"I thought the ring is supposed to know what it is I want above all else," Christine pointed out. "The ring is omniscient, is it not?"

Since none of them knew what *omniscient* meant, they did not disagree. At the four-minute mark, the girls' expressions began to fall. Christine hated to crush them with facts, but it was best they learned the hard truth of life now. The clock continued to tick away the seconds, and Christine was impatient to remove the ring. Whatever she wanted most in the world had best make an appearance in the next thirty seconds, because the ring was about to come off.

But just when Christine was ready to remove the ring, a sharp knock at the door startled her. A collective gasp sounded. Even Christine froze.

"Aren't you going to answer the door?" Dolly whispered when Christine made no effort to move.

She pushed away from the desk. "Pull out your tablets," she said. "This performance is at an end."

Not normally superstitious, she could not entirely ignore the shiver that suddenly went down her spine as the door loomed in front of her. What exactly did she want more than anything?

Good grief, I am as bad as my students are.

She opened the door.

Lord Sedgwick stood in the corridor.

Chapter 3

"**L**ord Sedgwick . . . !"

Hearing Christine's voice catch on a gasp, Erik had the distinct feeling she was about to slam the door in his face. "What are *you* doing here?" she breathed.

Erik tapped a quirt against a tall riding boot. "Miss Sommers. I have not come at an inconvenient time, I hope. I did not hear noise inside and thought you might be alone." He peered past her into the classroom. Thirteen pairs of wide eyes stared back at him.

She stepped outside the classroom and shut the door, bracing the wooden portal with her body. "You most definitely have come at an inconvenient time. You aren't even supposed to be in this corridor," she rasped, even though he'd seen visitors coming and going through the main gate. "How did you get inside this building? How did you find me?"

Amusement lifted his brows. "This *is* Sommershorn Abbey, is it not? I rode through the front gate on my horse. The groundskeeper directed me here. I saw you from outside through the window." His mouth twisted slightly. "It is only business that has brought me to Sommershorn Abbey this day, Miss Sommers."

"Mr. Darlington isn't here, if that is whom you came

to see. In case you didn't know, he and Amelia eloped last night. Furthermore, I am teaching her class now. So if you will excuse me . . ."

He did not excuse her. In fact, he stuck his quirt between her and the doorjamb, preventing her easy escape. Conscious of the prim scent of lavender clinging to her clothes, he cocked a dry smile as she twisted around to confront his actions. "Thank you, Miss Sommers, for that bit o' information." His breath stirred the hair at her temple. "Is there a place we can speak privately?"

"I . . ."

Squeezed as she was against the corner of the door and the jamb, she gave him a vague smile. "What is it you want, your grace?"

"You, Miss Sommers. I need the opinion of an expert to tell me exactly what my people have found on my land. Honestly"—he shrugged, a surprisingly boyish action for the stern taskmaster of the Sedgwick empire—"you are the reason I came to London. You were the first person I could think to come to who would not think me completely mad."

"Then you give me more credit than I deserve." She paused and seemed to reverse her thoughts. "What is it you have found?"

"In private."

She peered up and down the hall. "Very well. Upstairs. My office is on the left, you can't miss it. We'll have privacy. Wait there." Her hand closing on the doorknob, she narrowed her eyes. "And don't *touch* anything."

Before he could reply, she opened the door, then shut it in his face. Both his brows arched. Her scent lingered in the narrow space where she'd stood. Feeling momentarily bereft of thought, Erik stepped away. Then he turned and looked toward the staircase. He was restless and his restlessness disturbed him.

He found Christine's cramped second-floor office at the top of the stairs. The door was unlocked and he stepped inside only to snag his boot on the carpet. Pulling aside the faded chintz curtain to let light inside, he returned his attention to the dull room.

Dusty old books spilled from overflowing bookcases and were piled high against the wall. Engraved plaques, diplomas, and etchings covered oaken-paneled walls, along with snippets of articles cut from newspapers and framed periodicals. There was not a hint of brightness on the floor or the walls or found on the shelves. He picked up a human skull sitting next to a stack of papers and a bound manuscript and turned it over in his hand. Some things did stay the same, he realized. Christine always did fancy the macabre.

"I found that skull in a cave in France," she said from the doorway, catching him like a child with his hand in the cookie tin after she'd told him not to touch anything. He replaced the skull where he'd found it. "I was eight at the time. Papa said it is probably thousands of years old."

She remained just outside the light filtering through the window behind him. "Everything in here is old," he said.

She twisted at the ring on her finger and seemed to hesitate as if debating the choices presented her. But obviously having no patience with coyness, she stepped into the room and shut the door. "I have a student watching the class, but I can't remain here long."

She placed herself behind the desk. Not only behind the desk, but also behind the cracked leather chair. Her hair looked on the verge of slipping her chignon and hung loosely at her nape. He'd never known a woman who could walk into a room no matter the occasion and always appear as if she'd just been tumbled in a loft somewhere.

"I don't expect that we are children or should go about behaving as if we should be strangers," she said. "Especially since we do know each other."

Intimately, her voice intoned and which he inferred even before he'd read the thought in her eyes.

She brought her attention around to the boxes stacked against the walls and frowned. "Would you care for a drink before you sit down and tell me why you are here? I think there is a bottle of Scotch somewhere around here. I'm sure I could find it."

"You need not go to the trouble."

They stood across the desk from each other. "You said you needed my opinion about something found on your land?" she asked.

With an impatient curse, he shoved his gloved hand inside his coat to remove the packet, the reason he'd made the trip to London—or one of them anyway. The other stood in front of him.

"Surveyors working for me found most of this some weeks ago." He set the palm-sized packet on the desk next to a taxidermied young caiman and unwrapped the contents for Christine to view. "An engineering crew for the railroad set off a massive landslide last summer. Since then my people have been finding all manner of ghoulish discoveries washing up on the bottomlands after the rains push the river from its banks. My sister is now an expert fossil collector." He stepped back to allow her to view the packet.

She stepped around the chair to better look at the bones and sundry other fragments, including teeth. The flash of a shiny bauble lured most women to men. But not Christine. Give her death and destruction and a bone yard to explore, and she was your friend for life. "Survey crew?" she asked.

"I am building a levee. I intend to shift the river in an attempt to save a thousand essential acres of bottomland."

He watched the corner of her mouth crook as she looked up from her study. "Leave it to you to presume you can change the course of a mighty river."

He eased his hands into his pockets. "Actually it is my intent to push the river back to its original course before that bloody, incompetent crew blew up half a mountainside to build tracks through the southern edge of my property. The levee project I'm working on is essential to the survival of a dozen farms that will not withstand another summer of flooding." He pointed to the loose pieces. "Work has practically halted since that was discovered."

She opened a top drawer in her desk and pulled out a large magnifying glass to resume her study. "Why? People are always finding such things. Britain is filled with archeological sites."

"Not like this one."

She peered up at him, her hair framing her face.

"This is different," he said. "During the past year two of my workers have simply vanished." He cleared his throat and walked to the window. "It seems the Sedgwick dynasty's curse now extends beyond my personal life." He turned back and faced her. "I came here because I don't have to worry about you believing in such supernatural rubbish. I need an opinion."

"I see," she murmured and returned her attention to the bones.

He settled his gaze on her profile. "I need answers."

"This is human and . . ." She held up the jaw fragment, to which all the upper teeth were still attached. She unwrapped the second specimen, raising it slowly to the light. "Obviously, not human."

Her interest piqued, she eagerly unwrapped the other pieces. "The explosion probably unearthed some ancient burial ground, which is why the two are mixed," she said to explain the human remains. "Not only is the rest *not* human"—he watched her hand hesitate on what looked to be a single five-inch-wide flat-pointed tooth. Becca had found it six months ago after a flood deposited shale and rock all over the bottomland south of Sedgwick Castle—"they look . . ."

"Like something never found before?" he said. "Something that might be found in your father's book?"

She raised her head. He glimpsed both the flush of confusion and excitement in her face before she tucked the emotion behind her blue eyes and straightened. "Where did you say you found these?"

"Near a riverbank about two miles from Sedgwick Castle. The river empties from the higher elevations surrounding my land, much of it inaccessible."

"This is why the Fossil Society interests you." Her gaze dropped to the human jaw fragment. "Yet why do I get the impression you aren't just interested in the paleontology aspect of this find?"

"True," he said. "That is my sister's passion."

"Then what is it you are after?"

He faced Christine with the desk a barricade between them and stepped nearer. "Answers," he said quietly.

"You think you know to whom these teeth belonged," she said.

"I do not *think* anything. I *know* to whom that fragment belongs."

"Your second wife."

He peered at her intently. Elizabeth had been missing almost seven years. There would not be much left to identify. But teeth were distinctive. He knew in his gut that upper jaw belonged to his wife.

"Why not go to your constable?" Christine asked.

"Because there is something on my land responsible for killing people. A cave, a hole, a crevice. Hell, some people think it is a monster, a ghost, or the Sedgwick curse. I need someone who knows how to follow the right clues and resolve this question. By the dimension of the tooth you are holding, something else *large* is buried up there."

"May I keep these for a few days? I would like to study this find."

His first instinct was to tell her no for she had already given him what he had come here for.

With the recent bones found on his property, Erik needed someone who could give him answers. But her request demanded that he answer to himself his real motives for being here, which had only partially to do with fossils and his need to absolve himself of a crime he did not commit. It had not been an accident that he had contacted Darlington after Charles Sommers passed away.

Erik picked up his hat and riding quirt from the chair and walked to the desk. He settled the hat on his head, then reached across the desk for the pen and dipped the nib in ink to scratch out his address in Mayfair. From the corner of his eye, he caught a glimpse of her skirt. In the dull light, he'd thought it a drab gray, but it was blue with little white flowers falling like random snowflakes. She was wearing a petticoat, one at most, for her skirt merely covered her hips and did not hide her shape. Following the path of this thought, he raised his gaze to find her looking at him with equal intensity.

The air seemed to warm around him, and over the smell of old books and dust that filled the room, something more enticing than a hothouse herbal garden touched his senses.

Forcing himself to concentrate, he scribbled on the piece of paper where he could be reached this next week. "I will be in meetings over the next four days," he said, writing furiously, "after that, I cannot tell you for sure where I will be. If you need to make an appointment, it might be best to go through my man of affairs." He held out the slip of paper and waited for her to take it.

There was a sudden heavy silence. She slid it from his fingers. "Your social appointment calendar must be brimming over."

His lips curled into a self-deprecating smile that briefly touched his eyes. "Are you asking in a polite, un-obtrusive way if I have come to London to secure myself another bride, among my other business of meeting with financiers, solicitors, and visiting you?"

She flushed, and he could see that was exactly what she was asking.

"Why?" He grinned. "Are you interested?"

"I most certainly am not."

Her reaction might have amused him had he suddenly not found himself insulted by the swiftness of her answer. But something told him Christine had not survived the last decade living in a man's world because her innards were made of fluff. She had learned long ago that there was no room in her world for frailty.

"What happened to you, Christine? You used to laugh and enjoy life. Where is your sense of humor?"

"Why are you here, Erik? Not in London. But why are you here at Sommershorn when you have the entire museum staff at your disposal?"

He set down the pen on the desk. "Besides the fact

that I need this find to remain secret, I came to hire the most qualified expert in the field to identify and trace the source of those bones. The work will be hard and arduous, as the crags around my home are not inviting of a Sunday picnic. Six months ago, I had written to your father about the possibility of his coming to Scotland. At the time, I did not know he was ill. He recommended Darlington."

The smooth line of her jaw went rigid as an ax. "As you already know, Mr. Darlington has been contracted by the museum for a dig in Perth."

Erik smiled, though no one of intelligence would construe the action as friendly. "I'm rich, Miss Sommers. I can offer him a hundred times what the museum is willing to pay. If I am not mistaken, my find will prove to be far more lucrative to his career than anything in Perth. Everyone has a price, Christine."

"You have not changed. You still think people can be bought and sold like commodities. Do you always win, your grace?"

He looked around the cluttered office that held the remnants of so much of her life, then at her. "Do you, *leannanan?*"

How dare Erik Boughton presume she was not qualified to lead an expedition, that she was too delicate to find her way among "arduous" Scottish crags, as if she had not climbed a *real* mountain before. His insult about her lack of humor came back to jab her as well and she sniffed in defiance of his insult. She had humor and laughed easily enough when she understood the joke.

Hurrying across the grounds, Christine paid little attention to the wind that had picked up since that morning and now whipped at her skirts as though the humidity and her emotions had conspired to create a storm. Head down, she persevered through the long grass as she swept past the pond.

How dare Erik give away quite possibly the greatest find of the century. Why would Papa even suggest Joseph Darlington's name? Men! Six of one, half a dozen of the other. They were all the same.

"Miss Christine! Miss Christine!"

She came to an abrupt halt and looked up suddenly at the heavy, black clouds forming on the horizon behind the wind-whipped oaks. Looking around, she caught her hair with one hand and vaguely wondered if she had imagined someone calling her name, or if God—or the devil—had whispered her name.

"Miss Christine!"

Christine turned in the direction of the school. Babs, Dolly, and the impish blond Sal, three of the girls who had been in class were running toward her with six other girls in tow. Only one thing in life struck fear into Christine more than standing in front of a classroom filled with intrepid students who asked a question she could not answer. And that was being caught outside in the open with those very same daunting students.

Putting on her optimum teacher smile, she greeted the girls. Dolly was the first to speak, her red curls bouncing around her flushed face. Each of them was carrying books. "You did not return to class. We have been waiting to speak with ye, mum."

All the girls flocked around her. "Everyone is talking about Lord Sedgwick's visit," Dolly said before Christine could find her voice.

"Will he steal you away from us, just like Mr. Darlington stole Miss Amelia?" Sal asked.

"It isn't stealing if she *wants* to go away with him," Babs said.

"But you believe in the ring now?" Dolly's hopeful voice persisted. "Why else would a rich, handsome *duke* visit Sommershorn Abbey?"

Christine had completely forgotten the ring. *Heavens.*

She stared down at the braided band of silver that seemed to be glowing blue in the dreary gray light. The thing had got stuck on her finger and she'd forgotten about it in her vexed emotional state.

"You must have been thinking about his grace before you put on the ring," Babs insisted, her voice fraught with awe. "Or he would not have appeared at our classroom door. What did you wish for, Miss Christine?"

Silence gathered around Christine at last, as anxious eyes awaited her reply.

It was true that morning she had been thinking about Erik, but that was only because of their meeting last night at the gala. She had merely been woolgathering this morning—something she rarely did—when he'd popped into her thoughts again. But thinking about a man did not mean she wanted him to show up on her doorstep.

And, yes, she admitted that she had told Aunt Sophie she wanted to make an earth-shattering discovery. *A discovery so magnificent . . . the entire world would stand up and take notice.*

Clutching the packet to her chest, Christine knew that what Erik had brought was indeed something magnificent.

She suddenly felt dizzy.

But none of this meant the ring was magic. The idea was ludicrous.

If the ring were magic, she'd be able to fly or turn invisible or possess some other power that would allow her to transcend mere human frailties. She would be invulnerable to doubts, her intellect intact, and she'd be perfectly cheery, like a dollop of warm sunshine on cobbles.

Taking in their determined expressions, she recognized the futility in glossing over reality. A reality born from the wisdom that came with age and experience, a wisdom that rebelled against a concept charged with fanciful notions. A wisdom acquired through life experience, and that refused to make her a co-conspirator with her students. And then she folded.

How could she be so cruel as to tell them the truth?

"It is not wise to believe in sorcery and fairytales," she told them instead.

"Why, Miss Sommers?" Babs asked.

"Because . . ." For a moment, Christine was at a complete loss as she sought to explain her logic. "Because we are sensible, and sensible people do not waste time on such piffle."

She started to step past them when Dolly spoke. "But Miss Sommers . . ."

Christine stopped. Something in her chest tightened. They looked so crestfallen, she felt a compunction to explain. "Lord Sedgwick and I used to know each other a long time ago," she said gently. "He and my father were in contact and we met again last night at the Fossil Society gala when Mr. Darlington introduced us. His grace then came to talk to me about . . ." she thought of the need for secrecy about his find, "something private. That is all."

Relieved to feel the first plop of rain against her shoulders, Christine looked up at the thunderheads. She told all of them to get back to their rooms.

"Go on now, get to shelter." She smiled encouragingly.

But watching them shuffle away, she didn't understand why she felt as if she had just crushed their hearts.

Christine could not remove the ring.

She used lard, tallow, ice, steam, Aunt Sophie's cod-liver oil. Nothing worked. In the end, Christine resorted to wearing gloves during class the next week and pleaded hard work in the laboratory to get Mrs. Samuels, her housekeeper, to deliver her meals in the evening while she studied Erik's tooth fossil.

She had not seen him since his visit to the abbey a week before. Not even a minutia of gossip appeared in the rags. Every day she had looked, expecting to see news that some aristocrat was offering up his poor virginal daughter to the devil duke of Sedgwick for perpetual bondage in the name of matrimony. But she'd read nothing.

Christine spent the last week evaluating Erik's find, poring over every detail in every book in her extensive library and that of the museum's, perusing every drawing depicting every documented fossil found. Today had finally been the last day of classes and, after collecting the students' books, she hired a hack and traveled a mile west to the church to see her father.

The old cathedral was a magnificent affair with seventeenth-century stained-glass windows and pillars carved from granite. It was the church where Christine had been baptized. Every Sunday since she had come to live at the abbey, she attended services at this cathedral with due diligence. Even Christine's father, who had been a free thinker for his time, and Aunt Sophie, who definitely held a particular bent toward one's spiritual freedom, had never risked their mortal souls. Still it had been a surprise to Christine that Papa had requested in his will to be buried here instead of the abbey. Aunt Sophie told her later that this cathedral had been the place her father had married her mother.

A wrought-iron fence enclosed the cemetery. Christine's father was buried near the rose garden. In all that time since Papa had passed, she had never seen another visitor to this sacred place. Today was no different. She removed the spent flowers she had placed in the urn next to his stone marker last week with a new bouquet she'd bought from the young flower girl hawking her wares outside the church. Then she sat on the stone bench.

What she wouldn't have given to show him the fossil tooth.

"We should have talked more, Papa," she whispered. "Why didn't you tell me you were corresponding with Erik?"

She suspected Erik had written to Papa about the discovery of the bones on his property. Then after her father had passed away, Erik had gone to Edinburgh and found Joseph. All of which had played a part in bringing Erik to Sommershorn Abbey . . . at the exact moment she had put on the ring, she'd reminded herself for days now.

The sunlight suddenly vanished briefly behind the clouds. She peered up at the sky as a voice behind her spoke. "Good day to you, Christine."

Reverend Simms stood beside the bench. She rose. He was a big man with gray hair and a gentle smile, the only man of the cloth Aunt Sophie ever tolerated lecturing her on the evil of smoking tobacco and drinking bourbon. Smiling, she held out her hand. "I thought you were in Westchester."

"I returned yesterday." He suddenly lifted her hand into a blade of sunlight. The ring shone nearly blue and warmed her finger. Raising his eyes to hers, he lifted his brows. "'Twas a gift," she said. Only a half lie. Her students had given her the ring. "The markings are some form of Gaelic," she offered to the silence, having already attempted to research the inscription.

"The words inscribed are Gaelic, the *markings* are Arthurian." He lowered her hand. "Sadly, even today, legends, and superstitions still surround the saga of Arthur and Merlin."

She brought her hand nearer to better study the ring. "You might know your seventh-century paganism. But not your metallurgy. This ring is not seventh century."

"I knew your papa," he said quietly. "The ring belonged to him."

Startled, she met his penetrating glance. "I thought the ring belonged to Aunt Sophie."

"Perhaps." His forehead wrinkled in a frown. "Your papa *did* give it back to her shortly after you were born. He told me he bought it from an old Gypsy trader who promised that the ring would give him whatever he wanted most in the world. What have *you* wished for, Christine?"

She smoothed her velvet skirts with suddenly nervous hands and laughed around the tightness in her throat as if he were being silly.

"You have always been able to put distance between yourself and others when it suited you, Christine. I would be more inclined to believe you have charmed yourself with your wishful thinking. Whatever that may be."

"Have you never believed in such nonsensical superstitions?"

He softened his tone as if he were speaking to a child. "Of course I have. For years when I was a child I never stepped on a crack for fear of breaking my mother's back."

She peered down at the braided silver band on her finger. Just looking at the ring filled her with a sense of purpose. And something akin to confusion.

After a moment, she unclenched her hand. "You married my parents to each other. Did you know my mother?"

"She was an actress," he said. "Your father defied common sense and his family to marry her. It was what he thought he wanted more than anything until it came to his next big discovery."

"Then in the end, the ring did not give him what he wanted most."

"Your father never considered that he gave more of himself to his studies than to his marriage."

Perhaps it is not enough just to want a thing," she said. "You have to be willing to sacrifice everything else to have it."

His brows lowered. "I have long since concluded that if someone believes something will happen, by their own actions, they can actually cause that event to occur, thus reinforcing their superstitions. No good ever comes from the belief in sorcery, Christine. Even if it *is* a figment of one's imagination."

And hadn't Aunt Sophie taught her how important it was to be sensible and logical? Persistence reaped its own reward. Isn't that what Papa had always promised? Though she hadn't always listened.

She'd told herself other things as well, as she spent last week evaluating Erik's find. Six days she had examined the evidence, daring to conclude that Erik was indeed sitting on what might be the greatest find of their age. Not since William Buckland discovered the first reptilian-like fossil bones at the Stonefield quarries near Oxford had such a discovery rocked the paleontology field.

She may have spent the last days of class teaching her students about the merits of hard work, but even she could not deny that Erik's arrival had occurred less than five minutes *after* she put on the ring. Christine had always thought she was too sensible to believe in such twaddle as spells and charms, but then her father had believed in the existence of dragons—to the dismay of all academia—and now she had a tooth in her possession that belonged to a beast at least thirty feet tall.

Christine spent the rest of the afternoon at the museum. By the time she reached the abbey, the sun had already set and a drizzle fell. Passing the caretaker's cottage, she picked up her step, her shoe heels clicking on the damp cobbles as she followed the stairwell down to the basement. She pulled her key from her pocket. A statue of Cerberus, the mythical three-headed dog that was said to guard Hades, sat in an alcove to the right of the doorway.

A solid twist opened the door. She blustered into the basement vestibule and slammed the door against the wind. She paused, leaning her forehead against the door before noting someone had lit the lamp. As thoughts tumbled through her mind, she turned.

Her scapegrace cousin leaned in the archway separating the corridor from the vestibule. "Hello, coz," he said.

His cologne overpowered her and she waved her hand in front of her nose. "What are you doing here, Gordy?" She adjusted her hat.

"Papa is in London. Parliament is in session. Your trust fund needs to be managed. All manner of business brings us to London." He suddenly laughed. "What is that on top of your hat? A *nest*?"

A lock of blond hair fell across his brow. He was considered by most to be dashing. He wore a shirt with a stand-up collar, silk cravat, and blue-and-white-checked trousers. He dressed like a deranged peacock. Christine possessed no inkling how they could possibly share the same grandparents.

She swept past him down the corridor to her laboratory. The door to her laboratory was open. A lamp burned on the table to the right of the door. Gordy had been inside!

Dear God.

She must have left the door unlocked.

She made a quick visual assessment of her workspace. The packet Erik had brought her remained wrapped in cloth beneath the top shelf where she had left it. Her research books lay open beneath where she had left them. It took all her will not to shove Gordy out of the room and lock the door in his face. "What are you doing at Sommershorn, besides trying to steal something?"

"This will all be mine someday. What is the difference if I sell bits and pieces of this room off now as later? It's only rubbish, old gel."

She swept past him and down the dais to her workbench. "Quit calling me that." She closed the books she'd left strewn over her workbench.

When they were children, he had taken great pleasure in throwing paste in her hair and tormenting her. Christine had been so grateful to her grandmother for leaving her a trust fund that would help her maintain her independence. She had used it to support Sommorshorn Abbey.

Lounging a hip against the countertop, her cousin leaned over her shoulder and picked up her C. A. Sommers's book. "Chasing dragons like your father, old gel?

"Why are you here?"

He sobered. "I heard Sedgwick was at the Fossil Society gala. Word travels. I also heard the bastard came here. Where have you been spending your time all week? No one can seem to find you."

"Perhaps because I have been teaching classes."

"Why was Sedgwick here?"

"He was in contact with Papa some months before he passed away. He merely came to offer his condolences."

"Is that *all* Sedgwick came for?"

"What does that mean?"

"The man has a reputation. He is dangerous. Just look at what happened to my poor sister who made the fatal mistake of marryin' the bastard."

"Charlotte died of scarlet fever. Don't be an ill-informed ass. Besides, I don't recall hearing you complain when you thought there was a profit to be made. You and your father liked him enough when you believed he was going to make you rich."

"What about his second wife?"

"Go away, Gordy. Annoy someone else. The night is still young. I am sure you can find someone receptive to your attentions. I am not."

"I only find it interesting that he came to see you." He slid her spectacles up the ridge of her nose before she could slap his hand away. "It ain't as if you are the crème of London's new crop of socialites, *old* gel." He shoved away from the counter. "Though you probably wouldn't be a half-bad looker if you took off those spectacles and did something different with your hair. Got rid of that hat."

Christine strode past him up the dais to the door. "Don't come down to this laboratory again without my permission. Nothing in this room belongs to you. I'll donate it all to the museum before I let you put your hands on anything."

He laughed. "You always did have airs, coz. I will tell Papa his control of your trust fund is still intact. He worries so for our security."

"Good night, Gordy."

After he left, Christine locked up the laboratory and walked upstairs to make sure he left the house entirely before she returned downstairs and worked another hour, carefully cleaning Erik's fossils with a small knife and brush. After supper, she grew tired and went upstairs to her room. Aunt Sophie was already in bed, so the house was quiet. Christine sank to the tufted bench in front of her vanity. It always bothered her when Gordy called her *old gel*.

For even at eight and twenty, she still suffered girlish freckles on her nose. After removing her spectacles, Christine took the pins out of her hair and let the length fall down her back. Her dark wavy hair defied the subjugation found in the soft feminine styles popular among the blond, fashionable set. She turned her head from side to side and tilted her chin. Her mouth was too bold and wide, perfect for shouting at rude hackney drivers but not necessarily pretty. Christine well knew she wasn't the embodiment of the classical beauty, but her imperfections had never bothered her before.

Papa once told her in a moment of whimsical intoxication that she looked like her mother, though Christine would not know. She barely remembered her mother and no one ever spoke of the base-born actress Papa had married and who had died somewhere in Italy with her lover. Christine turned down the lamp. She had not let herself think about her mother in years.

"Mum, will ye be needin' anything?" the housekeeper asked from the doorway.

Christine looked around the room. She relaxed a little when she found Beast asleep on her windowsill. She wanted only to be alone with her cat. "Go to sleep, Mrs. Samuels. I'm sorry I kept you up waiting for me."

Mrs. Samuels remained in the doorway. "Is Miss Amelia all right, mum? We've not heard from her in a week." Mrs. Samuels looked at Christine in the mirror, her gray eyes anxious as they met Christine's in the cheval glass.

"I'm sure she is enjoying herself and will want to tell us everything when she returns." Joseph would want to return as soon as possible to begin all necessary preparations for his trip to Perth.

After Mrs. Samuels shut the door, Christine twisted around and located the scratch paper Erik had given her with his instructions to have Joseph contact him upon his return to London.

She knew with the condition of the roads, a trip to Gretna Green and back could take over a week.

Christine studied Erik's missive she was supposed to give Joseph upon his return. Then she looked at the clock and saw that it was half past eight. Guilt over what she was about to do pulled at the strings of her conscience but only for a moment as she rose and walked to her dressing room to find her cloak.

Joseph had Perth, she told herself.

He had the museum's backing and support. He had entry into the Royal Geographical Society. The Edinburgh Scholars welcomed him with open arms.

Christine, on the other hand had sadly reached an impasse in her life where if she didn't do something brilliant soon, she would become irrelevant. Since her return to England two years ago, her prospects had already dried up, like a well in the Sahara. Her funds were not endless. She didn't want to live the rest of her life never venturing far from Sommershorn Abbey and die of old age without another single, solitary discovery— or friend. Her life and her work were unfinished. She needed Erik's find.

More than anything in the world, she wanted the beast of Sedgwick. And though her pride balked at the idea of pleading with Erik to put her in charge of the dig, she could *not* allow him to give this discovery to Joseph Darlington.

Chapter 4

Rain pebbled against the windows of the hack Christine had hired to take her to Mayfair. Lightning flashed in the distance, bringing a frown to her brow, but the brunt of the storm had yet to reach this part of London. Absently, through her kid gloves, she fingered the ring on her finger. A dozen times, she had fidgeted with the band of ancient silver only to pull her hand away. She leaned forward and stared out the window. She usually never did anything impulsive.

Streetlamps marked the shiny pavement as the hack turned off a busy street. It wasn't as if she were going to a bachelor's residence in the dead of night, she told herself. Lord Sedgwick's sister lived with him—and it was not yet nine o'clock. Any meetings he might have had during the day would be over. If he wasn't at some club, she hoped he was home reading in the library or playing chess with his sister. He had always enjoyed playing chess, she thought. A game of give and take that rewarded the best strategist with a satisfying win. Tonight felt a little like that chess game of old. She had to win.

After a few minutes, the hack finally rolled to a stop. Ignoring her racing pulse, she tugged the hood of her cloak over her head and stared out the window. A grove of knotty oaks and a rather large brick wall shielded most of the huge stone manse from the street. She glanced down one more time at the address in her hand to confirm she was indeed at the right residence in Mayfair.

Her eyes fell on her simple rose-colored gown. Only now did she think she might have better served her purpose wearing something less countrified. She had not thought to change from what she'd been wearing to teach classes that day, though she had repinned her hair. The door opened and the driver set out the step. It was too late to worry about such nonsense as her looks now.

"Are you sure this is the correct house?" she asked.

"We be at the right place, miss," the driver assured her, a hint of a grumble in his voice as he glared at the sky. "I told ye we would not beat that storm."

She shoved a coin into the driver's hand. "My business here will not take long."

He held up the coin. "You want me to stay? You'll pay me more than this here pittance, dovey. This won't even buy me time with me Delia."

She scowled over the rim of her spectacles at him, but deciding she needed this boor's services more than she wanted to argue fare, she gave him a second coin. "I will give you another just like it when I return."

She walked through the gate and into the yard, her sturdy half boots crunching on gravel as she followed the footpath toward the arched entryway. She hurried up the steps, stopped at the front door, and rapped loudly.

A moment later, the butler answered. He was a tall, aged figure with a head full of gray hair and a bushy white mustache that reminded her of an English general. Other than the rise of one brow, his face showed only the slightest expression. "Miss—"

"Sommers," Christine said. "I am here to see Lord Sedgwick."

His eyes went over her. "Is he expecting you, Miss?"

She had told Erik she would get back to him; she just had not told him when. Christine stepped past the butler into the foyer. "Yes," she lied. "If you will please inform his grace that Miss Sommers is here to see him, I am sure he will see me."

"Very well, mum. If you say so."

He led her into a tall foyer. A brilliant chandelier colored the walls in rainbows. Christine had barely registered her surroundings when the *clink* of silverware in a distant room stopped her. She turned and looked down the corridor toward the butler. "Wait!" she rasped. "Does he have guests?"

The butler turned on his heel, but before he could speak a young girl's voice came from above. "My brother will not mind the intrusion."

Christine looked up. Lady Rebecca sat halfway up the stairs looking down at her from between the spindles on the bannister, her curls wrapped in rags like some adolescent Medusa. She wore a pink wrapper buttoned up to her neck and tied at the waist with a sash. "Are you here about my tooth?" She hurried down the stairs in a swish of pink silk. "Erik said he visited you at Sommershorn Abbey."

"As a matter of fact, I *am* here about the tooth."

The girl peered at the butler. "Go tell my brother Miss Sommers is here. But walk slowly. . . . And whatever you do, don't say you saw me awake."

The corners of his stern mouth softened into what suspiciously resembled amusement. "No, miss, I would not dare."

After the butler turned away, Lady Rebecca stuck out her tongue at his back. "He is an informer. If Erik finds me, he'll know I lied about my dreadful headache. Then I will be subjected to another long and boring lecture."

Christine cleared her throat to cover her laugh. She pulled her cloak tighter over her gown. "Do you lie to your brother often?"

"Only out of self-preservation." Lady Rebecca lowered her voice to a stage whisper. "You have not met Lord and Lady Willows and their insipid daughter. They are even worse than the Marquess Elderbury's wife and daughter that we had over yesterday. Did you know they had never even *seen* a fossil? I showed them one of a partial skull and Lady Elderbury fainted." Erik's sister rolled her eyes. "If my brother takes either daughter as a bride, I shall . . . I shall surely leap off a cliff and drown myself."

"That is a little extreme, is it not?" Christine couldn't help her grin, before she realized the butler would be returning at any moment. "Perhaps I should return tomorrow."

"Oh no, that will not do, Miss Sommers." Lady Rebecca took Christine's elbow and led her down a hallway. "You cannot go yet. Not when you have come all this way about my fossil."

She branched left into a carpeted corridor and dipped into a white-and-blue parlor. Christine stopped. The walls were bright blue trimmed in white wainscoting. A marble fireplace covered one entire wall and warmed the well-ordered room. She had never seen such pure white curtains and polished furniture. Everything shone bright and new, completely opposite the chaos in which Christine reveled in her own life.

"Now tell me about my tooth before Erik finds us," Lady Rebecca said, her voice pulling Christine around. She stood inside the arched doorway as if on lookout. "Erik won't allow me down by the riverbed any longer." She lowered her voice. "By my estimation, the creature in whose mouth that tooth once belonged must be huge. Imagine a *beast* like that living in Sedgwick."

"Yes, imagine." Christine felt excitement escalating in her blood. "Tell me what else you have found."

She went on in detail about a second tooth and part of what she thought might be a vertebrae. The girl had no idea just how rare and magnificent a find like this was. Though Christine could hardly contain herself, she hesitated to say more until she saw everything for herself.

"But then Erik found . . . he found partial human remains."

"Yes, he told me."

Lady Rebecca's brown eyes widened. "Do you think that horrid tooth beast *ate* the unfortunate person?"

Christine remembered who Lord Sedgwick thought that "unfortunate" individual was. "No. I find it more probable the beast was dead many, many millennium before that particular person crossed paths with its grave, and the river has somehow dredged up both."

"Do you truly think so?" Lady Rebecca considered the statement but did not appear entirely convinced. "I wish I could be as logical about such things. But the idea of the beast has not made the tenants wholly confident there isn't another beast like it living in the crags."

"Why would they believe that?"

"You haven't walked the crags, Miss Sommers," Lady Rebecca whispered. "Some who have . . . never return."

"Lady Rebecca—"

"Oh, please, call me Becca."

Voices in the foyer suddenly snapped the girl around. She hurried to the archway and stared into the corridor. "He's coming." She looked over her shoulder at Christine. "I have enjoyed our conversation, Miss Sommers."

"Wait—" But Becca had already dashed out the door before Christine could glean more information about the other fossils.

Bloody hell.

She stepped into the corridor in time to glimpse a flash of pink vanish in the servants' staircase down the back of the hall. She turned at the sound of voices near the foyer. Apparently, Erik was searching the front rooms for her.

She stepped back into the parlor, out of sight. Her heart pounded as she juggled the idea of returning tomorrow when he did not have guests, but a glance around the parlor revealed no sign of a doorway that opened to the garden. Drawing in a deep breath, she smoothed her skirts and shut her eyes.

This is business, she thought. *Convince him you are the best contender for the job. We're adults.*

With that mantra in her thoughts, she took one more fortifying breath, turned and nearly screamed.

Erik leaned against the door, his arms crossed over his chest. Her fist flew to her breast. "You scared the *life* out of me, Erik."

His gaze traveled from the top of her square-shaped hat, down the tiny rows of buttons on her bodice to the damp hem of her skirt before he returned his attention

to her face. His mouth turned up at the corner. A little
thrill shot through her stomach. "Christine."

He was dressed impeccably in formal black, his white
shirt a stark counterpoint to the image of brute strength
he so casually conveyed in his easy stance. "It seems my
sister put you in a wing that has no escape door."

Christine's brows snapped together. "Your butler informed on her?"

"That she left me at the mercy of our guests on the
pretense of suffering a headache?" He smiled. "No, he
did not have to. I know my sister."

Evidently, his grace knew something about Christine
as well, to recognize that she would have escaped had
there been a door. "I came to talk about your visit to
Sommershorn Abbey. I know you said to go through
your man of affairs to make an appointment. I will
return tomorrow if that is your want."

"Did you give the tooth back to my sister?"

"No." She smoothed her gloved hand over her reticule. "My reasons for coming here tonight were spontaneous. I didn't think to pack up everything. I . . .
I normally plan such things with more attention to
detail." Nor did she normally blather about like a flit-
ting butterfly. "Your sister said that you had more specimens where that tooth came from."

He didn't reply, which doused her hope that he had
brought the entire cumbersome collection to London.
"If fossils have been washing up on one of your riverbanks, the source has to be from somewhere near where
the tooth was discovered. I want to examine all your
bones."

He suddenly pinched the bridge of his nose and quietly laughed. Her gaze of its accord moved to his lips.
And a random memory besieged her.

No one kissed like Erik. Not in her entire life had

any man touched all five of her senses with only a taste of his mouth. He could make her hot and buttery and certain of her desires. He could make her want more than she knew she should have. His eyes returned to hers, amusement in their depths.

The long-ago memory vanished, but not the heat it left behind. "What is so humorous?" she asked.

A strange, tender light came into his eyes. "All of this we could have discussed in the morning, Christine."

"No, we can't."

Christine didn't understand why this conversation couldn't have waited until tomorrow but something inside was pushing her forward, an ember of passion she had not felt in so long. Passion that was suddenly flowing through her veins and pumping her heart faster.

Her future was in Scotland. She knew it in her heart and her gut and she only had to convince him. "Have you ever believed in something that no one else did?" she quietly asked. "Ever *wanted* something so much, then suddenly find that by whatever fate it has dropped into your lap and your whole world changes?"

His silence seemed to tell her he was listening.

"I want to go to Scotland and find the beast," she said. "I am asking you to hire me. You cannot find anyone better qualified than I am for the job."

She withdrew a packet of folded papers from the pocket lining her cloak, outlining all of her qualifications and years of experience. Laying out in detail the last ten years of her life. All she had done since . . . since she and her father had boarded a ship to South America. Since she had walked away from him . . .

"I know what your qualifications are, Christine."

Christine felt a rush of heat to her face. But to her relief he held out his hand and took the slim packet. "I assume Darlington has yet to return?"

She had the sense to recognize that his hesitation might have something to do with her obviously stepping over Joseph, and how unfeeling it might appear. But in her mind, her case for doing so was strong. Joseph had Perth.

"Mr. Darlington is on his honeymoon. I can be ready to leave before he is," she went on in a rush afraid he would say no, unsure what she would do if he did. "That tooth your sister found might very will be the link for which Papa spent years searching. You must have known it or you wouldn't have come to me. At the very least you must have known what that find would mean to me."

"Go on," he said.

She took a hidden steadying breath. "Your beast of Sedgwick is going to help me prove that dragons may have once inhabited this world."

Silence followed.

Christine fought a frightening urge to laugh. "Not in the way that fables and mythology have painted them. But as you must know since you read his book, my father believed there were creatures as big as a house that once roamed the earth, a place far different from what we know today, the same creatures that eventually evolved into what we see today as birds."

Erik's brows lifted in a clear attempt to tell her he must have missed that chapter in the book. "You want to take Becca's find and announce to the world that dragons or something that might have passed for such once existed and are still here today having evolved into what . . . ? Chickens, or the red-breasted robin we see picking worms out of the earth?"

The theory had once sounded ridiculous to her as well. "If anything, whatever that tooth came from is huge. Bigger than anything ever found. In my world, it is more important being first at discovering a thing than in being right in explaining how it came about."

"Is it not pure hyperbole to make such a deduction from a single tooth?"

"My father believed in something that he could never prove." Moving nearer, she willed him to feel her passion. Her *raison d'être*. "He died a laughingstock to his peers. Disgraced for what he tried to teach. Have you any idea what it is like not to have anyone believe in you?"

Folding his arms, he looked away.

"You *owe* me this chance, your grace!" She blurted the words, then stepped back, horrified by what had come over her.

"I owe you?" he asked in a clipped voice. "How did you manage to come up with that conclusion?"

He *did* owe her, a part of her shouted at her to say the words again.

He owed her for breaking her heart, for marrying her cousin, for daring to think he could come back to London, taunt her with that fossil, and then tell her he wanted Darlington. He owed her for making her come here tonight and plead her case like a vassal bowing before her lord . . .

"Your grace." The butler suddenly stood in the corridor.

Erik straightened. "What is it, Boris?"

"Dessert is being served—"

Without taking his eyes from Christine, he said, "Tell them I have been called away. Bring my cloak. Have my carriage sent around," he said. "I will be escorting Miss Sommers home."

Boris stole a glance at Christine's pale face. "Yes, your grace."

After Boris retreated, Christine sidestepped Erik. "I can take myself home."

He caught her arm. "It is a moot point. Your hackney driver has been paid and already sent away. I'll not be missed here."

She doubted that. His absence would be like a large black chasm. She did not want him accompanying her. "You needn't go to the trouble."

"I do not trouble myself over anything I do not wish to do, Christine." He smiled his humorless smile. "I thought you would remember that about me."

Christine pulled her arm from his hand. She had no choice but to accept. Where would she find another hack in Mayfair this time of night?

Then they were outside scurrying through the drizzle and he was handing her up into the cab of a luxurious brougham, horsed by two magnificent blacks. Once inside, she attempted to relax against the velvet squabs, watching as Erik gave orders to his driver. The coach lamps hanging from the driver's seat cast a warm glow over his stark features, made all the brighter by the surrounding night. And as a gust of wind buffeted the coach, she felt the strange stir of something powerful.

For all of her fearlessness when it came to exploring dark, cold, and confining places where most people, especially women, would never go, all in the pursuit of her passions, her discomfiture around storms had always been something of a joke among those who knew her. But tonight she felt no fear.

Instead, she found the storm's energy seductive. It intensified her senses, as if something inside her had awakened. Something deep and dormant within her she was not sure that she welcomed.

A moment later, Erik climbed into the carriage and sat opposite her, filling the air around her with his heat and scent. He dimmed the single light in the carriage, causing the upper portion of his face to be darkened by shadow. The coach jerked forward and for lack of a place to set her gaze, she watched his house fade in the gaslight mists. The horse's clip-clop on wet cobbles pulled at the edge of her mind and she folded her hands in her lap, too conscious of him as a man.

She stole a glance at him and found herself looking directly at him. Tonight was a perfect example of how he treated people, she thought, the way he had abandoned his guests at his own dinner table.

"Do not worry about Lord and Lady Willows," he said, reading her thoughts. "I have given them the perfect excuse to discontinue our association without paying me insult. I find it disconcerting to be in the company of his wife, who thinks I am some monster ready to devour her precious daughter. Honestly?" He raised a brow. "It is a relief to carry on a conversation with someone who is not afraid of me."

He didn't seem relieved. He sounded cross.

She had never been afraid of him, despite what other people thought of him. She respected a man who could go against the grain of society and accomplish what he had done, caring not a fig that in the process he had greatly angered the mainstream. In many ways, he reminded her of Aunt Sophie.

But respect did not always equate to admiration and she would be a fool not to be cautious where he was concerned. After all, because of him, she had left England a long time ago.

"You have not given me your answer," she said.

"Why don't we continue to talk about your qualifications instead?" His smile was not kind, yet neither was it cruel. Only curious. "How close were you and Darlington? Were you too disappointed that he wed that pretty blond assistant of yours?"

"Of course not. I hope they are happy."

"You are good friends then."

"Yes, of course. Why would you think otherwise?" What did any of this have to do with her qualifications?

"Is that why you want to cut him out of any find you might make when you know he is as desperate for recognition as you?"

"He has an opportunity in Perth."

"Yet, you know I can give him a better one in Fife."

He was right, of course. Though Christine had not seen the other fossils, if they were anything like the tooth, they, too, would be a magnificent discovery. But this was *her* discovery.

Erik leaned forward, placing his face in the pale amber light. "Then do not for one moment think you and I are not alike in the pursuit of our goals, Christine. We are both selfish."

"What does that mean?"

"We are both willing to sell our souls for a price. Only I did it a long time ago and have become more adept at the game. You are just beginning your journey. Or are you?"

"You're . . . mad!"

He laughed. "Aye, that is what they say. But that is not why you left England ten years ago. Is it, now?"

Her heart racing, Christine recognized too late the trap he had set for her.

"I did not run away from you. I walked. Surely, ye do not still hold that against me?" she mimicked his slight Scottish brogue.

"Ah," he said quietly, amusement in his eyes. "But that does not explain why ye came back just one more time, now does it?"

"I should think what happened between us that night would explain it with clarity."

"Just one last *fook* for old time's sake? Was that it?"

Christine had forgotten just how far away from him she had run to forget him. Leave it to him to bring out the worst in her. She had never struck a person in her life, but she was suddenly balling her fist, prepared to give him a facer he'd never forget. He caught her wrist in midair. She would have struck him with her knees if she could have moved against the weight of her skirts. Her inability to defend herself only amplified her feeling of vulnerability and defeat and made her more furious. Until she had finally spent herself and he was no longer restraining her as much as he was using his weight to hold her in her seat.

Aware of a sudden burn behind her eyes and his breath against her temple, she lifted her chin.

She expected to see only anger equal to hers in his eyes, but in his dark expression, she saw something else entirely, something that reflected back into her own eyes, primitive and all-consuming. Recognizing that they were both capable of such violence frightened her.

"It is well and good that we finally clear the air between us, Christine," he breathed against her mouth.

Her lips parted, but whether in protest or invitation, she knew not. He seized upon her hesitation and covered her mouth with his. A hot openmouthed kiss that pinned her to the bench. Like the clever black-hearted devil he was, he swooped between the cracks of her defenses. She made a token effort to deny him. But he dragged her across his lap, bringing her down to the bench beneath his weight.

His tongue swept deeply into her mouth and met hers, a tempestuous battle that shattered all boundaries between them and made her earlier resistance seem childish. As if an earthquake swept through her psyche, the past crumbled, and she was without pride, returning the force of his passion and reveling in sweet desire. He tasted like rich coffee and brandy and hot gratifying sex in an elemental way that made her feel alive.

He groaned, his hand burrowing through her hair, dislodging pins. Their mouths angled, devouring, as if both of them had suffered in hunger for so long. His palm traced her waist and stroked upward to her breast. A tremor went through her and she gave a small gasp of surrender.

Her fingers curled against his chest and pushed. "Nay, Erik," she protested weakly, "I cannot."

Closing his fist in her hair, he drew back, their mouths so close they shared the same air. Their eyes clashed and held, crackling hot, but not as much from lust or the physical link they still shared as from the great purge of emotion.

He was like the vortex of a storm swirling around her, sucking and pulling at all of her senses. If she did not anchor herself now . . .

It was as if the past had snagged her, and the realization that his assessment of her character rang with truth. It was as if, from the moment she put on the ring and opened the door to see him in the corridor, she had gone back ten years to the point where she had been.

The very moment when, amidst the laughter of a thousand people, and from across a candlelit ballroom that glittered with gold-draped walls, she'd first glimpsed him standing alone near the French doors.

He'd worn his youth and solitude like a mantle of iron, as if daring a person to tear it off him.

That summer she had tried.

She'd lost her heart to the daring and defiant duke. She had been young and impulsive and so full of her sense of self-importance that she'd believed in fairytales. She would not allow him to steal her dream again. "I was barely eighteen, Erik," she whispered. "You were about to announce a betrothal to my cousin—"

"You've not been *barely* eighteen since you crawled into my bed the first time." His eyes burned into hers. "You not only left England, ye left this side of the world. I did not even know where you'd gone for a year."

She shoved against his chest. "You pined so much for me that you've been married? Twice? You correspond with my father but not me? You come here now to hire Mr. Darlington. . . . You make it too easy to forget we were even *friends*." Before they'd been lovers.

That she had taught him the names of constellations even as he had shown her how beautiful the stars could truly be.

"You make it easy to forget everything," she whispered.

He slid his knuckles beneath her chin and tilted her face into the misty light. "You make it too easy to remember. I am glad to see there is more than ice water still running through your veins." His tone was a study in composure, where only moments ago he had kissed her with hot, openmouthed abandon.

She splayed her fingers against his chest and felt the beat of his heart on her palms. "Loose me. Please, Erik."

To his credit, he did. She clamored from the bench back to the other side and straightened her clothing. Her lips felt swollen, pillaged. She felt self-betrayal, having succumbed to him like some demirep willing to sell her soul for a tuppence of pleasure. Or for a chance at his fossils. Shaken to her core, she would not let herself look at him until she had regained some semblance of composure, relieved to find the only damage seemed to be to her chignon, which draped loosely at her nape.

He reached over to the opposite window and raised the shade to look outside. She welcomed the darkness inside the carriage as she removed her spectacles and attempted to clean them. Somewhere across London, a distant flash of lightning marked the storm's fury, one that equaled the tempestuous, if silent, battle now being waged inside this coach.

She set her glasses back on her nose then raised her chin. Erik was watching her with an intensity that burned with familiar unwelcome warmth.

"I will give you your beast of Sedgwick, Christine," he said at last. "But it will be as my wife that you will come to Scotland and live in my home and around my sister and daughter. If you want this beast so much, you will wed me to have it. Those are my terms."

"Marriage." His words floored her. "Your terms? Just like that?"

As if she were one of his business acquisitions. Just that fast, he had homed in on her one weakness, sweeping down with talons outstretched like the hawk he was. Her eyes narrowed.

This was not a spontaneous decision. Erik Boughton did not act impulsively. He had not become known and feared in London society because he was reckless and soft. The devil duke of Sedgwick played chess like no man she had ever met. And he always played to win.

"Papa never suggested Darlington. He suggested me," she said calmly as much to herself as she spoke the words to him. "You've manipulated me. You must have known all along if you came to me with that fossil that I could not turn down the prospect of finding that beast. But you wanted more," she whispered in astonishment. "So you had to make sure I came to you. Make sure I understood what I had in my hands enough to . . . to . . . Is this some sort of punishment on your part to even the score between us?"

"No, Christine." He leaned forward, resting his elbows on his knees, his quiet tone demanding her attention. Nothing else would have forced her to look at him. "But I will admit that the idea of marriage to you began to weigh heavily after your father and I began to correspond last year. You were still unmarried. I am in need of a wife. But this is not something I take lightly. I was not sure until tonight that we would suit."

"Because we are both *selfish*?"

"Because we each can offer the other something in the bargain."

"You could not just ask me to wed you like a normal person?"

"You would have thrown me out of your office on my ear."

A week ago, she had wanted this discovery more than she wanted anything else in the world enough to sell her soul. Now he was asking her to do that very thing. She suddenly felt sick to her stomach as her thoughts went to the ring. "This entire evening is . . . it is not real."

"*Real?*" He leaned to take her chin and force her to look at him. "What happened between us tonight cannot be bought on the streets of Whitechapel. It cannot be faked. Would marriage to me be so abhorrent?"

"If I don't do as you say, then you will give the job to Mr. Darlington?"

"No, Christine. I meant it when I told you I needed other answers that have nothing to do with finding your beast. Until I find out what happened to Elizabeth, I am not ready to share that discovery with anyone else but you. Whatever is in those hills will remain there. At least during my lifetime."

"You would allow the greatest find of this century to be *lost*?"

She looked away from him in confusion. If he had threatened to give the find to Darlington, she would have been able to maintain her righteous anger, and her decision would have been simple. This she did not understand.

He sat back in his seat. A thump on the top of the carriage gave her a start. The coach began to slow, drawing Christine's gaze back to the window.

The rain had stopped, but the gaslights cast a wet sheen over the walks and illuminated the cozy elm-lined street now strewn with wet leaves and twigs. She saw the protective high brick wall that enclosed Sommershorn Abbey. She was home.

"You can tell your driver to let me out here."

She thought Erik would argue. He did not. He tapped the port behind him and gave instructions to his driver. The coach rolled to a shuddering stop. She reached over to open the door herself, but Erik's hand was on the latch an instant before hers. "My business in London will be concluded the end of the week."

He was telling her she had until then to answer him.

"I will need to get your fossils back to you before then."

"Christine . . ."

Impatient to be away from him, she flung open the door and descended without waiting for the driver to set out the step.

But even as she knew she must not allow the devil duke inside her head, he was already imbedded there like a burr by the time she reached her house and slammed the door. Aware that her own panic was driving her thoughts, she leaned with her back against the door and she shut her eyes—as if the action would block the taste of him from her lips.

Raising the brandy tumbler to his lips, Erik stared up at the stars and drained the glass. Outside his bedroom window, the clip-clop of horses' hooves mixed with an occasional hansom that was ferrying late-night party-goers to their destinations on wet streets. The witching hour, he thought, leaning a bare shoulder against the sash. Bemused by the path his thoughts had taken, he looked out on a world that rarely had been kind to him. Wearing only a pair of silk drawers tied loosely at his hips, he was conscious of the tension that arced through him, that had been there since he left Christine at Sommershorn Abbey.

He didn't know what had come over him tonight. Hell, he had taken her into his arms and kissed her as if ten years did not stand between them. As if she had not already *fooked* up his life once before.

Yet, as he stood there bathed in moonlight, he felt as if he were awakening from a long, dreamless hibernation. He might mentally consign his behavior to the night, but he knew one thing for sure that he had not known until she had opened her mouth and kissed him down to the soles of his feet. He did not regret his decision to make this trip to London.

With the recent bones found on his property, Erik had needed someone who could give him answers. Over the last pair of months, while Scotland was coming out from beneath its winter freeze, Erik had been learning bits and pieces about Christine's life. With *unapproachable* stamped across her forehead in bold block letters, her current vulnerability was an oddly compelling contrast to the confident woman he'd once known.

She had never married. Never veered from academia and all things archaeology related, including the infant offshoot of paleontology that specialized in *dinosauria* fossils. He'd learned about the subject from Christine's own unpublished manuscripts her father had sent him during many of their discussions last winter about the find on his land. From what Erik had seen of her work and what Darlington had told him, she knew her discipline. Yet despite her extensive knowledge, or perhaps because of it, she'd been shut out of the gentlemen's network and finally relegated to teaching young girls with no marital prospects skills to survive a harsh world.

When Erik had sought an invitation to the museum gala, in the beginning, he'd told himself it was for Becca. But seeing Christine on the steps of the museum, then at Sommershorn Abbey, and finally again tonight, had brought back more than memories lost in the ugly chaos of his life. Christine still stirred him. And while he could claim beautiful women in his life since he had known her, and indeed had wed two, no one had ever made him feel needful. He had made it a point in his life never to *need* anything or anyone.

"Erik?"

His sister's voice in the darkness behind him startled him as he turned. Erik padded to his massive four-poster bed and donned his robe. Belting it at the waist, he turned to the nightstand and lit the lamp.

Becca stood in the doorway, wraithlike in her white robe. He thought she might be asleep.

This wouldn't be the first time Rebecca had been found sleepwalking in the corridors. An "episode" was what the physician had called it years ago, that began shortly after Elizabeth's disappearance. And because of the fear she might harm herself or someone else, the doctor had suggested she would be better off locked away in an asylum under the care of people who could better deal with this manner of illness. Erik had fired the physician. But he always kept a maid near his sister at nights.

He turned up the lamp. "What is it, Elf? Another nightmare?"

"I'm not asleep if that is what you are thinking."

Becca's maid suddenly appeared in her white nightcap and robe. "I'm sorry, your grace," she said breathlessly, as if she had been running. She dipped. "I didna hear the lass get out of her bed."

He shifted his attention from Becca to the maid. "Go back to bed. I'll see she gets to her room."

Clutching the edge of her robe, the maid dipped again. "Yes, your grace."

After the woman left, he allotted Becca his full attention. "My bedroom isn't the place to talk in the middle of the night." He swept out his arm directing her toward the adjoining sitting room where he kept an office and conducted his personal affairs. Becca walked past him, and he followed her.

"I am a terrible bother," she said as he lit the lamp on his desk. "You worry about me. I wish you would not."

"Becca . . ." He replaced the dome of frosted glass on the lamp. "Asking me not to worry is like asking me not to care."

Her attention moved to the desk. She picked up the unfinished drawings and sketches he'd left there earlier before his distractions had driven him to the brandy.

This was a part of his life most people knew nothing about, one of the pleasures he'd lost over the years and had only recently attempted to take up again. He'd been educated at Cambridge, but many did not realize he'd also spent four years at Edinburgh University and St. Andrews studying civil engineering and architecture. The levy project on his property in Fife was his development, as was a long-ago renovation he'd done to Sedgwick Castle, and he was now attempting to design the new library at St. Andrews. But like most of the activities he'd started these past seven years, he had yet to finish.

"I believe I like this one best." Becca held up the drawing that had been on top. "It looks less like a medieval cathedral and more like a stone gallery from one of Sir Christopher Wren's visions, except with your personal touch. You are the best architect in all of Britain."

Placing his hand beneath Becca's chin, he lifted her face to his. "As much as I appreciate your faith in my abilities, I know you did not come here to talk about my work."

Tears filled her eyes. She suddenly stepped into Erik's arms and pressed her cheek against his heart. "What is it, Becca?" he quietly asked.

"I did have a nightmare," she said against his robe. "It was terrible. I don't want to lose you, Erik."

"Lose me?" His arms held her to him. "What is this about?"

She turned her face away and shook her head.

"Becca . . ."

"I don't want you to die."

His hands tightened on her shoulders as he looked into her face. "Someone told you I was going to die?"

She lowered her gaze to her slippered toe, making circles in the Turkey carpet. "Is it true what they say? You are cursed and no woman—?"

"Who has been filling your mind with nonsense?" His sister scrubbed her cheeks with the heel of her hand. "Look at me, Becca."

Her troubled eyes met his. "If you must know . . . Momma came by today while you were out."

Bloody *hell* . . . Erik's mouth tightened. He looked away.

"Why must you dislike her? She's your mother, too—"

"What exactly did she tell you?"

Hesitating, Rebecca studied the lace on her wrapper. "That you bear the mark of the curse. Every Sedgwick duke for the last hundred years who has borne the mark has never lived past his thirty-fourth year."

Becca was talking about the small silver patch in his dark hair just above his temple. Erik had listened to that same Sedgwick-curse rubbish his entire life.

No doubt his mother would like to see her words come true.

"I'm sorry. I invited her here. I wanted to see her. We had a good visit, Erik. And she misses me, too. She wants me to spend the Season with her."

"No."

Bloody hell, no!

Becca looked up at him, tears no longer in her eyes. "But Momma said she will give me my first Season."

"Becca." He did his best not to inject his own animosity toward their mother into his voice. "You are returning to Sedgwick Castle with me before the end of the month. I am not leaving you here in London. Secondly, we have already been over this. I will give you your debut next year. I promise."

His sister's brown eyes flashed with passion. "I have been out of short dresses for a year. I want to meet others my age, Erik. I had *fun* at the gala. Do you even know what that is like? You never laugh anymore. You rarely smile. If you have your way, I . . . I will perish an old maid."

"You will not perish an old maid. I promise. What happened to your passion for fossils? How is it a girl who thinks she has discovered a great beast in Fife worries that she will perish an old maid?"

She sniffled, straightened, and put on a brave face. "I like Miss Sommers. Do you think she will help us?"

"I believe she might."

"I told you I found something rare and magnificent," she said, some of her verve returning the color back to her cheeks.

"I should never have doubted you. For that, I apologize."

She grew quiet. "I will accept your apology only if you promise there is no such thing as curses."

"Come here, Elf." He pulled her into his arms. "Tell me you do not believe in such foolishness." It pained him to find he was suddenly sitting on the sharper edges of his temper again. "Tell me, Becca."

A shudder went through her body. "I don't believe anything they say about you. But sometimes people are cruel. I told Momma she musn't believe the worst of you. I know you are not a murderer. I could not love you if you were." Her arms tightened. "Do not be angry with her. I could not bear it if you were."

"No, Becca," he gently reassured her. "I am not angry."

He dared not be angry when he paid his dear mother a long overdue visit in the morning.

Chapter 5

Erik dismounted at the manse where his mother had lived since she returned to London years ago. Sturdy stone quarried from southern England fronted the quaint house that butted the gabled roof and framed the porch. He owned the dwelling where she resided, but he could count on one hand the number of times they had crossed paths in the last ten years. He handed the reins to the groomsman. "Rub him down," he said briskly. "He's been ridden hard."

"Yes, your grace."

Erik ascended the stone stairs to the house. He stepped out of the sunlight as the door swung open and the staid butler appeared. He wore the unique black-and-red livery worn by all his servants.

"Charles." Erik stepped into the house and while removing his gloves peered up the winding staircase. Sunlight from the large leaded-pane windows above the doorway spilled into the gilt-trimmed foyer. "Is the Countess Sutherland home?" he asked, handing the man his cloak, hat, and riding gloves.

"She is still abed, your grace."

It was not unlike his mother to be asleep at two o'clock in the afternoon. "Wake her."

"That isn't necessary." His mother suddenly stood at

the top of the stairway. Dressed in a red velvet morning gown, her thick blond hair pinned in curls at the back of her head, she looked first on him then on the butler. "I am quite awake, as you can see, Charles." She placed her hand on the rail and descended. "Bring honey and milk with my tea to the salon."

"Yes, my lady."

"And make sure the crumpets are properly warmed on the griddle."

Without expression, Charles turned his attention to Erik.

"Nothing for me," he said.

Nodding, the butler bowed out of the foyer, leaving Erik alone with his mother. She had stopped on the stairway a step above him, as if the added height afforded her some modicum of safety or privilege. At fifty-one, she was still considered one of the leading beauties of her time. He would agree with the critiques. It was an unfortunate circumstance she was a cold bitch, especially when she had been drinking. He could smell the sherry.

Erik nodded his head. "Mother."

"Really, Erik. You could have given me some warning that you intended to visit."

"Did you think I would not call on you today?"

Neither of them wasted breath on polite trivialities. The countess swept past him and down the corridor into the red salon. "If you are here to clap me in chains for seeing my Becca without first consulting you, then know that I did so at her behest, not mine." She dropped onto a red-and-white-striped *chaise longue* in front of the fireplace and crossed her legs. "What else would you have me do when she sends letters asking to see me? She misses me. Is it so much to ask my daughter to come live with me?"

Erik closed the door behind him. "Leave off the melodrama, Mother. We had an agreement. And if you think for one moment that I would allow her to spend a day alone with you and your crowd, think again."

"How could you possibly deny me my own daughter? You must know I have missed her terribly."

"You've missed her so much you could not bother writing her in five years? Now you want to play the matron saint while disparaging me in my own house. I am not going to rehash an old argument. We had an agreement."

"*You* had an agreement. One that you coerced me into signing. You have punished me long enough because I married a man of whom you did not approve. You cannot blame me for the past, when I have only done my best."

Allowing for some manner of calm to settle between them, Erik strode to the window. He rarely raised his voice. He did not lose his temper or his self-control. His entire life, he'd witnessed the effects of emotional anarchy and swore he'd never lower himself to a level where emotions ruled actions. God help him, he'd seen enough of that in his lifetime. "It is not my intent to embark upon a battle with you, Mother. That is not why I am here."

"Of course it isn't." She drummed her manicured nails in impatience. "You rarely crawl out of that wretched hellhole you call home. You must be as desperate for a wife as they said you are, seeing as you have to leave Scotland to find one. Are you here to announce you have found someone willing to wed you?"

Erik drew in a breath and swore to himself. Why did he continue to allow her to shock him? His entire life he had been only a means to an end for her. He no longer knew why he bothered with civility at all. "My personal reasons for coming to London are no one's concern. Certainly, they are not yours. I came here this morning because I wanted to give you the courtesy of informing you personally that I will be in London for another week at most. During that time, if you want to see Becca you may, but you will go through me." Erik moved from the window. "Do not put her between you and your hatred for me."

"I . . . I don't hate you. She asked about the Sedgwick curse. Would you have me lie? She is sixteen, not a child any longer. You will find that out soon enough one day when it is you she hates."

"I believe we are now finished with our conversation."

"Erik. Wait." She rose in a *swish* of velvet and hurried to his side. "Don't go. Please. Not yet." She twisted her hands. "Can't we talk? Won't you at least remain for tea?"

He'd stopped mid-stride and, against all better judgment and instinct, turned. "For what purpose would you want to have tea?"

Her chin thrust up. "Is it your intent to deny me forever?"

"I have never denied you anything, only the pederast thief you married. I can only thank God Becca never knew her father. Or the last two you wed."

She gasped. "You are cruel, Erik. Exactly as your father was." She delicately dabbed the corner of a handkerchief at each eye. "He took pleasure in his spite against me as well."

Erik looked away, refusing to allow himself to be drawn into a discussion about what his mother had been forced to endure with his heartless and arrogant father. He had long ago inured himself against her attack on a man Erik had never known.

"Wait. Perhaps if you gave me more income . . . I could travel. I could go away from this place. I wouldn't have to be a bother to you."

His mother detested traveling. She never went farther than the expensive and very private boutiques on Bond Street. "Have you already run out of your allowance, Mother?"

"You don't give me enough. I am a pauper among my peers."

"Three months ago, when we had this discussion, I told you I would not listen to your complaining. My accountants and solicitors go over your books and I have been reassured you have more than enough to live extravagantly. What I give you in a year is more than some families see in a lifetime."

"Truly." Tears filled her brown eyes and she looked away. "You cannot put me in the same category as a fishwife in Cheapside."

"I wouldn't insult the fishwife with such a comparison."

He walked to the door and called for his cloak and hat before facing his mother. "If you stayed away from the cards and opium dens, you would have more to spend on your parties and your wardrobe. You could have spent more time with Becca, and Erin, if you ever cared to acknowledge my daughter's existence."

"Despite what you think of me, I have done my best under the extreme circumstances fate has forced upon me. Besides . . ." She tucked the handkerchief in her sleeve. "You owe me something for keeping silent all these years about Lady Elizabeth—"

Erik slammed shut the door.

She visibly swallowed. "It is only my intent to remind you how easily secrets can slip. Loyalty deserves compensation. Do you not agree? Five thousand more pounds a year should be no hardship for you."

Bloody hell.

"Oh, Erik. Please." His mother wrung her hands. "It was never my intent to push our relationship to this point."

"What relationship, Mother? You have always been on the wrong side of every problem I have ever encountered in my life. You stood against me on the side of a man who could have hurt Becca."

"He was my husband. Have you considered that it is you who was wrong and misjudged him?"

"Your loyalty has forever been to yourself or to the bloody useless cretins you continue to marry."

"Please, Erik. I am in need. And I have kept your secrets."

He lowered his voice in menace. "Whatever was between Elizabeth and me, my daughter is an innocent. I will not have her parentage questioned by the likes of you or this ton. If you *ever*, and I mean *ever*, breathe a word about anything Elizabeth wrote to you . . ."

Lowering her head, she nodded. "I know. I'll do anything you ask. But I need the money, Erik."

"Are you sure five thousand is enough, Mother?"

To her credit, she nodded and did not push him further.

Withdrawing a blank bank draft from the leather pocket book in his jacket pocket, he walked to a small secretary near the window and scratched out an order for five thousand pounds to be presented to his bank. If this was what it took to rid Becca of her influence and protect Erin, he would pay ten times the amount. He tossed the pen on the desk and held out the draft. When she suddenly seemed hesitant, he raised a brow.

"Second thoughts?"

She eased her hand over the draft. He tightened his grip. "Know this now," he warned. "If I ever learn you have kept a single letter Elizabeth sent you, I swear you do not know the meaning of true poverty. I do not care if you are my flesh and blood, I *will* destroy you."

He walked to the door and slowly turned. "And the next impoverished lord you decide to marry will be the one supporting you for the rest of your life."

"You are an unforgiving and callous man, Erik. It is no wonder Elizabeth left you. What woman would have a man with no heart?"

Despite the traffic and length of time it had taken to cross London, it was still early in the afternoon when Christine finally arrived back at the abbey. She'd spent most of the morning at the museum working on an exhibit Lord Bingham had been panicked would not be ready for next week's opening. It annoyed Christine that she continued to allow herself to be at the curator's disposal. She shouldered through the garden gate, barely stepping aside as a doe bounded through the trees and nearly caused her to drop the armful of books she carried.

She edged her hat higher on her forehead and continued toward the house. Amid London's crowded urban sprawl, the enclosed abbey grounds offered a garden sanctuary to those who lived here, including the wildlife on the property, and like clockwork, the breeze brought the sound of anxious quacking to her ears. She spot-

ted the resident ducks waddling out of the long grass
to intercept her. Struggling to shift the books against
one arm, she tossed bread crumbs toward her growing
feathered entourage to keep them from following her
to the house. It didn't matter which gate she entered,
the ducks always seemed to know where she would be,
and lay in ambush for her. She'd finally simply given up
trying to avoid them and made an effort to buy bread
on her way home.

Her arms laden with books, her chin balancing
them, she hurried past a pond. Then she stopped and
backtracked three steps. A tall black horse lingered
beneath the branches of a sweeping oak. Someone
had gone to the trouble to keep him off the main
drive. Sunlight reflected off her spectacles. Then as
she looked toward the rose garden at the back of the
house, her momentary hesitation vanished and something else took its place.

Erik sat with his back against a white picket fence,
a blade of grass between his lips, watching her. As she
turned, he tossed aside the stem and came slowly to his
feet. His jacket was unbuttoned. He looked handsome
in his tall boots and dark riding attire. The collar of his
shirt was open, the sight of his bare throat uncivilized.
His sheer masculine presence was so incompatible with
Aunt Sophie's delicate rose garden, he looked almost
vulnerable to her as she approached and stopped in
front of him.

But it took only one look into his sherry-colored
eyes to make her feel like a blushing virgin. Because
of him, she had been unable to sleep last night. All day
her stomach had fluttered and her mind kept drifting
from her task as she went over time and again what she
would say to him when she saw him. She didn't want

to be eighteen again, when all he had to do was look at her and make her body want to violate every tenet of moral etiquette.

"Your grace."

Without asking, he reached for the books in her arms. "Why don't I carry these to wherever it is you are going?"

"Why?" She suspiciously watched her precious books leave her arms. "Do you intend to follow me?"

He was looking at her hard. "I think you know why I am here."

Despite her willingness to forgive him for last night, she felt her heart skip. He didn't ask if he was intruding on her time or offer apologies about his atrocious behavior in the carriage. Indeed, he looked as unrepentant as sin. But at the very least, she owed him back his fossils. For that reason alone, she chose not to argue with his presence. She could manage herself around him for one more day.

She cast off like a ship setting out to sea. "I am on my way to my laboratory. Your sister's fossils are there."

She walked in silence, staying ahead of him, conscious of the sound of twigs breaking against the weight of his boots, aware of the rasp of his clothes and his eyes on her back. At the back of the house, they descended into the stone stairwell until they reached the basement door. She stopped and withdrew a key. "If you will wait here a moment." The metallic click of a lock sounded. "I need to go inside first."

Before he could reply, she disappeared through the postern.

Adjusting the weight of the books in his arms, Erik looked back up the stairs behind him. Water dripped from a pipe to his left. He stood on a layer of green moss that had grown on the walk. He studied the stone enclosure where it met an ivy-covered wall, and he noticed structural cracks that came with age. He peered up at a second-story window with yellow curtains, then at the doorway as he heard Christine return.

"I have traps set up around my laboratory," she explained.

He stepped into the vestibule. "Rats?"

She reached around him, her skirts whispering against his legs as she shut the door behind him. "You can say that. One can never be too careful of wily family members." She led him down a short corridor and stopped at another heavy oak door that would have required a battering ram to break down. "Unfortunately, the only culprit I have thus far ensnared is my cat. Poor Beast has yet to forgive me for turning him green."

"*Beast?*"

The first hint of a smile turned up her lips. "If you see him, he will probably startle you," she said as if she were his own proud mam. "I had one occasion where a lady fainted. But he really is a pussy cat."

"Indeed."

"The fairer feline population loves him. His orange progeny run rampant on the Abbey grounds. He has helped us control our rat population."

Once inside the sizeable room that could pass for a vault, she lit two lamps, the smell of sulphur briefly eclipsing the other unpleasant smells that came with being around dead creatures and relics of the past. The walls were lined with wooden shelves bowed by the weight of dusty artifacts and wooden crates filled with petrified bones.

"I have to keep everything down on this stone floor," she said as if in explanation of the visual chaos surrounding him. She shut the door behind him. "The weight of all of this petrified bone would cause the floor above to collapse."

His interest moved to the surrounding workbenches. They were standing on a dais that looked as if this room had once served as a classroom. Four rows of parallel wooden workbenches ran thirty feet deep into the room.

"You will have to pardon the smell," she said, sliding out of her cloak and laying it on the table next to the door. "I don't usually bring anyone here. The dust makes people sneeze. Twice a year, I have to bomb the place with a cyanic compound to kill the vermin or they will eat everything. Once, they ate Aunt Sophie's mummy."

Shaking his head, Erik laughed. "And to think your family looks perfectly normal on the outside."

She suddenly stood in front of him, her chin level with his shoulders. "I'll take the books now."

Her hands brushed his. Just a whisper of a touch, yet, even through his gloves, he felt warmth flow through him. He did not pull back. "Tell me where you want them," he said.

He thought she might balk. She pointed to a cluttered table against the wall. "Over here."

He set down the books and she stood each one perfectly aligned with the others, certainly not concordant to the disorder surrounding him. But some people's chaos was another's harmony. He had a feeling everything in this lab, as in her life, had its proper place.

"Your sister's fossils are here." She led Erik down

two wooden stairs to one of the wooden countertops. "I have finished cleaning each one. If your sister is to become a collector, she will need to know how to care for her finds."

"Would you remove your hat?"

The intimacy of his request startled her. "Pardon?"

"I have a desire to see a person's eyes when I am speaking. That is all," he said simply, setting his gloves aside.

If he was going to negotiate for his future, he would bloody well look in her eyes when he did it.

Her hands slid a hat pin from its mooring in her hair. Carefully easing the hat from her hair, she presented him her face, spectacles and all. His gaze touched the freckles on her nose and then her lips. "Is this to your satisfaction?" she asked when he failed to reply.

"It is."

She turned abruptly and began setting each of Becca's fossils on a piece of soft fabric. Instead of staring at her, he took in various bins. "Is everything here yours?"

"Everything in the bins will one day be donated to various museums around the world," she said without looking at him. "I still have to finish cataloging what is on the shelves. To answer your question? No. Only some of what is here is mine."

He leaned a hip against the dusty countertop and, folding his arms, looked around for a possible sighting of Beast. After a moment, he found Christine staring at him.

"What is so amusing?" she asked.

He couldn't seem to take his eyes from her face. She looked out of place in this dusty hell pit. Like a solitary cornflower blossom on a gravel drive. His mouth crooked faintly. "I don't know what is more amusing.

That you ensnared a furry thief or that you named your cat Beast. I could use Beast's appetite for mice and rats at Sedgwick Castle."

Dropping her gaze from his, she finished wrapping Becca's fossils as if she were caring for pieces of fragile porcelain.

After a moment he said, "Have you ever been to Scotland, Christine?"

"Papa and I attended a lecture once in Edinburgh," she quietly said as she continued wrapping the fabric around the fossils. "My great-grandparents were Scots. Aunt Sophie was born near Dunipace."

"The reputed home of Merlin," he said, waiting for Christine to turn her head and look at him.

Her hands paused in her task. She turned her head and looked up at him, her eyes a smoky blue in the light. "Most consider Merlin a myth."

"Like dragons?" he challenged. "Beasts larger than a house? Do you want to know what Scotland is to me?" he asked, not wanting to digress, needing her to understand what he offered. To Erik, Scotland would forevermore be his home. "She is raw and moody. A fortress in a cloud. Brilliant summer sunsets. Storm-lashed coasts. She is like a temperamental queen, exciting and more beautiful than anything you will ever see."

She returned her attention to the fossils, but her hands were no longer steady. "We both know why I am here, Christine."

She snagged a length of twine from the shelf and wrapped it around the cloth. "It occurred to me while I was attempting to sleep last night that neither of us has been ourself."

"Do you think there might be a reason for that?"

She snapped her head around to peer up at him, eyes wide. "Do you?"

It wasn't a question he'd expected to be thrown back into his face. In fact he'd meant it rhetorically. But neither was it a question he could answer with clarity. "Last night, I asked you to marry me. I came here today to press my case in the hopes that you would listen to everything I have to say."

"You need not—"

"In any case, you will listen. You owe *me* that."

Drawing in her breath, she accepted his pronouncement with more calm than he had expected. Shifting his feet, Erik forced himself to look away. He picked up a stone egg atop the shelf level with his eyes. "Fossils are like rocks to me, Christine. Only when they are mixed with human remains do they take on importance." He studied the fossil egg, before setting it back down. "I meant it when I told you I needed other answers."

"You are referring to the human remains that you found with the fossils."

"You have never been the focus of malicious gossip. A circumstance that does not particularly bother me, but words can be a cruel thing. In Becca's case, they are worse. She was the last person to see Elizabeth alive. She has no idea that the remains I found probably belong to Elizabeth." With his backside to the countertop, he folded his arms but he did not look away from Christine.

Her lashes threw ragged shadows that shifted behind her spectacles as she blinked. The dull amber light coming from the single lamp by the door emphasized the height of her cheekbones and the bow curve of her lips.

"My first marriage, I hardly remember," he said quietly. "I wanted the vows done with so I could leave England. We had not yet reached Scotland when she became ill. My condolences to you and your family for her loss, but that is the way of it. I did not poison her or wish her ill."

"I know you didn't."

"Some claim I am cursed, which brings me to Elizabeth."

He looked away and wondered why it was suddenly so difficult to speak, why he'd lost the words he'd come to say. But he needed Christine to believe in him. After the most fleeting pause, he continued. "Elizabeth was the youngest daughter of the only man I ever considered a father, a man I looked up to for counsel on more than one occasion while growing up. I will not lambaste her character or tell you that the faults in our marriage belonged to her. They did not.

"Our relationship, if it was anything at all, was . . . tempestuous." And that was putting it as kindly as he could in describing the mother of his child. "After a particularly unpleasant argument, which she accused me of adultery, I took my daughter and left. For the record, I was never unfaithful. By the time I returned to Sedgwick, Elizabeth had already been gone two months. A year ago her bones started washing up on the riverbank along with those of your beast."

"Why are you telling me this, Erik?"

"Because after last night I have come to realize you and I are both still looking for something. I am no philosopher who contemplates the stars and speaks in antidotal verbiage that people find poetic and pretend to understand. Whatever happened between us might be in the past, but not forgotten. Last night proved that to me. I don't claim to know much about love. I doubt you do either. From what little I've seen of love in my life, it is overrated anyway."

She looked down at her hands lying folded atop the fossils. Erik studied her profile, defined by the pale light and a mood he wanted to understand. He wrapped his fingers gently around her chin and turned her face. "It is important that you do not believe what most say about me. And if I offended you last night—"

"I'm not offended, Erik."

"Then marry me, Christine," he said softly, his eyes locked on hers with a deep intensity. "Marry me and I will give you your dream. I will give you your beast of Sedgwick."

Chapter 6

Christine tried to turn away, but Erik's hand wrapped around her arm and stopped her retreat. "No, Erik," she said. "You can't know what you are doing. What you propose is mad."

His touch was neither harsh nor gentle, only unrelenting in purpose. "Would you believe my intentions more honorable if I knelt at your feet spewing romantic sonnets worthy of a Shakespearean melodrama instead?" She turned her head away, but he placed his hand beneath her chin, then splayed her cheek with fingers that should have been soft and unworked.

Instead, they had calluses like a man unafraid of toiling work. He smoothed the side of one hand across her cheek. "Neither of us has the luxury of time for me to court you properly," he said. "I have to return to Sedgwick."

"You need an heir. I don't know the least about children. I am merely convenient to this marriage you will ask of me." No longer sure of her own mind and unable to comprehend his, she struggled to make sense of the turmoil he created within her.

"Ours would be no marriage of convenience, Christine." He placed his palms on the countertop,

trapping her between his arms. He smelled of sunlight, like the woodsy, warm pine needles, the kind
that had cushioned her that long-ago day near the
lake near her uncle's home in Somerset, where Erik
had taken her to the ground and made love to her
with his mouth. When she had been too young, too
foolish.

"Look around this room, Christine. I can give you
what you want. Legitimacy. Respectability among your
peers. Your beast of Sedgwick. Tell me this is not enticing to you. I have an estate littered with the bones and
artifacts of the past."

"I do not believe this is happening."

He placed his hands alongside her head, and with her
back against the countertop, he gently held her face to
his gaze, removed her spectacles and set them behind
her. "You do not think me capable of proposing? Or
you do not believe any man capable of wanting you?"

A soft sound escaped her lips.

He pulled her against him while one hand slipped
to the nape of her neck, not to hold her captive but to
angle her head. "A partnership between us doesna have
to be boring, Christine." Slowly he bent and kissed her,
a breath against her lips. "It will be ours to do as we
please."

He pressed her to the countertop, his kiss breathy,
like a hot, humid dawn. The taste and texture of him
swept through her. Her own rapid heartbeat melded
with his almost as if some unseen force had wrapped
them in its palm, and all she was conscious of was the
rhythm of his tongue striking hers. She clung to him
because she didn't know what it was she wanted, and he
pressed her no further than she was willing to go. Just
enough to lay claim to her willingness at least in this.
She could never assert he'd forced her or seduced her.

But she could not do this. She had not thought this through. Had she?

"Erik . . ."

"Don't." His breath coming faster, he rested his forehead against hers as if he, too, fought for control. "Don't turn away."

She shook her head. Pins had loosened in her hair. "This isn't right. . . ."

"This is as right as it gets between us," he said, his voice urgent, and then he kissed her again.

He stepped into the juncture between her thighs and she nearly cried out. He was as fully aroused as she. A low sound of pleasure threaded from her throat. He enflamed her with feeling so intense it was almost painful.

She sank against his chest, his warmth as close to heaven as she had ever remembered being. She curved her arms around his neck. His hands roamed down her back, cupped her bottom and brought her up hard against his sex. She tasted more than him in her mouth. She tasted lust. Her own. She tore her mouth from his and took a step backward.

She touched a finger to her bruised lips. Confusion beset her. Looking up at him, she felt her chest constrict.

"Christine . . ."

She didn't want to need him. Wanting him was dangerous. "Why did you have to return? Why did you have to come to Sommershorn Abbey?"

She spun and practically ran to the door. She'd opened it only an inch before he slammed it shut and twisted the key in the lock.

"Lord, Christine." His heat limned her back. "Is a future with me so horrible to contemplate? Am I some wretched beast to be shunned by you as well?"

"No." She pressed her forehead against the oaken panel and fought against the stinging in the back of her eyes. "But we're not ourselves right now. Or we would not be doing this."

He braced his hands on either side of her head. "I have not been more myself, more confident of my decision, since the moment I saw you at Sommershorn Abbey, Christine. I know you felt it, too. This is not wrong. *I* am not wrong."

Groaning, she luxuriated in the feel of his chest pressed against her back. One strong forearm beneath her breasts held her to him. His erection was hard against her bottom. "I want to be inside you, Christine," he rasped against the corner of her mouth. "Deep inside you. I want your body to know mine again. I want to feel you around me." He pressed the heel of his hand against her most intimate place. "Tell me you don't feel the same." He splayed his other hand across her jaw and into her hair. "Tell me, Christine," he breathed.

With her cheek against his shoulder and the other moist with his breath, she turned her head. Lifting her chin, she sought his lips. He murmured her name as she opened her mouth to receive his thrusting tongue. With a predatory intensity, he'd eroded the certainty of her feelings, scraped at the heart of her emotions, made her forget his ruthlessness and the past.

Made her forget everything but this.

Beneath her bodice, her breasts grew heavy. Her head spun. His taste was like an intoxicating shot of scotch consumed in a rush, warmer and more invigorating with each draught she stole from the glass. She let him touch her anywhere he wanted. Her breasts. Her lips. Between her legs. Especially between her legs.

Even through her skirts his touch burned and excited her in every wicked way possible. She plundered his mouth, burning for his touch, no longer feeling submissive but assertive in her own needs as well.

She was on fire. Ravaged by heat. Lost in her own sensuality. And with her back still pressed against his chest she raised her arm and curled it around his nape, pulling his mouth hard against hers. Need drove her to rub her bottom against his sex.

He drew breath through clenched teeth. Then he was no longer kissing her. If one of his arms had not been holding her pressed against his chest, she would have collapsed to the floor in a puddle of muslin. He turned her roughly and pinned her hands against the door. Their moist breath came in gasps.

"God, has it been so long for you, Christine?"

It had been forever since she had allowed herself the freedom to feel this way, to let everything go as if tomorrow didn't matter.

His eyes dark and intense, he lowered his mouth to hers. "Say no, Christine," he rasped against her lips. "Or I'll nae be stopped."

"Don't stop." Her lips brushed his cheek and then his lips again. "Don't . . ." She no longer cared about tomorrow or the consequences of this moment. ". . . stop."

"Shh." The faint whisper was a vibration against her cheek.

His hands moved beneath her skirts, eased up her thighs past her silk garters. She watched breathless as he raised her skirts and found the slit in her drawers. She felt heavy, weighted between her legs. Hot. Alive. He passed two fingers through her moist curls, arousing a feeling so intense she barely caught her voice against crying aloud.

For a timeless moment, he stared into her eyes in such gentle opposition to her racing blood that she stood on her toes and pulled him into a kiss.

His finger slipped into her slick flesh, then another. She shut her eyes and heaved a breath. Bending, he guided himself between her thighs and caught her weight against the door. Her skirts weren't enough of a hindrance to impede his movements. His member, burning and heavy, pressed into her, filling her with an unrelenting pressure that stole her breath. He withdrew, gripped her bottom with one hand and lifted her higher onto him.

He pushed as deep as he could go. And stopped.

"Christine . . ." he uttered from deep in his throat.

Her thighs closed around his hips. With her back pressed against the door, he braced one hand next to her shoulder and thrust again, driving deeper. His body rocked against hers. Slowly at first as if savoring the pleasure of their rhythm. The sinews of his arms moved against her palms. Her lips parted. She heard her own soft moan and opened her eyes. He was watching her, his eyes heavy-lidded and dark in the shadows just beyond the light.

She felt branded by his possession, and wanted to brand him in return. His breath grew more ragged with each thrust of his hips. "Come to me, Christine." He spoke low and close, nudging her thighs wider, brushing his lips across hers. With each rocking thrust, blood rushed to her center and pulsed like a heartbeat. "Come to me now."

"Yes . . ." Her panting breaths steamed against his lips.

"Let me give you everything you want."

She wanted only to feel more. Every nerve ending seared her. Fire spread across her flesh.

The tension between her legs intensified. Her fingers entangled in his hair and she couldn't stop a sobbing outcry. "Yes."

His lips pulled and suckled. His tongue probed her mouth deeply, making love to it as he did to her body. Somewhere she thought she heard voices in the hallway outside the door. He must have heard, too, because he said, "Quiet, love." He breathed roughly without breaking rhythm. "The door is locked but not impervious to sound."

Helpless in her release, she pulled him into another soul-searing kiss and rode the currents of pleasure, arching her back as she came with the force of one blissful wave after wracking wave crashing on sand. His grasp tightened on her hips and he held her down on his sex, his guttural groan muffled against the naked curve of her shoulder where her gown fell open. She felt the shudder of his breath against her ear, and a white-hot rush flooding inside her, drenching her. Their breathing rasped in the heated silence.

Even as her mind-numbing pleasure eased to tiny pulses between her legs, she quietly sucked in air and listened to the voices fading outside in the corridor. Erik's forehead rested against hers. With his penis still heavy and thick inside her, they remained pressed against one another, breathing shallowly. In the aftermath, neither moved.

"What just happened between us?" she said when some semblance of sanity tried to reassert itself in her mind.

"I don't know." His voice sounded amused. "I think I just *fooked* you against the door."

A part of her welcomed his devil-may-care attitude and the way he could spurn convention. Yet, in many ways, Erik Boughton was as conventional an aristocrat, and archaic in behavior, as the new Queen herself.

When he finally eased out of her and lowered her skirts, she fell forward against his chest. Bereft of strength and aching with a new tenderness, she inhaled the musky scent of sex still wet between her legs even as she absorbed his heartbeat against her cheek.

What had he done to her? Wading through the mist of her emotions, she understood nothing but the feel of the shimmering rainbow that still seemed to surround her. She didn't want to let him go.

He spoke against the soft shell of her ear, his voice a hoarse whisper. "I will procure a special license. I think it wise that we be wed as soon as possible."

She pulled back. Her hands trembled as she worked to repair her clothes. "I need time, Erik."

His shirt hung loose and unbuttoned from his trousers. He looked as ravaged as she felt. "Time?" He laughed as if to say that ten years was more than enough time.

"I have . . . I have responsibilities to attend to at the abbey," she said.

"I won't force you, Christine," he said quietly. "You'll come to me willingly. Or you'll not come at all. Do ye understand?"

He would have no martyred wife in his bed. Theirs would be a marriage in truth, a partnership as he had said. A promise. Her eyes filling with tears, she touched the frown line bracketing one corner of his mouth. "I'm sorry."

"Christine?"

Erik was halfway to his horse when he stopped. "Devil take it." He did an about-face on his heel.

He'd be damned if he was going to allow Christine to walk away from him . . . *again*.

She, who braved a man's world with spear in one hand and a shield in the other, like one of Sparta's warriors at the pass of Thermopile. The woman who pampered old bones and relics as if they were her children, who set traps for thieves and named her cat Beast. She had fled him as if he were the plague.

One thing was for certain, he told himself as he traipsed through an overgrown garden in search of a path that would take him to the front of the house. He would be deceiving himself if he thought today's passionate sexual tryst precluded her from having any choice in the matter of her future. She did have a choice. At the moment, she was exercising that choice not to marry him.

Fifteen minutes later, feeling like a supplicant as he followed an addlepated housekeeper into the drawing room, he ran into Joseph Darlington and his blushing bride, Amelia. Their presence shocked him. He had not expected to see Darlington back from his honeymoon so soon. They sat in the drawing room having tea with Lady Sophia, Christine's maiden grandaunt.

The housekeeper announced his name and that he was here to see Miss Sommers. The angelically blond Amelia leaped to her feet first and dipped into a curtsey. Mr. Darlington rose. Only Lady Sophia remained seated.

"Your grace," Amelia replied. "We have not seen Miss Sommers."

"Perhaps she is still in the laboratory," Mr. Darlington replied. "I believe that was where she was fifteen minutes ago."

Amelia was studying the toes of her shoes. Remembering the noise he'd heard in the hallway when he and Christine were against the door, Erik looked from her to Darlington. He suspected these two had heard everything.

So be it, he swore to himself. He intended to marry Christine. But announcing that fact would not further his cause.

Lady Sophia watched the interchange over the rim of her teacup. He was sure Lady Sophia would have remembered him from years ago. How did one forget a man who had married into the family, then promptly lost his bride to a fever ere two weeks had passed? One did not, he suspected. "You are welcome to join us for tea, Lord Sedgwick. If my niece is in the laboratory she could be there awhile."

After an awkward moment where he declined tea and no one spoke, Erik returned his attention to Darlington. "You will be leaving soon for Perth," he said, remembering their conversation at the museum, and the look on Christine's face when Darlington had announced he had received the appointment. Erik had no idea why he should care. But he did.

When no immediate reply was forthcoming, Amelia slanted her husband a hesitant glance. "We will be remaining in London for a while," Darlington said.

"You will be remaining at Sommershorn Abbey," Lady Sophia told Darlington. "We were just discussing that very thing when you arrived, Sedgwick."

"I should let you return to your conversation." He felt out of place.

Erik patted his inside pocket. He hadn't brought a card or anything that would make this look like a planned social call as he stood in front of the threesome in his shirtsleeves looking more like a roustabout than an aristocrat calling on a young woman. "Tell Miss Sommers I was here," he said.

Erik finally bowed politely and left the trio to enjoy their reunion in peace.

He reached the tree where his horse should have been tied only to ascertain it had loosed itself from the branch where Erik secured him. He found the gelding's tracks in the dirt and discovered the horse had decided to quench his thirst in the middle of the shallow duck pond.

Erik's new Italian leather boots were still wet and caked in mud thirty minutes later when he reined in the bay just at the edge of the wooded parkland behind his house and swore softly to himself.

Now almost home, he'd remembered he'd forgotten to bring back Becca's fossils. With an oath, he swung the bay around.

Christine was suddenly in front of him, bringing her mare to a skidding halt before she collided with him. His startled horse reared, nearly unseating him. He brought his horse around as it pranced sideways into a mud puddle, sending a spray of black water up and onto his cloak, which now complemented the mud caked on his boots. But his anger died as quickly as it had come.

The first thing he noticed was that she was riding sidesaddle. For some reason he had expected to see her defying custom and riding astride. A jaunty straw hat covered her hair and the large blue bow at her chin framed her oval face. Her blue velvet riding attire hugged what he considered a perfect pair of breasts. No country bumpkin was the very fair Miss Christine Sommers.

He leaned an elbow against his knee. "Why am I not shocked that you are here without a groom?"

Her black tossed its head and danced a few steps. "Perhaps we are beyond being shocked with each other."

"Are we?"

Her flushed cheeks stood out in contrast to the white lace collar that buttoned at her neck. He suspected why she was here. Her presence had everything to do with Darlington and Amelia's sudden arrival at Sommershorn Abbey, but he only knew he did not care the reasons.

"I would have an answer from you." She waited for him to nod. "You have made it clear your only reason for marriage is to beget an heir. What happens to our marriage after I give you a son?"

"What do you want to happen?"

Evading the deeper issue of love, she attacked the primary topic of concern. The one she *could* control. "Any children we have will also be mine. I'll not leave them, nor be forced to do so."

"You think me so heartless?"

"The devil duke of Sedgwick is not known for his generous heart."

There was the briefest of pauses. "I will not force you to leave," he said quietly. "Nor will I force you to stay."

"I see," she said. "Then ours will truly be a marriage of convenience? A bargain met only in bed? You will have your life to attend to and I will have mine," she said. "Is that it?"

"Unless you know of another more suitable arrangement."

"Such an arrangement is not all bad," she agreed.

She fidgeted with the lace on her sleeve only to realize she was destroying her cuff. "You won't wake up tomorrow and realize you have made a terrible mistake?" she quietly asked.

Did she think so little of herself? "No, Christine."

"Then to that point, I have just one more request to ask of you."

"Will it hurt?" he asked.

Despite her unwillingness to smile, she seemed warmed by his humor. "I hope not. But this is important."

"What is it you want, Christine?"

"By law, Sommershorn Abbey will pass to my husband." She drew in breath as she pondered what his reaction might be to her request. "You don't need the property. I would ask that you put the school into a trust that cannot be touched except by the executor I appoint. I wish the Abbey to remain my legacy to the young women for whom my great-grandmother built the school. I want to keep the tradition alive. No woman should ever be allowed to feel shame for her intellect."

"As you wish, Christine."

"Thank you."

And for the first time since she'd ridden pell-mell into the glade, he felt the constriction in his chest loosen. "Is there anything else to which I should agree?" he asked.

"This may be business for you, but it is also my business. I will be an equal partner in all matters personal between us."

"All matters personal," he agreed. "In everything else, I have no doubt you and I can come to an equitable agreement. Do I meet your criteria?"

The wariness inside her eased. "I will marry you, Erik. Your solicitor can deliver the contracts. I will sign them."

She urged her horse back as if she might swing away, but he bent down and took hold of the bridle. He looked into her startled face, her eyes wide open and blue as a piece of summer sky.

Until today, he'd always considered himself a man of restraint and subdued passions. In his entire life, with only a few exceptions, he had never surrounded himself with anything that he could not live without.

"Do we have an agreement, your grace?" she asked.

His hand tightened on the bit. Even suspecting her reasons for accepting his offer and wanting to escape England, he would take her. "Aye," he said satisfied for now with the bargain he had struck. He released his grip on the bit.

"You have not told me where you wish to speak our vows," he said.

She toyed with her reins. "I wish to marry at Saint Jude's Cathedral off York Square. It is not far from here."

"Ah," he said simply and, despite himself, he smiled. "Saint Jude. Patron saint of hopeless and difficult causes."

She did not quite smile, but her expression became less tense. "Papa is buried there. I have known Reverend Simms my entire life. I would like him to perform the ceremony. As soon as possible." A blush stained her checks and she rushed to explain. "As it will take a few weeks for me to pack and settle my affairs at Sommershorn Abbey before I can leave, and I know you cannot remain here in London. I would not wish to change my mind while you are frittering away your time in Scotland waiting for me."

His gaze tracing the tiny curve of her smile, he lifted his eyes back to hers and recognized the comment for what it was. A self-deprecating fact. "I can have a special license in two days. We can be wed by the end of the week."

She seemed relieved to put the entire affair into his hands.

"Then we are in accord?" she asked.

"Yes." His thumb brushed her moist lower lip. "I believe we are."

Without giving her time to respond, he wrapped his hand around her nape and laid his lips over hers. He'd meant for the kiss to be simple, a bargain sealed. But somehow, his intent gravitated toward something far more complex and less governable, in a kiss that deepened into something rough. Her hand curled around his lapel. Heat clung to her like the sunlight warming his shoulders and she melted against him. Their horses stirred. Slowly, he pulled away.

With trembling hands, she gathered up the reins. "I will await word from your solicitor."

She swung her black around in a tight circle and, as he watched her maneuver through the trees the way she had come, an old adage nipped at his thoughts. Something about . . . the wolf eating the lamb that strays from the field.

He frowned and nudged his heels against his horse. Better that adage than the one that said *He who picks up a thorn has one less sin, for had he stepped on it, he would have cursed*.

It should not have mattered to him why she was marrying him, only that she was.

Christine arrived back at Sommershorn Abbey just before dark. Holding a package close to her chest, she shut the door then closed her eyes as if she could shut out the doubts as easily. After leaving Erik, she had not come directly home but had instead gone to a small lace shop near the cathedral where she would soon be wed. A true bride always wore a veil, she'd told herself.

Mrs. Samuels came bustling toward her. "Oh, mum, you are finally arrived. Lady Sophia is in the dining room waiting for you. Oh, dear, oh dear. Mr. Darlington and Miss Amelia . . ." Wringing her chubby hands, the housekeeper murmured in her doomsday voice, "Mrs. Darlington," she corrected, "also be with her, mum. And your uncle and that rascally son of his arrived twenty minutes ago."

"I see." She gave Mrs. Samuels the package to take upstairs. "Make me some tea. At least you can boil water while fretting. You don't have to be here."

"Yes, my lady. Thank you."

After Mrs. Samuels waddled away Christine removed her hat and hung it on a peg beside the door. She recognized Amelia's voice and Joseph's somber undertones coming from the dining room.

She drew in a breath. She had no interest in hearing about his week, nor was she interested in explaining hers. She would not even know how to begin.

And because no good reason could have brought her family to the abbey on a night like this and because she was a coward, she considered escaping upstairs to her room, before changing her mind. Except she had spent most of her life at the merciful whim of other people's platitudes.

Christine recognized the sound of her aunt's cane tapping the floor. It was muffled by the carpet, but it had no less effect on Christine than if it had vibrated the very air she breathed and she imagined Moses' staff when he parted the Red Sea. Her aunt appeared in the corridor and stopped.

Since she was six and had got herself stuck in a tree

while sneaking out of her room, Christine had not seen that worried look on her aunt's face. "We were about to call out a search for you. Come inside, child."

Aunt Sophie never called anyone *child*. Unable to stop the downward spiral of her emotions, Christine clutched her skirts and stepped past her into the dining room. Joseph and Amelia sat at the dining table. Joseph came to his feet. Christine's uncle, Papa's brother-in-law, the earl of Heath, and his wastrel son, Gordy, did not rise. She laid her hand on the back of the dining chair as she faced them all, like Daniel in the lions' den.

She nodded to Joseph and Amelia. "I am glad to see you both back." Her eyes on Amelia's face, she attempted to smile. "You are looking well."

Amelia lowered her gaze to her hands.

"Where have you been, Christine?" her uncle demanded. "Don't tell us you were at the museum. Mr. Darlington and Gordy just returned from there this evening. No one has seen you since this afternoon."

Gordy smirked behind his hand as if whispering conspiratorially to Joseph, "We shouldn't say 'no one.' "

Remembering just how much she disliked the little weasel, she narrowed her eyes on Gordy, then settled her fury on Joseph. How dare he stand on the side of her family? "Am I now required to consult with all of you whenever I leave the abbey? Since when has any of you cared what I do?"

Her uncle's expression darkened. "Since Sedgwick was here this afternoon. Since further inquiries have revealed this is not his first visit."

Gordy leaned forward on his elbows. "And in case you ever had a doubt, old gel, your laboratory activities aren't exactly beyond our hearing, you know."

Christine felt the awful rise of heat in her face.

"What were you *thinking*?" her uncle said. "Have you no ken what would happen to the repute of the school and all of us if anyone found out about you and that bastard? We would be ruined."

Christine pulled off her gloves, jerking one finger at a time as she worked through the panic that threatened her composure. "You needn't fear about your reputation. Any of you. I have agreed to marry him."

Shock silenced the group only momentarily. Then everyone started talking at once. "You have an obligation to the school" . . . "loyalty to the family to consider" . . . "The man has been accused of murder" . . . "His own mother wants nothing to do with him" . . . "He lives in the wilds of Scotland, a barbaric country."

"No decent woman dallies with the chap, much less marries him," her uncle blustered. "Good *Lord*! Society tolerates him only because his title and wealth make him powerful. He may not have caused the scarlet fever that killed my Charlotte, but he is responsible for his second wife's disappearance."

"Bloody hell, *coz*," Gordy said, "how could you possibly agree to marry the man knowing what you do about him?"

"They are right, Chrissie," Joseph said.

"Yet, you did not seem to care about his reputation, or ours, when you brought him to the museum gala and introduced him to Amelia and me. What does that make you but a hypocrite? Or worse. Tell me you were not going to ask him for his patronage?"

Joseph raked his fingers through his blond hair. "What would you have had me do, when he approached me about attending?"

He spoke with such fierceness that for a moment, Christine could say nothing.

"He and your father had been in contact for some

time before your father died," Joseph said. "Sedgwick has made substantial donations to the university in Edinburgh. Yes, I had talked to him about the possibility of his sponsorship."

"Even thinking him a wife murderer? Please spare me the sanctimonious drivel. All of you. You've lost your right to pass judgment on me. You more than anyone, Joseph."

"My *right*? We've known each other years. I don't have to be an expert to know the difference between seeking someone's patronage and marrying him. I care about what happens to you. I care about *you*. You cannot possibly think you would be happy with the man."

"And if you *truly* cared an iota about me, you would *not* have wed Amelia."

The words were out before she could stop them, and she would have given anything to take them back. Her gaze flew to her friend. "Oh, Lord." Shaking her head, she pressed the heel of her hand to her temple. "I . . . I'm sorry. I should not have said that. I did not mean it that—"

"Are you with *him* because of some latent, unresolved anger you have toward *me*?" Joseph asked as he came to stand in front of her. "Good God. Is that why you are marrying him?"

She stared up into his handsome face, his hair sweeping his brow like a troubadour of old, and saw the man with whom she'd thought to spend her life. Until he'd met Amelia and married her instead.

Until Erik had come back into her life and changed everything. Until she had put on the ring.

"Christine . . ." His voice lowered. "What would you have any of us say to you?" He swept his arm across the room. "Tell us."

"I would . . ." Tears burned in the back of her eyes. The fight suddenly went out of her. "You and Amelia will soon be on your way to Perth. I wanted that position. You know I did. But I am happy that you will be making a showing for the museum. You have *all* made decisions about our futures. I'm only asking that you let me now make mine."

She waited for someone to say something. Even Aunt Sophie remained silent, sitting on the settee beneath the window. Christine was suddenly exhausted and feeling entirely too isolated, unsure of herself and worried about the meaning of Aunt Sophie's silence. Of everyone in the entire world, Sophie's approval meant everything.

Her uncle rose and, with an oath, stomped from the room.

Joseph paused before her before he walked out of the room. "I wish you well, Chrissie. I really do."

The words hurt her more than anything else he could have said. Because they felt empty. Like a great tomb that should have been filled with gold only to be discovered empty upon excavation. She wondered how she could have ever thought she might have been in love with him. He lacked fortitude, the kind needed to claw one's way up a cliff. Joseph would let go and fall. Amelia rose and hesitated in front of Christine, tears in her eyes.

"Joseph's Perth expedition has been postponed indefinitely," she said. "He would have told you himself this afternoon."

Christine's mouth dropped open. "I don't understand."

"We went by Lord Bingham's home this morning. Joseph wanted to let him know he was ready to assemble his team as soon as such a meeting could be arranged. The expedition lost another one of its lead archeologists, this time to some French team in Greece. All hush-hush. Supposedly a big find is about to be announced. Everyone wants to be part of the group that unearths the next discovery. Perth is no longer of interest to the museum."

Christine felt her chest grow heavy. He had wanted Perth so badly and she hurt for him. "I'm sorry, Amelia."

But Amelia was already walking past Christine and out of the room.

Gordy chuckled. "You do realize, no one in this family will ever speak to you again. No more invitations to Christmas reunions. Your name will be stricken from the Sommerses' family bible." He chuckled as he lumbered past her to the door. "You've even rendered Aunt Sophie speechless." He lowered his voice. "I thought only a bottle of bourbon did us that service."

Christine strode past him to the front door and opened it for him. "Good-bye, Gordy. And do watch your step. The stairs are wet. I should hate for you to fall and break your neck."

He swept her a bow. "May you rest in peace, too, *coz*."

After slamming the door behind her cousin, Christine returned to the dining room to find Aunt Sophie had not moved. "I do not know if I should rejoice or weep at the turn of events this day," she said.

Christine could not bear her aunt's disapproval. At the very least, she hoped for neutrality. "Lord Sedgwick is not as people paint him," Christine said.

"Ten years is a long time to be away from a man and still think you know him. He may be more like the portrait that has been painted of him than you know. What did he offer you, dear?"

Christine shook her head, but no longer able to stand, she dropped into the seat beside her aunt. Aunt Sophie withdrew the cloth in which Christine had wrapped Becca's fossil. "This perhaps?"

Her heart gave a start. The amber light in the room seemed to embalm the tooth with sinister life. Erik had left the fossils in her lab. Christine did not bother to deny the truth as she took the fossil from Aunt Sophie. "He has found a beast on Sedgwick land."

"That explains why he contacted your father last year. Does Sedgwick know that *you* are C. A. Sommers?"

Christine wiped the corners of her eyes. "C. A. Sommers?" she said facetiously, "the infamous dragon hunter?" The malicious term the elite academia had labeled her father. "No, he does not. It wouldn't matter if he did learn I am C. A. Sommers. Though he might begin to care if people started laughing at him because they believed his wife was a loon."

"Your papa believed in you, Christine. Don't disgrace his sacrifice for you by mocking yourself. He would not have wanted that from you. "

"Papa died a laughingstock because of me, Aunt Sophie."

That beast-bird theory had never been her father's, but hers. After her discovery of similar skeletal remains off the Isle of Wight, it had been her initial hypothesis that the ancient creature held similar skeletal makeup to modern-day feathered creatures. Dinosaurs could be the ancestors of birds, a theory that Papa took to the Royal Society scholars, only to be scorned.

He'd believed in her enough to go out on the proverbial limb for Christine. And paid for it with his professional reputation. Even though the book won an award, he still died the butt of all the jokes among his true peers.

"Lord Sedgwick is not just any man, Christine."

"I want this discovery, Aunt Sophie." *I need this*.

"Nothing like *sticking* it in the eye of authority," Aunt Sophie said with gusto. "And what does Sedgwick want from you?" At Christine's embarrassed flush, Aunt Sophie nodded sagely. "I see. The proverbial heir," she said consideringly. "Then love has nothing to do with your decision or his."

"We will be business partners, Aunt Sophie. Nothing more." She scrubbed the heel of her hand against her cheek. "My decision is made. I hope I can count on your support."

Christine finally rose and left the room. Once in her room, she slammed shut the door. She washed and dressed for bed early. For some reason, having been walking an emotional tightrope all day, she just let herself fall off. Face-first.

But strangely, it was not her argument with her wretched or cousin or with Joseph, or Amelia's parting words, or even Aunt Sophie's lack of approval, that found her still awake at midnight when Beast deigned to leave his place on the windowsill and join her in bed.

Erik kept her awake. Erik, who made her heart race. Erik, who remained in her thoughts long after the time she should be sleeping peacefully—as he had from the moment she had first seen him climb down from the carriage at the museum gala. Erik, who promised her more than she dared dream possible.

Her hand pausing in the act of petting Beast, she splayed her fingers in the cat's fur where moonlight warmed the silver wishing band on her finger. With a groan, she turned onto her back and placed her forearm across her brow, aware that her own foolishness was driving her thoughts, reassuring herself that there were no such things as magical unseen forces that held the power to control a person's destiny. There were no such things as real dragons either, even though she was about to embark on a hunt to find one. No fairy tales either, even though she was about to go to Scotland and live in a castle.

Yet, the only thing she feared more than waking up tomorrow and discovering today had been one huge cosmic joke was that *Erik* would be the one to awaken first. Or worse.

The ring really *was* magic.

Chapter 7

The steamer packet carrying Christine and her small entourage approached Kirkcaldy, where she would meet the Scottish laird who was now her husband. He had gone on ahead of her while she'd remained in London these past weeks to finish her affairs.

A sudden gust of wind swept the deck and struck her full in the face. A storm off Holly Island had sent most of the passengers on the *Excalibur* to their cabins before dinner, but not her. With gloved fingers, she clasped her cloak as she huddled within its folds. As a blast from the stack bellowed their approach, she peered from beneath her hood across the dreary landscape, her eyes straining to see the Leith & Hamburg dock.

Several conveyances lined the wharf, apparently awaiting the packet's arrival. Her gaze landed on a dark carriage parked a short distance from the dock. A pair of figures stood beside it. She straightened as she recognized Erik's solicitor, Mr. Attenborough, and her husband. Erik wore a greatcoat and hat that cast a shadow over much of his upper face. He stood unmoving, like some medieval laird, much in accord with the storm clouds churning behind him.

She had not seen him since his departure from London. He had not written except to say he had arrived at Sedgwick. The note had been brief, formal in tone, utterly aristocratic, as if his arriving in Scotland had somehow transformed him back to the way he had been before coming to London.

Christine's mind spun backward and her memory filled with the recent events that had changed her life. A month ago, almost to the day, just after nine o'clock in the morning, beneath a trellis of lilacs outside St. Jude's Cathedral, Reverend Simms had joined Christine Alana Sommers forever to Erik James Edward Boughton, the twelfth duke of Sedgwick. Erik's sister served as maid of honor. He had worn an elegantly cut gray morning jacket, silk waistcoat and trousers, a stark contrast to her bright blue satin gown. She had entwined tiny white rosebuds into her hair, which seemed fitting for her wedding day.

With the breeze stirring the leaves of the large oak tree branches above where they stood, their hands clasped between them, they faced each other and spoke their vows. She promised to love and to honor him through sickness and in health until death they did part. His eyes dark and unreadable upon hers, he repeated the same vows and slid a gold band on her left index finger.

After Reverend Simms pronounced them man and wife, Erik bent and brushed his mouth across hers. "You owe me for this, *leannanan*." His velvet whisper mingled with her breath as his hand curved around her nape. "I must be the only groom in the history of Christendom to be wed in a cemetery."

She elected not to point out that they weren't exactly *in* the cemetery. Or that this close to the cemetery was an apt place for a marriage bought with gold.

Or that the cemetery was the only place she could think to be closest to her father.

Let her new husband be irked, she'd thought at the time. After what his solicitors had put her through for a week, for once, something would be on her terms. She realized her temperament deflected her own culpability. "The lilacs are in bloom," she told him.

"Lilacs hold nothing to you as a bride, Christine." His voice gently warmed as if he understood a part of her heart. "If your father were alive he would agree."

Whether it was his words, the smell of lilac lingering in the air, or the break in the clouds that suddenly filled her with warmth, she didn't know, but the knot around her stomach loosened.

Then just that quickly, with the slant of his lips across hers, the world vanished.

'Twas no chaste kiss he gave her, befitting a proper English gentleman, but an impassioned one, exactly what she expected from a Scotsman. The sheer primitiveness in that assault warned her to retreat and take stock of his actions. But she did neither. Instead, she rose on her toes, deepening the kiss. She kissed him just as she had that first night in the carriage, hot and urgent.

He slowly lifted his head. Their eyes met, searched.

Reason had told her to pull away on that fateful morning, but she could not disregard the underlying tension between them, nor ignore its source.

The ceremony, for all its significance to her future, had lasted a mere ten minutes. In truth, the words had been nothing more than a formality, a public declaration of their union. In fact, she'd belonged to Erik Boughton since the moment she signed and blotted her signature on the last of the thick sheaf of papers and official documents his many solicitors brought out to her in the days before their wedding, thus assuring him that she would be standing before him when the day of their joining arrived.

Among the *heretofores* and *moreovers*, the documents proclaimed that she would receive five thousand a year for the rest of her life and Sommershorn Abbey would remain hers. Her future husband had made her wealthy beyond her wildest dreams, giving her enough to keep the school open for her lifetime. In return, while Christine worked diligently to find the source of the bones he'd brought to her, she was to remain at Sedgwick Castle until she produced an heir. The devil had bought her soul, and she had willingly sold it to him like so much real estate in his portfolio.

She would have found it all more appalling than it was if she had not been a willing party to it.

He'd had to return to his estate. They had both agreed beforehand that while they spoke the vows at St. Jude, their marriage would begin in Scotland. They planned for her to remain a few weeks to finish her affairs at Sommershorn Abbey and then join him. Christine knew he was allowing her time to adjust, and she'd been glad for the reprieve.

As the ship nudged closer to the quay, Christine became aware of the rumble of the engines vibrating the deck beneath her feet. Over the sound of the wooden paddle-wheel churning through the white-capped water, she could hear the captain shouting orders to his crew.

Christine had already shipped most of her belongings on the 450-mile journey north two weeks ago, along with poor Beast, who had protested loudly at being stuffed into a wicker cage to suffer the indignity of traveling like luggage, even if he did have his own staff to care for him. Christine had filled her other trunks with her father's journals and her manuscripts. Crates of important petrified bones had also gone to Scotland. Everything else in her laboratory at Sommershorn Abbey she had donated to the British museum. She had only a single trunk in her cabin.

No one had come to the docks to see her off. Amelia still had not forgiven Christine for what she had blurted that night at the dining table. As for Joseph, Christine was sorry he lost his bid to go to Perth, but she could not let herself worry about his plight, any more than she should worry that Lord Bingham would never find anyone to replace her at the museum in time for his next grand opening. Or that her family had warned her that if she committed this folly, they would never speak to her again. Only Aunt Sophie had stood beside her this past month.

For the entire journey, Aunt Sophie and Mrs. Samuels had been hibernating beneath blankets with seven other trunks in the chamber that adjoined Christine's.

Christine turned to look around the deck to see if her aunt had come out yet, only to find her sitting on the wooden bench in front of the pilothouse watching her intently.

Christine joined her and took her hands into her own. "How long have you been out here in the cold?"

"Long enough to wonder how I ever allowed you to talk me into coming with you." Aunt Sophie sobered and looked toward the dock, where Erik stood next to the carriage. "And I say the time for second thoughts is past. It is about time you finally took it upon yourself to seize the moment. Though bugger me, I still don't understand how it all came about."

"Aunt *Sophie*!"

She patted Christine's hands and looked Christine in

the eyes. "No grandniece of mine who marries a cursed Scotsman had better go to the marriage bed with doubts in her mind, dear."

Christine caught herself before she lowered her gaze. Aunt Sophie was right, of course, and an unaccountable fierce sense of determination settled within her, lifting her precipitously sliding resolve. "Thank you. What would I do without your staid counsel?"

She sniffed. "You've been disowned by the family, dear. Who else do you have to counsel you on these things?"

Christine peered into her aunt's warm eyes. Surely, who needed a mam when she'd had Aunt Sophie's love her whole life? "I love you, Aunt Sophie."

"I know you do, dear. I have practically raised you as my own, after all. Now help me stand so I can fetch Mrs. Samuels out from beneath the blankets. I cannot feel my toes and I am looking forward to riding in your husband's warm coach."

Erik's solicitor, a short, stout fellow with white mutton-chop whiskers and wearing a woolen suit, met Christine first, on the dock as passengers from the steamer crowded past them. Mr. Attenborough had been the one to arrange all of her travel accommodations from London and she took a moment to thank him.

"We apologize for the rain," he said and bowed. "Unfortunately, even his grace can't control the weather."

Finding Mr. Attenborough's comment amusing, Christine glanced at her husband directing those offloading Aunt Sophie's trunks from the steamer to a nearby conveyance. "I hope our arrival has not been too inconvenient. A storm delayed us. We are late in arriving."

"We have been in Kirkcaldy since last night. With the condition of the roads, Lord Sedgwick was adamant that he be here when the packet arrived."

Again, Christine found her gaze wandering to Erik. Then Attenborough began talking. Her trunks would follow in another coach. Yes, Christine's belongings—and her cat—arrived at Sedgwick a week ago. No, chilly weather was not uncommon in June. "His grace has placed warm bricks beneath the seats for your comfort."

Christine turned and awaited her aunt and Mrs. Samuels's descent from the steamer deck. "They are in need of warmth, if you will, sir."

"Attenborough will see them to the coach." Erik was suddenly standing in front of her, blocking the cold wind with his body.

For just a terrible heart-stopping moment, as Christine turned and looked up at him, it was as if part of her mind stepped out of time. She was a wife now. Loath to admit that on more than one occasion she had wondered what it would feel like to be married, she now realized she had no idea how wives should behave with their husbands. Especially this particular husband, a man many considered a bastard, in the liberal sense, not the literal, and who by most accounts had been responsible for the death of his second wife.

Oh, for God's sake, she silently berated herself, suddenly overwhelmed by the ebb and flow of apprehension.

"Thank you, your grace," she said.

His eyes darkened at the formality. Then he looked over her shoulder as Aunt Sophie and Mrs. Samuels approached. "I trust you had a pleasant journey, my lady?" he asked.

"I barely survived with my fingers and toes intact,

young man," Aunt Sophie said stiffly. "Next time, I will take my chances on the road."

Erik smiled with sudden charm, his change of manner striking for a man who held himself apart from the world. "As unpleasant as it is arriving by sea, I guarantee the inquisition had nothing on the tortures you would endure traveling nine days on these roads, my lady," he humbly chided.

Not one to fall prey to charm, Aunt Sophie merely sniffed, but Christine had glimpsed the subtle warming in her aunt's eyes before Erik directed Attenborough to take Lady Sophia and her maid to the coach.

"You left your sister and daughter alone at Sedgwick?" Christine asked, casting about for something neutral to say. After all, she had not seen him in a month, and he did not seem in a hurry to follow Aunt Sophie to the coach.

He looked amused. "If you call being left with sixty-five servants, a butler, housekeeper and nurse 'alone,' then yes. They are utterly and completely alone."

The corners of her mouth lifted.

"Is that actually a smile I just glimpsed, Christine?"

She restrained the urge to look away, restless to get to the heart of her disquietude. "To be honest, we have agreed to enter into a partnership, yet, there is much about this matter between us with which I am apprehensive."

"That is the case with most marriages."

"Perhaps. But since this is my first, you will grant that I do not have your experience. I will admit to a certain degree of atypical trepidation. You will forgive me, if I do not yet *feel* married."

He fairly choked. When he recovered, he yanked down the rim of his bowler and considered her with mirth warming his sherry eyes. "It is my intent to give you a wedding night when we are alone to enjoy such. Unless you *want* me to consummate our marriage in full view of my liverymen and everyone watching from the streets. Your eagerness warms my heart, love."

"That is not what I meant." Christine thrust down a feeling of pique, only because she realized he read her mind with the intuition of a mystic. "Truly, your conceit is appalling, Erik."

Grinning, he opened his pocket watch. "We'll be stopping in a few hours at a quaint inn for the night north of Kennoway." He looked up at the sky. "If the weather holds that long."

"Perhaps you should command it to do so, my laird."

The inn was exactly as Erik had said. Quaint.

But it was more, Christine thought, as he handed her out of the carriage three hours after leaving the dock, and she gazed up at the beautiful Tudor relic, a throwback to a world where monarchs ruled their subordinates with iron fists, and an errant subject was as likely to be beheaded as he was to have his wife ravished by the reigning lord. Looking up at Erik as he issued instructions to the footmen who descended from the inn, she realized how easily he could fit the role of monarch.

After instructing Mr. Attenborough to help Aunt Sophie and Mrs. Samuels inside, Erik rested his hand absently at the small of her back and guided her forward. Night had fallen darkly upon them and they'd just arrived ahead of the storm that had been threatening all afternoon. The wind caught the hood of her cloak. Holding her head down, she let Erik whisk her into the inn. A gust of wind and rain slammed the door behind them.

Christine stood for a moment in the common room brushing the raindrops from her cloak, aware that Erik had moved no further. As she glanced up, she steeled herself. Those sitting at the tables closest to them had quit talking. The chorus of rowdy laughter slipped away. Since she could not concede she warranted such regard, she realized that it was not her presence but Erik's that had dropped the noise level in the room to dead silence.

"Gentlemen," Erik said.

A few men met his eye, then proceeded about their business, albeit in a more subdued manner. The door to the kitchen suddenly sprang wide. A stout matron wearing a white apron appeared. "Yer grace!"

Her face flushed, she hurried forward and snapped to one of the serving girls, who was holding a tray piled high with empty glasses with a frozen look on her face. "Get yerself movin', Finella, 'afore I take a bloomin' switch to yer backside, girl. It's his grace. Take him upstairs to the rooms we prepared."

The young barmaid scampered forward. Another maid, a younger red-haired image of Finella, entered the room and sidled past Erik to follow the footman carrying the trunks upstairs.

"Beggin' your pardon, guv'nor," the elder innkeeper nervously said, self-consciously patting the gray wisps of hair escaping from beneath her mobcap. "The weather has brought in a crowd tonight and I've 'ad to spend more time in the kitchen." She stole a surreptitious glance at Christine and then at Aunt Sophie before she hastily wiped her hands on her apron. "Supper will be to yer rooms shortly. I'll see yer favorite bottle of Lochnager brought up, yer grace."

Erik inclined his head. "That is why I always stop here, Bessie."

The matron blushed profusely. To Christine, she curtseyed. "Lady Sedgwick, it be our pleasure to welcome ye for the night. 'Tis a terrible night to be about and we've already warmed yer room."

Captured by the woman's kindness, Christine thanked her. "My wife would like a bath brought up, Bessie," Erik said, moving Christine ahead of him to precede him up the narrow wooden stairs. "See that my other guests are cared for."

Christine attempted to look over her shoulder at Aunt Sophie, but Erik's body blocked her efforts. "Your aunt will be all right," he said against her ear. The stairs creaked beneath their weight. His head brushed the rafters. "If there is anyone here who can take care of herself it is she."

Her hand locked in his and his other lightly touching her waist, like a brand, Christine felt him behind her the entire ascent and prayed she would not trip on her skirts. At the end of the narrow corridor, she finally turned to face him. Rain pebbled against the roof. She resisted looking up at the ceiling if only because the noise blunted the sound of her own heartbeat in her ears. He seemed so calm, completely inured to the attention, as if it were common fare that he halt an entire room of conversation with his presence.

"Is it always like this wherever you go?" she inquired.

"Like what?"

"Everyone knows you. Do you travel here often?"

"This is the only respectable inn between Kirkcaldy and Sedgwick Castle. Bessie has been curator of this establishment for five years. Her rooms are clean and she is a notable cook. I have stayed here many times."

She gazed up at him with a half smile. "Bessie seems quite in awe of you."

"I am the largest employer that supports this borough. Some years when the crops fail, I am the *only* one who can pay any wage. Hunger is a motivating factor to many to be polite and respectful."

"I didn't know Sedgwick land was so close to this place."

"This village is part of the Sedgwick duchy. We're *on* Sedgwick land."

"But I thought we were still a half day from Sedgwick Castle?"

"We are. But it is not a road any sane traveler attempts at night."

Christine was left momentarily speechless. She'd known the Sedgwick duchy was large, but for some reason she was not prepared to learn just how significant it was.

A gloved hand slipped beneath her chin, tilting her face into the sconce light. Both apprehensive and attracted, she fought the urge to melt against his powerful masculinity as her practical nature intervened to remind her that theirs was a partnership. He'd explicitly spelled out her purpose in their contract. "A maid is inside," he said, his voice intimate and hushed. "Will you need more than an hour for your toilette?"

"I've lived in jungles and deserts and shared quarters with snakes, centipedes and scorpions, not to mention bloodsucking sand fleas. The experience taught me well how to economize on my toilette."

Amusement in his eyes, his gaze lowered slightly to caress her bosom, suffusing her with an aura of warmth. He leaned around her to open the door, brushing his arm against hers. "Then I will return in an hour, madam."

She wrapped her hand around his arm. "Where will you be?"

He tipped his chin to the door next to this room. "For now? In the chambers next to yours." Then he released her hand from his sleeve and gently edged her inside the room. "Enjoy your bath, madam."

Chapter 8

Erik stepped inside the room adjoining Christine's and shut the door. A single lamp lit the room. He walked to the window and, pulling aside the curtains, peered outside. A lull in the clouds let the moonlight through and he looked out over an uneven landscape of stone chimneys and thatched roofs stretching into the sleepy village.

Raindrops that had gathered on his cloak had dampened the floor. Removing his hat and gloves, he turned back into the room, carelessly tossing each to a chair. His cloak followed. A bathing closet divided this room from Christine's and he reflected on the hour he had given her.

He had just stripped off his waistcoat when a knock sounded. Working off his cravat, Erik opened the door. Bessie's older daughter, Finella, stood hesitantly in the corridor. She carried towels and a bottle of Lochnager and two glasses. Head down, her bright blond hair framing her face, she murmured, "I brought yer drink, yer grace."

Erik stood aside to allow her into his chambers. Her chin shot up as if he had just invited her into his bed. He frowned. The top of the girl's head barely reached his chest. She looked all of Becca's age, perhaps younger, though it was hard to tell with her hair in her face.

Unlike other landed gentry who frequented this main road, he did not sample or abuse the local fare. Not that he had been chaste these last seven years—he had not. He simply did not use his power to mistreat children and servants. Erik considered her for a space, then took the towels from her arms and told her to set the whiskey on the table just inside the door.

The girl slid past him and did as he bid. "Is there anything else?"

The valise he had brought in last night and left here when he went to Kirkcaldy this morning had already been unpacked. His robe lay across the bed. "Attend to my wife's toilette, Finella. She is in the chambers next to this one."

Clearly relieved not to be doing whatever task it was she thought she should be doing for him, she scurried off, her threadbare shoes making only a whisper of sound on the floor. He had shut the door and started to undress, when another knock sounded. Down to his shirtsleeves, he rolled each to his forearms and swung open the door.

Mr. Attenborough stood at his threshold. "Your grace . . ." His solicitor had the good sense to look apologetic for the interruption.

"What is it now?"

"Lady Sophia has requested an audience with you."

"Tonight? Does she realize I might perhaps be occupied?"

"The innkeeper told her ladyship she was preparing Lady Sedgwick's bath and that you were not currently in the room. Lady Sophia was adamant," Attenborough said. "I think she must have been a sergeant-major in a past life."

Erik's brows rose. "Is she armed?"

Mr. Attenborough's stern visage cracked slightly. "I would not hazard to guess. But if you wish that I frisk her . . ." Color rose in his staid solicitor's cheeks. "Not that I would."

A corner of Erik's mouth moved. "Are you blushing, Attenborough?"

"No, sair. I am a lawyer, your grace."

A few moments later, Erik knocked at Lady Sophia's room at the top of the stairs and at her clear summons entered the small chambers. A fire in the stove against the wall took some of the chill from the room. Lady Sophia sat on a red-cushioned chair in front of the window, her back straight, and her hand resting on the top of her cane. She turned her head and, despite the harsh set of her mouth, the lamplight captured the softness of her face.

With her patrician features, her beauty in her youth must have been unrivaled, he thought.

Erik had once done his own inquiries regarding Christine's entire family, including her eccentric aunt. He knew Lady Sophia Sommers had never married, though she had once caused a scandal when she eloped with a naval lieutenant in Nelson's command. Her furious father had promptly annulled the marriage and exiled the beauty to Italy for a year. Three months after the event, her lieutenant died fighting the French fleet in Aboukir Bay at the mouth of the Nile. Lady Sophia had been eighteen . . . the same age Christine had been when Erik had met her his first year in London.

He could see much of Christine in the shape of her lips and eyes, but that was as far as the resemblance went. Christine had not yet developed the deep cynicism that had formed the deeper lines bracketing her aunt's mouth and that he knew reflected back at him.

"Is my niece going to survive, you think?"

Erik recognized that the question had more to do with Christine's association and marriage to him than with any physical condition she might suffer. Leaning an elbow against the dresser, he folded his arms. "Is she ill?"

Lady Sophia thumped her cane on the carpet. "That is *not* what I mean, young man, and you well know it. I know you have already spoken vows, but I will know your intentions before it is too late for my niece to change her mind."

"It is already too late, my lady."

Nor was he in the habit of explaining himself or his actions to anyone, especially when, in his opinion, he had already consummated the marriage many times, if one went back into their history, and tonight was a mere trifling detail.

But something in Lady Sophia's tone touched him. Though he could not help but admire her obvious affection for Christine, another concern that Christine might have voiced doubts nagged him. "What has your niece told you?"

"Nothing. She is taking this wedding business very seriously. Frankly, I have never seen her behave in such a manner. It's alarming."

Mildly relieved, he looked away from Lady Sophia's penetrating glance, but he was thinking of Christine. He answered in a serious tone. "Your niece and I are in accord over the terms of our marriage, my lady."

Bracing her hands on her cane, Lady Sophia sniffed. "She defended you to our family, you know. None of them will ever speak to her again. No great loss as far as I am concerned, they do not deserve her. But I will not have you be her greatest mistake. I will not see her hurt. Does she know what her father offered you to marry her?"

Erik tightened his jaw but did not look away. "I took nothing from her father, Lady Sophia. And I would take nothing from her. I have allowed her to keep Sommershorn Abbey. The land is in a trust. Should she ever need to return . . . for any reason."

"She would be crushed to ever learn that her papa went to you. Her pride would not stand the betrayal, you see. So if I seem harsh . . . it is only that Christine is not like me or her father or you, your grace."

"No daughter should love her father less for wanting to see her future secure. Christine is a big girl, my lady."

Lady Sophia suddenly rose in a swish of silk. "Perhaps you do not know that her mam left her and her father when she was five." Sophia walked to the window and looked at his reflection in the glass. "They were on a dig in Greece and the woman Christine idolized and trusted decided her life would be more exciting with a Shakespearean actor than with a husband and their child."

Bracing her weight on the cane, Lady Sophia turned. "I loved Charles but he was entirely too selfish, dragging Christine from one dig to another, mourning the loss of his marriage, never thinking that his daughter lost her mother. And Lord knows I am not the embodiment of feminine sentimentality. Charles lost himself during those years and it was Christine who pulled him from the brink. I believe he would not have been the paleontologist he became if not for her."

"Why are you telling me this?" Erik asked, more than aware of Christine's talents.

"Ten years ago, Christine had no idea that you made an offer for her hand. Her father never told her. You thought she rejected you," Lady Sophia said as

Erik shoved his hands into his pockets and turned away. "Then you signed the contracts for her cousin's hand and that godforsaken land in York, and it no longer mattered. You were gone from her life. Then last summer, your letter to Charles came from out of the blue. I know it was business about a find you had made on your estate . . ." Lady Sophia's study of him remained deliberate. "But whatever Charles had done in the past to Christine, he tried to make it up to her, you see."

A vast sense of anger swamped him. Not because Erik made the choices he had in the past, he was a pragmatist after all, he told himself. Wishing the last ten years stricken from his life would be akin to wishing his daughter had never been born.

His anger came because someone else had made a decision that profoundly shaped his life. Nor did he want Lady Sophia believing Charles Sommers had manipulated Erik into returning to London now. He had not. Erik truly needed help to deal with the bones washing up on his land from an expert, who—no one but he seemed to understand—was Christine herself.

Especially since he knew the reason she had wed him. He might need an heir to reassure that all he'd worked to build in his lifetime would remain with his family and his people, but Christine wanted her beast and her glory. Her passion had always been her fossils.

As he walked to the stove and stared at the flames contained within the iron grate, he said, "She would have turned down my proposal, my lady."

Lady Sophia held her silence for a heartbeat. "Of course. Everyone expected you would wed her cousin after all, and, like you, my niece is a pragmatist because circumstances required it of her. You went on with your life and she with hers. Christine is a woman who needs something to believe in, you understand." Lady Sophia drew in a breath. "But she is more fragile inside than you think, Sedgwick."

An hour later, her hair damp from her bath, and clad in a scandalous nightdress possessing the gossamer thinness of Babylonian silk, Christine stood in front of the long cheval glass.

Upon entering the chamber, she'd discovered the white nightgown and silk robe from her trousseau laid out on the bed. Almost afraid to touch her fingertips to the delicate cloth, she had a moment's doubt. The French modiste she had found on Bond Street to make her traveling trousseau had told her that a proper bride would never wear such a scandalous garment, but mistresses were constrained by no such barrier. Since Christine was not quite a bride or a mistress—she was both and neither as she was not sure where *partner* fit between the two—she had more freedom to choose. But as she peered at the unfamiliar woman in the glass, barely recognizable with her tumbledown hair to her waist, the color high in her cheeks, her schoolmarm appearance vanquished behind white gossamer, she wanted only that Erik see her as an equal and viable partner in this contract.

Especially since walking into the inn that night and realizing she'd never felt less like a duchess than the moment she'd stood next to Erik in front of those people sitting in the common room. She squeezed shut her eyes and opened them again, half expecting to see herself standing at Sommershorn in the dark of her laboratory wondering what madness had inflicted upon her.

The young girl who had helped with her bath had quietly left earlier. Alone, Christine turned to study the room. Dark paneling covered the walls. The foot of the plush canopy-draped bed opened to the hearth. The comforter had already been turned down revealing crisp white sheets smelling of lavender. A fire warmed the cozy confines of the room. A beautifully set table topped with sterling, crystal, and the finest porcelain glittered in the warm light.

With a small gasp, she straightened. Erik stood just inside the door leading to the bathing room. Leaning against the door frame, one hand holding the neck of a whiskey bottle, the other a glass, he raised the tumbler to his lips, and peered at her from over the rim. He had not undressed, and she did not know why.

"Madam," he said, the lazy grace of his stance conflicting with the heat she felt from his eyes.

She smoothed the fabric of her nightgown. "I didn't hear you enter." She panned her arm across the room. "The proprietress has gone beyond expectations. The room is beautiful."

She had the vague impression that he was watching everything about her closely. "I am glad everything meets with your approval," he said quietly.

She wished now that she had put on her robe. "Have you checked on Aunt Sophie and Mrs. Samuels to make sure they are saf—?"

"No one at this inn will harm them, Christine."

She believed him. Of the people she'd seen thus far tonight, she could not imagine a one who'd rather not jump off a cliff and dash themselves on the rocks below than dare draw the wrath of the duke of Sedgwick.

Yet, she had never been afraid of him. In fact, fear was the last thing on her mind as she stilled her racing heartbeat and pondered why he seemed hesitant when there had been nothing fastidious about him in London.

Taking a deep breath, but short of announcing that she was ready to do her duty by their contract, she focused her attention on the glass of whiskey in his hand and might have asked if he had another glass if she thought she could stomach the assault.

Then he was suddenly standing in front of her and her gaze rose in deference to more than his height. He slid her glasses higher on her nose. "When did you begin wearing spectacles?" he murmured.

She ruefully smiled. "When I woke up in a blur one day and realized it wasn't the effect of too much drink."

His hand moved to her chin and tilted her face. "As I recall, drinking was never your forte."

Her rebellious streak surfaced. But he was right. She rarely drank except for wine and an occasional glass of champagne, and doing so now would prove only that she was foolish. She wondered what else he remembered about her.

"You like stargazing," he said in response to her unspoken thoughts. "You are the only person with whom I have ever climbed a tree simply to get closer to the moon."

Christine had forgotten that silly night where she had tippled in wine, stripped off her petticoats, and climbed a tree. He'd followed and, sharing a stout branch above the leaves, she'd pointed out the Big Dipper and Pegasus. The whole universe had been staring down at her that night.

Erik moved past her. He set down the bottle and glass on the nightstand, retrieved her robe from the bed, and laid it across her shoulders. "We are about to be delivered our supper," he said.

As if on cue, a knock sounded on the door. His hands tightened on the fabric and closed it over her nightdress. "For my eyes only, *leannanan*."

He turned and walked to the door, leaving her to stare after him as he opened the door. She now realized why he remained dressed. The harried innkeeper and one of her daughters stood outside. The elder wheeled in a trundle cart topped with silver chafing dishes while the younger lit the candles and poured wine.

Erik helped Christine into her chair, his hands brushing her shoulders, then he moved to sit across from her. Christine watched as the innkeeper proudly displayed each dish, pleased pink each time Erik nodded his head in approval. Roast grouse and stovies on the side. "Yer grace," she said, presenting the final dish.

She deftly removed the lid and revealed a plate piled high with neatly arranged oysters on the half shell and shaved ice. Enough to feed a Scottish rebellion. Christine smothered a laugh as she raised her eyes over her serviette.

"That will be all, Bessie," Erik said bluntly.

The poor woman's expression fell as if the moon had dropped out of the sky. Clearly, she had not meant him any displeasure. "Yes, yer grace."

Christine watched the woman leave and shut the door. "We've hurt her feelings, Erik."

"You do not think thirty oysters somewhat excessive?"

The mere thought of consuming any slimy creature made her grimace. "Thirty-four," she corrected, inclining her head toward the plate. "Obviously, one for each of your advanced years."

She reached for the green leaves in a dish next to his plate and dropped them in his cup—"I believe a sprig of jasmine in your tea is supposed to accomplish the same thing. So I have heard."

"Thank God for that."

She suddenly laughed. As did he.

When they had both settled down again, his eyes found hers. Her smile faded. The desire blossoming inside her had been dormant for years and now that she had unlocked the cage again, she found she might not be able to rein the beast back inside. But her instincts, ever diligent in protecting her, rose to her defense.

"Do you still play chess?" she asked.

"No. There has been a dearth of worthy adversaries in my life of late."

His finger circled the rim of his wineglass and she followed the movement, wondering if, now that she was his wife, he regretted the contract between them. Except for the moment he'd set her robe on her shoulders, he seemed distant. Unlike he had been in London. She was uncertain if she had done something wrong. "I have been thinking about the fossils," she said by way of attempting conversation as she lifted the grouse from the trundle cart and spooned some into her plate, attempting to do her duty by Bessie and at least eat. "Aunt Sophie is one of the finest anthropologists in the world. I want to invite her into this investigation—"

"I prefer to keep that part of our understanding between us, Christine."

Christine set down the dish. "She won't judge you."

"I think when it comes to you, her opinions may be biased."

His words, as much as the tone in his voice, struck her. Though she'd never had a murder accusation tossed at her, she'd confronted enough prejudice to understand the isolation. "I cannot imagine what you must endure, Erik. People can be cruel."

His mouth quirked as if he found her concern an odd

thing to contemplate and he drank from his wineglass. "I have long ceased caring what people think of me, Christine."

"Why?"

"It is neither important nor relevant to my life. The people who are essential to Sedgwick's survival are well paid enough not to have an opinion. As long as I can give them what they need, they will pretend they believe me innocent."

"Everyone wants something—is that it? Give and take. No complications?"

A small smile lurking on his handsome lips, he considered her. "You are not satisfied with the terms of your contract then?"

She narrowed her eyes. "No one should ever doubt your generosity, Erik."

He laughed. "I believe you are one of the few who does not. I am not known in many circles for being either generous or nice."

Obviously, ruthlessness was not a trait he shunned. Nor was he bothered possessing it.

When she'd met him years ago, he was already infamous, having gained repute over his legendary war with his stepfather for control of the Sedgwick duchy. Erik had not only fought the powerful establishment at a young age and won, but he had also gained custody of his infant sister some years afterward. Truly, he was passionate in his fight to protect that which he loved, passion he worked hard to conceal in himself.

"And yet . . . you are both nice *and* generous," she accused him.

Leaning toward her, he braced his elbow on the table. "The business between us requires . . . shall I say, a certain degree of gentle persuasion on my part, a tactic I don't usually employ in my other business dealings."

Clearly, she had given him the false impression that he had a right to the platitude that purchasing her allowed him a certain degree of ducal ennui in her presence. But she would not allow him to convince her he had handled her ruthlessly. In addition, she was beginning to suspect that the only person sitting at this table displaying timidity about their contract sat directly across from her.

She, too, leaned forward. "We can both agree your gentle persuasion may not have been as swaying had you not dangled that tooth in my face and threatened to give the find to Mr. Darlington. But consider this." She peered at him over the rims of her spectacles. "I didn't have to marry you to come to Scotland. I would have come with or without your consent."

"Is that right?"

"It is I who has wed *you* for selfish purposes, not the other way around. As you have said, ours is a partnership based on mutual interests."

"Don't misinterpret my generosity for kindness. It would be a mistake."

"And don't mistake *mine* for cowardice, Erik."

Their mutual awareness sent a rush of heat through her veins, and, from the lazy-lidded look in his eyes, he, too, felt it. And seemed pleased.

"I can see I have erred in my attempts to play the gentleman," he said.

Before she knew what he was about, his hand snaked out and captured her wrist. Her heart skipped in her throat. He drew her around the table, pulling her across his lap, nearly upsetting the table and poor Bessie's dinner all over the floor. "What are you doing? Erik . . ."

He threaded his fingers in her hair. His other hand traced the curvature of her cheek and throat and laid claim to her breast. Her robe, a meager cover at best, fell open. "I intend to make love to you, *leannanan*."

And, in one gentle motion of his mouth, he extinguished her voice with a kiss. An unhurried easiness and contentment that warmed even as it calmed. That excited even as it cautioned. A flutter of anticipation heated her veins. She became acutely aware of his body, aware of the thickness of him against her bottom, the heat of his arms. She tasted wine on his lips and in her mouth.

He opened his palm and her breast filled his hand. Her body, already hungry for more than the tactile caress of his palm against her flesh, shifted in his arms. The freedom to simply enjoy his touch infused her with heat. And longing.

And her own hunger.

The linen shirt clinging to Erik's muscled frame yielded to her desire to touch him. He raised his head and looked down at her in his arms, his wild dark hair muted by firelight, and then he smiled wickedly, as if to tell her there was not an inch of her he would not touch in the next few hours.

He splayed his palm against her navel, then lower. She watched his gaze follow the slow path of his roaming hand, parting her robe for further exploration as he found the damp triangle between her legs. His blood quickened in his veins. Surged. He knew about arousing a woman's body, where to look, how to touch, just when to stop and allow her to feel. He knew all these things, when she knew so much less about him.

But whatever it was they'd once shared, whatever passion had been theirs, no matter the bargain they had struck, no matter the years separating them, they both knew fire still burned hot between them.

He kissed her deeply, first her lips, then the hollow

beneath her ear. Then he removed her glasses and set them on the table.

"*Tha sin a' còrdadh rium,*" he murmured ever so enticingly against her lips. The Gaelic endearment foreign to her ears, and yet, she understood the words as if she'd spent her entire life wandering Scottish fields of heather.

"I like this, too," she answered.

He slowly pulled back, his warm breath caressing her lips, as sensual as the heat reflected in her eyes. She smiled. "*Tha sin a' còrdadh rium,*" she whispered.

"Aye," he rasped. "Our arrangement will more than suffice, my lady wife."

He stood with her in his arms. He kicked off his shoes. Then they were on the bed. His hands sank into the mattress on either side of her shoulders. Her hair splayed across the white satin of the comforter. Her eyes lifted to his.

Her legs parted beneath the pressure of his hips. Only his trousers prevented full contact, flesh against flesh. His mouth closed on her breast, sensually laving her. With a deep groan he caught her lips, and lust coiled low in her abdomen. He gathered her filmy nightgown into his fist and drew it over her head, tossing it to the floor.

She had never been naked before any man except him. That he might not find her pleasing was indicative of the way he made her feel around him.

"Look at me, Christine."

She heard his voice through the thunderous rush in her ears. Her lashes fluttered open. The dark centers of his eyes made them nearly black in the shadows pressing against him.

All she could think about was seeing him naked too.

He sat back on his calves, stripped off his shirt, and flung it to the floor. Dark hair arrowed up his abdomen and sprinkled his chest. His stomach was firm, his chest and shoulders toned with an athlete's grace. His hair hung in his eyes as he yanked the buttons on his trousers. She sat up and watched the play of his muscles that moved with his arms. His penis jutted from between his thighs, rigid and hard. With one hand, he extinguished the lamp on the nightstand, leaving only the light from the hearth fire flickering on the walls.

Even June in Scotland was no proof against the chill of a thunderstorm. Erik dragged the eiderdown over them both, encapsulating them in the humid darkness beneath the covers, and braced his weight on his elbows. She couldn't see him in the darkness beneath the covers, but she could feel his body and taste the scent of him on her lips. He parted her with his fingers and eased into her. "I do not need oysters for this." One large hand enclosed her bottom and, with each move, he drove deeper inside her. "Or jasmine tea."

He sank hilt-deep inside her. She cried out, a soft keening sound, her hands clutching his muscled back. His mouth dipped to hers, taking the sound, open-mouthed and hungry as she. Then she was kissing him, wanting this always, the feel of him inside her, years of celibacy that had not been completely assuaged when Erik had taken her against the door made her think only of this. Her arms wrapped around his neck. She rocked with him. Savored him. In time, they found their blend of rhythm and melody.

The intensity of her orgasm was never more finite than the instant before it burst. She arched into the hard length of him, taking him deeper, shuddering around him, heedless of her panting, vulnerable to more than her passions as she let Erik rock her to sweet oblivion.

His back arched and his eyes half closed, he rose on his palms and spilled himself inside her. And when the throbbing ebbed, Erik remained braced on his hands, his face half hidden in the humid shadow beneath the canopy of the bed, but she could feel his eyes on her. Still buried within the wet heat of her body, he lowered himself to his elbows. When he did, a gleam of firelight touched his face.

Neither of them spoke.

Rolling off her, he sprawled on the pillow beside her, dragging her against him. A second passed, then two, where they both settled into the sanctuary of their own thoughts, a less volatile place to be. His hand moved into her hair and his lips touched her temple, the thickness of desire still between them.

"I didn't know you spoke Gaelic," he said.

"You're Scots," she said sleepily, wondering why such a simple feat as learning a language should surprise him. She only spoke a little. "It would be a dishonor to you if I did not prepare myself for my place here."

Christine pondered his silence but was not sure what she had said. Perhaps it was not that she was a quick study that perplexed him—surely he must know such things as learning languages were not difficult—but that she had cared enough about who he was to do so at all.

Chapter 9

Aunt Sophie's presence stopped Christine the next morning when she arrived downstairs dressed to depart the inn. "Mrs. Samuels has gone on ahead with the luggage," Aunt Sophie informed her, eyeing her carefully as she wriggled her hands into her gloves. "Mr. Attenborough said we will arrive at Sedgwick Castle late this afternoon."

"You needn't have remained behind because of any concern for me."

Her aunt sniffed. "I hope he has fed you, because the carriage is waiting, my dear."

"I have eaten, Aunt Sophie."

She stepped outside into the sunlight. Her husband stood near the coach speaking to Mr. Attenborough, looking every inch the devil duke people suspected him of being. With the exception of a spot of white beneath his jacket, he was dressed entirely in black, from his jacket that emphasized his shoulders to the waistcoat, trousers, and shiny boots that hugged his calves.

In the bright morning sunlight of the new day, only the tenderness between her legs had given hint of the many exceptional and unexpected pleasures she had shared with him last night and this morning.

As he turned slightly, his jacket opened to reveal a braided chain looped through his buttonhole to his pocket, and a shirt open at his throat. He paused mid-sentence when he saw her and her heart skipped childishly. His eyes raking her and the blue velvet traveling garment she wore, he dismissed his solicitor and approached. "Madam." He offered his arm.

Bessie and her daughters waited just outside the door. Christine paused to thank them for their kindness, her words leaving the timorous trio standing a little taller as she stepped past them. They had not moved from their place when a few moments later the coach lurched forward.

Erik braced his body against the sway of the coach, his arm across the back of the squabs and his hand casually resting against her shoulder.

Christine glanced at him but found him engaged in dialogue with Mr. Attenborough and Aunt Sophie sitting across from them. She was vividly aware of the warm, clean scent of him, her place beside him as comfortable as she could be, traveling by coach over bumpy roads, until his long fingers came to lay beside her jaw and turned her face to look up at him.

"You are comfortable?" he asked.

His voice caressed her much as it had last night while his hands and mouth had worked sinful magic on her body, the mere memory making her flush like a silly virgin bride in front of Aunt Sophie and Mr. Attenborough.

"I am merely admiring the view," she said, smiling at Aunt Sophie, who peered at her as if she might reach over and test Christine's face for fever.

"Just past that oak tree is where the first duke of Sedgwick was beheaded as a traitor to King Henry II for fighting on the side of the Scots during one of the many rebellions," Mr. Attenborough said.

"Good heavens!" Aunt Sophie gasped, pressing her nose to the glass. "Which oak tree?"

Mr. Attenborough pointed to the tall, sweeping oak they had just passed.

"What an ignoble beginning," Aunt Sophie said.

"Nae at all," Mr. Attenborough said. "Most Scots found it an honorable end to get themselves beheaded or drawn and quartered in their fight against the English. It was a mark of courage and their sacrifice for Scotland."

Aunt Sophie peered at Erik. "I thought the Sedgwick duchy was part of an original English patent."

"It is," Erik said. "But Sedgwicks have always been Scots."

To Christine, the countryside lay like a breathtaking tableau painted by the color of the sky and thick oak trees. They traveled a northeasterly road meandering over rolling hills and across sweeping vales that slowly receded and gave way to lonely crags, and climbed steadily higher. Furtively, she glanced at Erik, looking out the other window, his expression as remote as the landscape. Even in the daylight away from the shadows, he was compelling to her, and she felt a strange impulse to ask him what he was thinking. He turned his head, met her gaze, and she watched the corner of his mouth crook. Like her, he seemed content enough to let Attenborough carry the conversation.

"We've close to four hours of this," he said against her ear.

Tilting her head sideways as she stared up at him, Christine quietly asked, "Are you warning me or apologizing?"

"We're sharing a coach with a lawyer," he said in amusement, shifting so he could better adjust her against him. "You are welcome to use my shoulder if you want to rest."

She told him she could remain awake—after all, in her mind, he'd had the same night as she—but the carriage's movement lulled her, and her eyes drifted shut before a mile had passed. Her dreams were vivid and filled with a flame-spewing beast, sharp claws and wings extended. Not her father's vision of a dragon but hers, and this one frightened her.

Something jolted her awake and she opened her eyes, her head leaning on Erik's shoulder, her thoughts jumbled. Across from her, Mr. Attenborough and Aunt Sophie remained talking as if the world had not just stopped.

The terrain outside the window had become starker as they seemed to be climbing in elevation. Looking up at Erik, she met his eyes. His gloved hand came up and slid behind her head, resting at the nape of her neck, almost protectively as he gently stilled her.

"Rest, Christine. You have a long day ahead." The warmth in his lazy tone told her she had a long night as well, and he must have glimpsed the carnal awareness in her eyes. "My staff is fervently waiting to welcome you."

Unsure if he had just made a jest with that double entendre about his *staff*, she resettled her head against his arm, breathing him into her senses rather than challenging him with a smile. The beast in her dream faded into the mists, though she could not vanquish it entirely as she'd begun to recognize its source—a growing apprehension at the thought of her arrival at Sedgwick Castle. An edginess that had not completely solidified until last night when Erik had told her they were already on land that belonged to the Sedgwick duchy. The carriage would be traveling on his land for hours.

When she had agreed to Erik's proposal and later signed their contract, she had answered all pertinent questions she'd asked herself about being his wife, but she'd not soundly considered every detail about what it meant to be his duchess. Clearly, her title would not stop her from persuing her goals. She would discover her beast and make history, as long as she met her contractual obligations to him, which also included searching the estate for the bones of a past wife. Someone with whom he'd loved and had a child—*after* Christine had left him, all those years ago.

Absently, through her gloves, she fingered the silver "wishing" ring that had yet to come off her finger.

She'd never allowed herself to wonder what would have happened all those years ago if she'd remained in England and fought for the cursed duke of Sedgwick— and, if she had, would she have been the one who perished of scarlet fever? Would it now be her bones lost in the crags of Fife waiting to be found?

Even as she told herself the existence of magic and curses was about as likely as seeing a leprechaun, a kind of resolute logic had taken root this past month.

Because of Erik, she was on her way to getting what she had worked so hard to achieve her entire life, what she had sacrificed everything else to have.

So she did not understand her continued restlessness.

Finally, she gave up attempting to sleep, opened her eyes and rejoined the living, not realizing at first, that not only *had* she slept with her cheek pillowed against Erik's chest curled up against his warmth like a contented feline on a feathered bed; but he'd allowed her to sleep like that for hours. The terrain had changed dramatically. Somewhere a river roared and crashed in the form of a waterfall from the stone escarpment soaring behind her. She sat up abruptly, adjusted her spectacles and peered out the window just as the road came across the top of a basin overlooking the river valley. The verdant landscape vanished for a moment behind the trees, then slowly came back into view.

Sedgwick Castle sat in the distance in all its tempestuous beauty, half hidden in the mist and the glare of an outlying lake.

"Good heavens!" Christine heard Aunt Sophie's whisper. "Sedgwick Castle really *is* a castle."

"The tower is the oldest part of the keep," Mr. Attenborough said with his usual authority about all things Sedgwick as he pointed over Aunt Sophie's shoulder. "His grace rebuilt it some years ago to save it from crumbling to stone. We're still farther away than it looks. The river divides the bottomland. Since the flooding began last summer . . ." His voice faded in Christine's mind.

Sedgwick Castle was indeed a real castle, with its vine-covered towers and turrets built around an older medieval stone keep. Sunlight captured the visual melodrama, and Christine had drawn in a breath at the sight of the rugged beauty spread out before her. Distant crags spiked upward like sharp dragon's teeth against the turbulent sky—a perfect complement to the feudal citadel the hills protected. Unmarred by the opulence that usually plagued such ancient duchies, Erik's baronial heritage was instead a world captured in time.

Behind her, the laird of that castle had not yet spoken but she could feel his thoughts, his presence inside her head more dominating than the dragon haunting her dreams. She twisted around to face him.

Having just spent the past few hours declaring herself magic free, he had to present her with a world taken from the pages of Grimm's fairy tale, *Sleeping Beauty*. The irony did not escape her.

And she almost laughed.

A perfectly reasonable reaction in her opinion, except Erik, upon presenting her with his ancestral home, was looking to her for something more lucid than peals of laughter. But it was Erik who surprised her by chuckling first.

"No regrets, *leannanan*?"

This was the land he had ridden across as a boy. A world that had shaped him. A world she wanted to explore. She had no regrets.

The thought had no sooner formed and she'd spoken it aloud before the front wheel crashed into a deep pothole. The coach dipped, then lurched sideways, throwing her across Erik's lap. This was followed by a sharp resounding crack of the axle shattering before the carriage came to a shuddering stop.

"Are you telling me this might not have been an accident?"

Four hours after the accident Erik stood in his library and faced his engineering foreman across the desk.

Erik had put down two of his best horses tonight. He loathed killing any animal. He tolerated the loss of life even less if the accident had occurred because of carelessness and outright neglect. But deliberate sabotage would have been reprehensible.

Hodges tipped back his floppy hat with a finger. He wore a rain slicker in deference to the drizzle that had begun to fall shortly after the accident that afternoon. "I am saying we were up there last week to inspect the road as ye required of us. The pothole was not there.

It *could* have been man-made. We found a pickax in the woods not far from the accident. Mayhaps someone intent on doin' mischief. Lights have been seen flickering in those hills. Some credit the sightings to your late wife's ghost and . . ." Clearly seeing where this dialogue was heading, Hodges cleared his throat. "Or maybe there be highwaymen in these parts—"

"Hodges," Erik interrupted. "No highwaymen have been in this area for twenty years. And I find it highly improbable a ghost or anyone crashed the coach. That road is not the main one into Sedgwick or the surrounding hamlets and is rarely used by anyone, including me."

He tossed last week's engineering report he'd been reading on the desk. Most of that road, which cut through the crags separating Sedgwick from the rest of Fife, had been there for centuries, having been carved through the rock and forests by conquering armies that had overrun Scotland at one time or another. A rockfall had made an older portion of the road impassable years ago.

"Still"—Hodges scratched his bewhiskered cheek— "it would nae take much more than a gully wash to make a small hole into a crater. It was raining the evening before the accident. The horses come a cropper and went sailin', yer grace. Terrible waste of fine horse-flesh it was too."

"Get Bailey here from Dunfermline," Erik said. "He's the civil engineer who repaired that road last month and reassured me it was safe. I want him up there by next week. I want to know why there is a four-foot-wide pothole that nearly swallowed my coach. If someone deliberately did this, then I will know who."

"Aye, your grace." Hodges hesitated at the doors leading outside onto the terrace, clearly circumspect and considerate of the housekeeper who would not welcome the mud on his boots, and turned back into the room, aware of Erik's dangerous mood. "Will her grace be all right?"

With a taper of fire burning in the lamp on his desk, Erik could not see Hodges's face in the darkness. "She suffered a severe bump on the head. She is resting."

When the carriage had dropped into the hole, her head had slammed against the door with a crack that seemed as loud as the sound of the axle breaking. Erik still remembered the sound. The physician had been with her almost from the moment Erik's retainers brought her in unconscious.

Lady Sophia had reassured him she was still alive. His housekeeper had sworn she'd briefly spoken when they'd removed her gown and cleaned the blood from her hair. The physician told him that she did not suffer any broken bones and only needed rest.

But Erik had not been able to go to her room, stand over her bed, and look into her face. He wouldn't have been able to do so without wondering if he were somehow to blame . . . if he really was cursed and had doomed Christine by marrying her. No logical man would have given weight to these fears, but at the moment Erik was not feeling logical.

"Make sure Bailey contacts me after he finishes the inspection."

Hodges nodded then left by way of the terrace door. Erik reached for a glass and the crystal whiskey decanter on his desk. Movement behind him made him turn. His butler stood silhouetted against the light in the corridor. "I have lit the fire in your chambers and set out your brandy," Boris said. "Lady Sedgwick is asleep."

Erik considered the empty tumbler in his hand,

then set it down. "Do you believe in ghosts or curses, Boris?"

"No, your grace."

Erik's gaze went to the clock atop the mantel. "Has the physician gone for the evening?"

The doctor lived in the sleepy Sedgwick hamlet five miles east of the castle. If Erik had taken the main road around the craggy hills, they would have ridden through the village.

But Erik had been vain or foolish, perhaps both. He'd wanted Christine to see not just Sedgwick Castle but the entire valley as he saw it, as most had rarely seen it from high in the hills, wrapped in mist and sunlight. A moment of childlike whimsy, he thought in disgust, banishing the vision and pushing past the clutter of his thoughts.

Boris informed him that the doctor would return in the morning and that Lady Sophia was with Christine, most of the drama of the day now died to a whisper in the candlelight. "We have finally got your sister to bed," Boris said. "I believe Lady Rebecca will recover in the morning when she sees that Lady Sedgwick has not been felled by the curse." The elder cleared his throat. "Not that any of us believes such nonsen—"

"Have you located my daughter yet?"

"Yes, your grace. My guess is she is the 'ghost' that fairly scared Lady Sophia's maid to death earlier this evening and caused her to drop the tea service she was bringing to her ladyship. Fortunately, nothing was broken."

Erik had not forgotten his daughter in the melee of that afternoon's drama, but her absence was not abnormal, since she usually only made an appearance when she wanted to be seen. He knew most of her hiding places, but this evening he had been too preoccupied to find her until Boris informed him she had not eaten her supper.

"Where is Erin now?"

Boris cleared his throat. "That is what I came to tell you."

Five minutes later, Erik entered Christine's sitting room. Lady Sophia was seated by the fire. His gaze darted around the dimly lit room. He wasn't sure what he was going to find after following the line of nervous servants down the corridor. He felt his body relax slightly. He shut the door.

"Lord Sedgwick," Lady Sophia said without turning her head.

"I was told my daughter is being held prisoner in this room . . ."

Lady Sophia sniffed. "If you are referring to the owner of those little bare feet hiding behind the curtains, I will credit that you have come to the correct conclusion. We are in what one might call an impasse. *I* believe I am owed an introduction after having helped clean up the tea tray Mrs. Samuels dropped. The lady Erin believes she is hiding."

Erik's boot heels made little sound on the carpet. He slowly drew back the heavy drapery. His daughter stood there, clutching an old porcelain doll to her chest. Her chin rose. "Come now, Erin." He knelt in front of her and gently tilted her chin. "It is time to come out of hiding. Everyone has been looking for you." She shook her head as much from stubbornness as fear.

She was a wild-looking child with long, unruly blond hair to her waist and bare feet below her white nightdress. Balking at being pulled past him, she clasped his shoulder. He made a gentle motion with his hand. "Will you not say hello?"

Shaking her head, she mutely hid her face in his shirt. Erik shifted on his knee. "This is my daughter, Erin."

Lady Sophia approached and peered over her nose. "Can she not speak for herself? How old is the child?"

He smoothed the curls from Erin's face. "She had measles as a baby and lost much of her hearing. But she is very adept at communicating when she wants something, though you might not be able to understand everything she says." He turned to his daughter. "Do you want to tell our guest how old you are?"

Clearly, she did not.

"She is almost seven." He cupped her cheek and forced her to look at him. "Did you come in here to see the pretty lady in the next room?"

Her head shook more adamantly, and Erik knew it would be impossible to take his daughter into Christine's room until Erin was ready.

"Hmpf. Incorrigible, no doubt." Sophia studied Erin with more detail, but there was a new softness to the set of her lips. "She brought Christine a sprig of heather and set it next to her pillow. We didn't see her until after Mrs. Samuels stumbled over her in the darkness. I fear the collision scared them both witless." Her eyes narrowed daggers at him. "The child could have been hurt. Does she have no proper supervision?"

Erik stood. Erin clung to his leg. "I have a household of servants and a nurse who watches over her. Short of locking her in the nursery under restraints, I have found it simpler just to allow her to come and go. She would anyway."

"That is the most absurd thing I have ever heard. Why . . ." Casting about for words she sputtered, "A child needs boundaries."

Amusement quirked his lips. "You are welcome to try and give her some, my lady. But I think it might be rather like trying to put a harness on your niece."

Bracing her hands on her cane, Sophia suddenly looked toward the door leading into the bedroom. "My niece was awake earlier. She would not take the sleeping draught the doctor tried to give her. She ate a bit of supper." Lady Sophia's eyes came back to rest on him. "She does not blame you. She was worried that you might believe yourself cursed and that you were staying away from her while nursing some immense guilt. She wanted to assure you she has not died."

"She said all that, did she?"

"She will probably remember none of it in the morning." Sophie held out her hand to Erin. "Come," she said to Erin, like a seasoned army sergeant. "It is past your bedtime, young lady, and your papa has some place he needs to be."

Erin eyed Lady Sophia's outstretched hand as if it were a snake, mutiny flickering in her eyes. Erik gently pulled her face around. Her large blue eyes widened in growing panic. "Your supper is waiting for you in the nursery, Erin."

"I will see that she gets there," Sophia briskly replied before he could lift his daughter and take her himself. "Come, come, dear," she patiently insisted. "I am an old woman. You do not expect me to open that door on my own?"

Shoving his hands into his pockets, Erik stepped back. "Her nurse is standing outside the room."

Hesitantly, with a glance back at Erik, his daughter laid her hand in Sophia's. He watched the two walk across the room. Erin opened the door. His daughter did not look back at him. The door shut behind her.

Darkness fell over the room. Erik looked around him

at his shadow wavering against the walls, trying to remember the last time he'd willingly stepped into this room. The tall clock at the far end of the corridor began to chime, signaling the end to a very long day.

After a moment, he walked through the dressing area and into Christine's bedroom. He removed his jacket and dropped it on the chair. He stoked the fire back to life to chase the chill from the room. Then finally, he crossed the room and stood next to the bed. He looked down upon his wife.

Surrounded by velvet hangings, she faced the hearth, her hair a shadow across the stark whiteness of the pillow. The blankets did not conceal her body from his gaze, and though she wore a shift, she may as well have been naked to him. His gaze slipped downward to caress the shape of her breast, the curve of her waist and flair of her hip, her peacefulness in sleep a contrast to the wanton in his arms last night, completely unaware that she tempted him profoundly. That she had always tempted him in a way he did not understand.

Then her fingers folded around his, and he was suddenly staring into her blue eyes, holding his breath. A tremor passed through him that he was unused to feeling, and like a man in a trance, he surrendered to the gentle tug of her hand and sat next to her on the mattress.

"This is not how I had planned our first night at Sedgwick Castle, your grace," she said, her voice as smooth and warm as the amber firelight, reassuring *him* when he was the one who should have been comforting her.

"The physician said you will be up and about in a few days."

The lump on her head was visible even in the shadows, and he wanted to tell her he was sorry for nearly killing her, the notion absurd, since he held no sway over the weather or geological occurrences that would have combined to cause that pothole. He did not believe in curses and his nature did not lend itself to emotional soliloquies or apologies. He was not a man weakened by passion.

His passions were dangerous.

"Lie beside me," she murmured sleepily, her eyes already closed.

And he did as she asked, against all warnings, and because he was a fool and he was exhausted, he stretched out his body next to hers. Her fingers moved over his chest where his shirt opened. For eons it seemed as if his eyes assessed her, then he touched her with infinite tenderness as she settled against him. Fully dressed as he was, he did nothing more than hold her.

His well-laid plans always failed around Christine. The first time he'd met her she'd been trouble to him. Not because she played coy with his affections, but because she did not. She could not flirt worth a damn. Unlike her cousin Charlotte or, later, Elizabeth, she was not popular or wealthy. In his entire life, he'd never met anyone as oblivious to her own faults as she was secure with her differences. She was an outcast, without self-judgment or self-pity the least helpless person he'd ever known. She was what she was without apology, and from the first moment he'd met her in that crowded ballroom in Somerset, he'd been incapable of seeing anyone else that summer. They'd been friends before becoming lovers, the only person in his life who had asked nothing from him.

Years ago, he'd accepted that she had chosen her work over him, and he had never allowed himself to look back. Now he did.

And, as the hours waned into dawn and Erik left the room, he knew he would have preferred that Lady

Sophia not told him that Christine never knew about his proposal. He had thought it had not made a difference but he found it was a lie.

Christine awakened to the sound of thick, rolling purrs. For a moment, she thought she was dreaming and she did not know where she was. The purrs rumbled louder. Her eyes flew open.

Beast.

Easing herself around beneath the covers, she found Beast stretched across the white ruched satin comforter at her back, an undignified contradiction to his plush surroundings. He'd found her. She wrapped him in her arms, awake now as he butted his head against her cheek and buried his nose and whiskers deeper in her hair.

"You made it, good boy, you." She cooed to him and they snuggled together, enjoying their reunion. He'd not abandoned or forgotten her. "Did Lady Rebecca take good care of you? She must have. I swear you are fatter."

Fighting dizziness, she lay back against her pillow and looked past him to the room, wondering if she had imagined Erik in here last night. Her hand went to the lump on her head. A dull headache and tenderness on her ribs made her grimace. A forgettable beginning for her at Sedgwick Castle, when she had wanted to make a good impression. Now, with dawn on the horizon and no one guarding her, she reached for her spectacles on the nightstand.

Holding Beast in her arms, she padded barefoot across the room to throw open the sash. She frowned. Dawn colored the horizon, but a tree defeated her desire to see much beyond her tousled reflection in the heavy leaded glass. Disappointed, she turned back into the room. With its paneled doors and resplendent French bed and Teniers tapestries, her chambers were reminiscent of eighteenth-century gaiety and brightness. She moved into an adjoining chamber to look for her trunks. A porcelain claw-foot tub sat against the wall.

Candlelight flickered in glass globes. Someone had recently been in here. She could still smell a taint of sulphur in the air as if someone had just lit the lamps. A panel door suddenly opened behind her. Christine turned as a young serving girl, wearing a white mobcap and carrying a full pitcher of water, entered.

"Oh, mum. Ye be awake." She rushed to set down the pitcher on a nearby dressing table trimmed in delicate floral chintz. "I be Annie, yer lady's maid." The girl suddenly eyed Beast with narrowed eyes. "Oooh, he be a sly tom, that one is. Everyone 'as been searching fer him. He only comes out when he is hungry. 'E likes 'is cod well-cooked and with a dollop of sweet whipped cream, mum."

Christine raised her brow in amazement. "Your cook makes his meals?"

"Oh, yes, mum. He gets only the best at Sedgwick Castle. The master's wee sprite of a daughter 'as taken a fancy to him, too."

"Erin?" Christine said.

"Lady Erin is much like your cat. If she doesn't want to be seen, she won't be. Come. Ye must be chilled."

Wearing only her shift, Christine was chilled. The girl took her through an interconnecting door to a dressing room big enough to be a formal sitting room. She opened one of the mahogany armoires. "I 'ave unpacked the trunk what arrived with you. Everything else what come in last week is aired and pressed."

Christine stopped in the doorway. She admired the yellow-and-white walls skillfully over-painted with trailing vines that matched the white-framed furniture and plush yellow chintz upholstery. An off-white Turkey carpet covered the floor in its entirety. The room was beautiful.

"Lady Elizabeth painted all of her private apartments yellow and green to match the daffodils what bloom here in the spring."

"The former Lady Sedgwick lived in these rooms?"

"Beggin' yer pardon, mum. I didna' mean any disrespect to you. The master's chambers be right through those doors."

Christine turned, surprise momentarily etching her expression even as the quick movement sent a shaft of pain through her head.

Of course, Erik's former wife would have lived in the apartments adjoining his private rooms. She glanced at the room almost in regret, much of her appreciation of the furnishings suddenly spent. "I'm not offended, Annie."

Annie pulled Christine's pink wrapper from the armoire and began brushing away the wrinkles. "She was an artist, mum. Her work is all around Sedgwick Castle. Even after all these years we be admirin' it."

Beast squirmed and Christine set him down. She walked to the windows. Beyond the leaded-glass panes, daylight had begun to stretch across a moody sky. At least she could glimpse something now.

The room overlooked a mist-cloaked garden. Peering past the high stone walls half hidden in the hedge, she saw an octagonal dovecote with an arched cupola up top. Throwing open the window, Christine leaned outside. Milkmaids carrying pails, gardeners, and an assortment of other workers walked about the inner courtyard near the scullery. A descending stone staircase would take her down the castle's backside, past terraces overgrown with shrubs.

As the sun burned off the mists, Christine could see beyond the lake. On a distant hill she glimpsed what looked like a house. But even adjusting her spectacles, she could not be sure. "Who lives over there?" she finally asked.

"That be Lord Eyre's estate. Lady Erin's grandfather." Bess reached around Christine and shut the windows. "Fortunately, his grace can only see the house on clear days."

"Lady Elizabeth's family?"

"It be ol' Angus Maxwell, Lady Elizabeth's great-grandda, what put the curse on the Sedgwicks," her voice lowered to a whisper.

"I see," Christine lowered her voice as well. "And was this curse cast before or after the first duke of Sedgwick was beheaded?"

"Oh, 'twas much later, mum," Annie said in all seriousness. "The curse was cast only a century ago, for a hundred years."

"What happens after a hundred years pass?"

"A princess will come and awaken the sleeping prince with a kiss," Erik said from the doorway behind her.

Annie spun around. Erik leaned with his shoulder against the jamb, his arms folded across his chest. "Thus breaking the evil spell and saving the castle and the entire kingdom from certain doom," he finished. "See that my wife's breakfast is brought up here, Annie. She is going back to bed."

The girl dipped. "Yes, your grace."

Annie glanced briefly at Christine, then hurried across the room, pausing in front of Erik to make a brief curtsey and finally easing past him through the door.

Christine's heart did a ridiculous flutter in her chest. He wore a snuff-colored riding coat, dark trousers, and boots, and looked as if he was on his way to the stable. "Must you always sound so cross at everyone, Erik?"

"You, madam, are not supposed to be out of bed."

"You are not my physician."

"I'm your jailer. The one with keys to your chamber."

Undeterred by his unsubtle threat, she turned her attention to the pitcher and sloshed the water into a porcelain basin, conscious of Erik standing tall and lean in the doorway behind her as she performed her toilette. She brushed her hair and parted it down the middle, then the side, then finally off her face, careful of the egg-size lump near her temple. She had never shared her toilette with anyone. It felt strange doing so now. Erik had made love to her many times, done things with his mouth, but he'd never watched her perform personal intimacies. To her, these things had always been private, like her writing and her studies.

She finally set down her brush, found her spectacles on the countertop, and reapplied them to her nose, as if they would shield her, like a mask. Erik still had not moved.

Gradually he abandoned his indolent stance and approached.

For a moment, a heartbeat perhaps, she glimpsed something in his eyes. Something reflected from hers perhaps. Then he tenderly touched the bump on her head. "Does your head hurt?"

She admitted that it did. "A little. I am dizzy."

He walked her into her chambers. Placing his hands firmly on her waist, he moved her toward the bed. "When that knot is gone from your head and I am convinced you are well, then you may get out of bed."

Beast lay comfortably sprawled like a peasant king atop the white ruched-satin coverlet on her bed. She lifted him into her arms. Erik looked down at the ball of patchy fur glaring at him from the crook of her arm. She realized by the shock on Erik's face that he had never met Beast.

"Good lord." Erik's brows angled over the bridge of his nose as he moved closer. "What is it?"

Christine rubbed her cheek against Beast's head. "Don't be cruel, Erik. You know what he is. You'll injure his sensibilities."

Erik laughed. Christine watched his growing mirth with a narrowing of her eyes. After a moment he cleared his throat. "My apologies, Christine."

"Be gone, Erik. Five minutes with you and my head is throbbing again." She climbed into bed and set Beast prettily to the side of her.

Erik pressed his palms against the canopy above her head. "May I get you some water? Blankets? Are you warm enough?"

She eased her head onto the pillow and pulled the covers to her chin. He could climb into bed with her, she thought. "Will the summer eventually bring warmth to this chilly clime?"

His gaze moved unabashedly down the length of her. "The summer brings longer days and shorter nights, but a man's warmth in this clime is not found basking in the sunlight, my love."

He turned and strode to the door, only to look over his shoulder. His eyes touched the room as if reassuring himself naught was amiss. "Do your chambers meet with your approval?"

"I thought perhaps I would paint these rooms. If that is all right with you."

"All that I have is yours, Christine. If you want to

paint every room in this place, simply tell Boris the color."

"When can I meet your daughter?"

He inclined his head toward the nightstand. "She has already been here."

Someone had laid a small bouquet of ragged purple heather on the nightstand. Christine pushed up on her elbow and lifted the sprig to her nose.

"You can meet her when you are ready, Christine."

Then he was gone. The emptiness in the room seemed to increase tenfold, swirling like a chilly mist to encompass her.

Setting the heather on the nightstand, Christine looked around her at the beautifully painted walls and wondered if she should paint them after all. It now almost seemed sacrilege. Elizabeth *was* Erin's mother.

A woman who by all accounts was beautiful, delicate like a woodland sprite, who loved to paint daffodils on walls, and who had left Erik in the middle of the night—abandoning her child and her life to a terrible fate.

Why?

What had Erik done to make her hate him so?

Chapter 10

The first tinges of amber had tipped the clouds by the time Christine awakened from a nap and looked outside her open window. This was the first time in days she had opened her eyes without a headache throbbing at her temples or had been so stiff she could not move. She'd suffered less pain the morning after the accident than after Erik had put her back to bed and she'd awakened barely able to move a muscle. Aunt Sophie had told her shock had originally numbed the pain. Pulling on her robe, Christine padded across the room to the adjoining chamber that connected to hers through a panel in the wall.

Erik's bedroom was cold and showed no sign that he had spent any of the last five nights in his room. "Do not mind my brother's absence," Becca said from Christine's doorway. "I don't think he spends much time in that room except to change his clothes. He rarely sleeps."

Christine turned as Erik's sister swept into the room, looking pretty in white as she set a well-stocked tea service on the table beside Christine's bed. The table had been there since Aunt Sophie dined with Christine a few days ago.

She withdrew and shut the door behind her. It seemed as if her bridegroom was perfectly content to let his servants and family members care for her these past days, she considered, as she had not seen Erik since he had offended her cat, then put her to bed. Alone. The physician had been by to see her that afternoon, examined the bump, removed three stitches, and pronounced that she would live.

"If you want to find him, I suggest that you go to the library in the mornings." Becca poured tea into a cup. "He practically lives there when he is not at the levee site."

Christine returned to the bed and crawled beneath the covers to warm her feet, her back braced against the pillows. "He does a lot of reading?" she asked.

"In a way, I suppose. Erik is an architectural engineer. Quite a fine one if I can say so myself. Much of this estate has seen the benefit of his skill. He has been working on designs for a library at St. Andrews, though still unfinished. His work gives him purpose, I suppose." She sighed as she added a spot of cream to the tea and smiled warmly at Christine. "I am glad he has found someone who will love him. And who will love Erin and me . . . and everyone else at Sedgwick Castle . . . and all the tenants and the people of Sedgwick. I want you to love Scotland and never want to leave."

"Becca . . ."

She handed Christine the hot tea. "I know I am being melodramatic." Spooning sugar into her own cup, she smiled. "But I am merely happy, you see. I already feel as if you are my sister. I wish to become great friends."

Yesterday, Becca had also kept Christine company, the entire day. They had shared tea, lunch, and supper. Earlier in the week, Becca had introduced Christine to Mrs. Brown, the housekeeper, and many other servants, including the cook who braised fish for Beast. Despite Rebecca's inexhaustible aptitude for conversation, Christine had been happy for the companionship if only because Erik's sister gave Christine deeper insight into her brother.

But only a sixteen-year-old with a romantic view of the world could believe that one meeting between Erik and Christine on the stairs of the museum had been nothing short of "spontaneous combustion between two lonely souls adrift in the universe" as Becca so aptly framed the words, something Christine was sure must be a quote from Byron. Electing not to ruin Becca's biased view of marriage with the truth, Christine cradled the warm porcelain cup in her hands and said instead what was uppermost in her mind. "I was hoping to meet Erin."

Becca set a warm crumpet on a plate and laid it on Christine's lap. "Not that Erin dislikes you. She has been around watching you." Rebecca sipped her tea. "But it would do you no good to meet her until she's ready. Erik would have to chase her down, and no doubt a scene would ensue."

"Is she . . . ?"

Becca laughed. "Normal? Mrs. Brown calls her Sedgwick's fey child."

"I was told her grandfather lives in the manse across the lake."

Becca idly traced a fingernail around the teacup rim. "Yes. But only Lady Lara, Elizabeth's older sister, is allowed here. She is the only one who would have anything to do with Erik after Lady Elizabeth vanished. Everyone was terribly cruel to him and still blames my brother for her disappearance. Lara didn't. She visits on occasion to see Erin, but I think she comes here only to see Erik."

Before Christine could digest the comment, Becca set down the teacup with a *clink*. "He said you will hunt our beast." Her voice was infused with excitement. "You should have Erik take you to the river. Though you must never go alone. The river is quite swollen and over its banks."

"Yes, he said he is attempting to reclaim farming land lost after the Western Railroad blew up part of the foothills leading into Sedgwick."

"Their actions changed the course of the river and have caused other problems. Erik has been livid over the entire ordeal. To make matters worse, he is having trouble among his laborers since two have vanished and strange fossils have been washing up on the riverbank since last year. Levee work has stopped. He hasn't allowed me to return to the river since last summer. I'm hoping your presence here will change his mind."

Christine understood why Erik did not want his sister involved in this search, especially when the human remains washing up could end up being Elizabeth's. What young woman would not be traumatized by seeing someone she once revered reduced to scarred bone?

Early morning mists still clung to the ground when Christine awakened the next day with a gift set next to her pillow. It was a small child-like portraiture of her. She looked at he dead flower stalks on her nightstand. After Annie helped her dress, she finally left her bedroom in search of her elusive husband. She wandered down halls that seemed to have no coherent direction and ended up lost before a chambermaid directed her downstairs toward the dining room and to Boris.

At the bottom of the stairs, she came face-to-face with a red firedrake displayed in the coat of arms hanging on the wall—a giant quadruped creature, wings and sharp claws extended, a flame spewing from his snout. The crest was also etched in stone above the entranceway.

"They say the Sedgwick coat of arms comes from the Draco constellation, which wanders the sky over Fife in the wintertime," Boris said from the doorway. He held a tea tray. "For centuries all Sedgwick dukes have carried the dragon into battle."

She was astonished not to have known. Erik did not ride with a standard flapping on a carriage when he traveled. He did not publicly boast his rank. He never had.

"Mum?" Boris drew her around.

"Is Lord Sedgwick in the library?" she asked when she had found her voice.

"No, mum. He leaves for his morning ride just after dawn."

Nervously clutching the portraiture in her hands, she asked for directions to Erin's chambers. Christine felt silly constantly asking for directions. With a bit of sleuthing and following toys like bread crumbs to the third floor, she found Erin's apartments. Wooden toys and blocks littered the floor. Dolls perched prettily atop white shelves. Bright yellow-and-pink wallpaper covered the walls and met a pale pink carpet on the floor. Christine stepped gingerly over a jack-in-the-box and walked through an adjoining chamber and into a dressing room lined wall to wall with dresses, pinafores, petticoats, shoes, and ribbons. She stopped just inside the connecting door.

"Boris informed me you were up here."

Erik's voice startled her. She whirled. Her hand went to her heart. "Must you always sneak up on me?"

He wore a dark blue waistcoat minus the jacket. His white shirtsleeves were rolled up to his forearms as if he'd been interrupted in whatever task he'd been doing. "Boris was mistaken," he said. "I have not been riding this morning. I would have come to your chambers this morning to bring you up here. My apologies for neglecting you, but I have been somewhat busy."

It was not as if the rules of their contract stated he owed her his companionship, nor the courtesy of an inquiry about her health or an introduction to his fey daughter.

"Nothing too serious, I hope."

"Everything these days is serious." Then he shrugged sheepishly as if to apologize for his terseness. "This is summer, the height of estate repair work, including all my roads. My time is not my own."

Nor hers either, 'twould seem. "I received this on my pillow this morning." She presented him the portraiture. "Quite an excellent depiction," she said, thinking the artwork actually made her look pretty.

His grin softened the grim set of his mouth and fairly set her breath in her throat. Erik was unbelievably beautiful when he tossed away his mantle of somberness. He raised his eyes and found her staring. A strand of his dark hair brushed his brow. "Come," he said.

Erik walked past Christine into the adjoining bedroom. "Do not get up, Mrs. Whitman," she heard him say to someone and, as Christine stepped into the bedroom, she saw a gray-haired woman sitting in a rocker reading, near the window. "Is she painting still?" she heard Erik ask the child's nurse.

"Yes, your grace."

Erik strode around the corner. Christine leaned forward slightly and glimpsed a white lace and pink velvet canopied bed against the back wall. He stopped just on the other side of an alcove set in the window that looked like a window seat. White curtains draped the window in a waterfall of fine Belgian lace, and sunlight found its way into the room everywhere. Unlike the rest of the castle she had seen this morning, there was an air of perpetual sunshine in this room.

"There you are," he said to someone who sat out of sight of Christine. "I think it is time to come out and greet the pretty lady, Erin." He held out the small portraiture of Christine. "Did you paint this for her?"

He must have received an answer, for he knelt. "She has been waiting to meet you. She wants to thank you for the gift. Don't you think it is time you introduce yourself to her? Erin?" Her father tenderly bade his daughter forward.

After a pause, a girl of about seven timidly appeared. Aunt Sophie had already told her Erik's daughter was partially deaf. But Christine had not expected to meet someone so fragile, so breathtakingly beautiful, an image of the portrait Christine saw in the gallery on her way upstairs, which she now concluded was Lady Elizabeth. Erin wore an ankle-length pink calico and white pinafore. Her long blond hair had been swept from her tiny face and was tied neatly with a blue ribbon. Wide blue, furtive eyes stared back at Christine.

"This is Lady Sedgwick." Erik smiled encouragingly then looked up at Christine as he lifted Erin into his arms. "As you can see . . ." he thumbed a blue-and-pink smudge from her cheek . . . "She wants to be a great artist."

Like her mother, Christine thought, remembering the artwork on her own walls. This child was a prodigy. Christine approached and took the portraiture from Erik's hand. "I have never received anything so wonderful," she said. "I am glad to finally meet you, Erin."

It was a positive sign that the child did not turn away.

Erik's arm encompassed the room. "And this is the nursery. You are welcome here anytime."

"She is all alone in this wing?"

A slight smile curved the corners of his mouth. "Only until she gets another brother or sister," he said, pressing his lips against his daughter's soft curls.

Christine blushed at the carnal intonation in his voice. But strangely, the thought of having a child with him did not fill her with the same uncertainty she'd first had in London.

The little girl said something in his ear. "Ask her yourself," he encouraged.

She shook her head and buried her face against his shoulder.

Erik grinned. "I believe she has developed a *tendre* for a certain ugly-as-the-blazes cat." He gave his daughter a wink.

"Erik!" Christine said.

"She wants to know if you will let her have Beast."

Christine shifted her attention to the little girl, suddenly nervous that she would spoil this meeting. "Beast doesn't belong to anyone, Erin." She kept her words slow and precise. "You can't own him."

Her independent cat was rather like Erik in that respect.

You can't make him love you, an unfamiliar voice inside her said.

"You have to be patient," Christine added, keeping her eyes on the little girl's. "But I understand he likes braised fish." She made a wiggling motion with her hand. "Maybe you can bribe him."

A smile trembled on the girl's lips. She cupped her mouth and said something else to her father. Erik grinned. "I believe she said that both she and he like Cook's cream-filled crumpets."

Boris suddenly stood in the doorway. He held a note in his hand. "Mr. Bailey is here about the road, your grace."

"Tell him I will be down shortly," Erik said.

He looked over at the older woman now standing next to the rocking chair. The woman approached. "Come, Erin." He shifted her in his arms. "Mrs. Whitman will need to clean you up before your lunch."

As Erin turned her attention to the approaching nurse, her small mouth tightened. "Erin. You are covered in paint. You need to wash up before lunch."

Erin wrapped her arms around her father's neck and with her head on his shoulder, her eyes watched Christine as he followed Mrs. Whitman into an adjoining washroom. Whatever else the devil duke might be to the rest of Britain, his daughter obviously loved him unconditionally.

A gust of wind swept through the treetops and fluttered the curtains. Christine walked over to the windows. She glanced out at the junipers and milkweed that blotted the wind-beaten landscape. Hardly a second passed when another gust of wind pushed against the window; then Erik was suddenly standing behind her. "I have business to attend. You'll be able to occupy yourself today?"

"I will try not to be bored, Erik."

Less than a half hour later, Christine was dressed for exploring. From Annie she'd learned there was an old drover's trail that went up into the cliffs, but no one was allowed there anymore. She'd found Boris in the dining room preparing lunch for Aunt Sophie and asked if Lord Sedgwick had a topographical survey of the area surrounding the river that might have been commissioned for the levee work. A map? No one seemed to know.

Maybe she didn't need a map. Surely, someone other than Becca would know the place where she had found the first fossils.

Carrying an old canvas knapsack filled with tools, Christine made her way down the hill to the stables.

Two hours later, with a reluctant groom in tow, she reined in at the bottom of an old washed-out road that ended in the river. A cool breeze tugged at her hair. Behind her, the groom's horse shifted. At least today wasn't bone-chilling wet, she thought, as she adjusted the strap of her hard pith hat around her chin and patted her shaggy beast on the withers. She'd wanted a horse that looked experienced enough not to fall off a cliff. Miss Pippen had proven game thus far. Certainly more cooperative than the groom who had reluctantly agreed to bring her to the river. Thirty feet of swollen raging water might prevent her from crossing, but it did not end this outing.

"We best not be going farther, mum," the grooms-man shouted over the noise.

"Nonsense, Hampton. We've already been out here most of the morning."

She pulled out her compass and got her bearings, then removed the glasses from the canvas pack slung over her saddle and scanned the valley behind her. This entire area had been formed by a massive volcanic eruption an eon ago. Over the last millennium the elements had rounded the hills, and glaciers had carved a valley into the floor. Away from the domestic confines of Sedgwick Castle, the crags and windswept vales were a forbidding and lonely place. She eyed the escarpment a mile ahead. "That is where I want to go. We need to find a way to cross."

Hampton scrubbed a hand across his bristles. "He

won't like me taking you up there, mum. The riverbank where the fossils were found be *this* way."

"I have every intention of viewing that part of the river." She pointed to the distant cliffs. "From up there."

Despite his reluctance, Hampton did as she bade. He took her another mile east, to a bridge that had not been washed out this past year—the only one left that crossed the river for miles. Until last summer, the river had been low enough in some places not to need a crossing. Now it was too dangerous, he'd told her. Leading the way, Hampton took her on the old drover's trail that led into the foothills and then slowly snaked up the cliffs.

The river's roar funneled up the rock walls like thunder. They stopped and ate lunch from a basket that Cook had given Hampton. After meandering along the trail another hour, Christine found the place where she wanted to stop and she dismounted. She handed Miss Pippen's reins to Hampton and walked a goodly distance down the incline to the cliff's edge, stirring rocks and sending some rolling over the side. Mounds of loose scree had washed down from the upper hills, and she knelt to study the talus. The ledge was as uneven as broken teeth and looked to have been slowly peeling away for decades.

She knelt on one knee to study the rocks, then leaning slightly, she looked down at the white water churning in a large rock hollow below. She'd never possessed a fear of heights but she felt a shiver. By the look of the scattered tree limbs and bits and pieces of flotsam, some of which looked like the bleached wall of an old cottage, a great violence occurred here every time it rained. Nature's fury at its most brutal.

Sedgwick Castle sat in the distance like a moody mistress framed by the clouds. Looking at the stark and beautiful landscape, Christine contemplated all its untold secrets.

Truly, she could fall in love with such a place, and found easy admiration for the man who had clearly preserved every stone of his heritage as if it had come to him encased in amber.

She picked up a handful of talus and let it slide through her fingers. Somewhere out here her destiny awaited.

Without turning, she asked the groom, "In which section of this ravine were the original fossils recovered?"

"Fifty meters upstream," a familiar voice replied, and it did not belong to the groomsman.

Christine turned and rose abruptly. Erik stood above her on the hill. His cloak swirled about his ankles. The sun was behind him and so she could not make out his expression, though his tone was unmistakable. "Do you bloody mind coming away from the edge?" he said. "The entire face of this cliff is unstable."

Having made that assessment herself, Christine did not argue his point. Or the fact that Erik would risk his own life a thousand times over before he'd ever allow her to risk hers. Even if the cause was for them both. He had brought her to Scotland to help him find Elizabeth.

She dusted off her hands and began picking her way up the incline. "Yes, it is dangerous. More so if I tripped and actually *fell* off the cliff."

He grabbed her arm as she walked past—not cruelly, but neither was his grip gentle as he turned her to face him. "This entire area is unsafe." He aimed his fierce scowl over her shoulder at the groomsman standing where he'd tied her horse to the limb of a dead tree. "Or had you forgotten?"

"Thank you, Hamilton," she rushed to the groom's defense. "I have appreciated your expertise in helping me locate everything I needed to see this afternoon. My husband will see that I get home all apiece."

The man crushed his hat in his hands. "Yes, mum." He peered nervously at Erik before slapping his ruined hat back on his head. "Your grace."

Watching the poor man mount and then rein his horse around, Christine eased her arm from Erik's grip. "Hamilton brought me here because I ordered it."

"Do you see the old watchtower three meters beyond that ridge?"

Christine turned her head. "What ridge?"

"My point exactly. This entire area crumbled into the river last winter."

"And do you see the old drover trail behind you? The one that comes up from the valley. I believe you followed it to find me."

Erik merely narrowed his eyes. Unabashed, Christine continued. "According to Annie it is still a through trail to the coast. People may not be allowed up here, but that does not mean no one has been here. Including some of those missing." She swept her arm about her. "This is old volcanic terrain. There are lava chutes running throughout these hills. Such geological formations make for excellent conditions in the creation of caverns. If I were a wagering man, I would bet that is where both of us will find the answers we seek."

Looking suitably impressed, he tipped back his hat with his quirt and peered down at her in amusement. "You've learned all of that in the ten minutes you were on that ledge?"

She thumped his chest. "I learned all that the instant I looked *over* the ledge and saw the hollow below." She smiled. "Water isn't overflowing from the river *into* the hollow. It is flowing *out* of the hollow into the river. That is why we are seeing a huge torrent of white water below us."

His brows rose. "I thought white water was caused by water rushing over protruding rocks."

"The protruding rocks are covered in moss. The water is coming from beneath the surface and not over it. And if you look closer, you will see black dirt and rocks on the bank. *That*, my dearest husband and partner, tells me your river has found a lava tube in which to frolic."

Satisfied that she had at last left him suitably astonished, she rocked back on her heels. "When the river shifted its course, it must have found its way into a lava tube and further weakened the walls. The breach could be showing up now because this cliff is unstable or this cliff has become unstable because of the rushing water. The fact that it has collapsed in places demonstrates that much."

"I haven't had my engineer walk these banks recently but—"

"I am no engineer, but I know dirt," she said with no amount of humility. "I know the difference between volcanic dirt and plain old river wash. If you want to peer over the edge of the cliff and have a look . . . ?"

He glanced over his shoulder but did not appear inclined to look further. Smiling to herself, she lifted her skirts and picked her way over the rocks back to her horse. She'd worn stout footwear and pants beneath her woolen skirt, a feminine article of clothing that she intended to remove when the time came for her to climb down this cliff.

"When the river level has dropped, I intend to go down there for a closer look." Then, looking up at the gloomy sky, she turned on her heel as another thought struck her, and nearly collided with him. "There are days in a row where the sun *does* shine?"

His fingers encircled her wrist like a chain of velvet, and he pulled her against him. She felt the burning touch of his body against hers. "Go back to the part where you said you intend to go down there."

She didn't try to escape him, nor did she wish to. "I need to get closer to the hollow. Maybe there is a way inside from the cliff. Otherwise, we will have to find another way inside. It is too dangerous to try by boat."

"Dangerous?" The word was a mockery of her assessment.

She brought his gloved fingers to her lips. "Don't be difficult, Erik."

His fingers unfurled beneath her chin. Like the legendary black lotus, a fruit touted to induce a dreamy languor and forgetfulness. That was the way he made her feel now as she gazed into his face. Dreamy.

"When I gave you permission to look for bones, I did not mean for you to be risking your life," he said.

"I am not a novice climber." If truth be told, she was an excellent climber and only her modesty prevented her from bragging. Climbing cliffs was not unheard of and had become something of a sport begun a half century ago by daring-do Englishmen who scaled the Alpines. "Mr. Darlington and I have climbed far worse than this," she said.

Erik released her hand but nothing in his stance told her he had relented. In fact, his expression hardened. "Besides," she added with a hint of nonchalance, deciding it time to clarify certain issues between them, "we signed an agreement stating that in exchange for—"

"I know what I signed."

"I am to have access to your estate."

"I know what I signed. It is *my* contract."

"It *is* your contract, and you clarified the details of this partnership down to each period and colon." He'd practically done everything but offer to open the door and invite her to leave once she had fulfilled her side of the bargain.

For a week, he'd been too occupied to visit or inquire as to her welfare. *Now* he was concerned? "You paid a great deal of money to make this a partnership between us. I am merely reminding you of the rules specific—"

"I understand that we signed a contract. A contract that, to put it bluntly, we both know would not stand up in a court."

"It isn't the law or the action of a tribunal that matters to me. I know I am your property. Your *word* binds you," she said, then on a softer note: "This is my beast we are talking about, Erik." And Erin's mother, she started to say, a woman whose fate Erik had charged Christine to discover.

For a long time, he said nothing, and she started to feel a weight settle in her chest. "Trust my judgment, Erik."

His eyes were steady. "I do trust your judgment."

Her lips curved up at the corners, a concession to his surrender, the movement of her mouth drawing the full measurement of his sherry eyes. "You are bloody stubborn, Christine."

"I prefer to think of myself as independent."

"Independence does have its charm," he said.

"Truly? You are not just trying to flatter me?"

"Truly. I cannot take my eyes off you. I am"—he peered down the length of her and lifted her skirts—"in awe of a woman in trousers."

"Awed, indeed." She slapped at his hand. "You are laughing at me."

He did laugh then, the rich sound filling her senses with a sort of bleakness. Christine narrowed her eyes, noting that she was too often the source of his endless amusement. "*Charming, indeed.*"

She mounted her shaggy nag, the robust mare nothing like the sleek chestnut Erik rode, and suddenly, she felt very much like that mare. Shaggy and hearty. Slightly worn around the corners. Bedraggled and yearning to be more beautiful. An absurd notion, since she considered herself suitable enough.

Reining Miss Pippen around, she peered down at the horse's owner from her lofty height and waited for him to recover his wits.

His eyes warmed her. "You must allow that a woman in breeches has its *rustic* charm."

"Most men are only interested in what I have inside these trousers," she said. "I am glad to see that you are not cut from the same cloth. Considering how close you are standing to the edge of yonder cliff."

Having effectively wiped the humor from his face, she decided it was her turn to laugh. "Your grace," she added as an afterthought.

"And how many men *have* been in those trousers?"

Since she'd stolen these pants from a stable hand years ago, she could not rightly say. But the fact was that no other man but Erik had ever touched her intimately or done the things he had to her. No other man had made her burn with his hands and his mouth and the mere touch of his eyes.

Or made her as vulnerable to her own feelings as he did now. And while he could claim beautiful women in his life since he had known her, she could not claim other men in her life. Not even a bald, toothless one.

The mere thought of such a lopsided existence gnawed at her sense of fairness and dissolved some of the goodwill toward him she'd been inclined to feel the last five minutes since he'd been avoiding her all week. Her hands tightened on the reins.

Rather than answering with the truth that he had been the only man in her life, she said instead, "I own that at least one man has made it into these trousers. Though it was dark that night in the stable and I could not see his face."

"Is that a fact, *leannanan?*"

Before she could decide if he was mocking her or himself, she laughed. "Dinnae get yersel' in a fankle, your grace"—she affected her own Scottish brogue—" 'Twas long after ye married another."

There was heat in his eyes as they held hers. After a moment he said, "I am gratified to know that you are still honest."

"You think no man would have me?"

"You're a woman. From the moment a lad experiences his first erection, his predominant thought is driven by his want, need, and single desire to *fook* anything in skirts. I have no doubt half the men in Britain would have you."

"Only half, your grace? You do me an injustice."

"And you do me one as well." He lifted her hand, an action that made her wary if only because she detected his intensity beneath the indolence of his touch. "Ye misjudge me if you think I do not know you, Christine."

She misjudged herself if she thought she was not in danger of falling in love with him all over again.

"We'd best return," he suddenly said, contemplating the churlish graying-green clouds overhead as if they had somehow become an extension of his mood.

"You do not want to be caught up here when the rain begins."

She watched him swing up on the mount with athletic ease. Sitting astride the sorrel-maned chestnut, he stopped in front of her. The wind caught his hair and cloak and stirred the loose tendrils around her cheek. "You are welcome to ride anywhere you want, but never alone," he said.

"Do you have a topographical map of this area?"

"I have a survey crew working on the road a mile from here. I will see what is available."

He reached across her horse and loosened her hands on the reins, and she inhaled his warmth. His shoulder brushed her cheek. "Let Miss Pippen set the pace on the way down," he said.

Erik nudged his heels. Then, absently pushing back a rebellious wave of dark hair batting her cheek, she watched his horse move past her and down the treacherous trail.

While Erik's time was taken up the next few days with business, Christine had plenty to keep her occupied as she worked to settle into her life at Sedgwick. But by the time she'd pulled up her sleeves and finished digging books out of her trunks, and her gown looked more brown than cheerful yellow any longer, she realized she disliked this dour room Aunt Sophie had aptly called a crypt.

Erik's retainers had put her trunks in the guardroom, and, though she didn't mind being surrounded by medieval weaponry, she wanted some place that was her own. Some place she could turn into her own personal space.

Working her hair back into a chignon, she'd set out to find the housekeeper, when a glance out the window

stopped her. Her gaze landed on the old tower keep.
Standing five stories in height, the keep belonged to
the oldest part of the castle. Four turrets crowned the
battlements. Windows overlooked the countryside in
all directions. Her hands gripped the windowsill. With
her heart racing like a child having just discovered her
first cave drawing, she knew exactly where she would
settle.

"His grace is the only one with a key to get inside,"
Mrs. Brown said an hour later as they stood in a small
enclosed courtyard outside, staring up at the beautiful
ivy-covered keep.

"But surely he will not mind if I go inside to look
around."

"You will have to speak to the master, mum."

The place was certainly ancient. "Is it dangerous?"
Her heart raced in anticipation and impatience as she
stood back and let her eyes travel upward. "Someone
must go up there."

Scotland's flag, along with that of Great Britain and
Sedgwick's standard, flew atop the highest point of the
battlements.

"You will have to speak to the master, mum. I only
know that his grace does not want anyone in this courtyard either."

Christine looked around. Little light penetrated the
ivy-enclosed courtyard. But hidden in the shadows in
what appeared to be abandoned enclaves gone to weed,
the gardens looked as if loving hands had once tended
them. "Why ever not? This spot is charming. If it were
cleaned up a bit."

Or perhaps a lot. If someone had a large scythe to
hack away at the thorny vines that had come close to
blocking the door.

Why should such a place be forgotten and neglected?

Christine shaded her eyes as she continued to look around her. A warm breeze tugged at her hair and skirts. The housekeeper cleared her throat, snapping Christine's attention back to the woman.

"I will need the key back, mum."

Christine frowned. She had practically forced Mrs. Brown, the termagant housekeeper, to give her the key just to unlock the gate so she could get into the tower courtyard. She and Mrs. Brown were definitely not going to get along.

"How long have you been with Lord Sedgwick, Mrs. Brown?"

"My family has served the dukes of Sedgwick Castle for the last hundred years," she said as if she were the guardian of the eternal flame. "We have been here since the old Sedgwick laird stole Angus Maxwell's bride from the altar and ravished her, then got hisself and all his seed cursed for the trouble."

"I see." Moved by Mrs. Brown's passion, Christine found she wanted to know more. "Tell me about the curse, Mrs. Brown. Is it truly as awful as everyone seems to believe?"

"Aye, mum. A hundred years ago, the old Sedgwick laird and Angus Maxwell were cousins, but they both fell in love with the same woman. Angus Maxwell was so bitter that on his deathbed he cursed the man what had once been his best friend and who betrayed him. No Sedgwick duke would ever know love again. Those what carried the mark all died before the age of four and thirty."

"But this is the nineteenth century. Surely no one believes such rubbish—"

"Rubbish?" Mrs. Brown's chin jutted outward. "The master be the last descendant what sprung from the youngest of the old laird's three sons. The Sedgwick line will end with him. And when the last Sedgwick duke passes without an heir, a Maxwell will inherit the duchy, just as old Angus predicted. The master's thirty-fourth birthday comes the end of summer."

Christine opened her mouth to reply, but whether from shock, disbelief, or the niggling realization that Mrs. Brown believed everything she had said to be true, she didn't know. What had Reverend Simms said about the power of superstition?

"The master would never have forgiven himself if something happened to you, mum."

"I appreciate your honesty, Mrs. Brown."

After a moment Christine withdrew the key from her pocket and handed it over to the housekeeper. She took two steps, stopped and returned her attention to the courtyard. "This place is too beautiful not to use. How difficult would it be to get someone in here and begin cleaning?"

"His grace—"

"I will talk to his grace."

Christine found Erik in the library. But he was not alone. "I hope I am not interrupting, but I would have a word with you."

"As I would with you." Motioning for her to precede him, he invited her forward to meet his visitors. Her husband introduced her to Hodges and a man named Bailey, who was the engineer Erik had hired to work on the various road construction projects around the estate.

"They are at your disposal for questions and anything else you might need," Erik said.

After Christine greeted them, Erik turned to the desk. She saw the rolled-up parchment next to a stack of books. It took only a moment after he handed her the parchment to discover that it was a topographical map. Or, as she realized as she met his gaze, something even better. Erik was essentially giving her the keys to his estate.

"My side of our bargain, madam."

"Oh, Erik!" She held the map to her chest as if it were gold. "Thank you."

"You do not have to thank me, Christine."

The men remained standing. Conscious of their presence, she wished now she had dressed in a prettier gown and taken care with her hair before she ventured to talk to Erik. They still stood within sight of the others, but not so near that her conversation could be overheard.

"I would like to open the keep," she said, jumping right into the kettle. Better to boil all at once than simmer slowly, as Aunt Sophie would say. "Your housekeeper seems to believe I am some invading army, and has refused to allow me any farther than the courtyard." *Imagine that*, she almost said, sensing the sudden change inside him. "Mrs. Brown was concerned you would be angry."

"Yet she let you inside anyway." His voice was quiet, subdued.

Christine pretended to study a splotch of dirt on her cuff. "There is no reason the place should not be opened," she replied, set on swaying him to her side even as she did not understand his shift in mood. "Just standing in the courtyard, I could see the keep is perfect for my needs. The windows on all sides will give me the light I need. I have a view of the estate."

"No."

His vehemence startled her. She could see the tall stone keep from where she stood. It didn't seem fair that Erik should deprive her of such a wonderful place to work, especially since it was unused. "If you are concerned that it might need to be cleaned—"

"The keep stays closed. No one goes up there. Nor am I ready to open it. Not even for you, Christine."

And with those words, so went their polite camaraderie. "Why? That is a ridiculous edict. What could possibly be up there that I cannot repair?"

"I have given you access to my land and to nearly every corner of Sedgwick Castle," he said, his voice low, his eyes darkening. She glimpsed what it might be like to be on the receiving end of his anger, should he ever lose his temper. "The keep remains closed. I am not negotiating this, Christine."

Aware that they were the subject of everyone's curiosity, Christine tamped down her hurt and her disappointment and finally her anger as she held Erik's gaze.

"It is not an insult to you," he said quietly as if she could understand anything about him.

But rather than barter words, she inclined her head in acquiescence and, taking her map as if it were a gift of gold, she departed.

Erik could not find her later. Christine was not with Erin, Becca, Lady Sophia, or in the guardroom. A chambermaid had seen her cat in the kitchens but not the feline's mistress.

"She has not been to her chambers all afternoon, your grace," Annie said when Erik left Christine's chambers a second time and sought out the maid.

He'd been aware of the deepest sensation of guilt since she'd left him in the library, pondering his refusal to allow her to have the keep as her own.

Her request had hit him like a broadside, and he admitted he'd not handled it well. Only Hampton went inside that keep, and only because he managed the daily raising and lowering of the Sedgwick standard. The keep stood as a monument to Erik's failures. If he'd had the courage to tear down the thing, he'd have done so stone by stone seven years ago. No, it would remain locked.

Finally, a stable boy reported that she had left Sedgwick Castle on foot nearly four hours ago. Her cloak lay on a chair next to her bed.

Even in summer, the weather could change in a snap. Then there were wolves to worry about, and a thousand places a person could break one's neck if one did not stay on the roads. Erik cursed aloud, then ordered his horse saddled.

"We did nae know she were not supposed to leave, your grace"—the stable boy rushed to apologize, taking a step away as Erik mounted his horse—"You said she could go anywhere."

Given his current wrath, Erik understood why the youth considered his life imperiled. "*Escorted*. That includes on foot. Never again without escort!"

He rode out beneath the old watchtower gate, flinging up clods of dirt against the rain-moistened ground, and a half hour later thundered across the wooden bridge that spanned a stream that eventually joined up with the river. The brisk wind whipped his cloak behind him as he reined in his horse two miles from the castle, atop a knoll glazed purple with a carpet of heather. His world stretched out in all its vastness for miles around him. His horse pranced sideways. He saw her then, a bright speck against the darker ash and hawthorns on the horizon, walking as if she were returning from the riverbank. Something in his chest loosened as she stopped to pick a pebble from her shoe, paused, and straightened. As she tented her hand over her eyes, he knew she saw him. His body reacted as if she'd physically touched him.

Urging his horse forward, he nudged the stallion into a gallop. Did she even suspect just how much trouble she was in?

Chapter 11

Christine stood in the stable doorway looking doubtfully up the darkened path. A sheet of rain poured from the roof and had pooled into mud at her feet. Clutching her map to her chest, she peered over her shoulder at her husband, who was talking to Hampton. She could not hear Erik's words over the rain and thunder, but she sensed by the disgruntled look on Hampton's face that he was receiving a hefty reprimand because of her.

Her eyes lingered on Erik's broad back, shaped by the damp shirt clinging to his shoulders, before she returned her attention to the rain.

Erik had given her his cloak earlier. Whereas the woolen mantle struck him just below his knees, on her, it nearly dragged the ground. She'd welcomed the garment when the rain began just as they passed through the gates. Now she struggled to adjust the bulk on her shoulders.

Then Erik was suddenly standing beside her, the lantern he held spreading a warm glow around them. He looked vulnerable with no protection against the elements. She clenched her jaw in a false smile to keep her teeth from chattering and to keep her own anger at bay. "Erik, I am hardly cold."

He held the lantern in front of him as a flash of lightning silvered the sky. "You will be." He took her hand and moved with her outside.

The rain hit her face at once, and even he could not block it. All she could think to do was protect her map.

He'd been furious with her earlier when he'd found her. His silence more ominous as he'd looked down at her from atop his horse, then held out his hand. He'd lifted her into the saddle in front of him and they'd ridden back in silence. She was glad he arrived when he had, since it had started to rain.

His hand tightened on hers, guiding her up the trail. She followed closely behind him. No one had ever held her hand, except when she'd been a child. Papa used to hold her hand on busy streets, and once when she'd been lost, a stranger had brought her home to Aunt Sophie. The gesture left her feeling the same way now. A little lost. Her ribs were still tender from the jarring ride on Miss Pippen a few days ago and they began to ache more with the robust jaunt, but she did not want to complain.

She could not have voiced the words anyway in the face of the slashing, bone-chilling rain, and soon it was all she could do to keep her head down. For all she could see in the blackness, Erik could be leading her off a cliff.

Then a door slammed and the deafening roar of rain and wind stopped abruptly. They stood in a stone antechamber. Erik hung the lantern on a hook beside another door. He took her elbow and they entered into another foyer, smaller than the one through which she had left earlier in the day. This one was less ornate.

She heard him speak to someone, then felt the cloak being lifted from her shoulders. Cold seeped through her soaked clothes to her drawers and she stood shivering and stumbling on her wet skirts. He lifted her and walked with her in his arms up a stone staircase. "This is why you must never leave the castle grounds without your cloak," he said harshly, his wet hair dripping on her shoulders. "The weather changes quickly in this clime."

She was too cold to argue or agree as he carried her through the long portrait gallery. They passed through another corridor to a pair of tall oak doors that opened ahead of them as if by unseen hands. He ordered a bath and hot tea brought to her chambers. She heard him instruct Annie to fetch her robe. Fog steamed her spectacles. She removed them and saw a fire burning in the hearth. He brought her within its glow, lowering her feet to the ground.

She was no longer shivering from the Scottish cold that permeated her bones but from the Scottish laird standing before her.

She retracted her palm. He saw the movement for what it was. Desire. Anger. Her gaze rose to meet his eyes.

"I feel much recovered," she heard herself whisper, attempting to edge him away.

He pressed his palms against the chair behind her, caging her. "I am relieved, *leannanan*." His whisper was a brand against her lips. "Your welfare is as much personal as business to me. I have to protect my investment."

For what? She wondered hotly, since he had rarely come to this bedroom and not yet to her bed since she had recovered from the accident. She told herself she would not ask him to do so.

That side of the contract belonged solely within *his* purview. Not hers. But whatever reason he had for staying away from her, she suspected it went deeper than even he understood. She had not understood it completely until he'd come racing after her that evening.

The sound of movement behind her lifted his head. Annie stood in the doorway leading into the dressing room, Christine's robe clutched in her hands. She gasped, "My apologies, your grace."

"Stay," Erik instructed. He stepped back, the firelight limming his shoulders and waist through his wet shirt. "My wife needs out of her wet clothing. I'll have her supper sent up directly."

"I wanted to thank you again for the map," Christine managed to tell him.

He continued to the door connecting his room to hers. "You may need another copy. I am not sure how well ink endures against rain."

"Then you can draw me another one. You *can* draw. You are an architect."

He turned on his heel. "I design edifices. Surveyors draw maps."

"Thank you," she said quickly.

He stopped, clearly exasperated. "For what, now?"

She held up the map then set it on the table next to her spectacles. "For giving me an opportunity to prove myself."

"I would not have wed you if I thought you a twit, Christine."

"Thank you," she said again to annoy him, and this time she watched with satisfaction as his eyes narrowed. "For answering a question I have been asking myself since my arrival. I thought you weren't coming to me at night because I had disappointed you in some way. I am relieved to know your opinion of me remains high and that my *wit* and intelligence played some role in your choice to make me your bride."

He reclaimed his steps and stood in front of her on a carpet now sodden with water dripping from her skirts. "My opinion of you has never been higher. In fact"—his voice lowered—"I would like for nothing more than to *fook* you where you stand if it would not shock Annie, who still happens to be standing in this room."

Christine's breath left her in a sudden gasp and her voice came out in a heated whisper. "You might shock Annie, but you don't shock me, Erik. You are being purposely rude."

He snorted in derision and turned on his heel. "It is not your intelligence and wit that clenched my decision to marry you," he said over his shoulder, snatching open his collar as he strode away. "Though your knowledge was a factor in my decision to go to London, it was not the deciding one that made you my duchess."

Christine followed him into his bedroom. His shirt-front unfastened, he stood at the bootjack. "What was the deciding factor?" she asked.

His sherry eyes burned into hers. "*You* were the deciding factor. Seeing you at Sommershorn. Touching you in the carriage. Watching while you tried to convince me why you should be the one to come to Scotland. You've never needed to prove yourself to me. Don't ever demean yourself or insult me by trying to thank me for something you already have." He removed his boots and strode to another door separating his bedroom from his dressing room.

Before Christine could follow, Annie dragged her back into her room. "You mustn't make him angry," she whispered as she helped Christine out of her sodden garments.

"Why not?" Christine snapped. "He's only a man. Not some cursed beast."

Ignoring her state of undress and Annie's urge to give her the robe, Christine strode barefoot through the door into Erik's chambers. She stepped over his balled-up shirt, a pair of boots near the bootjack and his trousers strewn carelessly on the well-tread path to his armoire. She found him belting a tie around his black silk robe and glared at him as he turned.

"You demand that I have confidence in my character when you do not ask the same of yourself," she threw out at him. "I would never have wed *you* if I didn't believe in your integrity or your innocence or . . . your honor. A hive of dragons could be living in those hills and it wouldn't have been enough to make me wed you if I did not believe you principled. I know why you rushed out to find me today. But I am *not* Elizabeth. I was not running away from you—"

"Enough, Christine."

She jabbed a finger in his chest and backed him a step. "Nor did some ridiculous curse cause that carriage accident, over which you have obviously been harboring guilt."

"Christine," he warned.

"And for whatever reason you choose not to allow me to use the keep, I will not argue. This castle is big. I will find somewhere else. We have a partnership, Erik. No one has ever willingly *sought* a partnership with me and I am appreciative of the trust. If I want to *thank* you then I will bloody thank you and you will *not* tell me I can't!"

She had backed him into the armoire. They stared at each other in the heat of the room as the wind and rain wailed around the windows and beat against the glass with blistering fury. But it wasn't fury she felt from him.

Like a tiny electrical current that stirred the air

around them, awareness coursed between them. Hot. Cold. After a moment, his head lifted, he looked over her shoulder and spoke to the shadows in his bedroom. "Leave us, Annie. You, too, Boris."

Christine had not even seen Boris when she passed through Erik's bedroom to the dressing room. "Yes, your grace," came the masculine voice, and then the quiet click of a door closing as Annie shut the connecting door.

"My butler is also my valet," Erik said. "I fear I insulted him by undressing myself, which probably flew straight from his brain the moment he saw you come striding through the room."

She peered down at herself. She wore nothing but a shift and corset, and a blush as hot as a kiln.

Before she could finish that thought, he backed her against the wall, his body radiating heat, his hand slipping behind her head. Their warm breath mingled, until at last his thumb slid beneath her jaw, teasing the curls at her temple. Then slowly, he lowered his mouth to hers. "Tell me again that you believe I am confused about what I want from this marriage."

His long legs pressed to hers, she was conscious of his erection pressed against the juncture in her thighs. "Tell me, Christine." He kissed her with an intensity that caressed her fevered thoughts as it enflamed her with more than want and desire. Long hot, tonguing kisses claimed her mouth. She caught her breath as he raised his head and looked at her as if he didn't want to stop looking for a long time.

Her corset went first to the ground. He drew her shift over her head. Her breasts warmed beneath his touch and her nipples hardened. In the dim firelight, she was conscious of the tingling where his lips touched, and the low grumble of thunder outside that seemed to vibrate the floor beneath her feet. The tip of his tongue seared a path down her throat. Her head fell back and she allowed the tender assault as his caress centered upon the peak of each breast.

Somehow they had made it into his bedroom. He fell with her onto his bed; she atop him. As she caught her palms on his chest, her long hair, still damp from rain, fell forward across her shoulders. He cupped her face with his palms, bringing her lips down to his and she wrapped her thighs around his hips, a carnal invitation for him to indulge in his passion.

And indulge he did, guiding himself into her body, stretching her flesh to accommodate all of him. She became aware of nothing save the rasp of his breath, the pulse of his heartbeat, the feel of his flesh and sinew beneath the glide of her palms and his rhythmic movement inside her. She moved with him in a slow, sensuous push and pull of their bodies. She wanted to pleasure him, a desire so strong her breath caught, and she pushed up against her hands, raising her body to see his face, the exact slant of his mouth.

She savored the play of his muscles against her thighs, a small portion of her mind taking pleasure in her dominance. His fingers splayed over her bottom.

His eyes glinted as he watched her, with surety and profundity, a master of control, she realized in some distant part of her mind. He knew what she wanted of him, what he was still unprepared to give.

Turning her on her back, Erik caught her wrists, entwined his fingers with hers, and pushed back, raising himself above her as he drove himself into her. He did not seek her surrender. He did not want to conquer her as she did him.

He settled for her repletion.

And he watched her beneath him, heard her soft

cries of gratification before he took her pleasure and made it his own. His head bowed, his hair lapped at her breast as he drew her into his mouth. Instinctively she wrapped her legs around his hips, pulling him deeper still. With a final thrust, he poured himself into her, a deep growl coming from within his chest. His passion spent, he collapsed against his elbows.

Her arms around him, he listened to the muffled beat of his own heart, the sound of the wind and rain, and wondered what was happening to him.

"Did you really come to the decision to wed me when we were standing in the hallway at Sommershorn Abbey?" she asked some time later. "That day you came to ask me about the fossils?"

He raised up to look down at her in the dying firelight. "You answered the elemental question I went to the Abbey to ask."

She pushed against him to see into his face, but he kissed her on the forehead, a tender kiss. "Did you still want me? I asked myself," he said.

His penis had started to swell long before he breathed another kiss against her lips. "And you did," he said, proceeding to show her just how much.

Chapter 12

Erik skirted a grove of oaks and pines, pulling rein at the top of the wooded trail before descending nearer to the rushing river. The sound of it blocked out all noise, but he watched several elk drift slowly out of the wash and continue past him. He could dimly see the tracks left by another horse ahead of him. The trail wound around the glade and continued to the levee work site. There were a few scattered clumps of dead trees and debris where the river, during a storm last year, had swept away the road that once used to be here.

After another mile, he dismounted in front of a thatched cottage and tied his horse to a hitching post. His eyes settled on the single gray Arabian, chewing on a clump of wild grass. Normally the paddock behind him would be filled with horses. But work on the levee had halted this spring. Those few non-superstitious individuals who chose to remain lived in the large lodging quarters a half mile away. This cottage was where Erik worked when he was present at the site.

The door opened and a woman stepped outside.

"Lara," he said, holding the note she had sent him that morning. A note that had pulled him away from lunch and one that he had not been pleased to receive.

Her black silk gown swished with her hesitant movements. Black netting lay across her upper face and attached to her hat rim. Erik could not remember seeing her in anything other than black or dark blue for seven years.

Lara Maxwell, with her blond hair and blue eyes, was still a pretty woman. But all her life her younger sister, Elizabeth, in both appearance and personality, had overshadowed her.

Where Elizabeth had been like vibrant sunlight, all passion and flair and heat when she walked into a room, Lara had been much like a single burning candle, warm and inviting, but barely noticeable next to her sister.

Erik might have married Lara Maxwell had Elizabeth not returned that year from Paris, blowing into Sedgwick like a firestorm after her years living away at a school in France.

Lara opened the door for him to follow her. "I am so glad you came."

He grabbed her arm. "What is this note about?"

She looked over his shoulder as if expecting to see they were not alone. "I apologize for the subterfuge but I needed to speak to you in private."

"Why? You are welcome at Sedgwick Castle. We don't need to be meeting like this."

"Yes, we do. Please, can we go inside? There is a chill in the air."

Erik followed her into the cottage. His eyes took in the desk and wooden filing cabinets. Her reticule and gloves lay on the desk next to a standish. Other than the fact that the curtains had been opened to allow in sunlight, nothing had been moved or changed since he had been here last week. She had not even lit a lamp. Yet, he had the feeling she had been here a long time, waiting for him.

She fumbled through her reticule and pulled out a folded sheaf of paper. "I apologize for the subterfuge, I truly do. I needed to warn you. This came to our house yesterday. I intercepted it before Papa found it."

Erik took the letter and unfolded the sheaf, frowning as he read the words.

> Please be well, Papa, and stop looking for me. I am content and so very happy for the first time in my life. I know you continue to worry. I am asking that you do not. Please let me be in peace. I have been and always will be your loving daughter.
>
> — E

A chill went down Erik's spine. Then fury.

"Can you now understand why I do not want Papa to see this, Erik? Whoever is playing such a cruel hoax will only kill him. This is the second one in as many months we've received."

"Why haven't I been informed? Who else knows about this?"

"No one knows. Not even my brother. I came here directly this time. I couldn't tell you before because it was too horrible and I thought someone only wanted to hurt Papa. Then this one came yesterday."

"Lara," he said cautiously, "you do understand this is not your sister?"

Tears welled in her blue eyes. "In my heart, I know it to be true. But it's her handwriting, Erik. *Look!* People still claim to see her. *Why* must we be tortured in this way? I don't understand the cruelty."

"My guess is blackmail."

"Papa is desperate to believe she is still alive, that is

true, but we have no money to pay anyone for information about Elizabeth."

"Do you have the first letter?"

She shook her head. "No, I burned it at once. Are you going to give this one to the constable?"

"Is that what you want me to do?"

"No. But it frightens me. Have you considered what this can do to *you*?"

"I have always told you I can take care of myself, Lara."

She dabbed at one corner of her eye with her knuckle. "But you have taken the blame for everything already and paid for it dearly. I would not be responsible for hurting you again. Especially now that you have been forced by circumstance to remarry."

He shoved the letter in his jacket pocket. "Circumstance?"

"Everyone knows you need a son." She ducked her chin as she pulled on her gloves. "You must endeavor to introduce her to Sedgwick at the country fair next month. You have not been in seven years. It will be good to let people know you are among the living again. You have suffered long enough."

"Have I?"

Since most believed he was responsible for Elizabeth's disappearance, he doubted people considered he'd suffered at all. Other than business, he had not been received in anyone's house in seven years. Unfortunately, most of those who would cut him directly in public also needed his money, including Lara's father.

Lara pressed her cheek to his shoulder. "Papa is wrong, Erik. You could never have killed my sister. I know that you still love her and feel much guilt over what happened. It was never your fault."

Erik put his hands on Lara's shoulders. It was just such an occasion as this that Elizabeth had walked in on seven years ago. The only *guilt* he felt now was in allowing himself to take responsibility for an incident that was no incident at all. Erik gently pulled Lara from his arms. "You need to go home. As it is, you will barely get back before dark."

He walked her outside to her horse. "From now on if you have something to tell me, do so at Sedgwick Castle. Understand? We've nothing to hide."

She nodded and adjusted her hat atop her tightly coiffed hair. "Except that letter. Please don't let that letter find its way to Papa."

Erik gave her a leg up onto the saddle. She adjusted her leg over the horn. "You have been my closest friend, Erik. I don't know how I would have survived these past years without you."

"The guilt was never yours to carry either, Lara. Let it go."

Erik's mouth tightened as he watched her ride away, then went inside the cottage. He walked to the hearth and lit a fire among the peat, disposing of the letter in the flames.

He hadn't told Lara that he'd also received such a letter some weeks ago, shortly after his return from London. Clearly, whoever was doing this was not satisfied with Erik's inaction, and now wanted to provoke Elizabeth's father. Someone wanted people to believe Elizabeth was alive. Why?

After spending most of the afternoon with Aunt Sophie and toiling over her notebook detailing observations she'd taken about the cliffs and surrounding terrain, Christine gave up trying to work. Erin was napping when Christine went to the nursery. It was too late in the day to venture outside. Becca and the housekeeper had trekked to the village earlier, but Christine had not gone with them. Not so much because her backside was still tender from the hours she'd spent last week bouncing on the back of an ill-gaited mare, or last night in bed, but because Erik would be gone until nightfall and this was an opportune time to explore unhindered.

Christine found the library. After walking across a carpeted room and opening the heavy brocade draperies to the early evening twilight, she turned.

Erik's refuge was a throwback to history, an antiquated museum of Scottish artifacts and furnishings, from the inlaid baroque tables to the medieval chairs. She picked up a compass, then set it down. She slid a finger along the beveled edge of the mahogany desk. The top of the desk was empty of clutter and in perfect order, much like his household.

She pulled open the drawers, not sure what she was hoping to find. Secrets. Something no one else knew about him perhaps.

In the bottom drawer, her hand paused on a worn copy of C. A. Sommers's book, *No Beast of Myth*. In London, Becca had said Erik had read the book.

She started to lift it, then edged it aside. Erik's drawings were stacked neatly beneath the book. Architectural sketches. They were good, she thought, as she flipped through two dozen images of building designs in various stages of completion. Some looked years old. Most were unfinished, as if he'd reached a certain point in each, then stopped.

She had never pictured Erik as an artist of any kind. Artists seemed to be sensitive, emotional people. Not that she'd known many, but she'd followed Aunt Sophie to art fairs in Devonshire and Greenwich and had met some of those cheerless few who spilled their passions all over a canvas for the world to see. People who were far braver than she was.

She touched his charcoal pencils and tablets, then, resettling everything back in the drawers, Christine slumped in the high-back chair behind his desk.

Other than the drawings, she'd found nothing, no letters or personal correspondence, no secret notes tucked away in false-bottom drawers, no hidden clues that might reveal an undiscovered character trait. He was much as she saw him, his personal life like his business dealings. All the pieces fit together like cogs in a wheel and ran like a well-greased machine. Nothing was out of place.

As her gaze shifted to the mahogany shelves filled with books that encased three walls from top to bottom, she rose to her feet and, setting her hands on her hips, looked from one end of the room to the other. She wondered if there was anything in the world Erik did not have. "You must have every book ever written for the last thousand years, my laird."

"Not every book," Boris said from the doorway. He carried a tea tray. "I saw you coming this way, mum. You did not eat much at lunch and I thought you might need refreshment."

"Thank you, Boris," she said as he set the tray on Erik's desk.

Although bent with time and arthritis, he was still a tall man, and Christine found herself looking up at him. She smiled. "You aren't by chance making sure I am not doing anything untoward in here, are you?"

"No, mum. If Lord Sedgwick wanted to keep you out, he would lock the door and the drawers," he added, clearly ignoring the heat in her cheeks as he poured a cup of tea. "Have you had the opportunity to see all the estate, yet?"

Accepting a cup of tea, she laughed. "Good heavens, no. I have barely seen the entire floor where my apartments are."

"It can be rather daunting, mum."

With the exception of Annie, most of the servants avoided her. She did not imagine it was out of rudeness, for servants did not mingle with their masters—or masters' wives—but still it was nice to have a conversation with someone familiar with Sedgwick Castle.

She observed the room. "Lord Sedgwick must love to read."

"He is well-read, mum. When one grows up as an only child in a world filled with doting servants, one learns to entertain oneself. This has always been his favorite room at Sedgwick since he was a boy."

She looked at the cases, filled with the finest, rarest books in the world, all behind glass, and knew most were too rare and valuable and not touched in centuries. In truth, any normal person would be a little intimidated by this room. But then Erik was not a normal person.

"You have been with this family a long time, Boris?"

He returned his attention to the tray as he folded a serviette. "I was here when his grace first come to Scotland, mum. A nipper he was. No one knew the kind of steel inside that lad. When he was twelve, he discharged most of the staff for slovenly and disorderly behavior. I am one of the few that remained."

"And were the others disorderly and slovenly?"

"Yes, mum. The last Sedgwick duke was a wastrel and allowed the household to go into disrepair. Most of them underestimated their new master."

"Because he was young?"

"Because he was a Sedgwick. His grace's predecessor did much to continue the Sedgwick tradition of drinking and carousing. The bloke rode off into the woods one icy night and got himself killed when his horse broke its leg. We found the duke near the road, where he had frozen to death. Despite what people continue to think about the current Sedgwick duke, the master has done much to turn the estate around."

"He never speaks about his mother," she found herself asking.

"And he won't," Boris said. "There was bad blood between him and Lady Rebecca's da, his stepfather. Lord Sedgwick discovered he was stealing from this estate's coffers. Then one night the man was drunk and his grace caught him beating his mam. Sedgwick nearly killed him. He got himself an undeserved reputation that night."

"That is why people claim him violent and capable of murder?"

"His mam did nothing to dispel the rumor. Lady Rebecca's da is dead now, but his grace never forgave his mother for staying with the wastrel and supporting him over her own son when he took the man to court to remove him as tutelary of this estate."

Boris said nothing more. After a moment, he brushed off his hands. "Is there a book you fancy, mum?"

She remembered *No Beast of Myth* lying in Erik's desk, its presence reminding her of her purpose for coming to Sedgwick. "Since you are here and I am trying to find my way around, maybe you can help me locate Lady Rebecca's fossil collection."

Christine followed Boris through the bailey to the glass hothouse. She had never been back here and welcomed the fragrant breeze against her face, the scent of loam heavy in the air. "Most people do not come out here," he said, leading her past a row of planter boxes, explaining that the fossils were kept here because of the dirt that usually accompanied their find, and because many of the servants found it a near sacrilege to have dead things in the house.

Boris brought Christine to the back, where wooden shelves lined the walls. Dim moonlight filtered from a row of skylights in the ceiling. He set the lamp on the workbench. There were close to a hundred fossils lining the shelves. After a while Boris must have left her. Christine did not hear him go.

The find was incredible.

She had not discovered this many bones in one place, even at Lyme Regis, where she had found her very first iguanodon bone. What made these special is that most were not imbedded in rock.

She balanced the fossil of a tooth in her hand against the one Erik had brought her in London.

And she was swept backward in time as old dreams came rushing back, assailed her, as she recalled the first excitement she'd ever felt as her father's student. What? Twenty years ago? It didn't matter: her life had always been about discovery, discovery at its core. A thing found through uncovering secrets buried under dust and time.

Time had always meant nothing to her, until she'd run out of it and she'd ended up losing her father and her dreams, and then Erik came along with this pot of gold beneath his rainbow. But if someone came to her now and asked what she wanted most in the world, would her mind grab on to the mystery she was holding in the palms of her hands? The discovery of something never uncovered or encountered before. Or that which had once been discovered and lost.

Christine set out a canvas cloth and laid the bigger fossils on it. She would need to mark where each had been found. Gathering up the treasure, she doused the lamp, then made her way outside the hothouse. Night had fallen while she'd been inside. She was not paying attention to her steps as she rounded a corner and collided with Becca.

Both of them fell backward, shocked, but for entirely different reasons.

Becca looked so petrified that Christine felt her surprise fade and now looked behind Becca in the darkness. Erik's sister had not come from the direction of the bailey. "Are you just returning from the village? I thought Mrs. Brown was with you today."

"Oh. We returned from the village hours ago."

Christine studied Rebecca's appearance more carefully, noting the heavy cloak and gloves one might wear for a long walk in the evening. Behind Christine was the stable. "You aren't sneaking out, are you?"

Becca's laugh sounded forced. "Of course not." She peered down into Christine's arms. "You've been to the hothouse to study the rest of the fossil collection. Well?" she nervously prompted when Christine was not convinced by whatever act Becca was performing. "What do you think?" Becca asked.

"That if you were going someplace you would think twice about breaking your brother's trust. A young lady sneaking about in the night, no matter how innocent she thinks it is . . . is never harmless to those who care for her."

Rebecca's shoulders slumped. "He worries so. He still thinks I am a child."

"You are not a child. I think *that* is what worries him."

"I was only walking to the lake."

Christine peered up at the moon, then over her shoulder at the lake. "Then take Hampton or someone with you. You could fall and break an ankle."

"Now you sound like Erik. I am not to go to the river. I am not to remain in London. I am not to have a Season. I am to have no life and no friends. I am surprised he allows me out of my chambers." Folding her arms, Becca sighed. "All right. I will go another night, and not alone."

It wasn't all right, but Christine let the topic drop for now.

"You have an excellent fossil collection," Christine said. "Why don't we go inside, and you can tell me where you found them all."

Erik found Christine later that night sitting at a table in her bedroom, awash in amber light, the map spread out in front of her, distracted as if she'd lost herself in thought that had nothing to do with the fossils piled on the floor beside the chair. The pencil in her hand tapped impatiently against the table's edge.

Leaning against the doorway, he watched her and wondered at her thoughts. "Boris informed me that you asked Hampton about ropes and that you had gone through your trunks, preparing climbing gear," Erik said, startling her from her reverie. "Can you really do as you said? Climb cliffs?" he asked.

"Yes."

Beast bumped his legs. Erik had been tripping over the cat since Christine's arrival at Sedgwick. He lifted the one-eyed tom. He'd never had a pet. Wasn't sure what to do with a cat. Christine seemed to love this one.

But before he could figure out how to make the capricious thing purr, the cat was plucked from his arms, and Christine held it protectively against her, scratching his whiskers until the feline's purrs rumbled loudly.

Erik leaned a shoulder against the doorjamb. For an absurd moment, he saw himself as the world must see him in the face of that ugly cat.

"I hope you do not intend to stop me from going, Erik."

"No, *leannanan*. I intend to go with you."

Chapter 13

Erik watched Christine pause ahead of him, her mouth taut in concentration as she studied the ground, the waterfall roaring behind them. She lifted her head and saw him sitting against a moss-covered rock, one knee drawn up to his chest, admiring the scenery she presented.

Her chignon pinned in a thick ball at her nape and her eyeglasses gave her a bookish look, a direct contrast to the uncivilized Scottish backdrop that framed her.

Looking pointedly at their gear dispersed over the ground, she said, "You are in charge of setting up camp, Erik." She stepped past him and began rummaging through one of the rucksacks.

He edged up her skirts with his riding quirt, looking to glimpse the trousers beneath.

She sidestepped him and placed her hands on her hips. "Obeying orders from one of your minions is a novelty I am sure, but I warned you before you decided to send Hampton back yesterday, those are the rules."

He held up his hands in mock surrender and climbed to his feet. "My will is yours to command."

"Good." She brushed dirt off her hands and pointed

to the hill. "Now I need you to carry all of our things up those rocks over there. Unless you would prefer that I ride back and get Hampton for the heavy lifting."

He peered doubtfully up the hill and tipped back his floppy felt hat. He'd sent Hampton back because he'd decided he preferred to do this little outing alone with his wife, even if it meant lugging about every knapsack on their packhorse from here to the peak of the highest crag.

"And while you are doing that"—she released the ties at her waist and dropped her skirts, revealing her trousers—"I am going to look for a place to drive a stake into the ground."

There was nothing bookish about his wife, he considered, as he watched her walk toward the rock ledge. She was a woman in her element, and he'd spent three days playing guide and lackey, basking in the surprising pleasantries found in allowing her to take control. She had proven capable.

In fact, when he'd embarked upon this expedition, as she'd called it, he hadn't known what he'd expected.

This morning they had ventured off the road where his work crew had repaired the pothole that had crashed their carriage weeks ago. He and Christine had followed the drover's trail along the river's path. At breakfast, she had droned on and on about her plans for the next few days, frustrated that yesterday the riverbank had not yielded one secret in the two miles she had walked, any more than the cliffs had surrendered anything the day before that. She had sighted a cave this morning near the falls and they had spent most of the day reaching a point in the hills where she could climb down to explore the opening in the rock face. Without comment, he'd followed.

"This is not an exact science," she'd explained, as if he'd considered it otherwise, and he could tell she was excited about the cave.

After he finished setting up camp, she found him. She carried a thick coil of rope wound over her shoulder and an iron stake in the other hand. "I found someplace to put this," she said.

He slid the stake from her hand. "As long as it is not through my heart, love."

She laughed. "As if you would allow it, *love*."

She turned on her heel. He bent and picked up the sledgehammer lying among the other tools and followed her. She took him down a talus slope, dropped the rope, and instructed him to place the spike within the iron circlet she had already laid out on a specific place in the soil. Then she walked about ten feet, stood on a vertical wall of stone and looked down.

"The cave is thirty feet below us, if you'd like to see." She peered over her shoulder at him. "Chimney sweeps climb more dangerous heights than this," she said as if that knowledge should reassure him.

Chimney sweeps did not hang above a wall of crushing water.

Erik drove the iron stake into the ground with one swing of the sledgehammer. "I'll take your word for it."

She returned to his side and began looping rope through the iron circlet. "I am looking for a way into an underground cavern or lava tubes," she explained. "From the trajectory of all Becca's fossils and the human bones found along the river, we are in the right area." Her hands paused. "We crossed the old drover trail that leads to St. Andrews. Would Elizabeth have had a reason to come up to this area?"

"Inferring that she could have *reached* this area on

foot in winter? I no longer know what to think," Erik said.

"Have you considered if we do find her . . . ?"

"That I will give the constable ammunition to charge me with her murder? Or perhaps she despised marriage to me so much she chose to kill herself instead. I have already been condemned, Christine," he said simply. "Or have you not yet grasped that the real beast of Sedgwick shares your bed, my love?"

She reached up to touch his face; his hand intercepted hers. His action was not unkind, but neither did he welcome anything construed as sympathy. Not from her. He brought her hand to his lips. "We have a few hours of daylight left," he said. "We don't want to waste time."

She looked over his shoulder at the position of the sun. "When I get to the bottom, I will signal you," she said, having taught him how to belay and rappel yesterday on a less dangerous cropping of rocks. "Then you will bring up the rope and follow."

Holding firmly with one hand, she pulled a double length of rope between her legs and smiled up at him, that brilliant burning sunlight grin that never failed to heat him. "Did I ever tell you I once climbed up the side of our very tall house carrying an urn of tarantulas to my wicked governess? This is easy compared to that."

Christine went over the edge and, as she held the belay with one hand, he watched as she worked her way carefully down the rock face. She'd been a climber when he'd known her ten years ago, he mused, remembering she'd somehow talked him into scaling a tree outside her window at Somerset. The year he'd gone to Somerset House to wed her cousin.

He'd been twenty-four, a duke, and he'd sat on a topmost limb risking his life, stargazing with a woman who hadn't had the good sense to stay away from him. That night they'd talked about constellations. With whom had he ever talked about the stars? No one, he considered. Not before or since that night.

His eyes on Christine, he wondered jealously if she'd talked constellations with Darlington—or any other man for that matter.

He called down to her, "You told me you've climbed cliffs with Darlington."

"He taught me to climb years ago. It's all the rage these days," he heard her say. "There are climbing clubs all about Europe. Naturally, women can't climb, so are not allowed membership."

"Naturally," Erik murmured as she disappeared inside the cave and signaled for him to descend.

He didn't have to do this, he told himself as he pulled up the rope, then double wound the length between his legs and over his shoulder. Before he could question what the hell he was doing, he backed off the cliff.

The cave entrance was an outward slope, slanting downward about six feet before a wall of rubble blocked the descent. When Erik entered, he found Christine squatting in front of the crumbled rock, frowning with disappointment.

By the look of the mix of crushed granite, bird droppings, and dust that layered the floor and walls, the cave-in was not recent. He could see evidence of habitation, the remnants of an old fire, a rusted mace. But if this cave had ever led to a larger cavern as she'd hoped to discover, it had not been in this century.

Clearly, Christine was disappointed. She had worked hard and had held high hopes. The sun was a giant orange ball in the sky, hovering just below the misty line where the distant lake met the sky by the time they had finished their climb back to the ridge. Erik found her sitting on the rocks in a shallow wading pool, washing her hands and legs and feet. She had stripped out of her clothes—all remnants of Christine the paleontologist gone—and wore only her shift.

The ancient mace she had brought up from the cave lay beside the rocks. It was a heavy medieval war club, missing half its spikes and mottled with age and rust, yet she'd protected and coddled it as she did that dreadful cat of hers.

He squatted beside her as she continued to scrub. "I know you are disappointed."

"Don't coddle me, Erik."

"Look at me, Christine."

She scrubbed her arms more vigorously. "I must be missing something."

"Searching for a forgotten or never-before-discovered cavern in a land where long ago, Picts and outlaw Scots' survival depended on knowing the whereabouts of such caves is a forbidding task for anyone."

He was not expecting miracles.

Nor had he expected to enjoy himself or to stay three nights encamped beneath a sky full of stars with Sedgwick Castle only a few hours away. But he *had* remained.

"Do you think me odd? You must," she said. "You have been patiently following me, taking my orders for days and we haven't a fossil to show for our efforts."

"I think you are *the* most interesting individual I have ever known."

It was the greatest compliment he could pay her, he realized, for her expression became less guarded. *Interesting* implied someone special, out of the ordinary and relevant. She was also passionate and loyal.

"This mace must be three hundred years old," she said after a moment, lifting it to examine it more thoroughly in the fading sunlight.

She could see by the amused look in his eyes that he conceived the piece worthless. "I have never understood the public's infatuation with antiquity, the need to reach out and touch a long-dead past, as if it could give meaning to the present," he said. "I don't understand it."

"You must have *something* you are passionate about."

"Aye." He laughed quietly, studying her face, noticing the smattering of freckles across her nose, before he looked away.

"I understand the value of this land in a different way," he said. "I look at it as a way of sustaining lives. Not just mine, but also thousands of others who live in this valley."

"Tell me, your grace," she asked, "do you *do* anything for merriment? Something with no purpose other than the pursuit of your leisure?"

Do you? he'd wanted to ask, for she seemed less adept at having fun than he did. "I'm here with you."

The sun was at her back, a light so powerful it silhouetted her body through the thin transparency of her shift. "This mace belongs in a museum," she said, clearly appreciating the bit of history this represented to Sedgwick, even if he did not understand the sentiment.

Instead, he kissed her.

He was not an archeologist or paleontologist. He did not seek his fortune in fame though infamy often found him.

He only knew as she opened her mouth and deepened the contact between them, her touch did not so much defeat him as it conquered him utterly.

But even as she drew him deeper into the sensuous fantasy swelling between them, he felt her pull back and raise her head. Their warm breath mingled until at last his thumb slid beneath her jaw and tipped her face up.

"I know you dislike being thanked," she said. "But thank you for believing in me."

In the beginning, he'd carried all the gear because it amused him to do so. Then as the days had passed, he had done it because he enjoyed being outside the walls of his life, watching Christine work, enjoying Sedgwick in a way he'd never allowed himself to do before.

He'd learned he could roam these grounds for a hundred years and still not discover all the treasures buried beneath his feet.

"Do you believe in magic, Erik?" he heard her ask against his lips as he carried her back to their camp and laid her on the blankets.

"Hmm," he said, shifting her body against him. "As they say, one man's charm is another's curse."

Her eyes opened. "Who says that?"

A shudder that was more than desire went through his body. "I do."

He brushed his fingertips against the cool tips of her wet hair before he drew his hand over her breast and down to the dampness between her legs. He touched her everywhere with his hands and his lips.

Somehow her fingers laced with his. Then he was pressing into her, filling her, merging his body with hers until he was so deeply joined to her that it no longer mattered whose mouth kissed, whose hands touched. There was only her.

And above them the night stars shone and the sound of the rushing waterfall faded in the rhythm of her breath against his lips.

Later he held her, and she talked about tomorrow.

But in the days that followed the river continued to run too high to safely venture on its banks, and he knew until it receded they would most likely find nothing new.

Christine flung open the large double windows in her sitting room and stared across a sun-dappled valley stretching out before her beyond the high stone castle walls. She could barely make out the colorful tents in the distance. The summer festival had arrived in the valley.

She'd been told that the fair came every year at this time and though it was not a grand party thrown for her, she found herself hoping that it might feel that way.

A line of honking geese flew overhead, and Christine watched them until they dwindled to pale specks in a bright blue sky. At least the day was warm. "Your grace," Annie said from behind her. "Lord Sedgwick wishes to know what has detained you."

Christine turned back into the room. This was the third time in the past hour she had been summoned by her husband. She made one final stop in front of the long silvered glass. She wore a dress of bright green crepe de chine stripes. Her hair was too thick to lie in perfect curls atop her head and Annie had folded it under and pinned it in a roll at her nape.

Erik might accept their attendance today at the festivities as commonplace, but Christine did not. She had spent yesterday making sure she wore the right gown and had changed it twice already this morning. This from a woman who had made her one sensational splash during her only London Season by wearing black to her debut ball, because she thought the color made her look regal.

"Mum, your cloak," Annie said, rushing from the dressing room carrying the garment. "The sun may be out, but the air can still be a bit nippy."

She accepted the cloak over her shoulders. "Thank you, Annie."

Aunt Sophie, Mrs. Samuels, and Rebecca had already gone ahead. She and Erik would be arriving at the festivities in the official Sedgwick coach.

Sweeping around the corner and appearing on the landing, she saw her husband pacing at the bottom of the stairs. They both came to a stop, his hand on the carved knoll of the banister. His eyes slid over her appreciatively.

Her eyes widened. *Good heavens!*

Her husband was not dressed in any such English garb as mundane as hers. Standing below her was a powerful laird. Erik wore a breathtaking tartan of hunter green, ancient red, and black, trimmed in tassels of gold. The pleated kilt reached his knees and was finished off by a sporran and a ceremonial waistcoat and jacket trimmed with gold buttons. All he lacked was a claymore and battle-ax.

The man was magnificent.

He held out his hand. "The festivities await, madam."

She glided downstairs on slippers she worried would begin pinching her feet before the afternoon was gone. "Your grace," she said softly and dipped in a playfully regal curtsey. "You look . . ."

"Like a laird?"

"Indeed, you do. We don't match. Am I dressed correctly?"

"Do I sense doubt in your tone?" He sounded astonished, as if she had never doubted herself. "You look charming, Christine."

She wanted to be beautiful to him. "I am only slightly ignorant of fashion, which makes me somewhat less than knowledgeable. But Aunt Sophie's London modiste assured me this gown is the top of fashion. I would not wish to embarrass you, Erik."

She had removed her spectacles, and he eased them out of her gloved hand and returned them to her nose. "Put them back on if they help you see," he said. "You will pass just fine as you are."

He could say that with casualness. Erik was the master of all he surveyed, after all. He had been the duke here since he was two.

Yet, for the first time since being a girl in her teens, she found herself willing to remove her spectacles and be blind rather than be different from everyone else. She should have worn blue rather than green. Or something less extravagant. Or English.

The carriage ride to the large hamlet of Sedgwick some miles away took less than an hour. She had visited the market and shops here over the last month, but today it was as if she were seeing the thatched cottages, brown chocolate-box houses, and winding streets for the first time. People stopped to stare as the carriage rumbled down the narrow cobbled main street and, as the coach and four slowed to a more sedate pace, she better glimpsed the faces of those who lined the road. Not all seemed welcoming.

She stole a nervous glance at her husband sitting quietly on the bench beside her. "It is not you they dislike," he said.

She would almost have preferred that it *was* her they disliked or mistrusted. Erik did not deserve it. This past month had taught her that much. "How long has it been since you have been to the fair?" she asked.

"I have not been in seven summers. I thought perhaps it was time I finally introduce you to Sedgwick. You needn't worry for me, Christine."

She smoothed the folds of her expensive cloak, one that Erik had presented to her only last week, and touched the diamond bobs in her ears and the one that lay above her breasts, feeling very much a lady of consequence.

She had been receiving many gifts these past weeks and now understood a little more why. None of the gifts had to do with any desire Erik might have to put her on display. Indeed, unlike his generous marriage contract, these gifts were not tied to promises or partnerships or to the passion they shared in bed. These were more personal. He did not so much *expect* her to like the gifts, as he *wanted* her to like them. He was seeking something deeper from her in the only way he knew. And it was suddenly *she* who did not feel worthy of *his* affection.

A line had formed by the time they reached the fairgrounds. Erik helped her down from the carriage and they both turned and faced the silence of the crowd. He introduced her to neighboring landowners, business associates, tenants, sheep farmers. He knew everyone in some form or another, though he seemed close to no one. His solitude had never been more evident, and she wondered at the boy he had been, growing up here. He never talked about his childhood.

But the day remained warm and the sky bright blue and free of clouds. Soon the novelty of the Sedgwick duke's presence faded and the crowd returned to their entertainment. Christine continued her tour of the enormous fairgrounds, walking among the people on her husband's arm. They watched an opera rendition of something that might have been Macbeth. She didn't care that at the end, she was the only one who clapped.

Erik paid them well for their performance, and as the afternoon wore on there was jousting, dancing, and games to attend. Jugglers and acrobats moved among the crowd.

The evening crowd was a mixture of members of high society, lower-born individuals, and dozens of barefooted children who laughed and followed the ropedancers as they wound through the busy aisles. Hundreds of booths were set up to sell wares. Woolens, leather, copper, and trinkets were all displayed.

In the background of it all, like a historical tapestry, Sedgwick Castle sat on the distant hill bathed in the glow of a misty sunset, an ancient reminder of the people's fealty to their laird, and his to the land that supported them all.

Erik watched her now in that way of his that made her wish she could read his thoughts. A frisson of lightning seemed to shimmer between them.

"Would you care to join me in a high-stepping rigadoon?" he asked.

Christine looked past him at the dancers as musicians played their lutes and pipes, inviting others to join the circle with carefree abandon.

"I would love to dance."

Erik took her hand. She was not an experienced dancer, but tonight her toes tapped to the tune of the beat as if she had spent her life dancing, and her eyes sparkled with delight. Shoulder to shoulder she went with her husband to the beat of the music. Her feet flew. Her laughter sounded, drawing the curious gaze of bystanders as many stopped to watch their laird. But Christine didn't notice.

She couldn't remember another time in her life when she'd enjoyed dancing this much. When the music changed, so did their tempo. The fire seemed to grow stronger and hotter. She looked into her husband's sherry eyes and felt the same burning heat where his gaze touched. They stayed the evening among the dancers until neither of them could spring another step.

"You dance well," she said, breathless, when they stepped away into the cooler shadows an hour later, away from the light of the fire and many of those who had stopped to watch them.

He did not reply and Christine had a feeling he had not danced in years either. Perhaps he'd even surprised himself that he still could.

"Ah, Sedgwick." A voice turned her.

A balding middle-aged man, possessed of an impressive set of whiskers and mustache, stood next to the penny beer tent as if he'd been waiting for Erik to see him, and when that failed he finally summoned up the courage to step forward. A smile on his face, he swept up Christine's hand and muttered that he was pleased to meet her. "Lady Sedgwick. Ye be lovely if I say so myself."

Erik smiled and introduced the older gentleman as a neighboring farmer who bred the finest hunters outside of Ireland. Bowing his head in gratitude, the man lightly clicked his boot heels. "Thank you, your grace." He rolled his r's with gusto. "And to that point, I have brought the prized mare ye were interested in looking over," the gent said. "Do ye like horses, Lady Sedgwick?"

She didn't have the heart to tell him that horses were only one rung above a camel on her favored list of temperamental hairy quadrupeds with large teeth. She liked her Miss Pippen. "Of course," she said. "Who does not enjoy a great mount?"

The moment she said the words, she felt the rise of heat. She stole a glance at her husband, but at that moment, she thought she saw Lady Rebecca duck between two vendor tents.

Ever since they'd collided outside the hothouse, Becca had been acting strangely. She was supposed to be with Aunt Sophie.

"Go on," she told Erik, glad for an excuse to escape a visit to the tent housing the horses. "If you will excuse me, I'd like to check up on my aunt."

Erik grabbed her arm, his touch startling her. He looked over his shoulder.

"Go," Christine said quietly, when it looked as if he might argue with her. "I will find you after I have eaten a candied apple."

With that pronouncement, she swept through the crowd after his sister.

Chapter 14

Christine lost Becca in the crowd. But she did find Aunt Sophie tippling near the whisky barrels.

"She be buying her own keg," Mrs. Samuels said, wrapping her shawl about her ample bosom. "But first she 'as to taste everything from 'ere to kingdom come. We've already been 'ere most of the night."

Christine peered worriedly at her aunt. Mrs. Samuels patted Christine's arm. "Ye don't be worryin' about Lady Sophia, mum. I won't let her wander off and get lost."

"Have you seen where Lady Rebecca has got off to?"

"That child be a handful of trouble, mum. She went into the woods 'bout ten minutes ago."

"Alone?"

"Yes, mum."

Christine walked a goodly distance through a copse of firs away from the noise. Needles cluttered the ground and cushioned her step with a pungent evergreen fragrance. Alarmed, she stopped when she glimpsed a horse and buggy through the trees.

Lady Rebecca stood near a pagoda with an older, fashionably dressed woman wearing royal-blue velvet and a wide hat that dipped to the side of her head.

The woman's hair was coifed in a plaited bun at her nape. Both women turned as Christine walked into the clearing.

Erik's sister visibly started. Her hand went to her breast. "Christine . . ."

"Rebecca."

The other woman did not move. Closer up, the woman's features were more distinguishable. By the tilt of her eyes and shape of her mouth, she looked remarkably like Becca. In fact, Becca introduced the woman as the Countess Sutherland, her mam. "Oh, please don't tell my brother you saw me with her," Becca pleaded, then promptly wrapped her arms around her mother's waist. "Mam is here to see me. That is all. Not to cause trouble. Please, you must promise not to tell Erik."

"Becca . . ."

"My daughter is right to be concerned," the countess replied, her arms tightening around Becca. "My son will not countenance my presence here."

Her heart thudding, Christine stared from daughter to mother, and suddenly felt sick. This was *not* what Christine had expected to walk into. "Why the subterfuge, my lady? You are her mam. Simply come to Sedgwick."

"She can't," Becca quietly said. "They do not get along."

Christine's gaze confronted the countess's with far less compassion than she'd felt a moment before. "You are his mother as well."

"Erik doesn't like complications. You will learn soon enough that everything must have its proper place in his life. Mine is in London, out of his way. If you tell him you saw me tonight, you will only make it harder on Becca by forcing her to defend me."

"Mam . . ." Becca whispered. "Please."

Christine's heart clenched. "Surely he will know you are here," she said. "This village is not so big that you will pass unnoticed."

The countess smiled. "I have not been to Sedgwick in fifteen years. Most do not know me. I am staying in a cottage across the lake." The countess took her daughter's hands into her own. "Go back. We have visited long enough."

"Find Lady Sophia," Christine said. "I will speak to you shortly."

Becca turned pleading eyes on Christine. "Please." A frown failed to detract from the fragility of her age or the beauty of her large brown eyes, which slanted upward from beneath delicately sweeping brows.

Christine remembered what Boris had told her. Erik and Rebecca did not share the same father. But remembering her own mother's abandonment, she suddenly did not want to see Rebecca suffer in the same way.

"Go now," Christine quietly said. "I won't say anything to your brother."

Rebecca pressed Christine's hands to her cheek. "Thank you."

After Becca reluctantly departed, the countess turned the full force of her attention to Christine. "I would warn you not to betray my son with a deception except that my daughter would only be hurt if he discovered hers. Rebecca is sixteen and still very much a child in many ways. She doesn't understand that there will never be any reconciliation between her brother and myself."

"Perhaps he has changed, my lady. Maybe you should offer to try."

"Erik is incapable of forgiveness. He has paid me a

great deal of money not to try. It is a simple thing to take his gifts, I suppose. He is a very difficult man to love."

Christine bit back an angry retort in defense of the man she had come to know very well. "I suggest you leave if you wish to keep your presence unknown to him."

Countess Sutherland walked past Christine to the buggy and turned, her gaze startlingly direct. "I was curious about the woman my son would marry after his torrid marriage to Elizabeth."

"And what have you discerned, my lady?"

The corner of her mouth crooked. "That you are not she."

That you are not she.

What the blazes did that cryptic nonsense mean?

Watching the countess climb into the buggy, Christine found herself frozen in place by her own misgivings. Erik deserved more, she thought, as she struggled with her own culpability. She had taken as much as anyone from him.

She turned to find her way back to the grounds before Erik set out looking for her, little realizing she had only been gone a half-hour. She found Aunt Sophie and Mrs. Smothers and asked them to take Rebecca back to Sedgwick. The night had not aged another five minutes by the time Christine found where the livestock was housed.

No one harassed her as she walked across the crowded grounds toward the large canvas tent erected to keep horses separated from the pigs, bulls, goats, sheep, and chickens. She finally found Erik near the last stall.

He saw her and beckoned her nearer. "I was beginning to wonder what happened to you." His gloved thumb brushed her bottom lip. "No candied apple?"

Christine shook her head. "No," she said. "I found Aunt Sophie by the whiskey kegs."

He chuckled, then before she could pull him away to a quiet corner, he raised his chin and nodded to someone behind her. She turned as a beautiful mare came into view. The man she had met earlier held the bridle, clearly having brought the high-stepping horse from the stall so Christine could examine her. She had never seen a more striking horse. She was nearly black and silky smooth with a coat that glistened in the lamplight.

"Do you like her?" Erik asked, watching her closely.

She met her husband's eyes. Then, realizing the mare's owner was holding the bit and anxiously awaiting her response, she said, "The mare is the most beautiful horse I've ever seen."

"She's yours if you want her."

She was too taken aback to respond or to hide her thoughts, as she looked at the mare. The horse *was* beautiful beyond compare. She had never seen its like.

"You don't have to do this, Erik," she said quietly. "I have Miss Pippen."

The creases around his mouth deepened. "You do not like the gift?"

"It isn't that." She folded her arms across her heart, and stared reflectively into his face. "Who would not love such a horse?"

He nodded to the man behind her. "Deliver the mare to my stables."

"Yes, your grace." The portly gentleman's cheerful reply tempered by a worried look in her direction, he led the mare away.

When she and Erik were alone, she faced her husband, "As I have told you before, you are most generous."

"I have insulted you. Why?"

"You have not insulted me. The last thing you have done is insult me."

"Christine . . ."

Whatever Erik had been about to say died as he looked up.

A man and woman stood next to the stall where the mare had once been. The pair wore simple clothes, but of a finer cut and cloth than the tenants and villagers she had met. The lantern light dappled the man's handsome visage. He was not much younger than she. The dark sweep of his hair dipped into a widow's peak and framed his face. He and Erik could have been related.

"Look who has come to our country fair, Lara," the man said to the woman beside him. "It has been a long time, Sedgwick."

Shaking off her trepidation, Christine remained next to her husband and waited for an introduction that did not come.

"Maxwell. Lara," Erik said.

"We have not yet had the pleasure, Lady Sedgwick," the other man said. "But if your husband won't introduce us, I will do the honors." He presented her a courtly bow that for all its mockery boasted of rank. "I am Lord Johnny Maxwell. This is my sister, Lady Lara. We live across yonder loch."

His was the estate she could see from her window. "Maxwell?"

"The Maxwells and Sedgwicks share a distant great-great-grandfather, and more. Elizabeth is our sister," Maxwell said, his eyes a clear blazing blue. "What your husband has neglected to say is that we are all family."

The fair-haired woman nodded at Christine. The woman's hair was too tightly coiled at her nape. She wore a dark blue dress devoid of lace or other adornments. Her appearance couldn't be more stark, but for one moment as she'd glanced at Erik, her face had come alive.

Erik moved behind Christine. "We were just leaving, Maxwell."

Maxwell stepped in front of Christine and she felt Erik's body tighten. Lara put a hand on Maxwell's arm. "Johnny—"

"Imagine our surprise to learn Sedgwick had not only found someone in London to wed him," the man continued, "but that he had done so in such an efficient manner. Like magic—" Maxwell snapped his fingers. "Poof. He has another wife." He stared shrewdly at Christine as if seeking the flaw that must be present in her character. "How much did you pay her to wed you, Sedgwick?"

Christine could only gape at the man's gall, as she stood shocked that he would bait Erik in such a manner, as if he expected—nay wanted—Erik to strike him. A sudden vision of bloodshed filled her mind.

But Erik did nothing.

Nothing.

Christine lacked the same restraint. But before she could reply, Erik's hand went beneath her elbow. Maxwell saw the movement and grinned. "Is it that you have no honor left for her to defend, Sedgwick? Or are you a coward who only takes his vengeance out on women?"

An audible gasp sounded from around Christine, and she realized there were others in the tent near the stalls.

Erik had not moved, yet his very stillness brought a hush down on them all and silenced his adversary. People nearby had started to back away as if they expected guns to be drawn. Whatever this confrontation was between the two men, it was not new and went beyond the bounds of hatred.

"Are you finished, Maxwell?" Erik asked.

"Am I? You tell me."

Lara suddenly turned into her brother's arms. "I want to go home now, Johnny. Please. Papa will wonder what has become of us."

Her panic evident to her brother, his expression suddenly softened. "It's all right, Lara."

She clutched at his waistcoat. "Please, let us go from here, Johnny. Before it is too late."

Johnny finally lifted his gaze. To Christine, he bowed gallantly. "We are the beggared in-laws, Lady Sedgwick. We are allowed certain liberties with our laird. Especially one who has not ventured among us in some time."

Thirty minutes later, she and Erik were in the carriage and crossing the bridge to Sedgwick Castle.

The carriage bounced over a rut, and his shoulder bumped hers. Turning her head, she peered up at Erik's profile. They had not spoken a single word since they'd left the tents. She'd been too angry. Tucked in her cloak, she looked outside.

"How could you allow him to humiliate you?" she asked without turning, looking at his reflection in the glass.

His arm braced on the back of the seat, he bent and turned down the lamp. "Worse has happened."

"Has it?" She faced him in the darkness. "Why would you not defend yourself?"

Why had he not defended *her*?

"Why, Erik? How could you have not felt anything at all?"

"Should I have called him out, Christine?" he said after a moment. "Would that make everything better?

Soothe injured feelings and sensibilities? A little blood-shed to cleanse the palate? If I called him out, one of us would die. Are words worth killing another man over? What is it you want?"

"What is it *you* want?" she flung at him. "No one should be allowed to insult you in such a manner. And you just let it happen. Why?"

Tears burned in her eyes, but she did not move to swipe them from her cheeks. She did not want him to see she was crying.

He was not even defending himself—even from her!

"Are we fighting, *leannanan*?"

The mockery in his tone was too much an affront.

But the depth of her feelings stunned her, not only because their argument left her hurt and confused, but also because she did not understand him. How could he not have defended himself? "You are either blind or a coward, Erik," she whispered. "You allowed Johnny Maxwell to make a fool of you."

A long, ugly silence followed and Christine regretted the words ere they left her lips. The carriage stopped and she realized they had arrived in the inner court-yard. No one had come to open the door.

"It appears we have arrived home, madam."

"Home?" she said in an unsteady voice. "Is that where we are?"

Most of the rooms were closed off and still covered in shrouds. He wouldn't allow her in the keep. He spent half his sleepless nights in the library. He was estranged from his mother, practically so from his sister whether he realized it or not. No one came to visit. "The only one who seems able to tolerate your behavior is your daughter."

His face hidden in the shadows, Erik opened the door. He stepped out easily, being of a height that did not require the use of a step. He set his hands on her waist and pulled her out of the carriage with little effort, his touch scalding her even through layers of fabric. She strode past him, only to have him snatch her arm and spin her about. "I am still your husband, Christine," his voice was soft, not with tenderness, but a warning she had never heard in his tone before.

"And you would think of me as chattel, like all your other possessions. You do not own me."

"Aye," he said, laughing. "But I can buy your services well enough. Tell me," his breath brushed her hair just above her temple, "what exactly did Maxwell say that was not the truth? Are you more embarrassed because he made a fool of me? Or because I did not grab up the gauntlet and slap him for you?"

Her face burned at the truth of his statement. He had turned her angry words inside out and flung them back at her where they pricked her with scorn. That was the crux of her anger. Her fury.

Johnny Maxwell had spoken the truth when he had asked how much Erik had paid to purchase her for his wife. But it was Erik who wounded her deeply.

She yanked her arm from his grasp. "If I were a man, I would have . . . I would have—"

"Shot him between the eyes? If you were a man, you would not be my wife and therefore would not be here at all, Christine. Darlington would. I could have hired him for a lot less trouble."

"Let go of me."

She would have struck him had he not been standing so close with his body pressed against hers. "Take my restraint as a wedding gift, my love. For had I touched Maxwell, I would have killed him in front of a dozen witnesses. Then a widow you would be when they hung me from the gallows for the cursed deed. Not even a laird or a peer of the realm is immune from the law when it comes to murder."

He let loose her arm and she stumbled back. Turning on her heel, she took the stairs. The door opened and she swept inside past Boris, caring little that she left her husband outside, staring at her back. She took the flight of steps to the second floor and found her way to her chambers. Her hands shook when she slipped the key into the lock and did the same for the other door. She didn't wait for Annie to help her undress. She slammed the door to her dressing room and wriggled out of her gown, and finally, garbed in her nightdress and robe, she pressed trembling fingers to her temple and berated her idiocy.

No light shone from beneath the door connecting her room to Erik's, but she heard him stirring inside. She should have been more circumspect with her temper, she thought, burying her face into her pillow.

Later, her eyes clear, she faced the door. But the only beast in the castle who came to her bed that night was her cat.

By early afternoon, the Sedgwick carriage had come to a stop at the end of the circular drive. Erik descended the coach. Absently clutching a lion-headed walking stick, he tipped up his hat as he peered at Eyre Hall.

Constructed of honey-colored stone and bleached gray by time, the once grand Eyre Hall had fallen into disrepair. A medieval chapel stood at the far edge of the property protected by tall pines and remained as it had for hundreds of years. Erik had married Elizabeth there.

"Will you be wanting me to remain at the carriage?" Erik's driver said from beside him.

No liveryman came to greet them. The roads being

what they were, it had taken half the day to get here by coach. He could have just ridden here by horseback but he had wanted the formality. He was, after all, who he was. In the beginning, he'd allowed the Maxwells a certain leeway. But last night would never happen again. "Remain here," Erik said.

He reached the top step when the door suddenly opened. The butler stood there, speechless. Lady Lara suddenly appeared.

"Erik"—she stepped outside and shut the door behind her but kept her hand on the latch—"please, you mustn't be here. You should not have come."

"Where is Johnny, Lara?"

Her eyes widened. "He isn't here." She opened the door and edged back inside. "It is not safe for you here. You must go away."

Erik placed his hand on the door to keep her from slamming it in his face. Her face snapped up to his, alarmed. "Then I will see your father."

"He is abed. Your presence will only add more strain to his heart."

"More strain than he has already endured because he has refused to allow Elizabeth to die?"

"Please. I will not be able to defend you to him this time."

"I have not asked you to do anything for me, Lara. I have never asked you to stand between your family and me."

"Then be grateful that I have. I have been your only friend."

"Grateful, Lara? I took your advice once long ago when you asked me to give your father time. And then it was too late."

Lara's wet, luminous gaze dropped to her hands. "I am sorry for that. But Papa would rather blame you

than accept his own culpability in my sister's death. He
is like you. Stubborn. He even wants to believe she is
still alive because he needs to believe in something, or I
fear he will die."

"Are you the one responsible for the letters?"

"I swear I have written no letters. I swear on my life,
Erik."

"Just like you swore on your life that you and I were
together the night Elizabeth vanished."

"We *were* together. I saved your life, Erik. They
would have arrested you that night."

"Or you saved your own life. For Christ sakes, Lara,
tell me you are not involved in this insanity?"

Erik looked over his shoulder as a horse approached
at a clipped pace up the drive. John Maxwell reined
in near the carriage and in a single fluid motion was
off his horse, then walking in long strides toward Erik.
He stopped at the bottom of the stairs. "What are you
doing here?" Maxwell demanded.

Lara moved between Erik and her brother. "Nothing, Johnny. He is leaving."

"Then why are you crying, Lara? What did he say
to you?"

She touched the corners of her eyes and looked oddly
at the dampness that came back on her fingertip. "I think
. . ." She lifted her head and looked at Erik. "I think he
believes me responsible for those letters, Johnny."

"You came all this way from your castle to insult
Lara? The one person in this bloody family who has
ever defended you?"

"Are you going to call me out, Johnny? Did you not
try to do that before?"

"Did you not run like the coward you are?"

Erik came down a step and met him at the bottom.

"You're hotheaded, Johnny. Ye always were. When you defend another's honor, know what it is you are defending. Know the difference between a truth and a lie."

"The truth?" Maxwell grit out. "Have you not already destroyed one of my sister's lives. And are now trying to destroy the other?"

Maxwell lunged. Erik stepped aside, caught Maxwell's ankle by the hook of his walking stick and pulled. The man sprawled face-first into the overgrown flowerbed. He lay there a moment, stunned. He rolled and came up to his knees.

Erik raised his cane and held it out with both hands, firmly gripping each end. "Just because I allowed you to vilify me and mine last night does not mean I will allow it again."

"Bastard!"

Erik propelled the cane like a staff and knocked Maxwell against the collarbones, then thrust in an upward motion against his chin, snapping back his head, landing him again in the mud, this time on his backside. The third time Johnny rose to strike, Erik hit him in the jaw with his fist, the impact throwing him beneath his horse. The stallion reared. Erik stepped over Maxwell's prone form and took the bridle with one hand, calming the horse with gentle words. He looked over his shoulder at Maxwell, who remained on the ground, and Lara weeping and kneeling at his side, her gray gown spread around her like a cloud. Maxwell brought the back of his hand from his lip. Blood oozed from a cut.

"Go away!" Lara beseeched. "Before there is nothing left of our lives."

Erik dropped the reins of the horse atop Maxwell's

mud-caked chest. "Count yourself lucky I did not kill you last night. If you ever insult my wife again I will not show the same restraint."

Erik turned on his heel and came to an abrupt stop.

Robert Maxwell stood at the top of the stairs. He was a big man, his red hair lighter than it had been years ago, but still fit for a man in his sixties. He looked from his two children to Erik. Then he peered across the lake at Sedgwick Castle, a small blur in the distance, as if confused by Erik's presence.

But to Erik it was as if the whole world had aged a hundred years while he had been asleep and he had just now opened his eyes. He felt . . . alive again, as an unfamiliar montage of emotions spilled through him.

"You and I can still find peace between us, Robert. For the sake of my daughter, your granddaughter. For the sake of the relationship we once shared, we can sit down and talk. Something we should have done years ago."

Lord Eyre's eyes darkened. "The relationship we once shared? Peace? I wish to God I had never known ye, Sedgwick. Now get off this land."

Erik's eyes fell briefly on Lara and Johnny. Both had come to their feet. Lara lowered her gaze. Johnny did not look away. Erik expected to see hatred in the man's eyes, and that was exactly what he got.

With one last glance at the old manor house, Erik lifted his cane from the ground, then stepped into the coach.

At one time he would not have blamed any of them for their mistrust and anger. Now he accepted the problem as theirs and no longer his. Though he did not acquit himself of his responsibilities in the events that had changed their lives, he accepted that he had taken the first step to heal himself—at least—realizing that it was not so much that he had to forgive them, but that he needed to forgive himself.

A fierce storm battered the vales and craggy cliffs of Sedgwick for a week. The winds and rains swept across the loch like a fierce, angry beast testing its power over the besieged castle and all its occupants, before retreating again to hide behind the face of a bright blue sky.

Christine lay across the settee in the sitting room. She'd been two weeks late, and for a brief period these past few days she thought maybe . . .

She disliked this time of the month. She cried too easily. She ate the wrong things. Her clothes did not fit properly. And as she lay in bed with a wet rag on her face, she knew it was moments like these that handicapped a woman in a world run by men.

Annie brought her meals to her room. But by the third evening, Christine had pulled herself out of her doldrums. She was a Sommers, by God, and Sommers women endured. The next day she went downstairs and set to work organizing the contents of all the trunks she had brought with her from London. Her manuscripts and fossil specimens had been too long consigned to oblivion, stacked in an old room, ignored by her and the rest of the world.

By the end of the week, Christine decided it was time she found the housekeeper again and view the rest of the castle. She needed a room with ample light and large enough to accommodate her collections, and with a floor strong enough not to collapse beneath its weight. Others might never read anything she had written or see anything she had found, but Christine refused to see her life's toil banished to trunks and crates because she could not find an adequate place to work.

Armed with newfound purpose, Christine untied the

scarf from around her head, unpinned the apron from her gown and left the rooms where her crates were being stored. She climbed the stairs to the main floors. She stopped a chambermaid carrying an armful of linens and asked where she would find the housekeeper at this time of day. She ended up on the second-floor corridor.

Christine came to an abrupt stop when she nearly tripped over a fish lying on the floor. On further inspection, she saw that it lay atop a tin plate attached to a braid of long twine. Following the string down the corridor, she saw that it looped around a corner and into Aunt Sophie's chambers. Her aunt sat on the floor working over a ball of twine.

"What are you doing, Aunt Sophie?"

Aunt Sophie quickly put a finger to her mouth. "We are catching ourselves a cat, my dear," she whispered.

A child's giggle sounded from behind Christine. Erin sat crouched next to the wall, watching the hallway like a scout for Wellington, on the lookout for French troops.

"That beastie of yours doesn't want to play today," Aunt Sophie said. "So Erin went to the kitchens and found herself a fish."

"Have you considered that the fish was in the kitchen for a reason?"

"Sssh." Aunt Sophie waggled her hand. "You're the one who told the child to bribe the cat. Now off with you. You are making too much noise."

Christine looked from her outlandish aunt to the little girl sitting next to the wall with a huge smile on her face. She giggled and covered her mouth when she saw Christine's eyes on her. She and her aunt had clearly struck up an odd friendship. Christine was surprised, since Aunt Sophie had forever resisted teaching at the abbey because she abhorred children. Was this all it took then, to recapture one's fading youth? To get down on one's hands and knees and see the world again through the eyes of a child?

Christine sighed. Poor Beast was doomed. His days of independence were numbered, she thought, as she hunted down her cat and brought him up to the corridor so he could discover the fishy lure for himself. Anyone who worked so hard to woo the beast's affections surely deserved a chance to win his heart.

Chapter 15

Christine stopped just this side of a double doorway.
"The ballroom, mum," Boris said.

With a nod, Christine turned. "Thank you."

Her first glance into the ballroom touched a pair of
Venetian chandeliers overhead. No draperies marred
the view where a long row of French doors opened to
the terrace and sunlight pooled on the floor. Erik stood
at the opposite end of the room across the polished
oaken floor, his sword in momentary riposte and another short sword angled just at the level of his head.
He lunged and retreated as he performed some sort of
master's wheel. He looked to have been at the ritual for
a long time. Sweat dampened his hair.

He wore no shirt. His leather breeches were cut close
to his thighs. Those were no safety-tipped foils he held,
but heavy steel-forged swords, and still he moved across
the floor as if he performed nothing more strenuous
than a waltz.

This was a man in control of his body. A man who
could easily have broken John Maxwell's neck with his
bare hands.

As Christine observed him, Erik saw her and stopped.
Her chin lifted as he lowered his arms to his side and

something indiscernible seemed to burn the air between them. His muscles rippled with barely detectable movement as he stood watching her. Then he turned and walked to a table against the wall. He set down the swords and, slapping a towel around his neck, waited for her approach.

Though she'd oft heard him now in his private chambers next to her own apartments at night, he had not come to her bed since they had argued. She should have sought him out earlier, she told herself, as she stood hesitantly on the threshold mustering the courage to approach him.

Christine strode across the polished floor and stopped in front of him. Up close, he smelled salty and hot, and she found herself trapped by her need to touch him. She would rather have his hate than the indifference she sensed in him as she approached. Yet, it was not indifference she saw in his eyes now.

"You are very adept with swords," she said.

He chuckled. "Is that a compliment I hear coming from your lips, *leannanan*? Or an insult?"

She folded her arms. "I am just surprised, that is all. I would have a word with you."

He waited as she struggled to form her thoughts. "As you can see, my schedule is clear today," he prompted. "I am at your leisure, Christine."

"I would apologize for my behavior this past week. I should never have called into question your courage, Erik. You are the last man in the world I believe a coward. I overstepped my bounds by involving myself with something that was not my concern. Our contract does not give me the right to interfere—"

"*Fook* the contract. I don't give a fig about the contract between us."

Taken aback by his vehemence, she inhaled her

shock. She had seen him show less emotion facing John Maxwell. "But we have an agreement."

"Agreements can change."

Would he remove her from the estate, prohibit her from hunting her fossils? Shut her out of his life as he had his own mother? "We *both* signed that contract. No more. No less. Isn't that what you told me?"

Boris entered the room just then, escorting Erik's solicitor, the verbose Mr. Attenborough, and another well-dressed gentleman. "Your grace," Boris said. "Mr. Attenborough has asked to speak with you."

Without looking at them, Erik bid the men to remain where they were. "I accept your apology, Christine," he politely said. His hand stopped her from leaving. He presented his cheek for a wifely peck. "If you will?"

"I will *not*," she whispered.

"As stated in *our* contract I believe you are supposed to cede to your husband a certain amount of warmth while in the company of others so as to convince nay-sayers ours is a love match."

She'd put the clause in as a jest, nay revenge, for his coldhearted handling of the entire proposition. Love matches were so tedious to the *ton* as to be practically scandalous. She'd never thought he would actually agree to the silly clause.

"Tsk, tsk, my love," he admonished, and his heat sent shivers over her body. He offered her his cheek again, which he fully expected her to kiss with wifely affection. "Everyone is watching. We would not wish the world to believe I dragged you unwillingly from England with every intent to fatten you up for my next feast."

"You are a fraud, Sedgwick. Do you have to resort to blackmail for that which you cannot buy? Is nothing around you real?"

Her words merely amused him. "You are real enough. And I can attest to the sounds that come from that lovely mou—"

Christine kissed him full on the lips. She placed one palm on his cheek and held him there with the pressure of her mouth, and hoped she adequately shocked him.

Let them go back to their wives and gossip about that, your grace!

But in the end, her anger tightened her throat and she could not voice the words. Pulling back, she peered into his shuttered eyes.

"I do not understood what you want from this marriage," she whispered.

She did not understand him, she realized, perhaps because she did not understand herself. "You ask too much of me, Erik."

"As do you of me."

She whirled on her heel and escaped him by way of the garden terrace. She turned and looked back as he'd expected her to do.

Gripping each end of the towel about his neck, Erik watched her, content, despite himself, that he could claim some ground beneath her cool façade as his own.

He would claim all of her if she allowed him to do so.

He knew he had always asked more from people than he'd been willing to give in return. Until now, it had been easier to keep himself locked away. He wasn't locked away anymore, and he wanted more from his wife than her signature on a contract.

"What is this?" Erik demanded.

He faced the burgh constable from across his desk in the library where he had gone after changing his clothes. Mr. Attenborough stood beside Erik, his face buried in the papers the constable delivered.

"We warned ye afore ye went to London, your grace—"

"*Warned* me? Now, I am no murderer but a bigamist? Which is it? I cannot be both, can I?"

The constable cleared his throat. "If her father says they've received a letter from her, we have te take this seriously, your grace. The only reason Lord Eyre has na' brought murder charges against you these past years is that he has always believed her alive."

"He has not tried to bring charges because he has no case."

Elizabeth was no more alive than that bloody doorknob across the room.

"Last year Lady Elizabeth was seen near the loch," Erik said. "Before that it was the cliffs above the river, and let me remember . . . where was she seen two years before that?"

"Edinburgh, your grace," the constable sheepishly murmured.

"And Glasgow, St. Andrews, and Kirkcaldy. With all that traveling about, do you not think *someone* would know where she lived by now if she were really alive? This is a blatant attempt to lay the groundwork needed to question the legitimacy of any children born from my marriage to my wife."

Erik crushed the writ in his hand. They were telling him he was a year short of the seven he'd needed for the high court to declare Elizabeth legally dead. *A bloody year!* Like hell, he was.

"If one or both parties are already legally married, the second marriage shall become bigamous and void," Erik's solicitor read from the sheaf in his hand. "Lord Eyre believes it will be a simple matter to render your recent wedding invalid. But considering the circumstances, I doubt the magistrate would dare bring charges of bigamy."

"Of course no charge will be filed. I am an English peer. I cannot be tried for bigamy in Scotland even if Maxwell owned *all* the high court rather than just the Lord Advocate."

For a long, horrifying moment his fury defied his effort to breathe. Erik walked to the window, where the sunlight colored the heavy leaded glass. Thus far, Maxwell had yet to truly taste Erik's fury. But if Lord Eyre succeeded in having his marriage to Christine invalidated, then Old Angus Maxwell's curse would hold nothing over Erik's wrath.

It wouldn't matter that Lord Eyre had once been the closest human being Erik had ever had to a father. Erik would destroy him. He would go after his financial holdings, his reputation, his family, and everything else the man held of value. He would own all the Maxwells' lives by the time he finished.

But first Erik would go to Dunfermline and deal personally with the adjudication of the matter. Lord Eyre's brother would have better served himself had he upheld the law rather than bent it to favor his anointed Maxwell clan.

"Get out," Erik ordered the man who had come with Attenborough. "The next time you show your face at Sedgwick Castle doing Maxwell's bidding, you best have a warrant for my arrest. I have been as tolerant as I am going to be."

"The closer the lines are together the higher the elevation," Christine said.

She and Rebecca were bent nose-first over the topographical map Erik had given her and which she had already marked up and triangulated where caverns could exist. She shifted. The cellar area where she had set up a laboratory remained dark and dank, even with three lamps lit.

"Whom do you think he was yelling at?" Becca asked.

Christine's hand paused on the map. "I don't know."

"He never yells." Becca traced her finger along the edge of the map. "At least he hasn't in a very long time."

"Whatever has happened, I am sure has nothing to do with you."

"Still, he is too overprotective."

"You are his sister. His family."

"Mam is his family."

"I will not pretend to understand everything in your brother's complicated life. Or agree with his handling of certain affairs. I allowed you to suck me into deceiving Erik once when it comes to your mam. I will not allow it again. I told you, she needs to come here if you are to visit. Or I will say something."

Christine returned her concentration to the map. She was doing anything rather than worry about whatever was taking place in the library. "When the river changed course, the water found its way into an underground cavern—"

"It's my fossil."

"I know it is, Becca. And I will never take your credit for its discovery."

"Mum," Annie interrupted from the doorway. She stood with a burly footman, carrying the last of her trunks from upstairs. "Do you wish this set against the wall with the other trunks?"

Christine rubbed her neck as she pondered the lack

of space. The movement made her flinch. Earlier, she, too, had begun hauling trunks and crates into this room. "That contains books. Put them in the adjoining room."

She had brought a settee and serviceable furniture out from beneath storage tarps in one of the closed rooms upstairs and arranged something that resembled a sitting room in what used to be the castle dungeon, resplendent with rusted iron rings and chains still attached to the stone walls. In truth, she thought it rather cozy.

Christine returned her attention to the survey map and collected the threads of her thoughts. Becca touched her forearm. "Thank you, for caring enough to discuss this with me."

Christine sighed. "There have been times in my life I would have given anything to see my mam one more time," she said. "But you must do this correctly or you will only lose what you seek so hard to gain."

Becca leaned her elbows on the workbench. She dawdled over the map. "Mr. Hampton said you have been working up at the falls."

"I will be returning there when the weather clears."

"Hampton said you are riding Miss Pippen as your mighty steed."

Nonplussed by the humor in Rebecca's voice, Christine began rolling up the map. "I am not interested in speed, only surefootedness."

"Did Hampton tell you Erik named her for his beloved childhood nurse?"

"She must not have been *too* beloved."

"Oh, but she was." Rebecca lowered her voice. "From what I understand, Miss Pippen had large brown eyes like a cocker spaniel and that my brother was in love with her. Puppy love." Becca smiled at her own joke.

"Imagine that. My brother had a heart when he was ten." She spun and faced the door. "Isn't that right, Erik?"

He stood in the doorway, his arms folded across his chest, leaning against the jamb. "Is what right?" he asked. "Did I have a nurse named Miss Pippen, or did I have a heart?"

"Both." Rebecca toyed with the lace on her sleeve. To Christine she said, "Ask him what happened to Miss Pippen."

Christine's gaze fastened on Erik.

"I'll tell you," Rebecca answered, "She died at a young age of a broken heart in her loneliness. 'Twas a terrible tragedy."

"She passed away a few years ago a woman of sixty," Erik calmly said. "I believe she is buried in Aberdeen near her sister's family."

Ignoring him, Rebecca primly fluffed her skirts. "I like my story better. If someone were to immortalize *my* memory, I should not want it bestowed on an old plow horse."

Christine rubbed her palms across her soiled skirts. Conscious of her dusty attire and the red scarf that covered her hair, she worked to finish rolling up the map, anything to appear busy.

"If you are finished with your nonsense, I would have a word alone with my wife."

Becca lowered her gaze. But when she swept past Erik, he gently grabbed her arm, turning her. "It is not my intent to hurt your feelings."

Nodding stiffly, she stepped past her brother.

"You can't protect her from life forever, Erik. Eventually you are going to have to trust that you raised her properly and allow her to begin making her own choices and decisions."

"I did not come down here to speak about my sister."

Christine walked into the adjoining chamber. She had forgotten Annie's presence. The maid was crouched next to a bookcase, unpacking the last of Christine's trunks.

Seeing Erik step into the doorway, she dropped the books in her hand, rose, and dipped. "Your grace."

"I will finish, Annie," Christine told the girl.

"Yes, your grace." Annie hurried from the room.

Erik remained in the doorway. Aware of his eyes on her, aware of the race of her heart, Christine knelt and finished shelving the books Annie had dropped.

"I have business to attend in Dunfermline," he said after a moment. "I will be leaving in the morning. I may be gone a week or longer."

She absently brushed the dust from her hands and raised her eyes. "I see." She rose.

"I have issued orders that you are to be given whatever you ask for as needed," he said. "You have only to make your wishes known."

They faced each other across what used to be an old torture chamber. As his gaze touched the manacles and chains on the walls, the irony of it must have struck him as well, for when his eyes returned to hers, she glimpsed amusement in their darkened depths.

"Is this where you intend to set up your laboratory then?"

Lamplight glowed in the semi-darkness and cast shadows on the walls barren of any amenities. Her gaze followed his hands to the table beside the door as he lifted the tablet containing her renditions of the beast she'd visualized finding. One looked forged in the fires of hell with its thick lizard-like skin, long snout, and teeth large enough to tear a man asunder. He flipped through each page in the tablet, his expression revealing nothing of his thoughts. His hand moved to her drawing case and opened the mahogany lid, his fingers touching those possessions that gave her life meaning, much as she had done to his things in the library.

"What happens if you do not find your beast, Christine?"

"What happens if I cannot give you a son?"

The silence between them was not so much uncomfortable as it was revealing. Neither of them knew how to answer that question.

"I suppose we can seek an annulment and you can buy yourself another bride," she offered.

"I have found that there is little my wealth cannot buy, Christine. People hate me for it, but no one has yet to turn it away."

Since Christine fit into that category, the arrow hit where he must have meant it to go for he watched her flinch. But it was not satisfaction she glimpsed in his eyes as he returned to his restless meandering.

"You did not come down here to engage in some sparkling repartee with me. Why are you suddenly on your way to Dunfermline?"

"I had a visit from the constable this afternoon. I intend to be in front of the bench tomorrow to see the matter of Elizabeth's disappearance put to rest."

He told her about the constable's visit and about the letter his former wife's family had received and various "sightings" people had made of Elizabeth.

What Erik did not tell her was that he could not be married to two women, but he did not need to. His very silence on the matter told her.

"But if the coroner's inquest concluded their investigation in May and issued her death certificate before you went to London, how can a magistrate reopen the case? The Lord Advocate must think Elizabeth could still be alive."

"The Lord Advocate is Robert Maxwell's brother."

"Robert Maxwell? Elizabeth's father? Why would he reopen the case?"

"Lord Eyre believes she is alive and he is attempting to invalidate our marriage. Maxwell inherits the Sedgwick duchy if I die without an heir. The letter is a hoax, Christine."

"Have you considered that the culprit perpetuating this hoax is playing into the Sedgwick curse? For seven years, you could not remarry. Seven years from Elizabeth's disappearance puts you at your thirty-fourth birthday. Who does not think you will implode and expire before the end of summer?"

Shaking his head, he suddenly crooked his mouth. "I haven't heard the matter of my imminent demise put in quite those terms."

"It isn't amusing."

"It is the only thing in this sordid affair about which I am capable of laughing. Allow me to savor the moment. But I agree with you."

Christine's fingers wrapped around his upper arm. "The bones you found could belong to someone else. You've said yourself, other people have gone missing. What if Elizabeth still *is* alive?"

"Then you must consider me a dissolute rake who would think nothing of robbing us both of our self-respect. Not even taking into account what such an action would do to my family. I would not have wed you had I a doubt. The remains are Elizabeth's. Do not ask me how I can know for sure. I just do." He leaned his backside against the workbench and folded his arms. "I just wanted answers, Christine. Closure. One day Erin is going to ask. I don't want her to believe her da is a murderer."

"What happened in the keep tower, Erik?"

He stared at her, but her question was neither a demand nor a desire to pass judgment. Then suddenly he shook his head. His chest rose and fell. He leaned with his palms pressed against the workbench. "Many years ago I decided that I had a great, big castle with many empty rooms to fill. I was young and possessed with a sense of my own importance. I wanted a beautiful wife and children to fill my life. As you can see, acquiring such a paragon has not been a particular skill of mine. I have discovered myself better suited to business than dealing with the women in my life."

He lifted a paperweight beside his hand, a mosquito encased in amber. "You asked once if I was in love with Elizabeth. At the time, I believed I was.

"I married her two years after Charlotte's death. I might have wed her sister, Lara, had Elizabeth not come back that summer from France. The last time I had seen her she'd been in short dresses. She was beautiful and filled with this . . . this spark for life. Her father married her to me because I had wealth and a title and because our two families were as close as two families with shared pasts could be. She did not want to wed me. And I regretted every day afterward.

"I rebuilt the tower keep and wanted to live there with her. I had never done anything with my hands and discovered a particular aptitude. When it was finished, she hated the place. She despised anything I loved, including Erin, who was born almost nine months to the day we spoke our vows. She became worse after Erin was born. Elizabeth was adept at hiding that side of herself from everyone but me.

"And so after a rather nasty argument where she accused me of adultery with her sister, she went up to the tower and destroyed everything I had built. My work. My books. My designs. My life."

"What happened after that?"

"In the end, she walked out of the keep and perished. I am convinced the only reason Erin is still alive is because I took her with me when I left. Lara later found me in Italy and told me Elizabeth had been missing since the night I left. When Erin and I returned, many assumed Elizabeth's accusations of adultery were true and looked at me for her disappearance. I hired anyone with the skill to follow a cold trail to try to find her. Only after that proved futile did I file a deposition with the burgh constable in St. Andrews asking for help. By then almost a year had passed. Now six years and some months after she vanished, her remains begin to wash up on the riverbank about two miles away from the castle. Along with those of the beast." His mouth crooked. "It does not seem fair that your beast has to share its legacy with my tragedy."

"It does not seem right that your tragedy should give rise to my legacy."

He had somehow restructured the boundary between them. She could no longer remember any of the reasons why she'd been so angry with him. "You confuse me, Erik." She wiped her nose on her sleeve.

"Good God, Christine." Not nearly appalled as he sounded, he whipped out a handkerchief from inside his jacket. "Whoever taught you to wipe your nose on your sleeve?"

She snatched the handkerchief from his hand. "Heaven forbid that I ever learn to cry like a proper lady." She blew her nose and glared up at him with determined, watery eyes. Then did something she had never done before.

She stepped into his arms. Not because he so obviously needed comforting—though clearly, he would never ask—but because she did, and his arms made her feel safe. She remained there without speaking or daring to breathe for fear of breaking the spell between them. Somewhere behind her, the glass-dome clock ticked away the seconds and resonated like the beat of his heart against her cheek, as if telling her she could not remain in Erik's arms forever. "Thank you for sharing your secrets," she said.

"I have never told another soul what I told you," he said. "Hell, I do not know why I told *you*, except I owe you some manner of explanation."

"You are kind to think so."

His chuckle bordered on satire. "I told you once before I never do anything out of kindness. I have my reasons for everything I do."

A tightness squeezed her chest. She pulled away. "Why do you behave as if you do not care what I think about you? What anyone thinks of you."

"Then allow me to recuse myself from any further comment on the topic of my confession, madam," he quietly said, his eyes touching hers, "for fear it will prejudice you more against my character."

"You *fear* too much, Erik. It is too easy to hide behind fear and guilt."

Cognizant of the heavy thudding of her heart as he laid a knuckle against her jaw and tilted her face, she tried to look away. But he would not allow her. "And what do you fear, *leannanan*? Where do you hide?"

There was heat in his eyes when they met hers. He tucked a wisp of her hair behind her ears. "I don't know what you are talking about."

He picked up the C. A. Sommers book he'd been fondling earlier. "Behind your father's work perhaps? Or should I say, *your* work? Christina Alana Sommers?"

Tears filled her eyes all over again as she looked away. How could he know she was C. A. Sommers?

"He let me read your manuscripts. Your voice is all over that book."

She shook her head. "I don't understand."

"Your father and I were in contact for a year before he passed away. I got to know you again through him. But I did not know for sure you were C. A. Sommers until you told me about his dragon. That theory had never been your father's. But yours. He is the one who went out on the proverbial limb for you."

"And paid for it with his professional reputation and his health." She pressed her nose into his shirt and sniffled again. "When you came that day to the school with the tooth, it was like a miracle."

"I don't want to be the one responsible for crushing your dream. Go find your beast, Christine."

And it was as if time had momentarily stopped and encapsulated them within its warm embrace. As if life had breathed springtime into her heart.

As if all her questions were suddenly answered.

If only all the answers were simple.

Her palms lay abreast of his thudding heart. "I don't want to lose you."

She felt the tremor that went through him, as if he read her thoughts in her silence. His fractured breath caressed her lips. Reaching his hand behind her nape, he drew her against him. "Know this now, my love. No matter what the future may bring, I consider you mine in every way. And our bargain has yet to be met."

He lowered his mouth to hers. She was conscious of the primal need to have him even as she knew much remained unsettled between them, yet, knowing at least in this, tonight they were partners in every way. The fingers that splayed his chest, closed into a fist that gripped his shirt. No longer content just to touch him, she deepened the kiss. A slow, guttural moan escaped him, and her world spun as he pushed his tongue deep, tasted, and finally sipped.

Slowly, he raised his head, focused on her lips, then looked into her eyes. She inhaled the scent of rain that dampened his clothing and his hair, and tasted him in his senses. Her name on his lips, he explored the contour of her cheeks with his palms, the softness of her skin with his fingertips. There was heat in his touch. Heat in his body pressed to hers and in the hands that framed her face and, for a moment, as he traced his thumbs along the outline of her lips, she believed that she, who believed in dragons, truly feared nothing.

Threading his fingers into the thick mass of her hair, he loosened the scarf until it drifted to the floor in a streamer of blood-red silk. "Look at me," he said.

She did as he bid, lifting her lashes slowly to peer into his eyes. She had expected them to be hooded, his thoughts hidden. Neither was the case. "I need this to be your choice. I cannot guarantee the future," he said.

"Then I will guarantee it for us," she whispered against his lips.

Her hands were already sliding his jacket off his shoulders as he carried her to the chaise longue. His hands worked the buttons on her bodice. With each sensuous push and pull of his lips on hers, she traced the play of his muscles on his back and his arms, their mouths hungry and searching. His shirt, only half unlaced, fell around her as he held himself braced with one hand above. She could feel her pulse pounding and the touch of his hand between her legs. He kissed her stomach.

"Is this still your time of the month?"

She shook her head, shocked that he would have known. "No."

Then he was between her legs, low over her belly, releasing the tension of his thumb, he gently kissed her cleft, preparing her by the slowest degrees for his invasion. He brought her legs up over his shoulders and without preamble or seduction, he replaced his fingers with his mouth, the sheer force of his oral penetration driving her hips upward. His tongue flicked against her clitoris. She cried out, breathy and shaking. Her fingers curled in his hair.

She thought she might scream and yet she held him there lifting herself higher so he could suckle all of her. He slid his tongue around the nub and then inside her, pulling, tasting, she could not decide if she should cry out in pain or pleasure. In the end, she did both as the pressure inside her released. Still rocked with tremors, Erik rose above her. He kept his eyes riveted on her face until she looked up at him, half-naked, her skirts rucked around her waist, her hair spread over the chaise and trailing to the floor.

"Mayhap there is one consolation for us, my love," he whispered against her mouth, spreading her thighs as he pushed inside her. "We are made for this, you and me."

Erik made love to her. Or she to him.

Christine did not know. Nor did she care.

She had come to Sedgwick to find a dragon. Not a myth, but one that might have once truly existed. It was the reason she married Erik.

And the reason why she later came awake in his bed upstairs in the darkness as warm arms encircled her and gently turned her on her back, and she felt that melting pleasure inside her all over again.

Christine cradled Erik's head against her breasts, feeling his tongue against her hardening nipples. Then his mouth was hard against hers and her arms wound around his neck. He caressed her buttocks as she moved against him, opening her legs to join with him, and within minutes he had filled her, and the dragon in her dreams became the one in her arms.

Chapter 16

An hour before dawn Erik rang for Boris. Erik had left Christine asleep in his bed where he had carried her earlier. He'd finally risen and dressed.

Now Boris stood in the doorway of Erik's private sitting room. Wearing a nightshirt and stocking hat, the aging man was a thin silhouette framed by the light behind him. "Did you summon me, your grace?"

Erik glanced at the clock on the mantel above the fireplace. "My apologies for waking you so early, Boris."

"Yes, your grace. I came. I thought perhaps there might be a crisis."

"It is too early for a crisis, Boris. I have personal business with which to attend and will be away from Sedgwick Castle. I need you to see that Lady Sedgwick gets this in the morning." Erik handed him a wooden box holding the heavy iron key to the tower. He could have been handing over the key to his heart for all he knew. He'd felt strange all evening. "The place will need to be cleaned. But you stay out of the tower yourself. Too many bloody stairs, else someone will be calling me to bring an undertaker back."

"Yes, your grace. Thank you."

"Do you mind not calling me 'your grace' with every

single syllable you utter, Boris. It is not necessary. And I find myself tiring of it."

"Yes, your . . . sir," Boris hesitated. "You have packed?"

"My valise has already been removed to the coach. I can see myself downstairs. I do not want the household awakened."

"Yes. Very well."

Erik pulled on his leather gloves. "My wife goes nowhere without Hamilton to escort her."

"He will guard her with his life."

"Thank you, Boris. I appreciate his loyalty. Just see that Hamilton keeps her safe. That will be all."

"Good morning then."

Erik turned back into the room. She lay on her side watching him.

He sat on the edge of the bed. His gaze slipped downward to caress the naked curve of her waist and each breast. "I'll be back as soon as I can." He pulled the covers over her shoulders. "The keep is yours to do with as you will, *leannanan*."

His gaze hesitated on the hand that came to rest on his. A small corner of his mind cherished the urgency in her touch. "Thank you," she said.

Erik pressed his palms against the pillow, bracketing her between his arms and his body, teasing the curls at her temple with his breath before he kissed her one more time. "Sleep."

"You will keep yourself safe?"

Their warm breath mingled until at last, his thumb traced her bottom lip and he kissed her lightly. "Always."

Erik walked the corridor to his daughter's rooms, the cloak billowing out around his calves with his stride. Quietly opening the door, he let himself inside.

A lamp burned on the table just inside her room. He walked to her bed. The doll she usually slept with no longer lay beside her. Instead, her arm lay protectively wrapped around Christine's orange cat. Both slept soundly. For a moment, shaking his head, all he could do was stare down at her, then he bent and gently kissed her curls.

She didn't know just how many times he had come in here during the night to watch her. He had never been very good at expressing tender feelings of affection. Never whispered the words *I love you*, to anyone. Not to Becca or Elizabeth or his own daughter. He didn't even know if he knew how.

Once outside, he greeted his driver and footman with a nod, stopping briefly to glance up at the tower keep before he climbed into the carriage. As the coach rolled away, he dimmed the lamp and stared at the rivulets of rain slanting across the glass. He understood why the people of Scotland were known for their fierce resilience and independence. The weather alone bred stamina. A person had do grow tough or perish.

He was relieved that Christine had never been the type to simply surrender to circumstance and perish.

Christine stopped on the top-floor stair landing, then stepped into a room shrouded in a gloomy shadow, unsure what she would find. Having left Mrs. Brown and Aunt Sophie on the second floor, she had come up here alone to look around. She tied back the heavy curtains and, after coughing and choking on the dust, put her hands on her hips and surveyed her surroundings. Weak light stole through the leaded windows. Dust coated everything. Yet even through the grime, Christine could see that with a solid cleaning, the room could be magnificent again. The keep itself might be a throwback to the days of fifteenth-century medieval warfare, but the old master's chambers inside had been gently tamed by modernization. The floors were carpeted in the colors of autumn. Corinthian stone columns supported the airy Wedgwood-style papier-mâché ceiling, in juxtaposition with the wild landscape outside.

Christine walked into an adjoining sitting room and tied back those curtains as well. She could make these upper rooms her workspace. They were big enough for her needs, the lighting ideal and the gothic ambience a perfect suit to her tastes. Still, there was a sadness in the cold shadows that pervaded her thoughts as she touched a hand on the wooden seat just below the window.

From the sitting room she continued her exploration higher into the tower, slowly climbing the circular stairway to an upper room. Here she glimpsed her first hint of the destruction of which Erik had spoken. A chair and table were overturned. A lamp shattered. Her feet crunched on glass and, startled by the sound, she cautiously lifted her skirts. She moved into the chamber and came to an abrupt halt.

Several tall glass-fronted cabinets lined the wall, their doors shattered. Tables were upturned. Papers and books raked from the shelves and strewn in heaps over the debris-ridden floor. Nothing had escaped the inhuman destructive force that had gone through this room and the adjoining one.

Knowing who had done this only made the scene more horrific. Saddened by the destruction, Christine backed away and returned to the floor below.

She would take out the bedding, tapestries, the draperies and all the carpeting. She would remove the furniture. She would make these rooms alive again.

The sound of clacking against the stone stairs leading into the lower bedroom drew her around. She hurried downstairs and peered into the circular stairwell.

"Good *God*, girl!" Aunt Sophie gasped. "You will be the death of me!"

Christine hurried down and took Aunt Sophie's elbow as she helped her the rest of the way upstairs. "I told you not to come up these stairs."

"And how exactly did you plan I should get here? Fly?" Leaning against the silver head of her cane, she waved away Christine's concern and looked about her. "Do not tell me you intend to live here. Why, the servants will rebel and throw you off the battlements."

Christine walked to the window and looked out across Erik's world. "But you can't deny the beauty of the scenery. These rooms are perfect, Aunt Sophie. Not just to work in, but to live in as well."

Christine leaned against the glass and looked down into the unkempt courtyard. "I shall surprise him when he returns from Dunfermline."

Daylight seeping in through the leaded glass touched the silver band on her right hand, drawing her out of her daze.

She found herself tracing the ring on her finger.

There was a reason she had always lived by certain rules of pragmatism, she told herself. Rules kept her from behaving like her idealistic students who believed in such silly things as magic, curses, and one's destiny being divined by a braided band of antique silver. And yet, pragmatism aside, she did believe.

She believed so hard and with such passion, she knew everything *must* work out. Christine closed her eyes. "Have you ever wanted to touch the wind, grab on to it with all of your might, and let it take you wherever it willed?"

When Aunt Sophie failed to respond, Christine dropped back down to earth with a mental thud. She slowly turned. Aunt Sophie was sitting in a high-back velvet tufted chair, like a queen on a throne, staring at her. "I have suspected all along that something was wrong with you," her aunt said. "I should have checked you for a fever and put you to bed with a cold compress long ago."

"Do you believe in magic, Aunt Sophie?"

Aunt Sophie crossed her hands over the silver knob of her cane. "Do *you*?"

Toying with the ring, Christine found herself hesitating. Aunt Sophie's gaze dropped to Christine's hand.

The room seemed to grow quiet. "Come here." Aunt Sophie motioned for Christine to stand in front of her. "Let me see what trouble you have got yourself into now."

Christine did as Aunt Sophie bid, feeling much like a child called to task for disappointing her elders. She knelt beside the chair.

"Give me your spectacles," Aunt Sophie said. "It's about time I saw the world around me a little clearer."

Christine eased the glasses off and handed them over to her aunt. Aunt Sophie applied them to her nose, tilted her head up and down, then took Christine's hand and examined the ring in the light.

Christine had always wondered how her aunt could see so well at her age and now realized she could not. Aunt Sophie's vanity surprised her for Christine had always thought her aunt immune to the opinions of others.

She caught Aunt Sophie peering at her from over the top of the spectacles. As if she had read Christine's mind, she said, "It is not my vanity that keeps me from wearing spectacles. It is admitting to myself that I am old."

With a sigh, Aunt Sophie returned Christine's spectacles and sat back in the chair. "I gave that ring to the granddaughter of a friend of mine as a . . ."

"Joke?" Christine helpfully supplied.

"I am hardly that cruel. Babs needed a lift. Something to get her mind off her mam's passing. She needed a miracle and I gave her one. At least in her mind."

"Her mind? Babs's wish to come to school at the abbey came true."

"Pah! There was no magic involved. I already knew she'd been accepted at the abbey. I am the one who paid her tuition to remove her from beneath her father's thumb. They had no money. He was preparing to send her to a workhouse."

Christine paled. "But Amelia and Joseph . . ."

"Were making eyes at each other before he went to Edinburgh. You were just too blind to see anyone or anything outside the walls of your laboratory."

Christine shook her head, refusing to believe that the simplest of explanations could account for everything that had happened to her since Erik had knocked at her classroom door. Her heart began to race.

She *needed* to believe. Aunt Sophie did not understand what was at stake. "There is power in this ring, Aunt Sophie. I know there is."

"The ring did not bring Sedgwick back into your life, dear. He had been in contact with your papa for months about fossil finds on this estate. There are no special powers that made you his wife and brought you to Scotland."

Christine refused to be dissuaded. There *was* magic in this ring. There *had* to be. She rose to her feet in a whisper of burgundy silk and white lace. "My entire life I have been searching for what I have before me now."

"Are you referring to Lord Sedgwick or your beast, Christine? A few months ago Sedgwick was not in your life."

Christine pressed her thumbs to her temple and wanted to tell her aunt to stop it! *Go away.* "*Why can't I have both?* Don't you understand, I *have* to believe, Aunt Sophie."

"If all of this is magic, what happens when the ring comes off?"

"*Why* must it come off? See?" She held up her hand. "It is on my finger."

"Then what?" Aunt Sophie quietly asked. "Sedgwick falls in love with you and you spend the rest of your life happy, or do you spend it doubting yourself? And him? You must be worthy of your wish."

The tenor in Aunt Sophie's voice both startled and frightened her because it suddenly answered a question. "Papa did not get this ring from a Gypsy trader, did he?"

Aunt Sophie waved her hand dismissively. "It is a silly ring with a silly Arthurian legend attached to it I found in my great-grandmother's hope chest. Your father discovered it one day. He must have been only twenty at the time. Always searching for that elusive magic elixir that would make his life complete. He had two passions in his life, archaeology and your mother. In those days, there was no paleontology or name for people who hunted fossils."

"Mam left Papa after he took off the ring . . ."

"You can only want *one* thing *most* in the world, Christine." Aunt Sophie rose. "And you must be worthy of your own wish. Spells and enchantments are all fine and well, but for all the magic on King Arthur's side, in the end, Britain's mighty savior lost his Guinevere, and his life, and the sword went back into the lake. Nothing will endure if you are not first worthy of your own wish."

Beast had abandoned her.

Christine recognized desertion when she saw it, and, a fortnight later, as she was making her way to the stables to meet Hamilton, she finally saw her traitorous cat following Cook down into the scullery that led to the kitchens. He hadn't made so much as one visit to her since she had moved into the tower.

Hamilton met her at the stable door. Miss Pippen was saddled, ready and standing next to his shaggy gelding. Hamilton dropped into step with her as she passed him to the mounting block. "You are up early again, mum. Will we be off to the same place as we were yesterday?"

Christine pulled on her gloves. "No, I think we will move east."

Seven days in a row, Christine had pulled poor Hamilton out of his bed before dawn. Yesterday he'd fallen asleep on a bed of pine needles, and Christine had had three hours to explore the higher elevations without having to worry that the lumbering man would break his neck attempting to follow her into the rocks. She'd wanted to find a better view to see the surrounding crags and dips. She'd mapped out trails on Erik's estate that needed closer inspection. At this rate, she could be here a decade and not see all the sections.

Erik couldn't wait that long for answers.

Last week, she had written to Joseph and Amelia and asked them to come to Scotland. Joseph Darlington had been a decent geologist before he'd specialized in paleontology under her father's tutelage. Tenting her hand over her eyes, she peered at the distant crags. If she had to share her dragon, then she would have it be with Joseph if it meant answers. She had not found one fossil.

Not one.

"You can only want one thing most in the world."

Looking up at the sky, she mounted. Today was a clear blue so bright the sun hurt her eyes. She adjusted her hat and nudged Miss Pippen forward with the heels of her boots. In no great hurry, the horse walked out of the yard, and only after they had reached the stone gate did the old mare pick up her pace.

"Miss Pippen might be a dawdler, mum," Hampton said. "But she be of sturdy stock. There be nothing wrong with sturdy stock."

The equipment she'd bundled in a knapsack and tied to the back of the cantle rattled with the choppy gait almost as loudly as her teeth did.

She had spent two hours last night grooming the mare Erik had given her, but she had not been able to make herself ride the beautiful horse. It was just a horse, after all, she'd told herself. Christine smoothed the aged woolen cloth of her skirts. Besides, she was more like Miss Pippen than the delicate mare. Hardy.

"There be a crew up on the high road again," Hampton said. "We might want to bypass."

"I thought Hodges told Lord Sedgwick the road had been repaired."

"Hodges thought at first someone be makin' the potholes mottling the road, but now he does not think so. There are more of them than before. He is recommending closin' the road permanently."

"More potholes?"

Christine reined in Miss Pippen and pulled out her map. The road connected to the drover trail and sat between the waterfall and the cliffs. She'd already surveyed the area where the carriage accident had occurred, but that was shortly after the road had already been repaired. Her heart began to thump.

Time and man had carved the high road over the crags. It would not take as long for rushing water to carve through weaker substrata beneath. Water flows toward the area of least resistance. Perhaps the reason why no more fossils had been washing up on the riverbanks was because the water had already eroded and perhaps expanded the lava tube enough, thus minimizing the powerful ebb and flow of water against the walls. Yet with expansion . . .

"Did Hodges say what is causing the abundance of new potholes?"

"He thinks there could be a sinkhole beneath. That's why he called back Bailey, mum. Hodges already sent a message to his grace in Dunfermline to inform him."

Another rider suddenly approached. Christine returned the map to her knapsack as Hampton moved slightly in front of her. She let him, as he was single-mindedly devoted to protecting her from all threats, seen as well as imagined.

"It be Lord John Maxwell," Hampton said.

Indeed it was. Christine tipped back her hat and awaited the miscreant's approach. He looked handsome atop a sleek bay hunter. He might sit a horse well and look distinguished in black. He might even resemble Erik from a distance, but there was nothing about him she liked. Today he was without his sister, Lara.

Reigning in his horse, he tipped his hat, his eyes a

deep cobalt blue beneath the narrow rim. "Lady Sedgwick. How fortuitous that we meet again."

Johnny Maxwell might be related to Erik by marriage and even be some distant cousin by blood, but the man was no relative of hers. She was not required to be polite. "Considering you are on Sedgwick land, I do not find it *fortuitous* at all," she replied.

He feigned injury. "You are still offended over my comment at the festivities," he said. "I would hope you know they were not aimed at you."

"Your barb was indeed aimed directly at me, sir. It just didn't have the result you wanted."

Maxwell rubbed his chin. "You think not?"

"Why are you here?" she asked. Maxwell must have known that Erik was not here.

Maxwell looked around him. "I've been informed you have been digging near the falls."

"Have you now? Considering only a few people know that, I'm rather curious to learn how you came about that information and found me."

"If I tell you, will you allow me to accompany you?"

She could not believe he had the audacity to ask. "I would not."

"May I inquire then, what are you searching for up at the falls? Rumors say you are a hobbyist fossil collector looking for the great winged Sedgwick beast. Me? I think you are searching for my sister, and I would ask to be included in that search, too. I want to know what you know."

Christine did not intend to allow him anywhere near her search. "Then you are not one of those who believe Lady Elizabeth is still alive, haunting these crags and sending a grief-stricken parent letters?"

"I am one of those who believe your husband had much to do with her demise. Maybe you are just a little curious, too. I wouldn't be surprised if he isn't the bastard who sent that most recent letter to my father to throw the scent off his back. My father is in frail health."

"How fortuitous for you then, since you will be next in line for the duchy."

Maxwell's eyes narrowed. "Perhaps if Sedgwick had been more generous to my family, his grace would not be in the predicament he is in now." Maxwell leaned forward. "By generous, I mean kinder to an old man who wants to know his granddaughter. You want the real beast of Sedgwick, look no farther than your bed, sweetling."

Christine's hand tightened on the quirt. "You may go, Lord John."

"Or what? Hampton will throw me off precious Sedgwick land?"

"Your rank may forbid Hampton from laying a hand on you, but it will not stop me. Or Hampton from defending me should you attempt to strike me back."

Eying her quirt, he laughed. "I believe you *would* strike me." Grinning, Maxwell leaned a forearm on his thigh and said, "Since you are about to find yourself out of matrimony, I believe I might decide to court you myself." He laughed and swung his horse around. "Even if you are an odd one, your grace."

She hated that his words made her flinch. *Out of matrimony.*

Watching Lord John ride away, she frowned. "Have you told anyone what I am doing in these hills, Hampton?"

He blanched. "I would never say anything, mum."

She reined around Miss Pippen to head back to the stable. "I think I will postpone our outing until later today."

"Where is Lady Rebecca?" Christine asked Becca's maid, catching the girl belowstairs.

Christine had left the stables and gone directly to Becca's chambers. When she found the door locked and no answer to her summons, she went to the dining room. No one had seen her since yesterday evening.

Becca's young maid folded her hands nervously in front of her. "Mrs. Brown told me I was not to disturb her, mum."

"Does Mrs. Brown often give you these dictums to leave her alone?"

"Only when Lady Rebecca awakens in the night with one of her nightmares, mum. They have become more frequent of late."

"I don't understand. Does his grace know she suffers these afflictions?"

"The doctors wanted to put her into an asylum but he would not allow it."

"Find a key and open the door."

Wide-eyed, the girl bobbed. "Yes, mum. Follow me."

Boris was standing outside the door when Christine arrived with the key. "Mrs. Brown was concerned you would awaken Lady Rebecca, your grace," he said. "It is always better after an episode that she sleep. She has been asking for her mother, mum. All day she has been asking. She has only just now returned to sleep."

Christine chewed on her lower lip. "What is wrong with Becca, Boris?"

He shook his head. "The nightmares began shortly after Lady Elizabeth's disappearance. She never remembers waking up or sleepwalking."

Erik had once told her his sister had been the last one to see Lady Elizabeth alive. "What did Becca see that night, Boris?"

Boris looked uncomfortable. "You will have to ask his grace, mum."

Chapter 17

Three days later Erik returned. Christine had just come down from the hills when she saw the Sedgwick coach in the carriage yard. The horses had already been led away to the stables, and men carrying buckets of soapy water were scrubbing the wheels and doors.

"He arrived home a half hour ago, mum," one of the livery boys told her as she slid off Miss Pippen's back and dropped to the ground.

Erik was home!

A moment later, Christine was rounding the third floor in the tower, slowing as she peered up the stairwell. She gathered her skirts and took the final flight of stairs. At the top-floor landing, she walked to the doorway opening into the bedroom. Only then did she dare pause and catch her breath. Whether from her exertion or seeing Erik, her heart thudded in her chest.

He stood in the middle of the master's suites, his hands at his side as he turned in a slow circle. He still wore his cloak and gloves as if he had come up here almost at once upon arriving. Holding her breath, she watched the play of his expression in the light filtering through the leaded windows, waiting for him to see her. Her hand stripped the scarf from her hair . . . and suddenly she was looking into his face.

Before she could dwell on the weight against her heart, she said, "I hope you do not mind the changes I have made up here."

She hurried to stand before the bed and brushed her hands over the emerald velvet draperies. "These were in another bedroom in another part of the castle. We painted the walls. Have you been upstairs? The shelves are repaired. New glass for the cabinetry will be installed next week. We had to send out to St. Andrews for a suitable glassmaker. You have your room back." She began to run out of things to say to fill the void she knew would follow in the silence. And then he would tell her what happened in Dunfermline.

He came two steps nearer. She took a step backward.

"Christine—"

"Don't say it, Erik. Do not come up here to my tower and tell me that with all your wealth and riches you could not buy us a reprieve."

Amusement softened his eyes. "*Your* tower, is it now?"

"You gave it to me." She scrubbed the heel of her hand against each cheek. "You said I could have it to do as I would. So now I have it and it's mine."

As you are mine.

"And I will not relinquish it."

He withdrew a handkerchief from inside his cloak. "What have I told you about wiping your nose on your sleeve?"

She snatched the lacy cloth from his gloved hand and glared at him. "Do not lecture to me about my lack of decorum. I . . . ."

He pulled her into his arms, and with his hand, he pressed her cheek against his shoulder. His cloak cocooned her against him, and there she remained, unable to say anything more.

"I do not believe I have ever had anyone fight for me that I did not well pay for the service." He pressed his lips against her hair. "You honor me."

She held her wet nose against his waistcoat. "You *have* paid me. You gave me this tower."

His chest vibrated against her forehead. After a moment, he said, "It is beautiful up here. I had forgotten."

The windows looked toward the distant crags. Piercing sunlight created a flawlessly blue sky, perfect in every way. She could see for miles. "I would have you live up here with me, Erik."

His hand framed her cheek as he lifted her face. Before she could breathe or whisper his name, his mouth was on hers. He kissed her with infinite gentleness. She could feel the solid beat of his heart against her palm. He pressed his lips to her hair. "I'm sorry you have been through hell over this," he said. "If I were anyone else, our marriage would not have been an issue. But because of who I am—"

"You are no longer my husband."

His mouth moved across her temple. "I am your husband in every way, Christine."

"Oh, God, Erik." Her knees nearly gave out. "You have no idea how I have worried over this issue. Why didn't you tell me the moment I walked in here?"

He lowered his arms and walked to the window. He braced his palms on the sill. "A hundred people have sworn they have seen her, Christine. I read eighteen witness depositions from the past few months alone. These were journeymen, tenants, ordinary people who *swore* on a Bible that they had seen her in the hills between here and St. Andrews. I saw the letter written to her father that said she was alive and happy and that he should no longer worry for her. It was her handwriting. Lord Eyre truly believes Elizabeth lives."

"What do you believe?"

"I believe the Maxwell clan will soon learn a hard and costly lesson about the follies of waging a war with me."

"That is not what I asked."

He slowly turned his head. Christine saw the flash of pain in his eyes and knew she could not possibly understand what it must feel like, blaming yourself for some horrible tragedy that might have been prevented had you *just* done something, anything, differently. Finding Elizabeth alive could take away that guilt and pain inside him. "Are you truly beginning to question this yourself?" she asked.

"The fact remains that despite the legal inconsistencies regarding her date of disappearance, she *has* been absent seven years and is not my wife any longer."

She laid her hand on his arm. "If the letter is a hoax, then it must also be aimed at Elizabeth's father. Have you considered that? What could anyone hope to gain by that manner of cruelty, Erik?"

"Robert and Johnny Maxwell are the only two who have anything to lose should you conceive my heir. They need our marriage nullified."

Still, the pieces did not fit. "No one can expect you to remain bound forever to a ghost. What can the person who perpetuated such a hoax expect to happen in the next few months to change anything?"

"I believe I am expected to die in the next few weeks, madam."

Christine gasped. Erik pulled her into his arms. "Ah, love, it is not my intent to make light of the curse. I do not want you hurt by this." He framed her face with his hands. "But even if I could go back and change the past few months . . . I would not do anything differently."

"I am relieved to hear that." She dabbed the handkerchief at her nose. Her chin tilted. "We are partners, Erik. I am not going to allow anyone to run me away from here. I think it is time we bring Aunt Sophie into the fold. She is an anthropologist. I want her to examine the human jaw bone and teeth you found last spring. Let us make sure. She has been saying it might be time for her to go. This will be a reason for her to stay."

Pausing, she gnawed at her lower lip. "I also wrote to Mr. Darlington and Amelia and asked them to come here." A smile trembled on her mouth. "If Elizabeth is out there, we'll find her and the answers you seek. I promise."

Erik shook his head but whether in disbelief or amazement, Christine did not know. Yet, suddenly the world seemed less bleak than it had when she climbed the stairs to the tower, barging in like Attila the Hun prepared to do battle on his behalf. He wrapped her in his arms, so close that she found herself no longer afraid.

"You honor me, Christine. I . . . I do not know what to say."

"I love you" would be a start.

I love you would be a beginning.

"Da!"

Erin's voice came from the stairwell.

Erik stepped away from Christine. His daughter's blond head appeared in the stairwell, then suddenly she was standing in the doorway. Wearing a red dress and white pinafore, her face lit with a smile. "Da!" she ran across the room and flung herself into her father's arms.

Her nurse huffed up the stairs. "Lady Erin!" Her face red with exertion, Mrs. Whitman caught her hand on the door. "I am sorry, your grace. The lass heard ye had come home and couldna' wait to see ye."

Erin wrapped her arms around her father's neck. He picked a cobweb out of her hair. "And where have you been playing this morning?"

"She has been following the dreadful cat, running through the servants' corridors. We found her in the kitchens again."

Erik tipped his daughter's chin. Then peered over at Christine. "Your cat is a bad influence, madam."

Mrs. Whitman cleared her throat. "Boris is downstairs waiting for you. Mr. Hodges is here. Since I was on my way up, I said I would inform you."

Still holding his daughter, he walked to the doorway. "Tell my sister I am back and would have her join me later for lunch."

Mrs. Whitman cast a brief glance at Christine. No doubt expecting Christine to be the first one to tell Erik his sister was in the village with her mother. Christine knew in her heart she needed to tell him about Becca.

But first, she had something else important. "Mr. Hodges is here about the road, Erik. That is where I have been the last few days. We found something."

"Do you want to tell me what we are looking for?" Erik's voice came at Christine from the ledge above.

She tented her hands over her eyes. "Take the rope," she suggested. "I've latched it to a solid root. It will hold your weight."

He worked his way down the slope. "And if it does not?"

She looked over the ledge at the river twenty feet below. Fast white water spumed up against the slimy face of the rock. "Then you will end up down there. Though it does not look too deep, it does lead to the waterfall."

They'd left their horses tied to the lower branch of a tree, and tramping through newly leafed oakbrush, walked down the hillside to where part of the rock face had slipped away into a river below. Shreds of talus rattled beneath his steps. She looked over her shoulder just before she moved lower on the slope.

She had been taking him along the rift in the road toward the sound of the waterfall. Two days ago, Christine had taken one look at the cracks in the now impassable road and recognized that more than the most recent spate of storms caused the damage. She stood and followed the narrow rim until she had found what she was looking for and sat. The evening air was cooler near the river.

Erik suddenly dropped down on the ledge beside her, sending scree over the edge. "Lord, Christine—"

"Look here." She pointed to a slim crevice in the rocks on her right.

He leaned around her. "What am I looking at?"

"A *cavern*, Erik."

He gave her a skeptical look. "If that is a cavern, then it is the bloodiest smallest cavern I have ever seen."

"Put your hand over this place here."

She helped him remove his glove, edging his hand across her lap to reach the crack. She knew he felt what she had felt, a strong draft, which meant air entered from some other access, picking up speed and strength as it funneled into the narrow crevices seeking an escape, much in the way air escaped from a hole in a hot-air balloon, following the path of least resistance.

They were a quarter mile from the cliffs and ancient drover trails she had been working around these past weeks. Now more convinced than ever a lava tube of some sort interconnected this entire area, she felt the excitement in her voice as she spoke, despite the grimness of the news. "A fissure has appeared since your crew repaired the road."

He scooped up a handful of scree in his gloved hand, letting it slide through his fingers. She knew a visual inspection of the road had been performed before he'd left for Dunfermline. "Fractures must have been present deeper down in the rock. If I were a bird, I could look down upon this entire region and give you a more thorough assessment."

He slung away the dirt. "Are you bloody telling me we might have some geological disaster in the making?"

"No. But this area is part of old volcanic terrain. Fissures have probably been present long before water began threading through these cliffs. This kind of rock formation is ideal for an underground aquifer that has probably been feeding the loch for eons. My guess is that the railroad opened something akin to a dam. The pressure has leveled off in recent months, but not before doing damage. The only thing we can know for sure is that there is a cavern beneath us."

She turned to assess his silence and found him looking down at the river. The river fed the waterfall. "I have already looked in the area behind the falls," she said. "There is no cave entrance."

"Is this entire area in danger of collapsing?" he asked.

"From what you have told me, some of it already has."

He swore, then lay back against the incline. She joined him. Shoulder to shoulder they both stared up at the sky. He didn't speak for a long time. Then he turned and rose on his elbow. A cloud smothered what remained of the sunlight passing over them. "What happened to Becca while I was gone?" he asked. "I saw the look Mrs. Whitman gave you."

"Becca is suffering nightmares. Mrs. Brown spent two days with her."

Erik sat up. The skin across his cheekbones seemed to grow taut. His wrist laid across his knee, he looked away. She pushed herself up. "You once told me your sister was the last to see Elizabeth alive. What did Becca see the night Elizabeth vanished?"

Shaking his head, he studied his hand. "I can only conclude she saw me arguing with Elizabeth. I can't explain what else Becca saw or didn't see that night for she has never spoken of it. She was young and the doctors feel the entire ordeal traumatized her. My sister has always believed in my innocence, but at a great cost, I fear."

Christine brought his hand to her cheek and wanted desperately to tell him everything else. "Erik . . ."

Talus suddenly trickled down the slope from above them. Christine looked up and saw movement among the trees. Then it was gone. Beside her, Erik had not moved. "Your men must be walking around wondering what has happened to you," she said. "We should probably be starting back."

Erik stopped her as she reached for the rope. "Wait. I sent my men back already. No one should be up there."

Christine's hand froze on the rope. "Maybe one of the horses has got loose."

He jerked the rope taut as if testing it. It held. He tugged again.

"Erik . . ."

"Wait here."

"I will *not*. Are you armed?"

He arched his brow. "Allow me to check my boot for the blunderbuss I keep stashed there."

"That isn't amusing, Erik. I am serious."

"As am I. Wait here."

Without using the rope for counterbalance, he started to stand. She snatched at his cloak to stop him. Something in the trees moved across the light. Miss Pippen suddenly lumbered into view. The tension drained from her muscles. And she fell back against the incline.

"Oh, lord . . . 'tis only my horse." She held a hand to her heart. "I must not have tied her securely. For a moment I was afraid."

"Fear is healthy, madam," he said, his eyes still on the ridge. "There is a reason I do not want people roaming about these hills alone."

"We are not alone. We're with each other."

He smiled faintly, then looked off the edge behind him. Something in his stance made her uneasy. "What is it?" she quietly asked.

Erik was clearly as conscious as she of the fact neither of them had a view of the place where she had anchored the rope. If someone *had been* up there . . .

"Have you ever swum in freezing water?"

His tone held faint amusement. Was he *joking* with her? Or was he taking the edge off his own discomfiture? His mouth crooked, as if he hadn't been uneasy, too. "I only ask because the river is bone-chilling cold."

Christine hiked up her skirt and tucked it in at her waist, making it knee length. "In that case, I should go first, your grace. I'm lighter. You can catch me."

Without waiting for him to argue, she took three quick steps up the incline. She didn't trust the rope and would not allow him to go first. She dug her half-boots into the talus. She held her breath, half afraid as she stretched for the first handhold in the rocks. "Dammit, Christine," she heard him say.

Then Erik gave her a foot up and she found a solid grip. He knew she was right. If the rope's integrity had been compromised, it was best that she go first since she was lighter. Besides, a person could find enough places to grab on to without taking hold of the rope in order to make a safe ascent. They weren't on a cliff, after all. Erik would follow easily behind her.

To her left she caught a glimpse of a jagged edge of rock and stunted trees. Her hand held fast to an odd-shaped rock that cut into her palm. It took her only a moment to realize what it was as it came loose in her hand. And then her foot slipped. She grabbed the rope and it took all of her weight. Erik would make sure she did not fall.

The thought had barely crossed her mind when the rope snapped.

Chapter 18

E rik hit the frigid water and went under. Sucked down by the undertow, then pulled by the current and the weight of his clothes, he bumped against the rocks. His feet finally found purchase against the slippery bottom, and he rose. The water was glacier cold. The river went barely to his chest, but standing was not simple as he at once searched for Christine, unsure if she had followed him over the bank's edge. She had fallen from the slope and he remembered shoving her forward into the incline. His effort to save her had been his doom. The momentum caused by that action had shoved him backward into the river.

With an oath, he wiped the hair out of his eyes and braced one boot against the rocks to keep from being swept underneath again. He struggled to remove the clasps on his cloak. He still wore one glove. Over the roar of the river and the waterfall in his ears, he sought to orient himself, realizing the current had dragged him down the river and to the opposite side. It might as well have been a mile from where he'd been when he'd gone over the ledge. He couldn't get back there. Even if he weren't wearing boots, he would not have been able to climb the lichen-infested rock.

He finally worked the sodden cloak off his shoulders. The current took it from his hands. He made it to the high bank at his back. He looked around for a hand-hold. And didn't find one.

He thought he heard Christine's voice. He looked over his shoulder and saw her on the opposite bank. Relief warmed him. She had not fallen. Though her hair and gown were damp with mud. Her soggy clothes clung to every line of her body. He wasn't even going to ask how she had made it this far downstream.

"I am hurt you did not jump in to save me, love," he called out.

"And drag us both under?" Her voice trembled. "You are taller than I am. At least you can stand."

He touched his hand to a cut on his forehead. His fingers came back with blood. "Hell."

"I see a place to your left, Erik. The bank is lower."

She was correct. Erik finally found a handhold. After fighting the current, he pulled himself up on the river's slippery stone bank. The sharp edges of rocks shoved against his hips and elbows as he rose to his knees. He'd injured his thigh as well, he realized. His trousers were torn. The cut did not seem too deep. He struggled to get to his feet, surprised at how weak he felt. He faced Christine on the opposite bank, his eyes at once searching the road above her.

"I want you away from here now. The river parallels the road for about a mile. Follow it," he said. "When you get out of the woods, you will see Sedgwick Castle."

"What about you? I am not leaving you."

"Unfortunately, my way back to Sedgwick Castle will take longer. I have to find a place to cross."

She pressed her palm to her chest and looked up at the sky. "You'll need to dry your clothes, or you could suffer a deathly chill. You need a fire."

"And what do you propose I use for matches?"

"Once when I was on a dig in Australia, Papa used two sticks to start a fire," she said unable to hide the tremble in her voice in her failed attempt at humor.

His temper softened. She didn't want to leave him. "Is there any place you have not been, *leannanan*?"

They both laughed at the absurdity of their conversation. He looked back toward the point where they had been standing, then up the steep hill toward where their horses were. Neither of them wanted to be the first to admit the possibility someone had been up there and cut the rope. Christine remained on that side of the river. He wanted her away from here as quickly as possible.

"It will be dark in a couple of hours. You will need every minute, or you won't make it back before nightfall. Go, Christine. I will be all right."

"Erik . . ."

"Go and get help." His voice came out sharper than he intended.

He did not plan to stand there while she could still be in danger. He wanted her safe and gone from this place. "If I make it back to Sedgwick before you do, I will be most unhappy."

"I will bring back help."

He walked with her until they were each forced by obstructions to move from their respective banks. "Now go. Stay parallel to the river until you get to the open." His shout carried across to her.

Then she was running, and a moment later gone.

Only then did he stop and lean against a large rock outcropping. Blood warmed his leg where it trailed down his thigh into his boot. The effort to open his trousers sapped some of his waning strength. He had torn a gash in his thigh. Watching the road for movement, he set his teeth against the length of his shirt and ripped out a strip of cloth, then bound the gash. After a while he climbed the bank and began working his way toward Sedgwick Castle.

Erik didn't know at what point over the next two days he realized he might die, that the curse would prove true after all. He suspected the idea began to take root shortly after the sun went down the first day, and he'd come out of the woods in a remote area near the cliffs just as a gust of cold wind hit him. Then the storm hit and he'd huddled in the shelter of a rock overhang away from the trees, pounded by the rain. Even in August, the evenings could be cold, and Christine had been correct about the life-threatening chill, especially coupled with wet clothes and the loss of blood. The injury on his leg had been worse than he'd first thought. It should have been stitched. He wrapped it instead in the river-water-soaked cloth he'd ripped from his shirt. A mistake.

With blurred vision and a debilitating headache, he knew he was in trouble when fever set in the next morning. Worried about Christine and lacking the patience to wait for someone to find him, and wondering why they had not, he chose to cross the river. The worst that could happen was that he would end up at the levee site a few miles away and his men would fish him out before he found himself eventually dumped into the sea. If he had been thinking rationally, he would have realized the error of his judgment.

The worst that had happened was that the river was a cold bitch and wanted to kill him. He made it across, but not before the current had swept him a half mile, and he had been slammed against rocks hidden beneath the surface and broken his ribs—or at least it had felt that way to him as he clung to the other side, with water rushing over him. He'd climbed up onto the bank and remained where he'd fallen for a day.

He'd awakened just before sunset and first glimpsed Elizabeth standing on a distant grassy knoll, watching him. He remembered staring at her and feeling nothing—not even surprise. He'd often heard that the angel of death visited a person just before he expired. Elizabeth had found her true calling then.

Then he'd awakened to discover a blanket lay across him. Yet, even with the added warmth, the shivering would not stop, and he forgot to care that a ghost did not carry blankets.

Erik remembered little after that. Somehow, his men had found him. He remembered Christine holding his hand, then discovered it was Elizabeth who sat beside him in the cart—no, not Elizabeth—Lara, his mind realized.

But then maybe he had imagined all of it, because when he awakened again, a blazing fire burned in a hearth, and it was his mother sitting on the chair beside the bed. His first thought was that he had truly descended into hell.

His movements stirred her, and she pressed a cup to his lips. It was daylight, and from the comfort of the bed, he guessed he was in his own room. His head and arm ached with a dull throbbing pain.

"Erik . . ." She softly coaxed him to drink. "You must finish this. The doctor does not want you moving about."

He pushed the cup from his lips. His weakness weighed down his limbs. "*Fook* the doctor." His words, little more than a rasping whisper, hurt his throat. "Where is my wife?"

"Erik . . . please. Won't you accord me some manner—?"

"Mother." *Christ* . . . his head hurt just to talk. He closed his eyes again and waited to awaken from this new unpleasant nightmare.

"I am at least trying," the voice said. "I have soup for you, and tea. Most of this needs to be warmed." He opened his eyes. She was indeed beside him, not an illusion. "You have given everyone a scare, Erik. Me especially."

"I don't know why you are here, except you must think I am about to die. I don't know what else would bring you to Scotland."

"That isn't fair to me, Erik," she whispered, staring at the cup in her hands. "I am your mother."

How could she have gotten to Scotland so quickly?

She couldn't have. His gaze took in the rest of the room before coming back to rest on her. "How long have you been here?"

She set the laudanum-laced drink on the nightstand. "Since you went missing. Becca brought me here. She needs me, Erik. You must understand . . . a mother needs to feel needed sometimes. She needs her children around her."

Erik pressed his fingertips against his temple. The last time she had needed him so much, he'd given her five thousand pounds. A bandage covered his head and wrapped his chest. "Where is Christine?"

"She is currently with Lady Sophia and Mr. Attenborough."

Erik tried to remember why that should alarm him. Attenborough wasn't due back until the end of the week.

Unless it was already the end of the week and his solicitor had received judgment back from the Commissionary Court.

* * *

Christine sat in Erik's library stone-still and learned that her marriage to the duke of Sedgwick was not legal.

Until the moment Erik's solicitor read the decree handed down after a preliminary examination by a magistrate in Dunfermline, Christine had not believed it to be true.

"His appeal failed," Mr. Attenborough said. "I warned him that it would. It was a simple matter for Maxwell to have the death certificate nullified and hence render your recent wedding invalid. But considering the circumstances, the magistrate will not bring charges of bigamy."

"Lord Sedgwick knew about this appeal when he returned from Dunfermline?" she asked.

Clearing his throat, Attenborough stole an embarrassed glance at Aunt Sophie. "Considering the seriousness of the original edict, I thought he would have told you, mum."

"No," she whispered.

"How long before all of this nonsense is settled and they can remarry?" Aunt Sophie asked.

"His grace will be legally free to wed in a year. We could get no magistrate to agree to conciliation even with a monetary settlement to Robert Maxwell. Lord Eyre still believes his daughter is alive."

Aunt Sophie drew herself up. "If this Lord Eyre person is claiming his daughter is alive, he will be greatly disappointed. Surely he wants something."

"Lord Eyre wants his granddaughter, mum. He will agree to the settlement and remove all claims if he can have his granddaughter. I believe when his grace learned of this request he said something to the effect that it would be a cold day in hell before Eyre ever saw that happen."

Christine studied her hands in her lap, folding and then unfolding them. She hadn't slept in a week. Only this morning, she had left Erik's bedside, reassured by the physician his fever had broken. She reached out her hand and touched her aunt's sleeve. "I don't feel well . . ."

"Of course you don't, dear. First, you nearly lose your husband and now you *do* lose your husband in the most idiotic of circumstances." Aunt Sophie glared at Attenborough. "You are supposed to be the best solicitor in all Great Britain. Surely you could have found some legal loophole—"

"Aunt Sophie"—Christine clutched her aunt's arm—"the matter is finished for now. Truly, I need to lie down."

A knock sounded on the door. Boris entered the library. "Your grace," he said to Christine. "Lord Sedgwick is awake and asking for you."

Christine rose. "How is he, Boris? Is he well?"

"Yes, mum. The countess is still with him."

After Becca had come to her the night Erik had been found, Christine had allowed his mother into Sedgwick Castle.

Christine still had many questions for mother and daughter, and though Christine did not trust the countess enough to leave her alone with Erik—a servant was always nearby—the woman was still Erik's mother and had pleaded her case successfully. The questions regarding any association the countess might have with the Maxwells would have to wait. Though in light of today's events, Christine was not even sure she held the right anymore to query his mother on the issue.

Turning her face away from the concern she glimpsed

in Boris's eyes, she knew if she faced Erik now she would likely wrap her hands around his throat.

And do what?

He'd lied to her that day in the tower, yes, and told her they were still married. But not because he'd wanted to hurt or deceive her. He'd lied because he cared for her.

"Mum . . ."

Christine nodded. "Please tell him . . ."

Aunt Sophie rose in a *swish* of bright blue and green taffeta. "Please tell his grace that my niece is not feeling well, if you will, Boris. She will be in to see him as soon as she is able."

Christine leaned against the tower window and stared into the darkness. The heavy leaded glass cool against her cheek, she watched the moon chase the clouds across the sky. She could not sleep. She'd been staring outside for an hour before she realized it and, with discontent, she gathered her robe about her and returned to the workbench. The aroma of that evening's uneaten meal still lingered in the chamber.

Bracing her elbows on the workbench, she turned up the lamp. Shadows danced on the walls and the ceiling as the flame wavered in a draft that came up through the cracks in the stone. She had made this room into a laboratory of sorts, with two workbenches near the windows. At night, the lamplight reflected off the glass and made the windows like mirrors. Tonight she would rather not be looking back at herself.

She still had not gone to Erik's room. Boris had reassured her when she had awakened from her nap in Aunt Sophie's room that Lord Sedgwick was doing well. But after that afternoon, Erik had not asked to see her again. She did not expect that he would. It would be beneath his station to do so.

Drawn back to her work, she'd finally returned to the tower. Alone in her laboratory, she removed the oilcloth she had placed inside a chest, then brought everything to her workbench. This was the first time she had unwrapped the cloth. Becca's tooth fossil lay at her elbow and she set a second one beside it—the one Christine had found at the riverbank just before she had fallen and nearly killed Erik. It was a tooth as big as her hand, bigger than the one Becca had found.

Christine had told no one of the find. Two reasons kept her silent. She wasn't sure what she had found, and she was awaiting Joseph's arrival.

But another reason, one she refused to admit to herself until Erik's recovery, was the realization that someone might have been on that cliff and cut the rope that day. Had she gotten too close to something someone did not want her to find? Had it been an accident? Or had someone simply wanted to kill Erik? She would never know for sure, for the rope had gone into the river where Erik had gone.

She heard Beast's meow, just before he bumped her leg and twined around her calves. Christine smiled and picked up the cat, welcoming his purrs as tears flooded her eyes, and she quietly wept against his fur. As usual, she had no handkerchief, and Erik's words about her lack of decorum flashed through her thoughts. She smiled against Beast's neck, hesitating as she looked over the top of his head.

Lady Erin stood half hidden in the shadows, peering around the doorway, watching her with saucer-wide blue eyes. A purple ribbon loosely restrained her long, curly hair, but only enough to keep the length out of her face. The child's feet were bare and, wearing only her nightdress, she looked like an escapee from the Sedg-wick nursery.

Christine straightened on the stool and wiped at her eyes. "Hello," she said. "Did you bring Beast up here to see me?"

"Beast sad kitty."

Christine had never heard the girl speak a sentence before and was surprised that her words were better formed than Christine expected.

A smile trembled on the corners of the child's mouth. She stepped around the door and, scooting against the wall, she tucked a doll close to her chest. Then offered it to Christine. "Cwistine sad, too."

"Cwistine?"

The girl nodded. Christine set Beast on the stool, walked over to where Erin stood, and knelt in front of her. Erin petted the doll's hair, then offered Christine the gift. "Cwistine."

Christine examined the worn ruffles and curls. She gently smoothed the hair. "I've never had a doll named after me."

She'd never had a doll. Period.

She'd been much too old even as a child to play with dolls. Papa thought it was more important for her to read Latin and study her numbers than play with toys and dolls. Touched by the simple gift, Christine raised her gaze. "She is beautiful. Thank you."

They remained in the shadows of the room, just out-side the reach of lamplight on the workbench. What must Erin be thinking? Had anyone spoken to her, ex-plained about her father's accident, or allowed her to see him yet?

"Have you been to see your da today?"

Erin lowered her eyes.

"Why has no one taken you to see your papa?"

The girl's beautiful face brightened. "Cwistine take me now."

Lord, she was insane, Christine thought fifteen minutes later, as she and Erin crept up the servants' stairway leading into Erik's corridor like two criminals. How had she allowed Lady Erin to talk her into this madness?

Christine stopped and knelt in front of Erin so that she could see her mouth and better recognize the words. "Quiet." She put a finger to her lips. "Shhh," she demonstrated, then pretended to button her lips.

Holding Christine's hand, Erin nodded. "Shhh," she repeated.

It was after midnight. The clock rang the hour as she and Erin entered the hall. Christine felt even more like a co-conspirator to a crime as she eased open Erik's door and followed Erin inside, careful to make no sound lest they awaken the sleeping dragon ensconced within the velvet draperies of his bed. A low fire burned, easing the chill from the room with gentle flames.

Christine was surprised and annoyed that no one was in here watching over Erik. Did they think two days' recuperation enough? Erin tugged on Christine's hand, and Christine realized she had stopped.

"Shh!" the child said loudly, as if Christine had made a noise. Then she giggled, and with infinite gentleness pulled Christine toward the bed.

Erik was propped halfway up the headboard against four pillows, his dark head bandaged. He wore a nightshirt laced at his chest, and she could see the fabric beneath. The physician said Erik had also suffered bruised ribs. The doctor did not think the ribs had broken or Erik would have been coughing up blood. The fever he believed came from the injury on his leg and from exhaustion.

Yet, in truth, Christine knew Erik was lucky to be alive. During the days of his absence, when no one could find him and the weather had turned, Christine felt the entire household go into mourning. They had done everything but lower his standard and put a placard on the garden wall next to Elizabeth's. The only person she was surprised *not* to see had been Robert Maxwell, ready to declare himself the new duke.

But Erik *was* safe and alive. The issue with their marriage would be settled in time. Strange that it worried her less than it should have. She had found something potentially huge in the ground—a discovery. So why did she continue to feel as if she might at any moment shatter into a thousand tiny pieces?

Why had the ring not yet loosened? Why wouldn't it let her go?

The floor creaked beneath her slippered feet, and she froze. Movement in the bed stirred in the shadows. Erik turned his head.

Erin laughed. "Da!" She climbed into bed to snuggle with her father.

His arm went around his daughter. He pressed one hand against the mattress and eased himself higher against the pillows. "It is about time, imp," he said, kissing the top of Erin's head. "I was beginning to think you had not convinced the princess to come down from her tower."

Christine stared at the two in disbelief. "You *tricked* me."

Neither one looked the least penitent. Erin took Christine's hand and pulled her nearer so that she was forced to sit on the mattress. Then, settling her head against her father's shoulder, she lay comfortably between them.

"She shouldn't even be out of bed at this hour, Erik."

He was a terrible father for allowing a six-year-old to wander free.

"What can I say?" His hand lifted to pull her chin around. "She escaped her nursery."

Christine's mouth pinched, but now that she was here, she wasn't all that angry with him. Certainly, she wasn't with the child, who had brought Beast up to the tower and given Christine her very first doll. "That isn't fair," she murmured. "Using your daughter against me."

"You have been avoiding me, my love." His fingers reached out to twine into her unbound hair. "Desperate times strive for desperate measures."

"Shakespeare's *Hamlet*."

"Hippocrates: Extreme remedies are appropriate for extreme diseases."

"Am I the remedy or the disease then?"

"Both," he said.

The tone in his voice as revealing as his words, his eyes held hers or hers held his, she no longer cared which, or that her heart should not be beating so hard or that she should at least summon some high-minded response in her own defense. She had missed him. They had a thousand things they needed to say, should say but could not without feeling hampered by her trepidations.

Erin had shut her eyes and her even breathing told Christine she was already asleep. Christine smoothed the hair from the child's face, then finding Erik watching her, placed the back of her hand across his brow. "You still have a fever."

He took her hand and pressed it to his lips. "I should have told you the truth when I returned from Dunfermline," he said.

"Yes, you should have."

His hand wrapped around hers and he waited until she finally lifted her gaze before he spoke. "Will you trust that it will not be a year to settle this matter? It will not be a month."

Christine looked away. How could he be so sure, so confident of everything, when she continuously found herself struggling?

"I do not want you going back to look for that cavern," he said.

Her mind frayed by the mêlée she'd endured the past few days worrying over him, and now this conflict—the one between her heart and her honor—refused to do battle with him now.

"Are you the one who lowered the drawbridge and let my mother into this castle?" he asked, pulling her down beside him and Erin, and bringing the comforter over them all.

The child stirred as Christine set her head on the pillow and looked over Erin's head into the eyes of the man she still considered her husband, no matter what some magistrate said to the contrary. Tomorrow, she would scandalize the servants when they walked in and saw her sleeping in this bed.

"Do not worry, Christine." Erik's recognition of her thoughts illuminating the darkness between them. "Boris knows you are here and will keep everyone away until you take Erin back to the nursery. For now, sleep, *leannanan*."

And she did.

Chapter 19

Christine awakened just before dawn and realized she must have shut her eyes long enough for Erin to curl against her and put her arm to sleep. The fire in the hearth had died. The room was now chilled.

Erik was gone.

Christine pushed up on her elbow. Someone was in the dressing room. Easing out of bed, she shoved her feet into her slippers, wrapped her robe tighter about her waist and padded across the room. Boris was inside, laying out a razor and soap beside a pitcher of water and a bowl.

"My apologies," she said, keeping her voice low so she did not awaken Lady Erin.

"The master is downstairs," Boris said. "He said for me to let you and the young lass sleep, mum."

Christine scraped a hand in her hair. She had not slept well. Nothing between her and Erik had really been settled. "Should he be out of bed?"

"No, mum. But if he is set on doing a thing, he'll see it done."

"I will take Lady Erin back to her bed," she said after a moment.

The little girl barely stirred when Christine lifted her. She stepped into the corridor and had reached the staircase when distant voices sounded from somewhere to her right. Lights shone from a room downstairs in a corridor mostly darkened with predawn shadows. Christine walked to the landing. She glimpsed movement from the room just off the entry hall, as someone passed in front of the light. Voices carried. Erik was speaking to Hampton and Hodges, two of the men who had found him near the river, but though she recognized the impatience in Erik's tone, his words were indistinguishable. *He should not be out of bed,* she thought. *And he expected me not to take risks with my life.*

She tightened her arms around Erik's child and turned toward the nursery, slowing as she padded through the portrait gallery and peered up at the last Sedgwick family portrait that hung on the wall, its ornate gold frame bright against the oak panel wall. It was a painting set in the gardens, with Erik and Elizabeth, who was holding their daughter in her arms and staring back at Christine with painted expressionless eyes. The portrait had been completed only weeks before her disappearance.

Aunt Sophie had examined the bones Christine had brought her. She could say with certainty the partial jaw belonged to a person of approximately nineteen to twenty-five years old. The former Lady Sedgwick, Elizabeth Maxwell Boughton, had been twenty-two when she vanished.

Up the stairs and just before she reached the nursery, Mrs. Whitman came around the corner. Still wearing her night clothes and nightcap, she nearly collided with Christine. The woman saw Erin in Christine's arms and burst into tears. "Oh, mum," she gasped. "Ye found the lass. I thought something terrible had happened . . ."

"Shh," she hushed the distraught woman.

Christine walked past Mrs. Whitman into the nursery. The nurse strode ahead of her and into the bedroom. She rearranged the bedcovers. Outside, daylight pressed against the windows. Holding a finger to her lips, Christine left the bedroom. Behind her, Mrs. Whitman shut the door.

"I awakened when I heard a noise in the nursery," the nurse said. "The countess was here. She didn't see me. When I discovered the tyke gone—" she pressed a hand to her heart and Christine worried that the woman might collapse— "I did nae know the tyke was gone. I thought the worst . . ."

"Because Lady Erin's grandmother was in here? Surely that is nothing that should frighten you."

"It is just that seeing anyone in this nursery is unusual. Even Lady Sophia does not go into the child's bedroom without asking me first." Drawing in a deep breath, Mrs. Whitman straightened. "Where did you find the wee lass this time?"

"She was with her father."

"I should not have panicked, mum. I apologize. You are correct. The countess is Lady Erin's grandmother."

Christine did not return to Erik's chambers. Instead, she ran up to the tower, found that Annie was already awake and preparing her toilette. Christine washed and changed into a dove-gray morning gown. The chilly morning air made her move more quickly.

"We must do something about the temperature up here, Annie," Christine said as the girl finished pinning up Christine's hair.

She needed to appear regal this morning, but after an hour of preparations was on the verge of expressing impatience, when Annie announced she'd finished. Christine made her harried way down four flights of stairs. She found the countess sitting alone in the dining room, eating a poached egg and drinking tea. Her head lifted at Christine's entry.

The chilly morning air outside contrasted with the warmth and smells of warm bread within the dining room. "My lady," Christine said. "You are awake early this morning."

The countess set down the serviette in her hands. "I thought I would see what it is like to awaken before afternoon tea. My son had no need of my help this morning, so I came in here. It has been a long time since I have eaten a meal at this table."

Christine served herself at the breakfront and sat across from the countess. The chair where Erik usually sat remained empty. "Boris took him his meal," the countess said.

What she did not say was that Erik wanted nothing to do with her.

A child's laughter outside the doors drew the countess around. Lady Erin was awake and with her nurse. The countess rose and walked to the windows.

Christine didn't know why she suddenly felt sorry for the countess. She was in this large room all alone, trying to be part of a family she did not know, and mother to a son who did not like her.

Christine thought of her own mother, dead and buried somewhere in Italy. Christine had always thought it was her fault that her mother left. That Christine had not been good enough or pretty enough or had misbehaved one too many times. All silly observations in hindsight, but to a little girl they had been real. Now she realized that sometimes mothers just left, and there was nothing Christine could have done differently. Having a child was no measure of a woman's character.

After pouring a cup of tea, Christine walked to the window. Erin and Mrs. Whitman were leaving the gardens.

"She is the image of her beautiful mother," the countess said. "I do not see any of Erik in her face."

"I understand you went to the nursery this morning to see her."

The countess returned to the table. "I wanted to see Erin before the household awakened. I would not have disturbed her sleep. If you must know, my son has given me orders that I am not to be alone with her. I am sure the only reason I have not been thrown out since he has awakened after the accident is because of you." More than bitterness tainted her words. Pain filtered into her voice as it wavered slightly.

"Me?"

"My son seems to hold an unusual fascination for you," Countess Sutherland said. "He has been on his best behavior. How would it look if he tossed me out for no apparent reason?"

"If he wanted to toss you out, you would be gone, my lady. I hold no sway over his actions."

"You do not think so? Have you been here long enough to see the castle?" the countess inquired, stirring milk into her tea as she observed Christine. "All of his life, he has been a connoisseur of beautiful things. Becca said that after Elizabeth's passing, he closed nearly every room in the castle and covered every piece of furniture. Now he is opening some of these rooms. Why is that, do you suppose?"

Christine suspected the countess knew exactly why Erik had closed off that part of his life, as if by hiding it away, he could hide himself from his feelings. She *had* taken note that some of the coverings had begun to come off the furnishings. "Perhaps he chooses to no longer blame himself for her disappearance."

"One cannot deny the effect you have on him. Whether he has found something new with which to indulge his passions, or if he is running away from the old indulgences and you are as far away as he could run, does not matter to me."

The barb hurt, and Christine did not entirely understand it, before she realized the arrow had not been aimed at her heart as much as it was aimed at her son's. "You do not like him very much, do you?"

"I cannot be faulted for loving my daughter more, if that is what you mean, when my son has done everything in his power to push me away. My daughter needs me. My son never did. I need to feel important, you see. I cannot bear the thought of growing old alone."

"Maybe if you were not so self-involved, you would see that it isn't about your needs at all."

The countess set down her cup. "When is anything we say or do *not* about our needs? We are all selfish in our way. You cannot tell me you married my son on the pretext of some great affection for him. You have not known each other that long. Yet you wed him. So do not speak to me of selfish needs. Has he told you that Erin is not his?"

Shock stilled her breath. "I don't believe it," she whispered.

"Then ask him yourself. He married Lady Elizabeth anyway, knowing that the child was probably not his. I tried to warn him the chit was not for him, but he gets his mind and heart set on a thing . . . He's about to take on the Lord Advocate himself over the issue concerning your marriage. But once

Lady Elizabeth fails to materialize this time, Lord Eyre will bring charges of murder down on him. He'll do whatever it takes to get his granddaughter. He'll bring up Erin's parentage. A scandal will ensue. Erik claims that he does not care what people say about him, but he will care what they say about Erin. He'll care when she is shunned by polite society, as Becca already is. Why do you think he has not allowed her to have a Season?"

Christine did not reply at first. Not because she didn't know what to say, but because she knew exactly what had to be said.

"You are saying I should leave here and spare him. Do the honorable thing to protect everyone?"

"I am saying that my son is fighting a losing battle. Yes, perhaps there is honor in such a decision. You would not be thinking of yourself."

"Then I should inform you that you have erroneously attached some form of nobility to my character if you think I will bow out. Doing so would not save him and his family the embarrassment that will ensue when he legally challenges the Lord Advocate's judicial involvement in something over which the man should not have held any sway."

Christine moved to the table and set down her teacup. "You see, I am also one of those who feel the Lord Advocate should be removed from power, as he has clearly proven he is prejudiced by his relationship to his brother, Lord Eyre, and prone to bribery. He has no business being in any position of judicial authority since he cannot perform his duties."

Blanching, the countess came slowly to her feet. But Christine was not finished. "Or do you think I should go to my husband and beg him to allow Lord Eyre near Lady Erin? If Eyre is such a vindictive man as you claim him to be and would threaten to humiliate his own granddaughter because of his war with Erik . . ." Christine could hardly say the words. "*I* would not even allow the man near the child."

"Then I misspoke. Lord Eyre in not vindictive. He is desperate."

"I spoke to Lord John Maxwell last week and he knew all about what I have been doing at the cliffs. Becca is the only person who knew I was looking for the Sedgwick beast. Did she tell you? And did you then tell him?"

"Our families are not strangers," the countess whispered. "Lord Eyre has been more Erik's father than ever any man alive. What has happened is not all Lord Eyre's fault."

"Pah!" Christine brandished her hand dismissively at such drivel as if she were channeling Aunt Sophie. "Where were the both of you when he needed you most? Where was anyone? Do not talk to me about being alone now. As my Aunt Sophie would say, 'You reap what you sow.'"

Tears of fury welled in the countess's blue eyes. Eyes very much the same shape and color as Erin's. "You cannot talk to me in this manner, young lady," the countess said. "You . . . you aren't even my daughter-in-law anymore."

"Then no one can accuse me of being disrespectful to a family member." Christine took a step nearer. "And before you say anything else to malign Lady Erin's parentage, I suggest you take a closer look at the child. You may not see Erik in his daughter's face, but you will see some of yourself. Look at her again and tell me that you believe she is not your granddaughter in blood and in name. Then try telling yourself Erik is not her father."

Christine had said enough. Aunt Sophie always told her to leave an audience wanting more and if you could not do that, then leave them shocked. Her only regret as she swept out of the dining room through the glass French doors was that she could not slam them in her exit.

Erik did not move from his place beneath the trees as he watched Christine disappear around a bend in the path. He felt something stab low in his chest. Something that had nothing to do with lust, but with longing of a different kind.

Something that should have been unpleasant to him, yet wasn't. His senses followed the soft pad of her angry steps on the sand-and-crushed-brick pathway until he could no longer hear her footfalls. He turned his attention to the open French doors leading into the dining room. His mother stood just outside, on the terrace. It took him a moment to realize she had not yet seen him.

He did not make it a habit to eavesdrop, but he had heard their voices, and so he had stopped in the gardens, leaning on his crutches because his leg throbbed abominally. Then he had remained and listened.

Maybe he'd been used to having his way for too long in this life. These past months had certainly been a reminder that his future was as fragile as his past. What he couldn't remember was the last time anyone had ever waged a battle on his behalf.

He stumbled three steps to the tree trunk, set his palm against the rough bark, and stared off at the distant crags steeped in mist, wondering how many hours he'd stood in this exact spot contemplating the choices he'd made in his life, contemplating his incapacity for compassion and forgiveness, and the realization that he had no idea how to truly love.

Yet even for all of that, the world suddenly seemed less bleak than it had just five minutes before—even when he returned his attention to discover his mother standing at the edge of the terrace where the garden began, he did not feel his mood or temper darken.

She delicately tapped a finger to each corner of her eyes. "I suppose you heard everything?"

"I heard enough."

And he was ready to be rid of her presence from his life forever as he awaited her excuses or some derogatory comment about Christine's character. But her understanding of the situation showed with vivid clarity in her blue eyes. She had but to utter one harsh word . . .

"She was right," his mother suddenly said. "Everything she said was the truth. I deserve to be thrown out of here. I deserved it before."

"Bloody hell yes, you deserved it." Hadn't he told her once before if she ever spoke to a soul about Erin that he would sever his ties with her?

He leaned his weight on the crutch and stumbled again, and she was suddenly beside him, propping her shoulder beneath his. "Why is it you insist on trying to kill yourself?" she snapped. "You have never been considerate of those who worry about you."

"Aye, Mother," he laughed with masculine scorn. "It has always been my intent to hurt you by maiming myself, as I am happiest lying in bed suffering."

"Oh Erik." At her behest, he sat on the old stone wall and took the pressure off his injured limb. "No matter what I say, I seem to mangle the sentiment. Believe it as you will, I meant only that I worry about you."

"And here I thought ye cared only for yourself," he said.

"It is not so much that I care about myself. It is that I have found it easier to blame everyone else for what is wrong in my life. You might be surprised to know I have not unpacked and had intended to be gone before you were on your feet. I told Becca this before she brought me here."

"How long have you been in contact with Maxwell?"

She crossed her arms. Her sleeves billowed over her wrists and she brushed at the lace. "When have I not been in contact with the old curmudgeon? We have been family friends since you were in short pants. Who do you think has been keeping me apprised of the events here? I was living at his boat house on the lake until we had a disagreement about you. You might be surprised to know I have since moved into a cottage near the hamlet."

"You? Living in a cottage without an entourage of servants? I gave you enough money to purchase your own estate should you want one."

"I did not take the funds you gave me. I would have gambled them all away. Nor have I had a single drink since that day you came to see me in London. I came to Scotland to be near you and Becca. Though I will admit I had not believed I would be offered the chance to be near you."

"Then the recent slate of events has worked in your favor."

"Only because I had unfettered access to you for an entire two days. I have not had that much time with you since you were practically stolen from my arms and brought here as the new duke of Sedgwick."

Erik knew that his mother had barely been a widow of two months when that event had occurred. She'd been eighteen with no family support upon which to draw who did not want a piece of the Sedgwick name and fortune. A part of him even understood how she would have involved herself with a man like Becca's father, this estate's former administrator and the man who had held legal guardianship over Erik. Erik had literally been taken from her.

Women did not possess the same power as men when it came to controlling their future—even an independent woman like Christine. The proof lay in the fact that she had married him for the reasons she had. None that had to do with love.

His mother started to turn away and Erik took her arm. She startled at his touch. When was the last time they had touched?

He lifted his gaze and looked into the face of a woman he had barely allowed himself to know and, as he and his mother faced one another, a new kind of silence fell between them.

Perhaps for the first time in his life, he looked at his mother with emotions no longer weighted by the baggage they both carried from their pasts, his lightened considerably by Christine's presence in his life.

Maybe almost dying had softened him.

Maybe falling in love—deeply in love, something he had never felt with this kind of intensity—had given him a new perspective on his other relationships, made him take stock of his faults. The man staring back at him from the mirror of his soul was not one he particularly liked. Certainly he was not one Erik welcomed any longer. How many wars in his life would have been averted had he just made some conciliatory move first? What would happen if he did so now?

He still did not trust his mother with an open invitation into his life, but neither would he send her packing and on her way from Sedgwick as he had done so many years before.

"Do you want to remain for a few weeks?" he asked. "I do not expect you to stay the winter . . ." Small increments, he told himself. "But a summer's visit—"

"Oh, Erik, I truly do. A few weeks would be wonderful."

Again, he told himself he could do this. He *needed* to do this. "I will send someone to the cottage and retrieve the rest of your belongings."

Erin's distant laughter suddenly signaled his daughter's approach up the garden path. She and Mrs. Whitman were returning from their morning constitutional. Beside him, his mother stilled. He could almost feel her panic.

"Have you spoken to her since your arrival?" he asked.

"She doesn't know me, Erik."

"Come." He pushed himself up on the crutch. "It is time to meet your granddaughter then."

An hour later, Erik left his mother with Erin and Mrs. Whitman outside in the garden, painting portraits of butterflies. He'd slipped away without either noticing, and stopped at the French doors in the dining room as he looked back at them.

"This arrived by special courier." The butler gave Erik a letter.

Without looking at the front, Erik turned the letter over in his hand and flipped open the seal. The note was from Joseph Darlington and addressed to Christine. He hadn't paid attention to the name on the missive when he'd turned it over. He tapped the letter impatiently against his palm. "It seems guests will be arriving tomorrow."

Chapter 20

C hristine's voice touched Erik first, a moment before she and Joseph Darlington entered the stable, where he'd gone shortly after breakfast. Sitting on a three-legged stool in the stall that housed Christine's mare, he stilled the pick in his hand. He lowered the horse's front hoof and rose to his feet.

Darlington and Amelia had arrived two days ago. For two days, his entire staff had been buzzing about in a state of eagerness. Sedgwick Castle finally had *guests*! At Christine's direction, the coverings had been whisked off much of the furnishings and rooms no one ever went into had been prepared as if the queen herself were visiting. Christine had spent all hours of the day and night with Joseph and Amelia in her laboratory in the tower. She had tried to include Erik. But his knowledge about paleontology could fit into a thimble.

She and Darlington had paused in the entryway and were talking to Hampton, asking about the quality of the rope stored in one of the outbuildings behind the stables. She stood in a wedge of sunlight, the only warmth to be found in the stable, as if a pair of hands had reached into the doorway behind her and parted the murky air like a curtain.

She walked to Miss Pippen's stall and pampered the nag with a handful of cubed sugar, while at the same time Erik was absurdly jealous that she had not paid that manner of attention to the mare he had given her. Erik watched as Darlington made a remark about the horse and her defense of the old mare.

A natural energy added to Christine's beauty and, more than once these last few days, Erik had caught Darlington's eyes on her face, and an odd look in his gaze as if he were seeing someone he'd never seen before.

Finally, brushing off her hands, Christine turned and saw him. Her hand went to her chest. "Erik," she gasped.

The chill had brought the apples to her cheeks along with a blush. Leaning against the warm girth of the mare, he could not help it as his gaze went over her, before shifting to Darlington.

As cynical as Erik was about Darlington, he was also equally primal, male, and possessive. Darlington must have recognized the look in Erik's eyes. "Amelia and I are elated about the opportunity you have given us here," he said after an awkward pause. "I have seen your sister's fossils. Chrissie and I agree that nothing like this has ever been unearthed. This is an enormous find."

"Thank my wife for your invitation," Erik said. "I had nothing to do with it."

Christine hesitated, clearly sensing the discordant undercurrent running between them, and not quite knowing why. Her eyes went over the horse. "I didn't know you were out here grooming the mare. Has the doctor given you permission to be up and about?"

"Since I pay his salary, the doctor allows me certain freedoms."

Christine's eyes narrowed. Darlington shifted in the silence. Then peering from Christine to Erik, he politely bowed his head and told them he needed to find Amelia. "The trip here exhausted her," Darlington said. "Mrs. Samuels assured me that she herself is still recovering and that I should not worry."

"I will be back to the tower shortly," Christine said. "We'll talk about our climb for tomorrow."

After Darlington departed, Christine took up a second currycomb and began grooming the mare beside Erik. She brushed and stroked the mare. He watched her hands as she spoke about her plans on the cliffs as if to reassure him—of what, he wondered, did he need reassurance?

"You may not know this about me, but horses have always intimidated me." Her voice was quiet as she spoke.

They faced each other across the back of the mare. "When I was fourteen, I was quite captured by my own brilliance and self-confidence. There was nothing I could not do. Until one night, I rode Aunt Sophie's prized stallion. She loved that horse. I killed it when it stepped into a hole and broke its leg. It would be the first of many lessons in the ensuing years that would teach me the peril of my own arrogance. And my own lack of significance."

She met his gaze. "You should not be jealous of Joseph."

"Jealous?"

Christine did not know him if she thought jealousy defined the depth of his feelings.

Jealousy meant one coveted something someone else had. He'd never *coveted* anything. He'd either purchased or owned a controlling interest in anything that was of any value in his life.

Indeed, he did not understand the concept of jealousy.

"Is that what you believe I am?" he asked. "Jealous?"

She stroked the mare. "No." Her voice remained quiet. "It is not jealousy that has made you churlish but your uncertainty in the face of, well . . . doubt."

"I knew from the beginning what you wanted from me, Christine."

He watched her hands pause. "I think what you have done for your mother is wonderful," she said after a moment.

Erik returned the currycomb to the shelf outside the stall, then worked the leather gloves from his hands. "If you are about to ask me to extend the same courtesy to Erin's other grandparent, don't."

Christine latched the stall gate behind her and laid the currycomb next to his on the shelf. "Would it be too difficult to try? Though I would not expect you to go alone."

He met the concern in her eyes. "Would you rescue me, my love?"

"That isn't what I meant." She brushed the hair from his brow and touched her fingertips to the silver at his temple. He gently wrapped his fingers around her wrist, arresting her movement. She wrapped both hands around his and pulled them to her cheek, where she held them pressed to the warmth of her flesh. "It is only that I want you to know you are not alone in this fight, Erik."

Not for the first time was he conscious that she stirred something deep inside him. He would not—could not—explain something he did not understand himself, and yet he found himself speaking the words anyway. "I need you, Christine." His voice was quiet, intense and, as he slid his hand around her cheek to cup her nape, the passion that he failed to hold back when he held her, made love to her, pummeled to the surface. "And I have never needed anyone. I am at a loss. Simple as that. My whole life has changed since you have entered it."

She pressed her forehead to his chest and, wrapping her arms around his waist became almost immovable. "Oh, Erik," she whispered.

He suddenly realized the front of his shirt was wet. He reached between them and tilted her chin. Tears swam in her blue eyes and spiked her lashes. Knowing her penchant for a lack of handy handkerchiefs, he could see he needed to find one, at least to help her clean her spectacles. "I hope those are tears of joy, love."

Her hands tightened in the loose fabric of his shirt. She shook her head. "They are tears of horrible guilt. I have something I must confess. Something I should have told you from the beginning."

A skein of alarm sliced through him. "What is it, Christine?"

"I fear I may have put a spell on you."

He didn't know if he wanted to laugh or weep in relief. "Aye." He pressed his mouth to her hair. "I am thoroughly charmed."

"No." The words brought a fresh rush of tears. She lifted her face. "You *are* under a spell. I don't know how, but you have been under one the moment I opened the door in the classroom and saw you standing in the hallway at Summershorn Abbey."

"Christine—"

"Look!" She held up her hand. "*This* is a magic wishing ring. It's an Arthurian antiquity. It belonged to my great-great-grandmother. The wearer gets what she or he wants most in the world."

He'd noted that ring months ago. More than that, he took notice of her words, and it was as if sunlight spilled into the crevices that had opened up in his life these past few days. "You wished me to your door that afternoon at Summershorn Abbey?"

"No." She scrubbed the heel of her hand at her cheeks. "You were the last person I wanted to see that day."

"You did not wish me to the door. And I was the last person you wanted to see. Yet somehow this ring did . . . what exactly?"

"Truly?" She straightened her shoulders. "I am not sure. But the fact that I am here and I am in love with you and you quite possibly feel the same must be the first clue that we have been charmed."

This time, he could not contain himself. He laughed. No simple laugh either. He felt a jolly deep release all the way to his sternum. "I do love you."

"Oh!" She pushed him. Stumbling backward, he caught his hand on the ledge of the stall before dragging her into his lap as he came to sit on a bale of hay. She pushed her palms against his chest. "I am confessing my heart and soul to you and you laugh."

"I am sorry, my love. I just told you the most profound sentiment I have ever told another human being, and I am then informed that the woman I love above all else is *non compos mentis*."

"I am *not* a raving lunatic." She again offered up her hand with the silver engraved ring as evidence. "Just *try* to get it off my finger. Try."

Erik attempted a sober expression as he examined the magic ring in question. He wanted to kiss her senseless. "Your finger is swollen."

She snatched away her hand. "My finger is not *fat*. The ring slid on my finger and tightened." She babbled on about someone named Babs and Sal, students of hers, he surmised. He heard Amelia and Joseph's name. Her father's. Clearly, countless believers had worn the ring. "This ring won't come off until my greatest desire is finally granted."

"Then theoretically, if it won't come off, maybe I am not what you want most in the world."

"But you are. I choose *you*."

"Christine." He slowly turned her in his lap. "I am honored by your confession. More than you can possibly know."

"But you *are* what I want most in the world. I don't understand. Perhaps in the beginning it wasn't or I did not think it was, because that tooth was very tempting, or maybe it was and I just did not understand the clues—"

"But then I won you over."

She lifted her eyes as if to say, "*yes*."

"Christine"—he wrapped her against him—"I do not need magic to tell you I love you or know that you feel the same. The magic we share is what we ourselves make between us. Let that be enough."

He spoke to her as if he were talking to his daughter who had lost her pet rather than a grown woman who had danced like a *houri* nymph for him last night, then pleasured him twice this morning.

"But what if it isn't enough?" she said, almost as if speaking to herself.

He finally found his handkerchief. "Then consider this, my love. In the eyes of the law, we are no longer wed."

A shadow passed across the light as someone entered the stable. Erik looked toward the doorway as Hampton entered. "Lord Sedgwick?"

Hampton spied Erik as he rose and set Christine on her feet. "What is it?" Erik asked.

"Boris sent a message from the main house," he said. "Mr. Attenborough arrived and requests an audience with you."

Erik's solicitor should have been in Dunfermline seeking an audience before the ruling magistrate in the Commissionary Court. His return *was* unexpected. Christine wrapped her fingers around his forearm. "Isn't it too soon to hear back from him?"

Once outside, Erik could see up the hill toward Sedgwick Castle. From where he stood, he glimpsed part of the inner courtyard. More than one carriage sat on the cobbles. "Did Boris say who else was with Attenborough?"

"No, your grace. He only said you needed to come at once."

Erik looked down at Christine. "Do a favor for me," he said with quiet intensity. "Find Erin and keep her with you."

"They have arrested his grace for the murder of Lady Elizabeth," Mrs. Brown said as she entered Aunt Sophie's chambers twenty minutes later.

Christine came to her feet. She had done as Erik asked and found Erin. Amelia held a finger to her lips as she shut the door to Aunt Sophie's bedroom where she had laid the child down for a nap. Mrs. Whitman remained in the room with Erin. "He is a peer. No one can just come to Sedgwick Castle and arrest him. On what evidence?"

Mrs. Brown lowered her voice. "Word is his sister be the one what condemned him for Lady Elizabeth's murder," the housekeeper said. "The constable has men downstairs and will take him to Dunfermline today."

"Lock the door behind me," Christine told everyone. "Do not allow anyone into this room."

Joseph stepped forward. His hand stayed hers on the door as if he would prevent her from leaving. "Chrissie, he must have known this was coming. Why would he have sent you upstairs? Maybe he knew something like this was coming."

"Let go of me. I won't let them do this. If you try to stop me . . ."

"Why after seven years?" Joseph asked. "Why now?"

"Because Lord Eyre hates him and would attempt to take Erin. I don't know, Joseph. But if you don't let me out . . ."

He looked over her shoulder at Aunt Sophie. "Go with her, Joseph."

Reluctantly, he opened the door. Christine grabbed her skirts and ran out of the room. She descended into the main corridor a few moments later. All she had to do was follow the line of frightened servants gathered in the hallway. Boris and another two dozen servants were milling just off the gallery.

Becca sat on a bench against the wall, her mother next to her attempting to soothe the distraught girl. The moment Becca saw Christine, she rose. "I am so sorry," she sobbed in Christine's arms. "This is my fault. All my fault."

Christine tightened her palms on Becca's shoulders and looked into the girl's tear-stricken face. "What have you done, Becca?"

Shaking her head, she murmured unintelligible words about having witnessed a scene long ago between her brother and Elizabeth. She wiped her nose and babbled into the handkerchief. "He told me to tell them, Christine. He *told* me. When the constable asked me what I saw that night, Erik told me to tell the truth. Afterward, Erik said I did nothing wrong. I condemned him and he said it was not my fault. Why would he say that?"

"Because he loves you, Becca. Because you have been holding a deep burden inside you. But whatever it was you saw that night, it was not your brother."

She wiped her nose and babbled into the handkerchief. "But it *was*, Christine. It was Erik. I saw them together. I saw them . . . !"

"What did you see?"

"It was near dark. I was sitting in the gazebo overlooking the lake. I heard Lady Elizabeth shouting at someone—a man. And so I followed the voices. The man wore a dark cloak with a hood on his head. Lady Elizabeth was upset about her sister. She struck the man. The hood came off.

"When it did . . . I saw his profile. It was Erik." Becca sobbed against Christine. "After that, I was too frightened and ran away. Erik didn't return for months. I never saw Lady Elizabeth again."

"Did the man you saw strike Lady Elizabeth?"

Becca shook her head. "No."

Christine looked at the countess. "Why would this condemn him in anyone's eyes?"

"Because my son told everyone he had not spoken to his wife after he'd left Sedgwick. He lied."

Christine's hands tightened on Becca's shoulders. "It must have been difficult for you all these years. You thought you were protecting your brother?"

Becca nodded. "I didn't want the rumors about him to be true. I could not have borne it. I told myself, I dreamed it."

"And yet you must have told someone about that night, else the constable would not have asked you these questions. Whom did you tell?"

She shook her head vigorously. Standing behind her daughter, the countess met Christine's gaze. "She told me."

"*You?*" Christine rasped, taking a step away.

"I told only my son what Becca told me." The countess's hand tightened on Christine's arm. "He is ready to have done with this, Christine. You must understand . . ."

Boris suddenly stood in front of her. "Mum," he said. "The countess is right. It has to be this way. Do not let him see you like this."

They are all mad!

The door in front of her opened. The noise in the corridor abruptly halted as Erik appeared, flanked by two burly men. He stopped when he saw her.

Behind her, the corridor grew quiet as the servants fell away and opened a path for their master. Boris, too, stepped to the side in deference. Erik said something in a flat, emotionless voice to the two men beside him, and they stepped away to give him room.

With a sob, Becca flew into his arms and clung to him. He pressed his cheek against her hair and said all would be well in time. His eyes on his mother told her to take his sister. The countess led Becca away. He spoke to Boris and then Hampton. Suddenly, Christine was the only one left standing in front of him. She was stepping into his arms. Tension gripped the corded muscles of his arms.

"I have failed you," she said. "I never found the answers for which you were searching." The words sounded faint. "Tell them you have done nothing. Tell them your sister was wrong. That it was not you she saw."

The palms of his hands were warm against her back.

"Shh." He pressed his cheeks against her hair. "I will be traveling in my coach with my own outriders." He placed a finger against her lips as she started to protest. "Look at the brighter side. No one can claim Elizabeth is responsible for sending any of those letters and then accuse me of killing her seven years ago. You have not failed me, Christine."

He scraped the hair from her face and held his palms to her cheeks. "I will welcome the truth that comes out in the next few days," he said softly. "But right now Erin and my sister need you." Gently, he caught her chin. "And understand this," his voice was as intent as his gaze, "I *will* be back."

"I just came from the library. These are old topographical survey maps." Joseph dropped three parchment rolls on the table behind where Christine stood in front of the tower windows overlooking the moonlit lake.

With her arms folded, she shifted her gaze from the lake to the hills, where a single star glittered like a drop of amber above the crag-lined horizon. Erik had been gone a few hours. He would reach Dunfermline tomorrow afternoon. Shortly after he'd left, the countess had also departed. *Good riddance*, Christine thought, swiping at the tears on her face. *Mothers are supposed to love their children. All of them.* "He wouldn't let me go with him."

"Christine . . ." Amelia said. "You must take your mind off your problems and come over here and sit down. "Joseph has something to show us."

Christine had come into the tower to get away from everyone. But it had proven impossible.

Joseph and Amelia were staying in the lower rooms. Becca was in the next room, still so distraught that Mrs.

Brown sedated her that evening with a sleeping powder. Erin had been tucked in an hour ago, into Christine's bed, where she had fallen asleep. Beast had been lying on her sill or twining about her legs and tripping her. Even Aunt Sophie had been here earlier, the only person at supper with enough spit and vinegar to tell everyone to quit moping and snap to. Joseph had done exactly that.

"I know you have a more current map," he was saying, "but I was hoping to find something older. A lot can change in a hundred years. I found this in the library." He pulled the lamp nearer to where he was working. He laid the older map across the table. It looked antique. "These maps show old roads and trails no longer in existence."

Christine's interest piqued. Her gaze had lifted in the glass and now she turned as he smoothed the corners of the map, inviting her to return to the table and see for herself. "This map was made forty years ago when some astute chap attempted to map the roads and trails in the hills."

Christine could read better without her spectacles, and removed them. "You were right that this kind of rock formation is ideal for an underground aquifer," he said. "Clearly the railroad opened something and it was that initial wash that swept through any lava tubes and abandoned caverns taking out the weaker stratum. This region has also had an overabundance of rain in the last few years." He shifted his stance and looked up at her. "I used to live in Edinburgh. Remember?"

She remembered.

After a moment, he picked up Becca's fossil tooth, assessing the discovery. He didn't know yet about the bigger tooth. She had not told anyone.

Joseph's expression sobered. "What happens if we find this Elizabeth person, Chrissie? What if the evidence does not bode well for his grace?"

"His grace will be exonerated," Amelia said.

"He came to me in London for answers, Joseph," Christine said. "He trusted me."

"We will find her. Then you will find this beast, Chrissie." Joseph pressed the tooth into her hand. "This is your dream. You will be famous."

She looked down at her hand then dropped onto the stool.

"This is what you want, isn't it?" Joseph asked.

"Of course this is what she wants," Amelia said. "Isn't it?"

Since Amelia had removed the ring months ago, Joseph's statement roused her. "Are you both happy?"

Amelia blushed. "Yes."

Joseph laid his hand atop Amelia's. "Even if I am just a simple professor. Who knows?" He looked at the map. "Maybe I will prove to be a better geologist than I ever was a paleontologist."

"The museum made a mistake canceling the expedition to Perth," she said in his defense. "You would have made an excellent team leader."

His mouth crooked with chagrin. "That must have hurt for you to say."

She drew in her breath. "Surprisingly, no." She wiped at her eyes with the tip of her thumb, for her thoughts were never far from the man she loved. "Now help me save my husband."

Joseph thumped his finger on the map. "We will begin here at first light. The Dragon's Lair," he said. "The name of this waterfall—" his finger tapped the falls depicted by a single blue swirl of color on the faded vellum. A hundred years ago, it was barely a stream.

"Dragon's Lair?"

Written in script next to the falls was the name *Dragon's Lair*.

Christine turned the aged map and stared in disbelief. "There used to be a connecting bridge of stone to the upper falls," she said, wiping her eyes, remembering what Erik had told her about parts of the cliff crumbling away.

She had searched the wall of stone behind the falls but never sixty feet above the ground.

Christine studied the map more intently. Then looked up at Joseph and Amelia, already having made her choice and knowing what she was about to give Joseph. Her only goal now was to find Elizabeth and free Erik from his past. She had no doubt that what she wanted most in the world she would give up everything else to have.

"I have a better place to begin our search," she told Joseph. They would begin where she'd found the second tooth. "*Then* we go to the falls."

Chapter 21

"They are inside waiting, your grace," Attenborough said. "The countess is with them."

"And Johnny Maxwell?" Erik asked. "Did my men find him yet?"

Attenborough shook his head. "No."

Erik had arrived at the Royal Burgh courthouse early. It didn't matter that he had been incarcerated in comfortable quarters; the last three days of inaction had not been easy to endure for a man who never allowed anything to chance.

But he'd had enough of the legal system and laws twisted to suit the interpretation of whichever bloody magistrate was hearing a case. In the end, he'd decided to fight Robert Maxwell in the only way he knew how—cease the fight. Surrender. If he could not confront Elizabeth's father one way, then he would do it in another.

Erik had known that, if Christine discovered what he was planning, she would never have allowed him to do this alone. And this was something he needed to do alone. He disliked having to deceive her, disliked even more putting Becca through hell, but as his mother suggested, the authorities needed to hear the story from her to make this work. Erik only knew his sister desperately needed to unburden her soul. It hadn't been until the incident at the river, and Christine's bringing up Becca's nightmares, that everything hit him with clarity.

After he'd begun to recover his memory and remembered more of the events of that day at the river, he began to do more than question Becca's memory. He knew now, Lara had saved his life. She had been no dream. To have known where to find him, she would have had to have seen him go into the river, which meant she'd either been the one to cut the rope on that ridge or she had followed the person who had.

If she had saved Erik's life, then he was counting on her to do the same thing now. If his gut was wrong . . . then he had just allowed his sister to condemn him.

Attenborough opened the door to the magistrate's office and Erik swept inside. The bailiff stood next to the door. Lord Eyre and Lady Lara were also present as was his mother. This morning Erik had received notice that Robert Maxwell's brother had stepped down as Lord Advocate and the magistrate who had been charged with hearing Erik's deposition had been replaced.

"Your grace," the new magistrate said, introducing himself as Sir Pritchard Wilson, the man now in charge of the case.

After thanking Erik for his time in coming to Dunfermline to close the case of one Lady Elizabeth Maxwell Boughton, he asked Erik to sit, which he was not inclined to do as he faced Robert Maxwell from across the space of carpet separating them.

Erik glanced at his mother, dressed like royalty in emerald-green velvet and a wide-rimmed hat cocked slightly to the left. "Lord Eyre has agreed to withdraw his petition to the Commisionary Court to see your marriage invalidated," she said.

"I am here of my own accord," Eyre said. "Lara told me of the letters Johnny has been writing. Though I am still not entirely convinced this is not some elaborate scheme to clear your name now." His voice wavered. "She has always shouted your innocence to the rooftops."

"Why is that do you suppose?" Erik demanded.

"You promised to listen, Robert," the countess said.

Lara's head lowered and she murmured tearfully to her father that she was sorry, but that she had tried to tell him the truth and he would not hear it. Erik looked at Lara's blond hair knotted at her nape. The shape of her face and eyes. "Tell him everything, Lara."

She looked at him and knew that he knew the truth.

"When your hair is down, you look like your sister," Erik said. "Why did you allow people to think you were Elizabeth, Lara?"

She lowered her head. "In the beginning it wasn't on purpose. But people noticed me. I could be beautiful when I was her."

"Lara," Eyre whispered.

"Have you no idea what it is like being her older sister? The beautiful Elizabeth Maxwell. The poor put-upon Elizabeth Maxwell. The daughter to whom you gave everything, including the past seven years? Johnny and I have been forced to watch and I have grown to hate you."

"Enough to make him believe your sister still lived?"

"Papa wanted to believe she was still alive."

"Just as someone wanted him to believe that Erin was not my child?"

"I cannot help what he thinks—"

"Just as you could not help that Elizabeth believed I was in love with you and carrying on an affair with you, her own sister?"

Lara blanched. "You *were* in love with me. If she had never made you look away from me, I would have been your wife."

"You must have hated her."

Lara's wet luminous eyes dropped to her hands. "I never hated her, Erik. I only wished I could have been her in your eyes. She was a silly child who refused to see the gifts she had been handed. I tried to tell her. The night you two argued so horribly . . . she was an utter fool."

"Did you do something to Elizabeth?"

She shook her head. "No."

"Did Johnny?"

"No."

Erik knelt in front of her chair. "At the river, you gave me a blanket and kept me from freezing. You did not want to see me die, did you, Lara?"

Her eyes wide, she shook her head. "I never wanted to see you die."

"Are you the one who cut the rope at the river?"

She shook her head. Erik's eyes remained on Lara's downturned face. She had not convinced him of her repentance and he had expected to be convinced. "You and I both know that it was not me Becca saw that night with Elizabeth. Have you told your da whom you have been protecting all these years?"

"Johnny didn't kill our sister. He didn't kill Elizabeth."

"What happened, Lara?" Erik asked.

Lara pressed her hands to her head. "He was furious with her for believing that you and I had an affair. He wouldn't let her leave Sedgwick. Her place was as your duchess."

"What are you saying, Lara?" Eyre asked. "That Johnny was the man Lady Rebecca saw with Elizabeth?"

Teary eyed, she beseeched her father to understand. "They argued. He left her there. He told me he left her there. She must have tried to follow Johnny."

Erik stood. "And you believe Elizabeth tried to walk alone ten miles around the lake to Eyre House at night wearing only her cloak for protection through hills where a twisted ankle could mean serious injury or even death if she could not get help? Wouldn't she have at least ordered a carriage brought around, Lara?"

"Johnny did not kill her. Why would he? She was his closest link to the duchy should she bear you a son or should you die. Either way, he would have had Sedgwick Castle in his hands."

If something had happened that night and Elizabeth *had* been killed, hiding her for seven years would do exactly what Christine had said to him once. If someone wanted to play into the curse and Erik died before his thirty-fourth birthday, the entire ordeal would be chalked up to Old Angus Maxwell's curse. How many people expected him to die in the next few weeks?

It suddenly bothered him that he did not know where Maxwell was. "Do you know where your brother is?" Erik asked, but she wasn't listening.

"He told me people would try to spread lies about him. And that I was not to speak to anyone. That no matter what anyone said, he was innocent. He pleaded with me. He was up at the river that evening because he had been following Lady Sedgwick. He did not cut the rope. I was there, Erik. The rope just snapped. He was frightened people would believe he tried to kill you."

"Yet, knowing all this, you came here today."

Her gaze fell on the countess. "I went to the lake house but the countess found me and told me I needed to come forward and tell everything. That if I loved

Erin, I would do everything in my power not to see her father harmed. And so I went to Papa, and we came here at once."

"Why the letters?"

"Johnny needed people to believe Elizabeth still lived. He couldn't take the chance that the curse might kill you and leave a son to inherit the duchy."

"Lord Sedgwick." Eyre rose. "In the name of all that is merciful, we don't know that Johnny murdered Elizabeth or the circumstances behind her disappearance. If he is guilty—"

"*Guilty*?" Erik demanded in utter disbelief.

Lara stood. "He is only guilty of defending what he believed should have been ours."

"Lara!"

Eyre stepped between Erik and Lara. "Your grace, if my son is guilty of murder, he will face judgment, but let it be from me, not from you. I ask that you allow me to bring in my son. I have been a bloody fool. Let whatever it was that tore apart our two families long ago end now."

For a space of a minute, an oppressive sense of tension filled the small white-walled office. Erik looked from Eyre to the countess. Erik knew when he walked into this room today, he'd been prepared to hunt down Johnny Maxwell and kill him for what he had put his family through for seven long, bloody years. For what Becca had suffered.

His mother had remained out of the proceedings and stood aside now, allowing him to make his own decision. He owed her a debt of gratitude for what she had done for him this day, in her way, giving him back his future by clearing his name once and for all. A future he wanted very much to own. Now that it was within his grasp to do so.

Months ago, he would have destroyed the entire Maxwell family as he had done to countless others who had betrayed him or trod on his toes, and would have relished their demise as justice owed. He had purchased more than one man's allegiance in such a manner. But thirty-four years had taught him the wisdom of looking before leaping into the fire. Three months with Christine had given him a reason not to leap at all. A second chance to begin life anew.

Yet there was something in his mother's eyes that told him she understood justice did not always favor the just or the right. She would support whatever decision he chose to make—and they would never speak a word of it again.

He shifted his attention to Eyre. "If my men find Lord John he will be brought to Dunfermline. If I find him near my family for any reason, I will not promise restraint. So, I suggest you find him first."

Sir Pritchard cleared his throat. The bailiff folded the papers on the desk and handed the sheaf to Erik. "You are free to leave, your grace."

Erik stared at the papers. Just that fast?

After seven years of hell? He was free to leave.

"Erik—" His mother's hand touched his arm. "You will tell your wife, I meant you no ill harm?"

Despite his need to get back to Christine now, he remained a moment longer with her. "I will tell her."

"If you don't mind, I will return with Robert and Attenborough. I am sure you will not wish to dawdle with us on the road."

As Erik strode out of the courthouse and into his waiting coach, he only knew that he needed to get back to Sedgwick Castle—to Christine.

* * *

Erik rode through Sedgwick's arched gates near dusk the next evening. He was already swinging off his horse before Boris appeared on the topmost stair. His butler came down the stairs murmuring his welcome and relief to see him. To Boris, Erik knew he must have looked like some highwayman of lore, unshaven and ragged, missing only a cocked hat and flintlock to complete the archaic picture.

The inner courtyard remained silent. No liveryman came to get his horse. He could see people atop the battlements with spyglasses and telescopes. "What is happening?" Erik demanded.

"They found her," Boris said. "Lady Sedgwick and Mr. Darlington believe they found Lady Elizabeth."

"Where is Lady Sedgwick now?"

"Her grace and Mr. Darlington have been up at the falls for three days. Lady Sedgwick has been working to bring out the remains they found in the cavern. Her grace did not want to tell anyone. She was concerned that you needed to see the body first."

"Clearly everyone bloody knows."

"No, your grace. Most everyone has gone into the hills or up to the battlements to watch the dig, hoping to glimpse the monster Mr. Darlington unearthed." Boris lowered his voice in excitement. "A creature that is surely not from this world. The people are terrified."

"But not so terrified that they haven't all run to watch the dig."

Erik was already walking toward his horse, his long strides eating up the distance in seconds. Mounting, Erik swung the horse around. "Where are my daughter and my sister?"

Having chased Erik across the courtyard, Boris

grabbed each breath. "Mrs. Whitman is with your daughter. I . . . Lady Rebecca is with Lady Sophia."

Twenty minutes later, Erik was mounted on a fresh horse and riding toward the hills. Another hour to arrive on the crowded scene at the crest of the road. An hour of hell, he thought.

He passed the place where the carriage Christine had been riding in upon her arrival crashed in a rut and the place where he had gone into the river. He slowed his horse to a walk as he turned off the road. Dozens of people stood huddled beneath overhanging tree limbs and pine boughs in an effort to stay dry in the thickening drizzle. No one looked in his direction as he dismounted. All eyes were anxiously looking down the trail.

Erik saw at once the object of their fascination. Lying atop a sheet of oilcloth was an elongated stone skull similar to that of a crocodile on display in the London historical museum. Only this one was larger, with more than a hundred huge, jagged teeth visible in its fossilized head.

He saw his engineering foreman at the trail's head just as the man looked up and spied Erik almost in the same instant. Startled, Hodges stepped forward in a fluster. "Lord Sedgwick."

All at once, others turned. The glade grew silent as people moved away from the trail to open a path for him. "We did not receive word you were returning," Hodges said.

"Where is Lady Sedgwick, Hodges?"

"Inside the cavern. We have done our best to keep people away. But you must understand everyone is curious. No one has ever seen the like of what has been found here."

There was no easy way to reach the falls. The ground

around this part of the cliffs was treacherous and slippery. A small path had been carved in the side of the rock, and a narrow rope bridge affixed to one side of the overhang just beneath the falls, which took him beneath a wall of water and into a narrow cave hidden by the falls. One could not get inside without becoming soaked.

Rubble had been painstakingly extricated from the entrance to the cave, which was now shored up with timbers and braces, an engineering marvel, as far as Erik was concerned. He removed his sodden cloak and left it on the rocks behind the wall of water he had just walked through. Hodges said his men had been responsible for the work.

Torches lit the damp walls inside. Water ran in streams around his feet. Lower down the noise grew louder and a platform had been built over a body of rushing water. Erik suspected this was part of the lava tube to which Christine had referred. There was not much to see but the wall of rock on all sides of him as he worked his way down the steep slope. Steps had been cut into the stone, and even he recognized the work was not recent. Raiders fighting the king's armies all the way back to William Wallace's time had probably used this cavern.

Once deeper inside, Erik looked up at the ceiling covered in cone-shaped stalactites, and all he could think about at that moment was the weight of all that rock precariously perched above his head. He did not like it down here. Then he turned . . . and that was when he saw it.

Imbedded in the hill like some macabre carving cut from stone and polished by eons of ice, wind, and water, was a massive skull from a beast he could not have conceived ever existed. It was similar to the one already brought out, only ten times larger, with plate-size vertebrae stretching six feet before disappearing into the rock. He could only imagine that the rest of it extended up the side of the hill covered by centuries of dirt and loose scree.

"Can you imagine living near the shores of the loch with a monster like that swimming about?" Hodges said. "Darlington said a millennium ago this entire countryside was part of the sea."

Dirt trickled over their shoulders. Hodges held out his hands, palms upward. "Darlington has kept most everyone out."

Even Erik could tell that water rushing through these caverns had compromised the integrity of the walls. They were standing in a tomb. Literally, he thought. Water seeped from the surface through cracks and disappeared into equally elusive cracks in the floor. Much work would have to be done inside here to make this place safer for excavation.

"Your grace," Darlington said from behind him, working his way up the incline. "Chrissie . . . Lady Sedgwick will be beside herself to see you. She and Hampton are farther back in the tunnel. Isn't this magnificent?"

Erik turned toward the tunnel. The ceiling was at a lower height as he descended. Halfway down the incline he was already sloshing in water. He grabbed a torch from the wall and noticed that the shoring above his head seemed sound.

"This cavern stretches a half mile in all directions," Darlington said behind him. "There is an underground river running beneath us and it comes up about a half mile from here, beneath the cliffs."

Erik held the torch out in front of him. "You are the one who discovered this find?"

"The credit is not all mine. Lady Sedgwick had an

idea where to look first. We found the first beast buried in the rock near where you fell into the river. We both found this cavern. A landslide had buried part of the opening probably hundreds of years ago. I was the first inside."

Erik turned and shined the torchlight in Darlington's face. Already they were both hunching over. "Is that right?"

"She injured her ankle. I would have taken her back, but she refused to go."

"She injured her ankle," he repeated. "Yet you brought her in here."

"She was thinking only of saving you, your grace. You needn't worry. She is much better now." Darlington stepped around Erik. "A larger grotto is in this direction. That is where she found the body. Part of the ground above the cavern collapsed and the body fell through. The woman she found had been wrapped in canvas. Lady Sedgwick has already discerned from the remains that the body was female. By the way she was wrapped, someone had buried her not realizing her gravesite was atop a sinkhole. Lady Sophia will make a final examination."

"Lady Sophia is down here?"

"We are working to bring the body through the collapsed part of the cavern. I would not have recommended that you come down here. We have not finished shoring up the ceiling in this section." Looking down at his feet, he said, "And the water is rising."

Turning, Erik ducked into the tunnel and sloshed through water. "Go on and get everyone out. I will find my wife."

A moment later, Erik was following the sound of Christine's voice. He heard the words, "Move to the left, pull, careful," resonating through the narrow corridor.

He entered the chamber and stopped. Fifty feet above Christine, part of the ceiling and wall had collapsed, exposing a five-foot-long horizontal crack of torchlight. The jagged opening was partially concealed by a fallen tree and backed up against a rock overhang.

The ropes attached to the shroud had been wrapped around a pinion of sorts in the wall and in the ceiling above the opening. Someone from above pulled. Christine managed the belay. He knew at once what the shroud contained. No matter what Elizabeth had done, she had never deserved this.

The shroud disappeared through the opening, bringing Erik back to the present and to Christine. As if sensing his presence, she suddenly turned. She wore a pith helmet to protect her head from falling debris. A long braid trailed down her back. Wearing trousers, she was coated head to foot with sticky mud. Hampton peered over the ledge.

"Your grace," Hampton said.

Erik's mouth crooked at the startled tone in the groomsman's voice. They had just brought up the corpse of a woman Erik had long been accused of killing. "Do not worry yourself, Hampton. I have been cleared of murder. Take the body to Lady Sophia. We are on our way up."

"Aye," Hampton said. "Not a one of us doubted you would be cleared." He ducked his head out.

Erik wanted to laugh at such new-found optimism. But when he returned his gaze to his wife, he suddenly did not know what to say.

"Your grace," she said as he approached her.

He still held the torch in his hand. With his other arm, he wrapped her to him and kissed her hard.

Erik's intent when he'd entered the cave to drag her out of this deathtrap had been fervent and selfish. Not just because he had raced like a lunatic to get back here and save her—when she clearly needed no one to save her. Indeed, she had never been the one needing saving. But because he loved her. She had changed something inside him from the man he was before to who he was now. He loved her more than he had ever loved anything or anyone, and that feeling had spread outward like the ripples in a pond, building momentum to finally crash like a cyclonic breaker against all his rigid perceptions of life. No one else had done for him what she had done.

Now, all he could think about was that she had come to Scotland to find her dragon, and that he had somehow been the one to fail her. A dream he'd once believed unimportant next to his own goals because it had seemed insignificant and odd to him. Because his view of the world had been handicapped by his own self-preservation, now altered forever, the instant he'd realized someone else would claim her beast.

He felt her gentle smile against his lips. "Oh, Erik, you goose." She pulled back and looked into his face. "We are standing ankle deep in bat guano and you want to get romantic?"

Looking in disgust at his feet, he grimaced. "I thought it was mud."

Christine took a steadying breath and held her gloved palms to his stubbled face. "It isn't." Her expression sobered. "You look as if you haven't slept in a week."

He cupped his palm beneath her chin. "I would have slept a lot less if I had known you were down in a hole like this, my love."

"Did you see the loch beast? Is it not magnificent? I believe Joseph will become famous."

"Christine . . . what happened? I thought you wanted—"

"I am all right, Erik. I really am."

And she was, she realized.

She had found what she had come to Scotland searching for.

They spoke for a moment about her week and he told her about his, neither really saying much when their eyes said far more, and when she would rather touch him than talk. They would speak later when they were away from this tomb. Christine asked him if he remembered how to belay the rope.

She climbed the slick rock. One hand over the other, she worked her way up the wall, when suddenly the rope went slack.

Alerted, she anchored her hands and turned to look over her shoulder as a shadow passed across the light above her. Johnny Maxwell squatted in the mouth of the opening next to the shoring beams. He'd cut the rope. Christine froze as he lowered a pistol at Erik. There was nowhere Erik could run.

"Let her finish the climb," Erik's tone sounded as dangerous as it was forced.

"I had heard they let you go, Sedgwick," Maxwell said.

"Did you think they wouldn't?"

The ground where he trod was unstable. Debris rained from the ceiling over Erik. "I was wondering how long it would take for everyone to figure out it was me your sister saw that night and not you. Everyone always said we looked alike from a distance." Maxwell rose and began to pace. He glared at Christine. "You should have let her stay buried."

"She deserved more than this, Johnny," Erik said.

"I didn't kill my sister. I swear it. I didn't kill her."

Christine's gaze tilted slowly to the sagging wall of earth above them. Even Maxwell must know he could bring this section of the cavern down on their heads. "You do not have to do this, Johnny," Erik said.

Back and forth, Johnny walked. "Do you think I care what happens to me? I can never go back now. Whether I live or I die here, I am dishonored. My own family thinks me a murderer."

"What happened?" Christine asked, desperate to pull Maxwell's attention from Erik. Make him stop pacing. Her arms had begun to burn. "What happened to your sister?"

Maxwell murmured that it was not his fault. Everything had been a tragic accident. "She asked for my help. I denied her." He wiped a sleeve across his nose. "We argued. She struck me. I swear, I warned her not to strike me again. I shoved her just to keep her off me. That was all. She fell and hit her head. Just like that. She was gone forever."

"If you say you did not kill Elizabeth, I believe you, Maxwell," Erik said.

"Why? Why would you or anyone believe me?"

"Because killing her would have made no sense," Erik said simply. "I think everyone has discerned that already. You speak of honor. What is the honor in doing this? So far you have not managed to *murder* anyone."

"Murder?" He waggled the gun. "I have waited patiently for the curse to do that for me. You have always had the devil's own luck. You with your *money* and your *titles*. Your bloody prestige. My entire life I have watched you lord over the world like a king. Do you know how many years it took to get you out of my father's heart? You, his favorite one. Elizabeth never wanted to marry you. But he forced her. No one despised you as much as she did."

He glared at Christine. "Why did you have to find

her? Why could you not allow her to stay buried?" He kicked out at the support piling beside him.

"Keep climbing, Christine," Erik told her. "Now."

"Why are you still alive, Sedgwick? Every other Sedgwick duke in the last century has succumbed. Why not you?" He raised his arm and aimed the gun at Christine. "Why not her? Hmm?" His eyes searched the shoring beams. "Why not the both of ye? Together?"

"Like hell, Maxwell!" Erik flung the torch in his hand.

It missed Maxwell, but just barely. He fell backward against a shoring post, sending scree tumbling over Erik. Part of the ceiling crumbled when the braces sagged.

Then silence. Christine held her breath in horror. Even Maxwell froze where he had fallen.

At first, she thought nothing happened. Then vibrations shivered through the air as if something around them shifted. Cold fear crawled over her skin. She looked up at the juncture in the crossbeams braced against the wall of rock above them. Maxwell scrambled away from the opening. Panic engulfed her. She realized what was about to happen. Erik must have realized it as well.

"Climb!" he shouted and hit the wall below her.

A long diagonal cleft to her left cut upward and she climbed into it, anchoring her grip on old tree roots. She didn't look down but kept climbing. The rock crumbled as she moved. Left hand in. Grip. Right hand pull. Her arms ached and burned. There was a sudden echo inside the curving stone wall above her where the air shifted, and the wind funneled out through a hole suddenly opening in the ceiling, which continued to grow as larger chunks of stone crashed to the floor. If she stopped, she would fall and die.

If she fell, so would he.

"Faster, Christine!"

Erik was already at her feet. She stretched forward to grip what she could of the ledge as rocks hit her arms and shoulders and the sound of the earth moving rumbled around her. Her foot slipped. The ceiling above the opening sagged.

Then suddenly, hands from above wrapped around hers, pulling her upward and over the ledge. She briefly glimpsed Hampton and Hodges as they dragged her out. Then Erik slammed her from behind and they were all running. Behind her, the ground shuddered, roared, and finally collapsed into itself, sending rocks and debris billowing upward. She tumbled sideways to the ground. Erik covered her body. The dirt in her mouth told her she was alive. The sound of voices and shouting all around them told her they weren't alone.

"Are you hurt?" Erik asked urgently.

Over the din in her ringing ears, she continued to hear shouting. She opened her eyes and peered through lopsided spectacles at his streaked face. Both of them rose on their elbows and looked behind them. The cave was a depression of rocks and dust. Debris continued to rain down upon them like a puff of volcanic ash. Hysteria nearly made her laugh. She'd lost her hat. The rope had, thankfully, come off her waist.

She frowned. "I hope the collapse does not extend farther."

"I told everyone to get out," Erik said. She suddenly saw Joseph and a dozen people running toward them from the woods. Aunt Sophie and Becca stood a few feet away, next to Maxwell's prone figure on the ground. Becca clutched a stout branch. Clearly, Maxwell had been whacked senseless over the head.

Hampton was kneeling beside him. "What do we do with the bloke?"

Maxwell groaned and stirred. "Bastard." Erik climbed to his feet but Becca threw herself into his arms.

"No," she said against his cheek, "he can no longer hurt us."

Christine placed her hand on his arm. "Becca is right. He is irrelevant to our lives, Erik."

Erik looked over his sister's shoulder at Hampton. "Is everyone accounted for?"

"It looks as if only this part of the cavern collapsed," Joseph said. "Maybe that's not such a bad thing."

For moment as they all stared at the depression, Christine knew everyone was thinking the same. It had been a grave for seven years. Then Hampton and Hodges dragged Maxwell to his feet. He saw Erik and began to struggle. "No. It wasn't my fault! No!"

Becca smashed him over the head again with the tree branch.

"Bloody hell!" Maxwell groaned.

"Bloody hell back to you!" Becca would have smashed him again, except Erik stopped her. "You have very nearly ruined our lives!" she shouted as Erik held her back.

Taking the weapon from her hand, Erik told Hampton to escort Johnny to Dunfermline. "Let his father deal with him," Erik said, and they all listened as Maxwell was dragged off yelling and cursing before Hampton tossed him to the ground and trussed him like a boar ready for the spit.

Erik turned his attention to Aunt Sophie and the weaponry still clutched in Aunt Sophie's hand like a medieval warclub. "You would have been proud of your sister," Sophie said.

"Aunt Sophie is the one who felled him first," Becca deferred.

"I merely helped, dear." To Erik, she said, "I have faced down cannibals. I would go into battle with her anytime."

Hodges came out and said you had returned. Then we saw Johnny Maxwell. "I thought he had killed you." She pressed her cheek against his chest. "Are you all right?" she asked.

"Are you, Elf?"

Her mouth turned up into a smile. "Yes. Yes, I believe I am."

With his other arm, Erik reached around Christine's shoulders, while Becca took Aunt Sophie's arm and they started walking. "Then let us go home to Erin."

After a moment, Becca asked, "Now that no one can think bad things about us any longer . . . maybe we can open the ballroom for my debut," she said.

Erik chuckled. "I think I will, Becca," he said, then brought his gaze to Christine's. "But I have something I want to do first."

Chapter 22

E rik and Christine tore up their contract that night. They were married a week later, repeating the same vows they had spoken months earlier.

No bargains. No contracts. A ceremony sealed by the love they shared and the promise that light shone on their future. Warmed by his strength, Christine faced him and repeated the words mirrored in his eyes. Aunt Sophie, Joseph, and Amelia and Becca stood around them. Erin her flower girl. Erik's mother had missed the proceedings, but only because she had taken her first trip out of the country in thirty years and did not return for months. But everyone else was present to share this moment. Christine had found new purpose. Or it had found her. She no longer cared to discern the difference or to sift through the logic of her happiness when nothing had turned out as she had originally planned. And, yet, nothing could have felt more right. More perfect.

The ring stayed on Christine's hand for one more hour that day, and then it just slipped loose and came off. She had not wept as the ring fell off her finger and into the grass, though the moment was bittersweet. Yet, she knew in her heart it was time to surrender the band of silver to whatever fate it would bestow on another. Still she kept it in her dresser for another week, looking at it, but discovering nothing new about what it really was. She only knew there was magic in her happiness. Her hand went to her abdomen.

That evening she knocked on Aunt Sophie's door. She hoped her aunt would remain a permanent fixture at Sedgwick Castle and Becca and Erin could become her students so Aunt Sophie could teach them both that the world stretched far beyond the walls of Sedgwick Castle, and that dreams were made, not born, and that anything worth having is worth fighting for.

Her aunt lowered the book in her hands to her lap as Christine knelt by her chair. A fire warmed the room. "What is it, dear?" Aunt Sophie asked.

"I believe it is time to give this back," Christine said, taking Aunt Sophie's hand and folding her fingers around the ring.

For a long time Aunt Sophie said nothing. But in those first few moments as her hand closed around the band of braided silver, the air stirred and hummed with electricity as if coming to life around them, and Christine wondered if Aunt Sophie felt it as well.

Aunt Sophie had not spoken anymore about the ring since that day when they had been in the tower. Now Christine asked the question that she had wanted to ask.

"You said the ring belonged to Great-Grandmamma. Will you tell me now where this ring came from?"

Sophie opened her palm and stared at the silver band. "I believe she found it in the vaults of an old abbey in Scotland. The entire legend of the ring began when she met my great-grandfather shortly after putting it on. He was a fierce Scottish lord bent on vengeance, which she somehow turned into love. She became the first archeologist in the family."

"What about you? Did you ever try on the ring?"

"No. I was afraid."

"Why? If you do not believe in its power."

Her eyes took on a faraway look. "My mother told me once that life takes us along paths we may not want to go. I was afraid of the choice I would be forced to make, fearing it would change who I was. I had important goals and dreams, you see. I did not want to take the chance on some unseen entity shaping my life. I was my own person, after all. Then . . . it no longer mattered. The choice was taken away from me when my Reece died. I did go on to become a well-known anthropologist. I did things few women dreamed of doing. I helped create the historical museum that now exists. I had your father to care for. And then I had you."

"But if you *could* go back and change the past, would you?"

Aunt Sophie patted Christine's hands. "That question is wrought with peril when one has already lived one's life and is nearing the end of that journey. But how does one change only part of the past without changing all one's future?"

Christine laid her head in her aunt's lap. "Oh, Aunt Sophie. Sometimes I think you are a victim of your own analytical thinking."

The Sedgwick curse died an ignoble demise the following week when Erik celebrated his thirty-fifth birthday in peace and harmony and utter lack of drama. Becca had her coveted debut the next month, the first ball held at Sedgwick Court in eight years, and Lady Rebecca Bonham, who turned seventeen the week before, danced her first waltz—even if it was with her brother.

Seven months after the ball, on one April morn, Christine gave birth to a beautiful daughter. Eleven months later, the devil duke of Sedgwick welcomed a son. Eventually Christine would bear another son and daughter, both dark-haired like their father. She never did become the renowned paleontologist that she had once thought she'd wanted more than anything in the world. But she did help Joseph Darlington become one. He and Amelia settled near St. Andrews, where he taught classes and raised their own three children. Christine and Joseph went on to discover more great beasts on Sedgwick land, spawning the myth that a great sea monster still haunted some of Scotland's lochs. As for Sommershorn Abbey, Babs and Dolly grew up to take the reins of the school, and Christine watched it grow into a fine institution, a haven for young women.

Then one summer evening, she and Erik returned with the entire family from St. Andrews after attending a formal ceremony commissioning the beautiful stone library he had designed for the university and which had finally opened to the world.

Christine had been sitting outside on the terrace watching Mrs. Whitman try to corral the children, the youngest of whom had just begun to crawl and had recently discovered the joys of eating dirt from the rose garden. And as old Beast curled up in Christine's lap, his rumbling purrs pulling Erin to her side, Christine wished her own father could see her now. For she was truly happy. Christine knew then that along with love she had been granted her greatest wish.

A family of her own.

An incomparable gift to her soul, and cementing her place in the world for generations to come.

It was quite late when Christine climbed the stairs to the tower room. She found Erik at his desk in the study. Because this was the only room in all of Sedgwick with windows so grand and large, she shared the space with Erik. Or he might argue that his small corner of heaven did not nearly equal her larger three corners that he seemed to jealously covet, since he had moved up here years ago.

His boyish grousing usually won him a sympathy kiss. But tonight he wasn't working over his designs. His elbows on the desk, he was reading something in his hands and did not hear her approach until she was leaning over his shoulder. "Why so serious?" she asked.

"Mother has announced her intent to wed again. She has asked us to lend our consequence to her upcoming nuptials by attending next summer."

Christine took the placard from his hand. "It should be beautiful at Eyre House in July." She peered over the rim of her spectacles at her husband. "They have been seeing each other for years, you know."

Erik grunted. Sliding into his lap, Christine wrapped her arms around her husband's broad shoulders. "Lord Eyre lost everything, Erik. He has done as you've asked and remained away from here. Perhaps it is time to allow Erin to meet her grandfather. He is old and he is alone."

Lara remained in a private asylum outside Edinburgh, and Lord John had died years ago during an outbreak of typhus while he had been awaiting trial.

"And your mother has not been inconvenient to have around when she visits. She *has* made a valiant effort. The children like her. And look"—Christine tapped the invitation—"she has asked you to give her away."

Erik lifted her hand into the light. "Whatever happened to your ring?"

She curled her fingers around his and brought them to her lips. "I returned it to Aunt Sophie, to whom it belongs."

His eyes captured the dim candlelight. Even after all these years, her heart never failed to skip a beat when he looked at her as if she were the only woman in the world. His sherry-colored eyes were now a midnight shade in the near darkness, consuming her with both tenderness and the fierce heat of his emotions. He still possessed the power to make her forget her name just by looking at her.

"You aren't about to tell me you have fallen out of love, are you?" She had meant the words as a jest, but deep down she had always harbored an inkling of fear that something catastrophic would befall her once the ring was gone.

The intensity in his eyes tightened the small knot in her chest. "And all these years I half believed that ring had made you fall in love with me."

"I thought you didn't believe in magic."

"I did not used to believe in giant sea monsters either." He pushed the hair from her face. A faint tremor went through his hands as he held her face in his palms. "Do you ever regret not finding your dragon?"

She nuzzled his palms, warmed by his touch and his concern. "My dragon found *me*, your grace. A big ferocious bull dragon and four little dragons have claimed me as their own, my love. I have been happily imprisoned in their lair ever since."

Impulsively she traced the tip of her finger along his bottom lip. "Besides, I have turned my attention to sea monsters."

The topic piqued her interest, much as it always did when it entered the conversation between them. "Did you know it is quite possible Joseph and I found a link between the sea monster he discovered in the cavern and a modern-day ostrich?"

Erik chuckled, then said her name softly, first against her hair and then her lips, diverting her before he received another lesson in bird anatomy when the only anatomical life form he wanted to explore sat in his lap. "I love you," he said fiercely. His tongue was hot and hard as he took her mouth in a kiss that devoured.

Erik had learned much in the years since he had married Christine. Twice.

Logic for his wife was not necessarily logic for the mainstream. Christine lived to the chords of her own melody. He needed that balance and her unique perspective. He needed her laughter. He'd never felt more alive when he saw himself in her eyes. Nor known a deeper peace in her arms.

After a long, hungry moment in which they shared a passionate embrace, he carried her down the stone staircase to their large bed, joining her beneath the goose-down covers. Instinctively, his hands moved over her body. She laid her mouth to the curve of his neck and suckled. He pulled her away and, turning her beneath him, lifted his head until he could see her lips and feel the rush of her breath against his mouth. "The last time you set your teeth to my neck, I had a bloody time explaining to our eldest why I had a happy face imprinted on my throat."

Christine's smile widened a fraction. He felt the primal jolt of more than arousal. "Tell me again how much you love me," she said. "And I will give you a happier face lower down where no one will see."

He slipped one hand around the back of her neck and kept her where she was, beneath him and weighted by his body. She was smiling up at him, a temptress bathed in moonlight. A beacon in the night. "I love you, *leannanan.*"

He breathed a soft sigh, answering hers as he nuzzled her ear. "I love you," he said again.

Inordinately humbled to know she loved him, too.

"I love you. I love you," he said the words a dozen times.

And Erik Boughton, the devil duke of Sedgwick, knew no bounds to the capacity of his heart. Growling softly he filled her with his heat.

He would be no true dragon worth his salt if he did not growl fire or shake his tail and, on very special occasions, fly her to the moon. Tonight he eagerly delivered all three.

Avon Romances

the best in exceptional authors and unforgettable novels!

AVON

978-0-06-083122-6

978-0-06-166244-7

978-0-06-164837-3

978-0-06-170628-8

978-0-06-171570-9

978-0-06-154778-2

At Avon Books, we know your passion for romance—once you finish one of our novels, you find yourself wanting more.

May we tempt you with . . .

- **Excerpts** from our upcoming releases.

- Entertaining **extras**, including authors' personal photo albums and book lists.

- Behind-the-scenes **scoop** on your favorite characters and series.

- **Sweepstakes** for the chance to win free books, romantic getaways, and other fun prizes.

- Writing **tips** from our authors and editors.

- **Blog** with our authors and find out why they love to write romance.

- **Exclusive content** that's not contained within the pages of our novels.

Join us at
www.avonbooks.com